The Banner Saga

The Gift of Hadrborg

By James Fadeley

Cover and interior art by Arnie Jorgensen

The Banner Saga: The Gift of Hadrborg © 2016
by James Fadeley

Published by Versus Evil

Second Edition
Cover Image: Arnie Jorgensen
Book Design: Arnie Jorgensen & James Fadeley
IBSN 13: 978-0692775080
ISBN 10: 0692775080

Follow Versus Evil at:
Twitter: @vs_evil
Facebook: https://www.facebook.com/versusevil/
Website: www.vsevil.net

Join the Banner Saga community at:
Twitter: @BannerSaga
Facebook: https://www.facebook.com/BannerSaga/
Website: www.bannersaga.com

For dad, who will always be missed.

Chapter 1

Stefnir winced as he squeezed his swollen shoulder, grunting at the pain within his muscle.

He had spent the morning both marching and being wary. Stefnir's shield bore several notches from fending off Olaf's "lessons," and the varl's deftly tossed stones were starting to wear the protective barrier away. The wolf pelt over Stefnir's shoulder obscured his peripheral vision, making it harder to notice Olaf's sly throws. Worse, Stefnir failed to block some of the rocks, and sported bruises on his legs and back as punishment.

"Well lad, seems we've lucked out," Olaf suddenly declared.

"Why?" Stefnir asked, turning his head. His shield arm shot up. The rock clattered off the barrier, nestling in the snow.

"Ha!" Olaf snorted. "You're getting the hang of it. Anyway, we're almost to Karlshus, with warm food and a fire to sleep beside. Sure beats that storm about to hit."

Stefnir spotted the brooding gray clouds in the dusky sky behind them. Despite their ominous appearance, no flakes had yet descended. But there was no question the matter was when, not if, the snow would fall.

Olaf pointed ahead. "That's where we're going."

Stefnir turned away from the horizon and peered into the encroaching gloom. He could see firelights and the outlines of buildings in the distance.

Something stung Stefnir's posterior. The boy shouted in pain as the stone fell off his back side. Olaf rumbled with laughter.

"Dammit!" Stefnir rubbed his rump to sooth away the agony. "Would you stop already? I need to sit down! And my shoulder is aching from lugging this shield for days!"

"Hey, you asked for it lad." The giant crunched snow beneath every step as he followed Stefnir, standing roughly twice the boy's height. "But carrying your shield is something you're going to have to get used to. We don't have a yox to haul our gear, and you should never be without your weapons anyway."

Stefnir continued to curse and swear under his breath as he walked. The varl shook his head with a smile.

"So tell me Stefnir, what've you learned from this? Figure it out and I'll give you a break until we're back on the road," Olaf offered.

"Never ask a varl to teach you anything," Stefnir muttered instantly, his face a scowl.

"Excellent! Now what was *today's* lesson?"

Stefnir rubbed his pained shoulder. "You were strengthening my arms for battle by making me lug this shield."

"Good point. But that was training for the body, not the lesson to be learned. You'll certainly need a firm shoulder." Olaf tapped his horned forehead while glancing down at the boy. "But a warrior's mind only comes in two varieties. Quick, or caved."

Stefnir said nothing for a moment, mulling over Olaf's words. "Vigilance. You were teaching me to always be on my guard, to be alert for danger."

Olaf nodded solemnly, the smile gone. "Now you got it. There's always something or someone who benefits from spilling your blood, lad. And I'm glad you've figured that out before we get to Karlshus. There are wolves in cities too."

Stefnir didn't ask what Olaf meant. The boy figured he'd find out soon enough.

Their trail of snow prints ended as they ascended the creaking wooden staircase to a mead hall. Stefnir could not read the establishment's sign, but the sigil bore a smiling bear holding a mug of frothing brew. Even before they entered Stefnir felt the warmth of the fire within. He could smell the honey-laced beverages and hear the guffaw and drunks singing.

Olaf ducked his head below the doorway's arch as he strode inside, Stefnir following behind. But the boy halted, stunned by a scene of debauchery.

A few long tables were laid out before the fireplace, seats and benches occupied by dozens of men, many of whom sported braids and vicious tattoos. The center of the room held the loudest and giddiest, where armed warriors surrounded and cheered on two bare-chested men. The pair grunted as they flexed their biceps, hands clasped in an arm-wrestling match.

A few serving maids worked the crowd, collecting coins and delivering drinks to men who ogled their rears. Often, the women asserted themselves and rebuked unwelcomed words and hands. But at least one maiden seemed to encourage and invite their raunchy statements, and was the most popular for it as well.

A few varl in the room kept to themselves at large round tables on the outskirts. They glanced up from their drinks to Olaf and gave him a respectful nod. Olaf returned the courtesy, the floors creaking as he walked towards the bar.

Stefnir followed but didn't hear Olaf's conversation with the bartender. After a moment the man jerked his head to his left, toward the back of the hall. Olaf faced the boy.

"You've no coin, do you?" The varl asked.

Stefnir shook his head.

"I thought as much." Olaf sighed. "Alright, hand me the wolf pelt. I have to barter with the owner for what we need."

Stefnir pulled the fur from his shoulder and the varl accepted it. Then Olaf reached into his belt pouch and pushed two coins into Stefnir's palm in return.

"Here, get yourself something in the meantime. Help put some hair on your face." Olaf chuckled as he walked towards the rear of the chamber.

Stefnir scowled and rubbed his hairless chin. The varl jested about one of Stefnir's quiet shames. His father had warned him that, like he and his father before him, Stefnir would likely not sprout whiskers for another few seasons, and the boy had yet to meet a raider who didn't sport a mustache at the least.

Stefnir shook his head and sought the bartender. The fat man scrutinized the boy suspiciously as the coins were set on the counter. He eventually relented and drew a measure of mead from a tilted barrel, setting a bone-carved flagon before his young customer.

Stefnir casually leaned against the bar and raised the drink to his lips. The last thing he expected was a cloying sweetness that was quickly chased with a bitter aftertaste. The sip went straight to the boy's senses and he almost sputtered. The bartender broke into laughter, and Stefnir realized he was probably given bad stock intentionally.

He lurched to his right and nearly spewed the brew out.

"Watch it!" A customer growled, narrowly avoiding Stefnir's jerky motions.

The boy swallowed and regretted it. The sweet-to-bitter flavor washed over his palette, intensifying the unpleasantness. His throat itched, and Stefnir wondered if bad yeast was somehow to blame. His vision watery, he squinted at the man.

A gaunt face regarded the boy with narrow, sky blue eyes under a hooded brow. Blonde braids ran down his shoulders, while his beard barely masked a snarl. All at once, Stefnir understood Olaf's statement about wolves in the cities.

"You sizin' me for a fight?" The customer growled.

Stefnir realized he was staring and shook his head. The customer's hand crept towards the axe at his belt. The boy's shoulders slunk and he bowed his head.

"I'm sorry," Stefnir explained. "Just a bad drink."

The blonde warrior sternly watched the boy for a moment, before the faintest smirk crept on his face. "I guess Geir's playing his old tricks again." He laughed and slapped a hand against the counter. "Geir! I'll have whatever he *isn't* having."

The bartender guffawed and Stefnir felt his face flush with shame. But to the boy's surprise, the warrior rounded about and extended a fresh flagon his way. Stefnir took it with a nod, putting the off-mead on the counter. "Thank you."

"Yer welcome kid." The warrior's smirk lingered. "Times are too tough with warrin' chieftains to lose yer head in a pissing match, anyway."

"It's well skinned," the mead hall owner, Broddi, admitted. He set the fur down to study the scroll unfurled over his lap. "Yes. It'll earn you a night for sure, Olaf."

The varl scratched his beard, studying the fat man seated in the leather and wood-framed chair before a fire pit. "My thanks, sir. But you seem more familiar with me than I you."

Broddi smiled. Despite being away from humans for some time, Olaf could tell his expression was genuine. "You don't remember me? It's been some forty years since last I saw you, and since you've been in this town."

Olaf stared for a moment, and then shut his eyes. He put his fingertips against his horned forehead as it came to him. "The bandit raid in Karlshus. Faen! That was an age ago!"

"Aye. I'd say I was about, oh…" Broddi put a hand just over his knee. "That tall. The way you and a few of your kind arrived and saved my family and hearth? Aye, a boy isn't likely to forget that."

Olaf nodded. The moment lingered, and the varl found himself somewhat uncomfortable as he dwelled on the praise.

"So what brings you to Karlshus anyway?" Broddi asked. "I know our mead is good but it's a long trip from the north."

Olaf's mouth drew into a line, his jaw rolling as he considered how to answer the question. Eventually he reached into his pouch and withdrew a piece of wood with roughly split edges. The varl raised it towards the owner. "I need to find whoever uses this emblem on their shields."

The sigil on the shattered piece was of a crude skull under a hammer and over an anvil, bronze over a background painted black. Broddi's jovial complexion instantly vanished. He fidgeted, rolling up the scroll in his lap before sitting upright. "What, um… what business would you want with those folks?"

Olaf lowered the shield piece. "They took something that belongs to me and my people. We intend to reclaim it. You're not afraid of them, are you?"

"No," Broddi replied, and then shifted in his seat. "Maybe. It's not quite that simple."

Olaf waited.

"You see…" Broddi cleared his throat. "Karlshus makes a fine swill but nothing worth a trip off the trade path, nothing you can't enjoy at home. So at my establishment, we do something unusual for a small village. We import a great deal of our mead from foreign sources, like Arberrang. And we get it at a fair price, too. Those people you're searching for happen to be my suppliers, and they're the reason that customers stop by Karlshus on their way to bigger settlements."

Olaf shifted his weight to the opposite foot. "There's only one port close enough that they're likely to visit. And if the prices are fair like you claim, then that must mean they're smuggling, bypassing the tariffs in Strand."

Broddi leaned back in his chair and sighed. "Listen Olaf, this is putting me in a bad position…"

"I realize." Olaf placed his fists on his hips. "And I'm sorry about that. I'm trying to deal with this quietly, because if I have to go back to Grofheim and get friends, they're more likely than I to get violent."

Broddi slumped. "I'll tell you. It's not like it's a huge secret, so you're bound to find out anyway. But my dealings with them are mutually lucrative. Just, don't mention my name, alright?"

Olaf nodded.

"They're a gang called the Mársmidr, or 'Corpse Smiths.' Their yox wagons come through here once a month, but you can find them in Strand if you just ask around quietly enough."

Broddi's voice dropped to a whisper, and Olaf could barely hear him over the crackle of the fire. "They're led by a man named Freystein. And if you meet him, that's when you know that business has gone bad."

"I didn't catch your name," Stefnir interjected. The warrior had launched into a tirade of drunken boasting and stories, never once actually introducing himself. Stefnir had politely listened through the rambunctious yammering, but used the pause his question created to take a cautious first sip of his fresh mug.

This time the sweetness was tame with little of the horrendous aftertaste, followed by heartiness that both soothed and warmed all the way down. Stefnir coughed but already wanted another gulp.

"This the first time you had mead?" The blonde-haired warrior asked, his smirk weakening as he scratched his chin. "And the name's Arnbjorn."

The boy nodded. "Thanks for setting my drink right, Arnbjorn. Anyway, you were saying something about warring chieftains?

"Ugh." The warrior took a swig, resting an elbow on the bar. "That's something a pup like you shouldn't get involved in. Especially one who can't craft a shield to save his life."

Stefnir blushed but didn't reply. His "shield" was barely more than a bundle of uncarved logs, clumped together by leather straps. Olaf had promised to show him how to make a better one later.

Arnbjorn leaned forward and whispered. "There are always some old feuds, grudges, and so on. But lately, it's been madness. Guys who dreamed of the Governor's seat have been reaching to usurp it. The triumvirate even made an attempt on the Governor-Prince's life about a year or so back, and Strand hasn't been the same ever since."

"Triumvirate?" Stefnir asked.

Arnbjorn blinked as though dumbfounded, and Stefnir suddenly wondered how drunk the man was. "Probably shouldn't have let that slip. Ah well, what harm could a kid like you do? They're some bad news they are, a group of three gangs. Alone, they were rough and dangerous. But together, they've been making some serious waves. Ahhh, I miss the old days when my brother and I were a part of it all."

Stefnir nodded, his eyes meeting Arnbjorn's as he listened with keen interest. "You were a member of one of these gangs?"

"Oh, you better believe it." Arnbjorn snorted and rambled on. "As of late, they've been trying to hire every decent axe-arm they can get in Strand, using their raids to pay for recruiting. They're gonna have themselves a grand army soon."

Stefnir put his mug down on the counter. "Have you ever heard of a man named Magnus?"

Arnbjorn gave the boy a sly look. "And here I was, thinkin' I was giving a whelp a few pointers. What's yer angle, boy?"

"I just heard the name whispered," Stefnir said, not lying but not quite telling the whole truth. His voice dropped a level. "I hear he's a slaver."

The warrior gave him a sharp appraisal but slowly nodded.

"It's been going on for some time. Magnus and his gang, the Vak'auga, are all about raiding and thralling. Usually going south to collect slaves and plunder, as the varl are often too dangerous to attack. Although I heard about one group, not Vak'auga but workin' for the triumvirate, that did go north. They were seeking a nice little prize from th—"

Arnbjorn stopped when a shadow fell over him. Stefnir spun around and realized it was Olaf.

"Any luck with the pelt?" Stefnir inquired.

"Got us some sleeping quarters, a meal and even a few coins out of it," Olaf replied, but his ash-colored gaze went from Stefnir to the interrupted warrior. "Hey, you there."

Stefnir realized that Arnbjorn was slinking away from Olaf and himself. The blonde warrior slowly half-faced them, fixing the varl with a dark glare.

Olaf wasn't intimidated. "I overheard the end of your chat with my friend here. Did you say something about a raid to the north?"

"*Olaf!*"

The varl stiffened as someone spat out his name with the challenging roar. Stefnir jumped, dropping his flagon and spilling the mead. Even Arnbjorn's hard stare disappeared as he looked to the source of the shout.

Another varl stood halfway across the silent and hushed room. The giant wore leather armor from chest to foot, his fiery red hair contrasting with his jade green eyes. Stefnir gulped as he watched the axe slung over the varl's shoulder, the weapon easily as tall as the boy.

"Ulfvalgr," Olaf mumbled, shock in his tone. "What're you doi—"

The opposing varl shot forth, streaking like a fireball at Olaf. Stefnir's mentor barely swayed from the punch aimed at his gut. Instead, Ulfvalgr's fist connected with an unfortunate drunk behind Olaf.

Ulfvalgr twisted to take a second shot at Olaf as the inebriate collided into a table of other patrons. Spilled drinks, smashed food, drunken wits and bad tempers swiftly combined and men began to fight amongst one another, misunderstandings fueling the chaos. Some jumped to the defense of friends while others reacted to perceived slights. The brawl swiftly escalated as other tables joined the fray. The serving maids wasted no time rushing to tell the owner.

As Olaf weaved and evaded Ulfvalgr's blows, Stefnir threw himself over the bar to escape the melee. Landing, he saw Arnbjorn hiding behind the counter as well. The warrior busied himself grabbing whatever he could from the mead hall's stock.

Arnbjorn noticed the boy and smirked. "Yer gonna be kicked out regardless, kid. So you best grab what you can!" With that, Arnbjorn fled towards the exit, clutching a mead barrel the size of his chest.

Stefnir realized Arnbjorn was right. There was no explaining or bartering their way out of this debacle. Undoubtedly, whatever deal Olaf struck was void given the damage the varl had unintentionally and indirectly caused. Over painful grunts, loud curses and the crunches of smashed chairs, Stefnir plucked cured meats and cheeses from the bar's shelves, stuffing the provisions into his pouch.

Stefnir caught sight of something in the corner of his sight and dodged back just in time. Geir's club whooshed over the boy's head, missing.

"Stealin' our goods?" The bartender snarled. "Not on my wat—"

Geir's jaw snapped shut as Stefnir slammed his slapdash shield into the bartender's face, blood spurting from his nose as he stumbled and fell. The force dislodged the bundled logs, which clattered against the wooden floor, leaving Stefnir holding only the strap. The boy spun and ran the same direction as Arnbjorn.

Outside Stefnir scanned about, eager to find any sign of the mead thief. But Arnbjorn was long gone. A chaotic mess of footsteps masked his trail, courtesy of the patrons who had also taken flight. Stefnir cursed. His chances of discovering more about the enslaving gang were dashed.

Creaking floorboards caught Stefnir's attention and he spun about defensively. Olaf rushed his way. "We're leaving!"

"Who was that varl?" Stefnir asked as he fell into step behind his mentor.

"He's only half our problems," Olaf explained as he led them toward the safety of the distant forest line. "Armed men burst came through the back and joined the fight! And they're *not* town guard!"

They entered the woods and came to a stop. Stefnir panted hard, holding his knees to prop himself up. Steam escaped his mouth with every breath. "Did we," he struggled to speak. "… Did we lose them?"

Olaf took deep gasps as he watched the town behind them. "I think so. I see no pursuers."

"Like it was ever that hard to catch you," someone spoke with a growl. Olaf turned to the origin, his features dropping.

Ulfvalgr stepped out from behind a stout pine tree. The handle of his axe was draped over his shoulders, his wrists over either end. The red-haired varl tilted his head to the side, upturned horns level to the snow. Stefnir cringed from the loud crack that emitted from the interloper's spine.

"I suppose I owe you some thanks." Ulfvalgr snarled. "Those men were on my tail for at least a day, but you gave me the perfect cover to slip away."

Olaf clenched his fists, his jaw jutting some. "What was that about back ther—"

"Where's the gods damned *heirloom*, Olaf?" Ulfvalgr took a stomp forth. The sheer *power* of his voice set Stefnir's hair on end.

Olaf winced and his shoulders slumped, defeat clear in his features. "The thief who took it went south to Halsar, where he was slain. I followed the killers' trail west, so I came to Broddi for answ—"

"Who and where are they?"

Olaf hesitated, trying to meet Ulfvalgr's scowl. "They're the Mársmidr, from Strand. Their leader is a man named Freystein."

Ulfvalgr snorted, before spitting contemptuously into the snow. "You always were weak, Olaf."

He began to march away when Olaf cried out a reply. "If they've gone to Strand, we should probably work together!"

The red-haired varl stopped but didn't face them. "And why would I do that?"

"You're alone. You can't fight them all off yourself." Olaf took a step forward with an opened hand. "You'll need a band of your own. You need our help."

"So what? You want to work together?" Ulfvalgr's fist visibly tightened around the shaft of his axe. "Tell me. Between a beardless boy and a feeble Shieldbanger like you, how would you 'aid' my chances at all?"

Doubt passed over Olaf's face. But Stefnir, having recovered his breath, lost his temper and replied. "Why would anyone want to work with *you*? If you're war incarnate, go get your prize yourself!"

Ulfvalgr bared his teeth as fury flashed across his countenance. Stefnir's hand instinctively went to the axe in his belt, but the boy knew such a fight would cost him his life. Olaf grasped the shield over his shoulder, ready to react.

Ulfvalgr did not move. Little by little, Stefnir thought he saw reason pierce Ulfvalgr's ardor. A dark chuckle grew from the varl's throat, his face relaxing, assuaged of anger. He turned his back on the two.

"Try to keep up then, whelp," Ulfvalgr said and set a brisk pace.

Stefnir and Olaf trailed behind. His mentor clasped a big hand over the boy's sore shoulder as they marched, leaning down to whisper. "Well done. I was at a loss on that one myself."

Stefnir nodded. "What's all this about an heirloom? And who is he?"

"It's a bit of a story lad, and not one I'm particularly proud of. But I'll tell you on our trip."

Stefnir's eyes bored into Ulfvalgr's back. "Can we really trust him? How do we know he won't just slit our throats when we sleep?"

"You don't," Ulfvalgr said without turning around. "But the armed men I ran from most certainly would have."

Stefnir's brow rose, and both he and Olaf glanced behind to Karlshus.

A massive column of smoke climbed the sky, black mingling with the gray of the overhead storm clouds. Stefnir couldn't be certain, but the fire seemed to rise from the mead hall.

Something cold touched Stefnir's face, and the boy raised his gaze skyward. The snow had begun to fall.

Chapter 2

Arnbjorn slammed his back against the wall of a hut, the mead barrel sloshing under his arm. He remained hidden, breathing hard until finally mustering the courage to peep around the corner.

Broddi's Mead Hall was a bonfire, the smoke rising to the sky which retaliated with a gentle snowfall. No dead were scattered around the hall, as most of the patrons had fled. Yet Arnbjorn could still see figures prowling about the blaze.

"Why hello."

The simple greeting chilled Arnbjorn in a way that winter could not. Slowly, he rounded and found himself staring into a disfigured countenance. A vivid scar ran down the man's brow, over his nose and passed his sneering lips.

"Ottar." Arnbjorn choked.

The ugly man was not alone. Half a dozen armed raiders stood by, dressed in dark trappings. One of the men cleaned blood from the edge of his axe, watching Arnbjorn with undisguised disgust.

"It's been a while," Ottar started. The crow's feet beneath his eyes appeared strangely jovial as he strode past Arnbjorn. "So, what stupid name do you go by now?"

"Arnbjorn." His attention never left Ottar. Although his instincts demanded he grab his axe, Arnbjorn resisted. He could not fight so many men by himself, but he might be able to talk his way out of this situation.

"That's not as bad as I worried," Ottar said. He turned and reached out with a black-gloved hand, brushing Arnbjorn's gold braids. "I must admit, I love what you've done with your hair. I think Broddi's daughter did the same with hers. Although, she was chattier after we threatened to gut her before her father."

A dark chuckle rose among Ottar's men. Arnbjorn did not flinch, but kept his glare as steely as he could. Even though his stomach felt of ice. "Did you hurt Broddi or his daughter?"

14

"Of course not. Businessmen are typically smart. After a few bloody threats and a little cut or two, he gave us what we wanted." Ottar cast a macabre smile toward the burning mead hall. "Family is everything, after all."

He returned his focus to Arnbjorn before looking downward. Arnbjorn followed Ottar's line of sight, and realized that he unconsciously tightened his own fist. Arnbjorn cursed his body for revealing weakness.

"Oh, poor Arnbjorn. I must have struck a nerve. Surviving without your clan is rough, without your brother taking care of you." Ottar laughed, his guffaw joining a chorus of the other raiders. "Perhaps if you didn't swindle Freystein's share, you wouldn't be in this predicament?"

Arnbjorn said nothing but shivered, the pent up rage building within him. Still he stayed his hand, forcing down the suicidal urge to strike at Ottar.

"Well. It's not like we came all this way to see *you*, 'Arnbjorn.'" Ottar scratched his marred mouth. "But, I suppose it's wyrd that we've crossed paths again. Tell me, how are your skills at tracking these days? Has too much alcohol dulled them? Or too many loose women?"

Arnbjorn's features tightened as he replied. "I could lead you to a woman if you wanted, Ottar. Not that you'd know what to do once you had her."

Catcalls rose from the raiders. Ottar flashed a sneer before settling into a grin, his cheeks flush from embarrassment.

"Good to see that tongue is still sharp at least," Ottar replied, his voice etched with chill.

"What do you want?" Arnbjorn asked. Glossing over the insult was the best way to see it forgotten.

Ottar tilted his head at the mead thief. "We came pursuing that red-haired varl. His name is Ulfvalgr, and he has something that Lord Freystein wants."

"What is it?" Arnbjorn asked, intrigued.

"Freystein is reluctant to give details for some reason. He said it was small, about the size of a man's hand. But Freystein warned us that Ulfvalgr likely hid it. We sought and infiltrated the caravan he travelled with to keep watch on him. At least until one of our men faened up and was slain while trying to search his effects. Ulfvalgr ran, and we tracked him here."

Ottar raised a hand to the burning structure behind him. "Clearly, the varl isn't likely to go down without a battle. We were moving on him when he started that 'fight' at Broddi's. It was a ruse to escape."

Arnbjorn laughed. "You're admitting you failed? To me?"

"It's time to switch tactics. This is a job for a thief and a liar…" Ottar smirked and gestured to Arnbjorn with an open palm. "So perhaps you could succeed where an axe could not. We need him alive."

"Taking on varl is kind of a risky venture," Arnbjorn replied. He wanted to ask why it was his problem, but thought it best not to twist the blade.

"Broddi admitted knowing the other varl, the one Ulfvalgr started that fight with. His name is Olaf, and Broddi pointed him to Strand. As they both disappeared at the same time, Ulfvalgr is likely with him now."

Arnbjorn said nothing, but remembered this Olaf as clear as day. Being in the midst of a varl brawl was not something even the drunkest of men could readily forget.

Ottar chuckled again. "Come now. You should see how badly Freystein wants this thing. He'd certainly forgive your transgressions and let you back into the Mársmidr."

"If they're heading to Strand…" Arnbjorn started.

"Fear not. We will return to call off the bounty, and ensure the rest of us know you're re-earning your place. Ulfvalgr will be avoiding the roads, so we should arrive in time to spread the word. You won't have to worry about someone collecting your pretty little head on the job." Ottar grinned.

When Arnbjorn remained quiet, Ottar continued. "You do want to see your brother again, don't you?"

Arnbjorn felt his expression softened at Ottar's words. "How is my brother?"

"Quite well, quite well." Ottar scratched his scarred lip. Arnbjorn knew this to be a frequent habit of Ottar's, a quirk exacerbated by the cold. "He recently pleased Freystein. Hoping for my job, I suspect."

Arnbjorn stood still for a moment, before his shoulders dropped, his head drooping. It was good to hear that his brother was doing well, but the loneliness seized Arnbjorn's heart. He ached to be reunited with his family again.

"That's a good lad," Ottar said with that sinister smirk, obviously knowing that Arnbjorn's body spoke for him. "We think they've gone north and east. If you hurry, you may find them.

"And be sure to keep them alive, Arnbjorn, at any cost. Freystein needs this trinket, and bumbling blindly through Strand is a fast way to end up dead in a ditch. Watch for our signs. If you can learn this treasure's location, do so. Otherwise, Freystein may want to take them captive. Personally."

Arnbjorn began to shuffle away, the circle of men opening to admit him an exit.

"And before you go."

Arnbjorn stopped and faced Ottar. The man seized the mead barrel from Arnbjorn.

"You had best travel light. Wouldn't want you bogged down or anything, so we'll take care of this for you." Ottar shook the barrel suggestively. His men laughed again.

Arnbjorn left the circle of marauders, bowing his head to hide his reddened cheeks. He marched through the falling snow in the direction of Strand.

Stefnir shivered as he followed the footsteps of giants.

It was merciful at least that their prints were large pits, craters that kept the snow from gathering over his shoddy boots and chilling his toes. But the wind cut through the scarf wrapped over his face. He crossed his arms, hiding his fingers in his warmer armpits.

It was a relief that Stefnir had lost his poorly made shield, his burdens eased. Olaf had told him to save the leather straps that once clasped it together. His mentor promised to teach him how to make a proper shield later, perhaps during a rest. But Ulfvalgr had driven them several hours into the flurried night, lit only by distant flashes of lightning and the torch that the varl struck after considerable reluctance.

"We've good and lost them already," Olaf spoke before a sudden gale stopped his words. When it died down, he continued, "We should make camp for the night."

"That's the third time you've pestered me about stopping." Ulfvalgr didn't change course.

"And I am no less right than the last two times."

Ulfvalgr halted and twisted about. His green eyes narrowed as he scanned the darkness behind them. The flurries were covering their tracks. Despite the occasional burst of wind and lightning from afar, the snow was otherwise falling gently.

Light suddenly appeared above, and the three raised their heads to the heavens. A break in the clouds exposed the moon's illumination. Stefnir used it to scan the area, finding nothing but snow and the silhouettes of trees.

Ulfvalgr grunted at the shifting weather. "As good a time as any."

"Where are we now?" Stefnir asked.

Olaf gave Stefnir a perked brow, his brown beard coated in flurries. "Use your ears boy. What do you hear?"

Stefnir shut his mouth and listened. He realized he overheard the trickle of water, as though cascading over rocks. "A stream? River?"

"The Red River, the body of water that runs between Strand and Karlshus," Ulfvalgr said. The varl lifted a massive hand and Stefnir flinched, fearing the giant would strike him. Then he realized that Ulfvalgr was pointing towards a patch of grass with just a hint of white. "The tree canopies cover that spot well. We'll pitch camp there."

Stefnir nodded and drew his axe. He approached a dead pine and judged its trunk to be as wide as a man's leg. Taking his weapon in two hands, Stefnir gauged his chop and struck hard enough to shake the branches, seasoning the snow with brown needles.

"What the faen are you doing?"

Ulfvalgr's words sapped Stefnir's confidence. He was certain he was doing the right thing. "I was just… getting firewood."

"We haven't all night to wait on you whittling the trunk down."

Ulfvalgr's words caused a lump of anger to swell in the boy's chest. Stefnir felt his shoulders tighten, but he bit his tongue rather than risk his life insulting the varl.

Olaf didn't.

"If he's terrible at it," Olaf scornfully rebuked, fists upon his hips as he glared at Ulfvalgr. "Then why not show us how a warrior like you would fell such a mighty tree?"

Stefnir smirked. At last, Olaf seemed to have regained some of the esteem that had dwindled since Ulfvalgr joined them. His friend's stern countenance gave Stefnir hope.

Yet when Stefnir looked at Ulfvalgr, hope vanished as the varl indolently rubbed his nostril. He drew his massive war axe as he sauntered towards the pine. Stefnir panicked and threw himself aside as the blade whooshed through the air.

Stefnir never saw the first strike, but he felt it. Buried face first in the snowy grass, the ground shook as Ulfvalgr connected, a root popping a few inches from the boy's face. Splinters rained down upon his hair.

The second strike finished what the first began. The tree fell, sounding like an aged yawn as it crashed into the earth. Stefnir blinked in time to see small critters scuttle and escape the tree's abrupt, violent fall.

Stefnir laid on the ground, stupefied. Eventually he glimpsed at Olaf, whose jaw dropped in shock. Ulfvalgr walked with casual ease towards the tree and sliced off two large branches. Strapping his axe behind him again, he unsheathed a massive knife from his belt— the size of a man's short sword— and began to whittle the cut branches into sharpened stakes.

"Make yourselves useful and have a fire ready by the time I get back from fishing," Ulfvalgr said as he faded into the night, in the direction of the river.

Stefnir stood and joined Olaf as he lumbered towards the fallen pine. The giant undid the knapsack on his back and dropped it in the snow-crusted grass. He withdrew a handle and an axe-head from the pack and set to work assembling the tool.

The two labored without saying a word, taking turns between stripping the large branches, gathering smaller twigs and then chopping and splitting logs. Between them, it did not take long to assemble a neat pile of fuel, kindling and dead pine needles for tinder.

Soon Stefnir was seated on a log, breathing heavily. His mentor knelt, striking sparks from flint against the pyramid-shaped bundle of wood.

"Olaf." Stefnir finally broke their silence. "Who were those men after Ulfvalgr? What's really going on between you two?"

The varl gazed at him. Even in the dim moonlight, Stefnir could see some of the sadness in Olaf's eyes. He reached behind his horned forehead to scratch his scalp. "Mm, I did promise to tell you when we escaped Karlshus, didn't I? A moment."

The varl went back to work and before long the tinder caught, though more steam than smoke arose. After a while, the flames danced upon the bark and dry needles curled into cinders.

Olaf stepped away from the fire, keeping a better distance than the boy, and sat down on the earth. Stefnir could feel the varl's reluctance to discuss his past as Olaf crossed his arms and rolled his jaw.

At last, Olaf sighed. "Truth is, boy… I failed."

Stefnir held his limbs close to the fire, but kept his focus on Olaf.

The varl leaned forward, his arms over his knees. "I'm Ulfvalgr's kendr… that is, the closest the varl ever get to being family. A blood-brother, you could say. We form relationships, and often the younger varl listen to the gray beards that our god, Hadrborg, crafted before us. Such was what Ulfvalgr and I do… did, with our elder, Torstein."

Olaf scratched his beard, his gaze keen on the flames as he went on.

"Our kind do not have parents as men do. But Torstein was like what you'd call a father to Ulfvalgr and myself. He taught us to fight. Taught us to survive and read. He took care of us and gave us a purpose. As our kind live such long lives, there is an ebb and flow of need to find a reason for life. It changes with the age.

"But we varl too, die. We fall in battle. To disease and accident. And after many, many lives of men, even we too will die of old age. When that time came for Torstein, he entrusted to Ulfvalgr and I an heirloom. A gift of great importance to us, not just Torstein's kendr and the kendr after, but all varlkind.

"Ulfvalgr and I were divided about how to protect the heirloom. I wanted to build a shrine to protect it, so should the time come when the varl needed it again, it would be at the ready.

"But Ulfvalgr had never been patient, and Torstein's death had left him with a terrible fury. He was not thrilled with the idea of being stuck in some isolated location for years. After much arguing and fighting, we came to an agreement. Carefully, we divided the heirloom in half, such that it could be reassembled later. Then we went our separate ways."

Olaf leaned back and raised his face to the moonlight. Stefnir just stared as the varl drew a deep, audible breath through his nostrils before exhaling steam from his mouth.

"And that's how it was for years, lad. Until one day almost two months ago, three men came from the south. They came, shields raised and weapons drawn. I knew what they wanted as they charged across the snowy plains, towards the stone and wood shrine Ulfvalgr and I had crafted to house the heirloom. As one they came at me, came for murder!"

Olaf shot out of his seat, his arms raised as though fighting the invaders then and there. Stefnir brows perked as he watched.

"The first man chopped his blade down, but I deflected it with the rim of my shield, using it to strike him across the face. Before I could finish him, my second foe shot out with his spear, and I ducked and weaved out of his range. He was skilled, and kept the pressure on me, keeping me out of striking distance. He wouldn't give me time to think, and just kept jabbing and jabbing while his kinsman recovered.

"Then he made his last mistake. I figured out his rhythm, and I countered his weapon with my shield. It snapped at the shaft, and cleared the way for me to cut him down!" Olaf swung his left forearm outward, following it with a slicing motion from his right hand. "The spearman screamed as he fell. But no sooner than I drew my blade from his body did the first man attack again. I barely managed to parry his blade with mine. He raised his shield, expecting me to smash him with my own again. The last thing the fool expected was the horns! Ha!

"Again and again, I butted and gored! I heard his helmet dent, his nose crack, then his jaw, until at last the man collapsed into the snow, unconscious…"

Olaf stopped, focused on the darkness ahead. Stefnir wondered what was wrong for a moment.

Olaf groaned. "That was when I realized the third man was missing. During the fight, the rascal had slipped away. I ran as fast as I could towards the shrine. When I arrived, the bastard grabbed the heirloom and a torch. He set the altar on fire, and I… I panicked. I had to get out of there."

Olaf stood still and dumb for a moment, before returning to his seat.

"I ran to the stream and drew buckets, trying to douse the fire and save the shrine. I didn't stop and think about what really mattered. When I finished, the shrine was damaged but intact, but the thief had gotten away. I found the other man, whom I had knocked unconscious, and beat him until he finally told me where his friend was going. Halsar, he said.

"After that, I took my prisoner to the nearest varl settlement. I told the elders what happened, so that they could pass word to Ulfvalgr should he return. I broke the prisoner's shield and took the emblem with me to show witnesses. But when I tracked the thief to Halsar, he had already left. I asked around, and the people told me they'd seen him going south… but they also said that I was not the only one to ask about him. A band of men also tracked him."

Olaf reached into his belt pouch and withdrew a piece of wood. He tossed it to Stefnir who caught it in both hands. Against the firelight, he saw it was black with bronze symbols of a skull between an anvil and a hammer.

"The townsfolk of Halsar said that the men who sought the thief also bore that very symbol, just as the thief's friend did. I followed their trail, back to…" Olaf stopped and glimpsed behind Stefnir.

The boy twisted about and saw Ulfvalgr had returned. Salmon dangled from the stick over his shoulder. Stefnir felt his chest tighten as he wondered if the varl was angry, if Olaf had overstepped his place by telling Stefnir about this heirloom.

Instead, Ulfvalgr walked around the boy, towards the fire. He laid his stake down and plucked the fish from it, drawing his knife to skin them. "Well Olaf. Don't stop a good story of your failure on my account."

Olaf frowned, his horns dipping a little. The varl glanced at Stefnir. "I followed them to Karlshus, where along the way I met you. While we were at his mead hall, I spoke to Broddi. He said that sigil belongs to a gang called the Mársmidr, in Strand."

Ulfvalgr raised his head from his grisly work. Stefnir found himself staring into a pair of angry, green eyes. "And we're going to find their leader, Freystein, and get back what's ours."

Chapter 3

"Go on Thorgils! Take a swing at the faen-faced yox yanker!"

A chorus of laughs arose from the crowd surrounding Thorgils. Drunk and giddy, the men of the Glotta-Ox gang delivered cheers and catcalls at their old rivals, the Oerr-Brandrs. Thorgils grinned as a rock flew over his shoulder and buried itself in the snow, but whether it was from his own Glotta-Oxs or his foes, he did not know.

"After I split your skull," Thorgils said as he lunged with both hands at the man before him. "I'll pay your woman a visit to comfort her!"

The shoved brawler flashed him a short-lived smirk, before he sneered and drew a dagger. Thorgils didn't know what the Oerr-Brandrs called him, but he dearly hoped Valgard would be careful with his blade this time.

"You trying to knife me, milk gurgler?" Thorgils charged. He ducked and slammed Valgard with his shoulder, just as they had practiced a dozen times in the last few weeks. Valgard's dagger arm came down. Thorgils shut his eyes, praying to the dead gods that his disguised friend didn't faen this up.

A man screamed behind Thorgils, who smiled. It must have been a member of the Glotta-Oxs.

"Kill 'em!" Someone shouted. The sound of steel being drawn followed drunken shouts and battle cries. The plan had worked. A drunken fistfight had become a lethal melee.

Valgard stepped back as Thorgils stood. Both men beamed at each other as they drew their weapons and joined the battle, though their axes fell more indiscriminately.

The feud between the Glotta-Oxs and Oerr-Brandrs went back years, always in the shantytowns just on the outer rim of Strand. Between stretches of untrustworthy peace and brutal short wars, the two gangs always competed to provide protection rackets for the few businesses in the slums, or sneak refugees under the city fortifications.

On that night, just outside the *Veggr Drinking Hall* where the argument first started, dozens of men from either gang maimed and killed one another. Fully half of both factions perished, and there would be no peace until one or both were dead.

"Faen…" A gang member from the Glotta-Oxs coughed a glop of blood onto his lips. "Ya bloody betrayed us, Thorgils…"

Thorgils put a boot to the man's neck, but hesitated to raise his axe.

"You best do it, Eirik," Valgard said. He leaned down to wipe his reclaimed, bloody dagger on the tunic of a dead Oerr-Brandr. "That gut wound of his isn't something he'll survive come morning."

"I'm sorry." The imposter "Thorgils" frowned as he slipped his axe's edge over the wounded man's jugular.

"Thorgils" watched the man as he died. The gang member futilely grasped his neck as the well of blood seeped over his fingers, trickled down his chest and reddened the snow. His pupils dilated, as though beholding finality and discovering the true meaning of death. Gurgling gasps and bloody bubbles escaped his opened mouth, until at last he laid still.

Eirik slowly raised his gaze from the man he had killed, and surveyed the area around the drinking hall.

By the light coming from the establishment's entrance, Eirik counted almost twenty bodies embedded in the snow. Puddles of blood gathered in myriad footprints. A few men still breathed, but from the wounds they cradled Eirik knew they would be lucky to see the morning, much less fight again.

Eirik shut his eyes and tried to blot out the groaning.

"Bad news," Valgard said. "We're short one man."

Eirik looked at his friend. "Which side?"

Valgard shrugged. He hooked his skeg axe to his belt and sheathed his dagger. "Doesn't matter. I thought the mead would dull their judgment and maybe we'd get them all. But if we're missing one, he must be running to get reinforcements."

"Then we best not be here when they arrive." Eirik slipped his axe over his back and took off, his cloak trailing in the wind as he and Valgard ran through a few alleys.

Valgard suddenly stopped and grabbed Eirik's arm. The two friends threw themselves against the wall of some hovel. Around the corner, Eirik caught a glimpse of figures bearing torches and drawn blades, running towards the massacre site.

"It'll be all out war now," Eirik spoke in a whisper. "I'd wager on the Oerr-Brandrs coming out on top."

"Aye, but they won't live long themselves," Valgard replied. "When they find neither of our bodies and we don't show up tomorrow, they'll know someone tricked them into battle. After that, they won't be taking recruits so readily. Without numbers, one of the bigger gangs will crush them before the new moon."

"So both are as good as dead." Eirik felt his mouth draw into a line. "But that just means someone else will seize control and extort this neighborhood."

The thought made Eirik's heart harden. A new clique claiming territory meant the need to make examples and show strength, often at the cost of innocents who thought themselves finally free of syndicate control. Perhaps it would be the Vak'auga, one of the strongest gangs that the Governor's Guard proved unable to stop. If it was, they'd have their own vision for the shantytown of Hundgaman; selling contraband goods and smuggled mead, hosting underground fights or finding late night "vocations" for the neighborhood girls.

That was assuming that the Vak'auga didn't just load the women onto their ships and sail south to sell them.

"Come on." Valgard clapped a hand over his friend's shoulder. "That's a problem for tomorrow, for we've done enough damage tonight. And I could damn well use some sleep in a proper bed."

The obnoxious racket at his bedroom door awoke Eirik. He cast off his sheets and sat up, regretting the action as a ringing ache rattled his brain. Eirik cupped his forehead in a palm, leaning forward and willing the pain away.

"I'm up, give me a moment," Eirik replied with a little more force than he intended at the persistent knocker.

"Apologies sir. Steward Olvir wants a word with you and Valgard as soon as you're able," the messenger spoke through the door. Eirik then heard the sound of footsteps travelling down the hall.

It took him a long moment to stand. Once he did, Eirik fetched his boots, tunic and cloak from the cheap dresser. The Governor's Guard had furnished him with basic room and board. Small as it was, it provided Eirik with the luxuries of a cot to sleep in and even privacy, benefits he never had as a child.

He exited his room as he fastened the cloak over his shoulders, crossing the hall and knocking on Valgard's door. He waited a moment but no reply came. He knocked again and then realized the door was unbarred. Slowly, Eirik opened it to peek within. "Valgard?"

His friend was in bed with his face opposite the entrance, a sheet covering his body. The floor was littered with uncorked, emptied bottles that once contained mead and ale. Eirik moved to enter when he saw another shape shuffle beside his friend, and a few long strands of blonde hair fell against Valgard's arm.

Eirik sighed quietly. Last night, their plan to return home was derailed when Valgard suggested "just one" victory drink at the *Skald's Scribbling*, which of course became several. He remembered seeing Valgard flirt with the bar maiden serving them, but didn't recall her following him back to the barracks. Then Eirik winced and rubbed his temple, realizing there was very little he could recall at all from last night.

With a shake of his head, Eirik shut the door to Valgard's room and resolved to meet with Olvir by himself.

"Eirik, good morning," Olvir greeted the Guardsman as he crossed the lobby of the Great Hall. Olvir was not alone but walked alongside a hunched, elderly woman who bore a long staff. Half her face was obscured by a hood.

"Steward Olvir," Eirik gave a slight bow, and again to the woman. "Mender Melkorka."

"Guardsman Eirik," the woman replied with a respectful nod. "He's all yours. I have some business to attend to."

"Of course, I'm sorry I couldn't help you," Olvir said as the woman turned towards the Governor's throne room and left their company.

"What did she need?" Eirik asked. Respect for the elderly had been so seared into his demeanor that Eirik couldn't imagine refusing a request for aid.

Olvir ran a tongue over his dried lips as he rubbed his wrinkled cheek. "She was curious about some of our recent activities and raids. Apparently, the Governor doesn't want to raise alarm amongst the court by asking himself, but you know how I prefer to keep information in controlled hands."

"Ah." Eirik shifted uncomfortably. "Then you're not going to enjoy what I ask either."

"Dammit boy." Olvir grimaced and took Eirik by the shoulder, guiding him to a corner of the Great Hall. After a moment of casting his brown eyes about and ensuring they were alone, he stared down Eirik. "Out with it."

"The raid today," Eirik's voice dropped to a whisper. "The Aetla Hilmir. I wish to join."

"Who told you about it? Captain Dylan?"

Eirik kept his features impassive. Lying was an art, but his position within the Governor's Guard had taught him the skill well enough. "Steward Olvir, it was my counter informant that tipped us off in the first place, before Valgard and I were pulled to go after the Glotta-Ox and Oerr-Brandr gangs. I want to be there for this."

Olvir sighed. "Eirik, you're smart, and you know better. We're having enough trouble as it is keeping the Guard's secrets. A watchman overhears. Then, if he passes the right tip along at the right time, his pocket suddenly gets a little heavier. Or he finds a woman waiting in his bed when he gets home."

For a moment, Eirik wondered if the girl that Valgard met last night was payment for information rendered. But he threw the idea aside when he recalled Valgard teasing and flirting with her all night. Eirik suspected that Valgard's fine face and honey-coated tongue could unlace any dress in Strand. The dead gods had given the man a knack with women that Eirik certainly never possessed.

"I'm sorry sir, it won't happen again," Eirik promised.

Olvir drew his mouth into a line. "Anyway. Speaking of those two gangs, I hear they're finished thanks to you and your partner."

Eirik nodded. "We started a brawl that finished off half of them and incited the others to war."

"Where is Valgard anyway?" Olvir's brow furrowed.

Eirik's features failed to remain calm as he scrambled to find an excuse for his friend. "He's… chasing a promising tail."

"Ah. Anyway, the City Watch detained some of the rest after a bloodbath at the Glotta-Ox's flophouse. Hundgaman is free of their influence again."

Eirik frowned. He always hated that name for the neighborhood, for it meant "dog's delight." But as long as crime ruled its street, it was as good a name as any.

Olvir raised a hand. "I know, Eirik. It won't really last until we've removed the root of the problem, which is why I suppose it's good you know of today's raid."

"Sir?"

Olvir nodded and put a hand on Eirik's shoulder, leading him through a nearby door and stepping outside. They passed a few watchmen, who stood with their spears and round shields at attention. The snow crunched as Olvir and Eirik walked towards the edge of the hill upon which the Great Hall resided.

"The truth is, you will be going after the Aetla Hilmir. Your information all but confirmed that they're behind this contraband coming in. The problem is, I couldn't risk them seeing you or Valgard. We might need to keep your faces fresh once we investigate, and perhaps infiltrate, them."

"Sir, I mean no offense, but that's a tall order," Eirik replied. "The Glotta-Oxs and Oerr-Brandrs snuck refugees into the city, which was a strong cover for Valgard and me to join them under debt. But of all the gangs in Strand, not one of them is as clandestine as the 'Fated Kings.' We wouldn't even know where to begin making the inquiries to gain admission into their ranks."

"And it may never be done, Eirik." Olvir took in the view of the clustered halls and homes below. "But if they know your face, it most certainly won't be. We've never really taken the fight to the Aetla Hilmir. But after today, we expect that they'll go to ground and start recruiting to replenish their numbers. I want you to head the investigation of what we uncover. Follow the leads to any and all parties they do business with. We'll rip out this weed at the roots, and reclaim Strand from this filth."

Eirik fought down the smile that would otherwise crest his face, but his heart still warmed with the thought of victory. He had waited a long, long time to finally take on Strand's greatest crime syndicates. Now, the tables were turning with so many of the smaller gangs being put down.

Soon, they would make Strand a safe city once again.

"Yes sir. What are our orders in the mean time?"

Olvir pointed to the horizon, over the distant trees to the southeast. Eirik peered out, spotting remote figures and yoxen-drawn wagons.

"We have an incoming caravan that should be here this afternoon," Olvir said. "Originally it was much smaller, but it met with another coming from the east and the combined group is quite large. The City Watch is understaffed to deal with inspections. As it'll be late when they arrive, there will be extra pressure to get them inside the walls."

"Which means some of the merchants are bound to expedite inspections with a little silver," Eirik said.

Olvir sighed. "If you see that, mark those carts. It could very well tip us off as to who is smuggling what. But above all, I want you and Valgard there to assist and be alert for any unusual activity."

Eirik bowed and took a final glimpse at the horizon before returning to the Great Hall.

Valgard threw Eirik a wink and then ran chalk against the side of the cart, creating a small mark on the plank. The City Watch inside the walls knew to stay alert for the symbol. They would stop the wagon and give the cargo a proper inspection, dashing the hopes of drivers who bribed their way past the gates.

Eirik scanned over the caravan awaiting entrance through Strand's huge wooden gates. It was forced into double lines for customs to examine, but a third, faster line had formed alongside this. This new line consisted primarily of hired guards and solitary travelers, scribes, couriers and specialists. Folks who had joined the caravan to avoid travelling alone but did not bring large shipments with them.

"Did you catch the watchman's name who took the bribe for this one?" Valgard asked as he returned from marking the wagon.

"Moldof, I think." Eirik jerked his head towards the burly blonde man who was busy arguing with another merchant.

"Course, he won't get fired for this." Valgard snorted.

Eirik shrugged. "Unless one of the carts that slip by happens to carry trafficked goods."

"Hey you two." Eirik and Valgard turned about to the watchman calling them. "Boss said this one can go."

"Of course," Eirik replied as he and Valgard stepped away from the wheel.

The driver flashed them a nervous expression before cracking his whip, driving the yoxen on. Eirik doubted the lumbering beast could even feel the lash under the mess of its shaggy fur and thick hide, but it began to move all the same.

"And the merchant?" Valgard asked as he gave the driver a false smile and a patronizing wave.

"If it's contraband, he'll be arrested and his goods confiscated. If he's just trying to skip the duty, he'll pay double. Add in the futile bribe, and this trip is likely to put his ledger in the red." Eirik perused the group of people trying to get into the city, staying keen for anyone strange or suspicious.

"It's all a waste." Valgard stroked his beard. "We levy taxes for the City Watch to fight the gangs and stop their trafficking, so then the gangs make a larger profit off of bootlegging and smuggled goods anyway."

Eirik considered it. There was certainly some truth to his friend's cynical words, but it didn't tell the whole story. "There's plenty of crimes worse than duty-free wheat, you know that as well as I. And that's Strand's real problem. We're what holds those men back from taking control of the city. What good are we if we cannot uphold Strand's law?"

"And they're the guys we should be pursuing…" Valgard grunted as he glared at Moldof. "Ah, sneaky devil did it again. Idiot barely tries to hide it…"

Eirik's attention was sharply on the crowd. "Valgard. Check this out."

His friend obeyed. "And what for?"

"Group of four. Three men and a girl. Aging man with a braid running behind him."

"Well faen me!" Eirik felt Valgard slap a hand on his shoulder. "It's old Leiknir! It's been a while since we've seen his face, hasn't it? He's gotten a bit pudgy."

Eirik felt his features harden as he recognized the man. Leiknir had a long nose and a stomach which had begun to protrude over his belt, his weight gain considerable since last Eirik had seen him. "I still owe that bastard for what he tried with Magnus."

Valgard scratched his ear. "Eirik, that was almost a year ago. We couldn't make our claims stick then despite your best efforts. But Prince Ragnar was fine, thanks to you."

"And how many undercover Governor's Guard were killed last year thanks to him? We both know that he's the gatherer of whispers for the Vak'auga."

Valgard inched a bit closer to Eirik and kept his voice down, just over the grumble of people trying to enter the city. "If we had a few of the boys with us, I'd totally be down with just following him into an alley. But those two thugs with him aren't drunk, and that girl with the javelins doesn't seem like one to be taken lightly. I don't think we should even trail them."

Eirik's body tightened. Leiknir turned directly their way.

He grinned. And even waved.

"That faen-faced bastard…" Eirik grumbled.

"That's not the only coincidence today." Valgard tilted his head to another group of people. This time it was a pair of varl; the first with fiery hair and carrying a massive war axe, the other had brown hair, and wore a large shield. The latter one twisted and chided a young man of perhaps no more than fifteen winters, his face bare of even a whisker.

"I admit that's strange, Valgard," Eirik said. "But hardly enough that we should investigate."

"Try again."

Eirik took a second look, and then he saw. A fourth man with blonde braids followed them from some distance. It was clear he was trying to be discreet by blending with the other travelers, but his trajectory was undoubtedly to follow the pair of varl and the boy into Strand.

Eirik smirked. "It's Hallvard."

"Now is that strange enough to act on?" Valgard asked with a wry smirk on his face.

Eirik cast a glance at the fading sight of Leiknir, then Moldof, and then back towards Hallvard. The man had a record as long as Eirik's forearm, and somehow Hallvard always slipped through the cracks. At least until he disappeared perhaps half a year ago. "It has to be something big if Hallvard is willing to risk returning. I think you're right. But what about the rest of the caravan?"

"There's not much left," Valgard replied, and Eirik realized he was correct. There were about a dozen more carts remaining, and the sun was already dimming beyond the western horizon. If they intended to get through before nightfall then they had missed their opportunity, any further bribery pointless. As for Leiknir, the spymaster had already spotted them and would be alert for any tails. To stalk him would be futile.

"Hey Moldof!" Eirik's voice turned the befuddled watchman towards them. "The rest get full inspection. Here. Understood?"

He shouted back. "And who the faen are you?"

Valgard chuckled at the man's obvious ignorance. "Do as you're told, or you'll be up to your ears in yox dung for neglecting your duty!"

Eirik couldn't resist a smirk as he pointed two fingers towards his own eyes, and then aimed them at Moldof. The corrupt watchman's mouth opened and closed like a fish out of water as it dawned on him just how much trouble he was in.

"Let's go," Eirik said. "Before we lose Hasty Hallvard."

"It's like he's gotten worse at this," Valgard said softly as they followed the scoundrel, who in turn stalked the varl and the boy through the streets of Strand. Hallvard seemed to stand outside cover just a little too long, stare at his marks more than he should, and take exaggerated movements. To Eirik, it was remarkably sloppy for a rogue of Hallvard's reputation.

They made a path through the poorer residential areas near the city walls, not far from the gang battle at Hundgaman the previous night. The house-halls barely held the warmth of their hearths, and the streets were little more than a scattering of stones set in frozen mud. It was almost nightfall, ambivalently making them more difficult to notice, but also making their quarry more challenging to follow.

At one point, they fell behind as Hallvard took a sudden set of twists and turns. Eirik and Valgard quickened their pace to keep up when they spotted hatching— gang markings and warning signs— defacing a wall. Eirik paused briefly to study the symbols, then rushed to follow their elusive mark.

When they caught up with Hallvard, he had slipped behind a hut. The varl ahead stopped to argue over something, and Eirik overheard questions involving lodging for the night. Valgard and Eirik took advantage of the lull to take position behind an old storage shed and turn their cloaks inside out. The different colors of their cloaks' linings were designed to throw off pursuers, or prevent their targets from recognizing a tail.

"They're heading into Kollsvein's territory," Eirik said, reflecting on the earlier markings as he raised his hood.

"I thought Kollsvein's crew was finished?" Valgard inquired as he returned his shield over his shoulder. He slipped to the corner of the shed to watch Hallvard.

"Almost. Another undercover team did them a number, so the gang has fallen back to petty robbery."

Valgard sneered. "Faen. If Kollsvein and his men are here, then this is going to get real complicated real quick. We should just grab Hallvard and make him squeal. If he's keen on these varl, he's likely to talk fast lest he lose them."

Eirik said nothing, but slipped a knife from his belt. With the softest footsteps he could muster, he slipped alongside the shed and approached Hallvard, who remained unaware. With one well-honed motion, Eirik's arms circled his target's head. The Guardsman muffled Hallvard's lips with a gloved hand while the winter-chilled knife touched the scoundrel's neck. He froze.

"Step to your right, real slow," Eirik whispered into Hallvard's ear. "We'll talk in private."

Hallvard obeyed, and the two men concealed themselves from the group ahead. Eirik heard footsteps behind him and knew Valgard approached. Eirik removed his hand from Hallvard's mouth and clasped his shoulder, turning the scoundrel around though careful not to slice his throat. Valgard plucked the weapon from Hallvard's belt.

There was a hint of wariness in Hallvard's eyes that eased into relief. "Oh, it's you."

"Always a pleasure." Valgard grinned. "How have you been Hallvard? Or are you calling yourself something different as of late? You're still quite popular here."

"Indeed." Eirik tilted his head. "Kind of stupid of you to come back, really."

"Okay, first." Hallvard raised a single finger. "Please, please call me Arnbjorn. And second, I have my reasons…"

"Which you won't mind telling us." Eirik pushed the blade against "Arnbjorn's" skin, causing the man to shiver slightly. "A number of skalds still sing stories about an indiscretion between you and a certain merchant's wife."

"Of course, anyone in the know understands that by 'wife,' they mean 'skimmed earnings'…" Valgard added. "And by 'merchant,' they mean 'your old boss.'"

A look of panic came into Arnbjorn's azure eyes. When he tried to peek around the side of the hut, Eirik suspected their veiled threat did not hold as much weight as first thought. "I think we should take Arnbjorn or Hallvard or whoever he is back to the Great Hall…"

"Wait." Arnbjorn opened his hands defensively. "Wait, wait, wait. Don't."

"That's a lot of waiting for someone hopping about with impatience," Eirik said.

"Alright, alright. It's them," Arnbjorn said, jerking a thumb towards the corner. "I got a deal with the old boss. I track these three, and all is forgiven. The bounty goes away."

"Ohhh," Valgard said with condescension in his tone. He glanced around the corner. "So if you lose them…?"

"What is Freystein after?" Eirik asked. "Out with it."

"I don't really know…" Arnbjorn hissed. "Bjorulf's blood! I don't know, Eirik!"

Eirik loosened the blade. "Sorry, force of habit. I suppose you won't mind us tagging along with you then, will you?"

"Eirik," Valgard said. Eirik faced his friend.

"This isn't the Mársmidr's usual business, Valgard. This is a lot of work, with unexplained motives. We must uncover them." Eirik gave Arnbjorn a hard glare. "So congratulations 'Arnbjorn.' Unless you want us to faen your plan, we're coming along."

Arnbjorn's mouth dropped a little, appearing worried, but he nodded. "Can I have my axe back at least?"

"No," Eirik and Valgard said as one.

Arnbjorn sighed, his shoulders sagging dejectedly. Eirik sheathed his blade, and the three crept into the night.

Chapter 4

With his back to Eirik and Valgard, Arnbjorn smirked as they discreetly made their way down the street. In truth, he had spotted the pair when he entered Strand and figured they would tail him. He nearly lost the duo entirely, until he saw signs of Kollsvein's Kin.

That was when Arnbjorn realized he might need the help of the Governor's Guard to keep the varl alive. As he followed Ulfvalgr's entourage, Arnbjorn considered the words that would convince Valgard and Eirik to join him. Ironically, the truth was the best bait to ensure their cooperation. All he needed was to feign reluctance and they would "force" his compliance.

The farther they followed, the more relieved Arnbjorn was that Eirik and Valgard had come along. The dilapidated homes were dark and abandoned, ideal for setting up an ambush. In the encroaching moonlight, Arnbjorn could see holes in the roofs and doors which had been splintered and smashed, perfect hiding spots. There were no warmed hearths, no sounds of families arguing or laughing, no sloshing of bowls filled with thin soups or cooked cabbage being split.

No witnesses and no one to call for help. All that remained were the rats. The kind that stood on two legs.

One such "rat" stepped out of a ruined home, his back to Arnbjorn as he gripped either end of the club slung over his shoulders. Beyond the bandit, Arnbjorn spotted the varl and the boy halting before a group bearing lit torches. There was little doubt, from their drawn weapons and the harsh tone their leader struck, that they had encountered Kollsvein's Kin.

Arnbjorn slipped behind a house, followed swiftly by Eirik and Valgard. The scoundrel peeked around the corner to watch, but was grabbed and gruffly tossed against the wallboards. Eirik took his place to observe.

Arnbjorn grumbled at the mistreatment, but with Eirik and Valgard's attention elsewhere, he carefully knelt and drew a subtle mark in the snow. He couldn't afford to let his trail grow cold.

"How many?" Valgard asked.

"Seven, at least," Eirik whispered in reply. "I think there's one more hiding in the house across the street."

"I've got a better idea," a voice boomed from the direction of the gathering. "How about you drop your blades and leave *your* purses instead?"

Arnbjorn felt pressure inside his chest. The voice likely belonged to the stubborn, fiery-haired varl.

"There's no way Kollsvein can afford to let them pass," Valgard said. "His crew must be hanging on a thread after their recent defeat. If he lets them leave without a toll, his men will desert or remove him."

"Go on, get them!" A man that Arnbjorn guessed to be Kollsvein shouted.

"Should we move to help them?" Valgard asked, his grip under the head of his axe. Arnbjorn knew he had to force their hand.

"I think we should see how well they do befor— get back here!"

Arnbjorn eluded Eirik's grasp as he dived after the bandit between himself and Ulfvalgr's group. Unarmed, Arnbjorn kicked outward, catching the man behind his knee. The bandit went down with a cry more from surprise than pain. Arnbjorn lifted his boot again and stomped on the fallen bandit's hand, forcing him to relinquish his cudgel. He followed the blow with a hammering fist against his downed foe's neck.

As he snatched the fallen club, Arnbjorn saw the angered Guardsmen approaching from behind. He smirked, leading them on a chase into the melee. Bellowing a war cry, he leapt with the club raised, cracking it down against the helmet of another of Kollsvein's minions. The highwayman fell, blood spurting from his helm's visor, crimsoning the snow.

Arnbjorn laughed, high upon the thrill of battle, and delivered a second bash that blasted the injured man against the road. The dented and blood-soaked helm skittered and rolled into the wall of a hut. Sure that the highwayman was finished, Arnbjorn surveyed the fight.

Kollsvein's Kin were clearly outmatched. Ulfvalgr was a seasoned warrior, keeping his enemies at bay with powerful, wide sweeps of his war axe. One thug made the mistake of coming within the varl's range, likely trusting his shield to protect him. Ulfvalgr's weapon shattered both his armor and arm.

Even Arnbjorn felt jolted by the crunch of bone sundering.

As the cleaved limb tumbled over the road, the maimed thug cradled his ruined stump. He did not scream, but his paled face wore a look of utter disbelief.

The rest of Kollsvein's Kin held back and kept the varl at bay with the tips of their spears. Behind them, Kollsvein screamed orders to go after the other varl and the boy. The gang hesitated to obey, maintaining grounded stances. The skirmish would be over if their leader was slain, but Ulfvalgr would strike Arnbjorn down if he drew too close, even in pursuit of their mutual foe.

Arnbjorn turned and panicked. A thug's spear thrusted towards his chest.

It would have skewered him had Eirik's axe not flashed down, severing the head from the weapon. Before the spear-wielding thug could escape, Valgard's skeg axe slashed across his chest. It sliced deep through the man's gambeson, spilling an arc of blood as he dropped.

Arnbjorn felt himself cringe before the furious glance Eirik gave him, the Guardsman's narrow gray eyes screamed danger. "What were you thinking?"

"You knew the stakes," Arnbjorn managed to reply, glad that Ulfvalgr's group was too occupied to overhear. Arnbjorn pointed a finger at Kollsvein. "Kill him, and you'll finish this."

Eirik and Valgard exchanged looks, before the latter shrugged. He stashed his axe in his belt and drew his dagger. Arnbjorn could see the man's unease as he lined up his shot.

"Too easy to hit the varl," Eirik warned.

Valgard said nothing, but took a step and hurled the knife.

It sang as it sliced through the air, spinning rapidly, yet managed to pass through the narrow opening between Ulfvalgr and his friend.

And sunk into Kollsvein's eye socket.

The battle came to an abrupt halt. Everyone's gaze went to the struck leader, who still stood for a moment. Blood dripped down the jutting dagger's grip, while the leader's mouth went slack. He fell forward, sinking to his knees. Then his face slammed the ground, the blade handle forcing his head to rest at an angle.

Kollsvein's men exchanged expressions and returned their attention to Ulfvalgr. The varl bristled, as though prepared for the fight to continue. Instead, the remaining thugs began to slowly step back.

"We're done here. Unless you're into justice or something," one of the highwaymen said, holding his spear at the ready.

There was a tense pause. Ulfvalgr jerked his head to the side. "Get lost."

Two of the surviving gang members gathered their injured friend, who had desperately tucked his stump in his armpit try stemming the blood loss. They did not run but faded into the slums, never turning their backs on their intended victims.

The two varl and the boy turned to Arnbjorn, Eirik and Valgard. Arnbjorn saw the surprise on the boy's face. For a moment he worried that the kid might give away his identity.

"And to what do we owe this timely salvation?" Ulfvalgr's jade eyes narrowed into dangerous slits. An inexperienced fighter would think the varl's stance relaxed, but Arnbjorn knew from the giant's posture that he could shift into a chopping motion with ease and power.

When Eirik froze and Valgard said nothing, Arnbjorn smirked. The Governor's Guardsmen were stuck, too used to planning and cultivating their false identities. They never had the knack for improvisation.

Arnbjorn strode forward, raising an open palm. "Collectin' bounties of course. That one who got his head stuck is worth a tidy payday for the trouble he caused."

Something flashed in Ulfvalgr's features, suggesting a hint of greed. Arnbjorn suddenly worried that his lie was about to backfire in a peculiar way when the other varl sheathed his blade and smiled.

"Well for what it's worth," the brown haired varl said. "Thank you for the aid."

Good. It doesn't seem like he remembers me from Karlshus, Arnbjorn thought. Likewise, Arnbjorn struggled to remember the giant's name. Then he realized that the solution was easy. Shoving his procured club into his belt, he slowly stepped forth and raised a hand above his shoulder, offering a palm for the second varl to shake. "I'm Arnbjorn, bounty hunter. And you are?"

"Olaf." The varl accepted and shook the offered hand. Arnbjorn worried that Olaf's gigantic grip might crush his fingers, but the varl was appropriately firm. "That's Ulfvalgr, and the boy is Stefnir. Who are your friends?"

"This is Valgard," Eirik said as he approached, tilting his head towards his partner. "And I am Eirik. Like Arnbjorn said, it's our job to hunt down these criminals and bring them to justice."

Arnbjorn gave Eirik a sly, appraising glimpse. It was at best a lie of omission, but the fact that Eirik had volunteered his real name suggested an intention to gain the trust of these people. Arnbjorn doubted that would be in his own interest. He would have to be prudent.

"Whoever tossed that knife, that was incredible," Olaf said, his brow raised appreciatively. "I've never seen a man taken down like that."

Valgard grinned and bowed. "Thank you kindly. I often practice over a drinking horn or seven."

Olaf stifled a laugh.

Arnbjorn noticed Stefnir staring at him. A few words from the boy and doubt could be cast on his freshly spun story. Arnbjorn winked at the kid. The nervous grin Arnbjorn received in reply allayed his concerns that Stefnir would talk.

But the biggest obstacle to trust was Ulfvalgr, who snorted. "Great. So thanks Arnbjorn. Now take this fool's head or hand or whatever trophy you need and go."

No one moved for a moment, until Eirik tapped Arnbjorn's shoulder. "Well? You heard him."

Arnbjorn's countenance dropped. He stepped towards the deceased gang leader and rolled the cadaver onto its back. Putting a foot against the corpse's bloodied forehead, he took the drenched dagger handle and tugged until it jerked free of the dead man's skull.

"What were you all doing in Kollsvein's territory anyway?" Arnbjorn heard Eirik ask. "Didn't you see the gang signs all over the place?"

"Neither Ulfvalgr nor I have been in Strand for some time," Olaf said. Arnbjorn glimpsed back and saw the red-haired varl give his friend a nasty stare, perhaps for revealing some perceived weakness.

Olaf continued. "Last time I was here, there was a thrifty inn around this neighborhood, with beds large enough for our kind. We haven't much coin to spend frivolously."

"We knew the place you speak of," Eirik replied. "Unfortunately, it burned down perhaps two years ago. Lots of people thought it was an accident. Others say arson, committed by a business rival. Regardless, it is long gone."

Arnbjorn swallowed and put the dagger against Kollsvein's temple. There was no serrated edge, so he put as much pressure as he could against the handle. The blade gradually sank through the cartilage of the corpse's ear.

"Still, you may be in luck," Eirik said. "It's unlikely that any other gangs will realize Kollsvein is dead until the morrow, and his men will probably gather what's left of their possessions and leave. You could probably squat in one of these abandoned homes for the night."

The dagger chimed slightly as it struck a rock, followed by the squelch of Kollsvein's ear plopping on the ground. Arnbjorn suppressed a wave of nausea, and cut some of Kollsvein's clothing into a rag to gather his grisly prize.

"Perhaps you should join us?" Olaf said. Arnbjorn swore he heard a hiss come from Ulfvalgr's direction, but Olaf continued. "The night is upon us, and we're less likely to have our throats slit if we're twice our number."

Arnbjorn noticed Valgard collecting the weapons of the fallen, adding credence to the bounty hunting story. Arnbjorn smirked, realizing that was a splendid idea.

"We would be delighted." Arnbjorn could hear Eirik's joviality through his words. "We'd love to hear tales from beyond Strand's borders."

The grin on Arnbjorn's face grew wider as he armed himself with Kollsvein's short sword. He wondered if he would need it tonight.

"Arnbjorn!" Valgard called out.

He cursed under his breath before replying. "Yes?"

"You know the rules. Eirik handles bounty trophies."

"Of course." Arnbjorn felt his features twitch from anger as he marched over to Eirik. With obvious reluctance, he gave the blade to the undercover Guardsman. Although Arnbjorn had a little revenge when he placed the small, bloody bundle in Eirik's waiting hand as well. "And here's Kollsvein's ear. Like Valgard said, you handle the trophies."

Eirik almost kept the rage from his face, but managed upturned lips against an ugly grimace. "Thank you, Arnbjorn."

Arnbjorn smiled with cheer. "You're welcome, boss."

"… after we joined the caravan a day ago, we arrived here," Olaf said, concluding his tale.

Arnbjorn sat on a creaky seat, listening to the account the varl told. As far as he could tell, the varl never outright lied. But even with what he knew, Arnbjorn picked out some vague details within the story. While traveling for "the sake of his kendr" might mean something amongst the ice giants, the concept meant very little in the realm of men. Of course, while Olaf mentioned stopping in Karlshus, Ulfvalgr's instigation of the bar brawl went unsaid.

After they had agreed to camp that night, they found a hall large enough for all of them— even the varl, once the horned giants ducked their heads beneath the doorjamb. It had taken a little scavenging, but they discovered some dried firewood and cooking tools. Eirik graciously offered some salted fish and vegetables from his kit. The provisions found their way into a kettle hanging over a fire pit, along with water to create a surprisingly savory-smelling soup.

"That's quite a trip," Eirik said as he spun the spoon in their nearly ready meal. "I apologize if Strand is not as kind as you might remember."

"You weren't even born when we last stepped through these streets, pup." Ulfvalgr snorted and took a swig from his drinking horn. Amongst the abandoned goods, they had discovered a few bottles of long soured ale, which Ulfvalgr drank without as much as a grimace. Arnbjorn once heard that such aged drink could be more potent than normal. But if the varl was intoxicated, he did not show it.

"Most likely. We could learn a lot from our northern neighbors," Eirik diplomatically said as he took a soft sip of the soup. "I believe this is as good as it will get. Valgard, bowls please."

Eirik's friend held up the hodgepodge of deep dishes and bowls. They had found only one of ideal size for a varl, so instead they filled a pan for the second giant. Arnbjorn eyed the portions and felt that the varl had been given an enormously generous share, even considering their girth. The boy was well fed too. Though to his credit, Eirik doled out equal portions for himself, Valgard and Arnbjorn. Generosity that Arnbjorn did not expect from the Guardsman.

While Olaf and Stefnir dived into their dishes, Arnbjorn couldn't help but note Ulfvalgr's reluctance to even touch his pan. Eirik, who also observed their guests before partaking, didn't seem to miss that fact either. The Guardsman took a long swig of his soup, supping from his bowl.

After swallowing, Eirik sighed in a manner that sounded content. "The secret is to cook the meat with just a hint of oil first. This unlocks the herbs and salts more readily, which mix with the rest of the base and vegetables."

"Eirik, you'll make a fine wife one day." Valgard smirked.

Olaf and Stefnir sputtered their soup from laughter. Arnbjorn guffawed. Even the unfriendly Ulfvalgr let out a sharp bark of amusement. Eirik gave his friend a look, although even he couldn't help but laugh aloud himself.

"Business for your lot must be booming," Ulfvalgr, uncharacteristically, added to the conversation. He had slurped down his meal after the jest, or perhaps because he had seen everyone else dine.

Eirik nodded with hesitance. "You could certainly say that. The City Watch have tried all kinds of ideas to slow the growth of these gangs. Curfews and patrols. They've even tried a tournament to mark the worst ruffians and get them to fight amongst themselves. But bounty hunting is rather effective, so long as you can match a name to the reward."

Ulfvalgr became bored with Eirik's conversation rather swiftly, his eyes half drooping. The varl downed the last of his soured ale then yawned heavily, covering his mouth with the back of his fist. He stood, ducking a little under the roof. "Well, it's been a fine evening. Thank you for the passable soup and hospitality, Eirik, Arnbjorn and…"

"Valgard," the man finished for him.

"Valgard," Ulfvalgr replied. "But I think I shall retire to the cellar for the evening. Not much room on this floor for two varl and four men to lay out. I would suggest you don't try to wake me. I have a habit of reaching for my axe when disturbed. Good night."

No one commented on the varl's rudeness as he opened a door at the rear of the hall and slipped through. Arnbjorn stifled a laugh when he realized the varl would have to crawl downstairs in order to fit through the narrow crevice. When the cellar door shut, all that remained was an unsettling silence.

After a while, Olaf sighed. "I'm sorry. My friend does not particularly trust anyone."

"That's quite alright," Eirik replied. "You have no cause for alarm in present company, I assure you, but that is a healthy attitude to take in Strand."

Olaf drew a sharp breath through his nostrils and rubbed the side of his face. "Still. I believe he has the right idea. It has been a long trip, a short fight and a good night in fine company. You would understand if we would have a lookout from our own party for the night?"

"By all means," Eirik said as he wrapped the kettle's handle with a rag and lifted it. He set the pot to cool in one of the chamber's corners, its legs thudding softly as it touched the stone floors.

"Stefnir, you haven't had anything to drink, so that will be you." Olaf stretched his arms as the boy's shoulders slumped. Dutifully, Stefnir nodded.

"Arnbjorn, would you care to have first watch tonight?" Eirik asked as he pulled thick blankets near the fire.

"Certainly," Arnbjorn said. It was a stroke of fortune. Stefnir had made no mention of remembering Arnbjorn during dinner, and Olaf had certainly forgotten their brief encounter.

They left the fire to burn. Arnbjorn took a seat near one of the windows, while the boy sat next to the entrance. They didn't speak, and Arnbjorn was content to leave it that way until he saw Eirik and Valgard's chests rise and fall with the steady rhythm of slumber.

Only then did he whisper to the boy. "Thanks for not saying anything about Karlshus."

Stefnir nodded. "You saved us, and I didn't think it would be ideal to mention old indiscretions."

"Atta boy. Anyway, I didn't expect you to be travelling with the same guy who tried to kill your big friend there."

Between the gentle moonlight from the window and the orange glow of the fading fire, Arnbjorn could see the kid's mouth draw into a line. "It's complicated… for all of us."

When no further words were forthcoming, he simply nodded with respect for the boy's business. In truth, Arnbjorn didn't care. As long as Freystein got what he wanted, and Arnbjorn got to rejoin the Mársmidr and his brother.

"What are you doing here anyway?" Stefnir finally asked.

"Hunting a bounty, of course. No trick. I get to town, spot the wanted poster. Threw my lot in with this pair of losers. And here we are." The lie left Arnbjorn's tongue with the fluidity of water. "After Karlshus, Strand was as good place as any to hide and avoid trouble. Broddi is… not very forgiving when someone makes off with his prized swill."

"Oh," Stefnir said. He hesitated before adding, "Thank you, by the way."

"For what?"

"Saving our lives."

A twinge of guilt suddenly sparked within Arnbjorn, and he felt his heart turn to lead. "Not a problem, kid."

Some time passed as they silently kept watch. The fire burned down to vivid embers, but the half-moon above compensated for the dwindling illumination. Arnbjorn remained patient until he felt the call of nature. "I trust you not to cause trouble while I yellow the snow."

The boy cringed at the metaphor, but nodded. Arnbjorn chuckled as he slipped out of the house, and went around the corner. He surveyed the neighborhood until he noticed a hut across the street. He examined it with narrowed eyes, and made his way toward the abandoned home, undoing his breeches.

Pain shot through his scalp as someone grabbed his hair and yanked him back. A cold, sharp blade pressed into his throat, but did not break the skin. Arnbjorn panicked, fearing that Kollsvein's men had returned for revenge.

"Just what the faen are you scheming, Arnbjorn?" Eirik's familiar voice whispered into his ear. "I saw the boy twitch and look at you when Olaf mentioned Karlshus, which is the same direction you tailed them from. What really happened there?"

"A fight, honest!" Arnbjorn struggled to keep his voice down, still startled by Eirik's violence. "I met the kid there at a mead hall. Just a casual conversation at first. Then his big friend showed up. Before I knew it, Ulfvalgr appeared and started a brawl. But anyone who has run a few cons in his time can spot a fake fight when he sees it.

"They got that place rowdy and bloody before taking off. I escaped and ran into Ottar, one of Freyste—"

"I know who Ottar is. Get on with it."

Arnbjorn gulped and tried to relax. He knew that the Iron Turtle was not beyond killing people when they crossed a line, the one which Arnbjorn now danced. "Ottar sent me after these three. Told me they were important, and need to be kept alive *at all costs*. Some varl relic they were after, about the size of a man's palm. That's all I was told!"

Eirik said nothing, but the blade pressed tightly enough to prick the skin.

"*I swear!*" Arnbjorn squealed.

After a tense moment, the knife was removed. "Finish your business and get back to the camp. I'll be taking watch from here on."

Eirik left. Arnbjorn sighed, his breath coming out as a mist. Glancing down, he cursed as he realized that he had relieved himself over his breeches. That was when he noticed the reply signal written on the frost-covered ground.

Slowly, Arnbjorn took a handful of snow and rubbed it on his trousers until he was content they were at least somewhat cleaned. Glancing up, he saw a short figure hidden in the abandoned home, his face masked the shadows of the rafters.

The man raised two fingers and tapped his chest. *Orders. We'll take care of the rest.* He made a circle with his fingers and thumb, and raised it. *In the morning.*

Arnbjorn made a half-thumb up gesture and then tapped his cheeks. *Understood. Will keep tailing them until then.*

The half-thumb movement was returned, and the short man faded into the darkness. Arnbjorn watched for a moment until he was sure the Mársmidr scout was gone. He smirked. Ottar had upheld his end of the bargain, calling off the bounty and ordering the Mársmidr to follow his signs. All was going as planned.

Arnbjorn pulled his breeches back up and returned to camp.

Chapter 5

Stefnir ran.

The wolves were on his heels. He could hear their panting as they sped across the snow, a howl making them sound ever the closer. Stefnir feared that if he were to look back, he would see the yellow fangs of the beasts just before they sunk their teeth into his flesh.

The faster he ran, the closer he got to the rising sun. When he crested a hill, the sunlight twisted from gold to orange and red, and the howl was overcome by screams of agony. He looked below and saw his village on fire. Men bearing shields marked with a baleful eye carried off women. Bodies of would-be defenders lay still, suspended in the air on tips of spears while their guts trickled down the weapon shafts.

But the always hungry wolves were still behind Stefnir. He turned, and realized the pack were upon him. Stefnir panicked as one bounded.

Until something swatted the beast aside. Stefnir saw a great, horned shadow over him, its grin like a crescent moon in the night…

The dream ended.

Stefnir rubbed his forehead. It was a new variation of the same nightmares that haunted him since his village fell to the slavers. The wolves however, were an incident that happened after he took his father's axe and ran.

Mom was gone, one of the few women slain in the fighting. Stefnir and his father had found her beheaded corpse near the ruins of their home, a hunting spear still gripped tightly in her dead grasp. She did not die easily, her weapon bloodied on two fallen raiders lying nearby.

Stefnir pleaded with his father, insisting that his mother was due vengeance. His father would not listen, explaining that the few survivors of the raid would need their help to survive. The raiders took the entire storehouse and burned the fields. Only hunting, fishing and foraging could sustain them until they could rebuild and resow.

His wife and the mother of his only child was dead, he told Stefnir. Slaughtering those responsible could not bring her back.

Stefnir couldn't let it go, and his anger only grew over the next five months. Finally, while his father was away on a hunting trip, Stefnir stole his father's axe and left, determined to chase down the slavers who bore the sigil of an eye.

On his own, Stefnir preyed on small game, fished and scavenged food as he ventured without luck, trying to learn the whereabouts of his mother's killers. His quest drifted to the north, sometimes doing odd jobs in towns for food and asking questions which earned him vague hints, including a name: "Magnus."

Then, almost two weeks into his journey, he was lost in the wild. His hunting bow had broken, and he could no longer easily feed himself. That was when he attracted the attention of a pack of wolves.

Stefnir stared at the snoring Olaf. It was only the varl's timely intervention that saved the boy from both the beasts and his own starvation. The varl fed him and teased him mercilessly when he begged to be trained as a warrior.

Somehow the past ended with Stefnir here, in an abandoned hut in Strand near a dead fire. Two of the strangers, Arnbjorn and Eirik, slept. The third, Valgard, kept watch as the sun peeked through the windows. Stefnir slowly rose, the blanket falling from his lap. The call of nature led him past the groggy Valgard, who perked as Stefnir left.

The sun had not yet cleared the eastern horizon as Stefnir found some privacy behind a tiny house. After a brief glimpse over his shoulders to ensure he was alone, he dropped the hem of his pants and relieved himself against the wall, sighing with comfort.

As he finished and pulled his trousers back up, motion stirred in the corner of his sight. He turned and spotted a feminine figure fleeing from one of the houses. The bundle of javelins on her back caused Stefnir to reach for his weapon.

Then she twisted, looking at him. Stefnir's jaw dropped with recognition.

She froze for a moment, then ran behind a corner. Stefnir left his axe in his belt as he chased after the girl. He took the same turn she had taken when something struck the wall and wedged itself in the stones, quivering.

The girl stood down the road, having already drawn another javelin and poised, ready to spear him down.

Stefnir grimaced as he saw her. Slowly, he raised his hands defensively. "Runa, please do—"

"That was a warning. If you move, I will skewer you. If you shout or do anything to call your friends, the same," Runa said with narrowed, iridescently hazel eyes.

Slowly, Stefnir nodded, keeping his hands high. He studied her. Since the attack on their village, she bore a heavy scar across her cheek. Her mixed, brown and blonde hair was shorter too, gathered into a side braid that hung halfway down her neck. She forewent customary robes for slacks and a tunic. Her frame was lean, with a wiry strength.

Despite her changes, she was the same girl from home.

"What are you doing here, Stefnir?" There was no compassion in her voice, even as she acknowledged that she remembered him. "You lucked out and weren't in the village when we were attacked. What the faen possessed you to come to Strand?"

"They killed mom." Stefnir lowered his arms with prudent stiffness. "I came here to kill the man responsible."

"Magnus," Runa replied.

Stefnir nodded.

Runa huffed as though suppressing a laugh, a sardonic grin on her face as she shook her head. "He'll kill you."

"How did you get here, Runa?" Stefnir asked.

Runa lowered her javelin arm and rested the butt of the shaft in the snow beside her boot. "Magnus took me prisoner. But when we got to Strand, he gave me to Leiknir, one of his lieutenants. Instead of forcing me to be a house maid or… other things, Leiknir freed me. When I asked him what I should do, he shrugged and asked if I had any skills of trade or value."

"You always were the best shot in the village," Stefnir said. He pondered what she meant by "other things" as he gazed at her facial scar.

Runa ignored the compliment. "When I showed him my fishing skills, he said I could work for him. I wasn't likely to get a chance to kill Magnus, but Leiknir took me in and cared for me. Now I'm his bodyguard and messenger."

"So what? You fall in with this Leiknir guy, and you forgive Magnus?" Stefnir couldn't help the derision entering his voice. "Magnus burned our village and just like that, you're cozy with one of his men? Were you tailing us?"

She sneered and pointed her javelin at him, not in a threatening manner but accusingly. "Stuff it, Stefnir. Give me a clear shot and I'll put it through Magnus' throat. I'm in a better position to pull it off than you'll ever be. Especially given who you're bedding down with lately."

Stefnir's eyebrow perked.

"The three men who joined you last night… two of them are members of the Governor's Guard, a group who will do anything to keep Strand safe. The blonde one with the shorter hair… I didn't catch who he introduced himself as but his real name is Eirik, and he's one of the Guard's best agents. They call him the 'Iron Turtle' because he always comes back from the slowest, ugliest jobs."

Stefnir kept silent, despite his initial instinct to defend Eirik. Stefnir knew he couldn't trust his face not to give away a lie, so he omitted the truth.

Runa stepped backward, spinning her javelin so the tip pointed to the ground. "The fact that you weren't slain or arrested just means they probably want something. But if you or Eirik come after Leiknir, I won't hesitate to kill either of you."

Stefnir swallowed. Her vicious countenance made it clear she would act on her words if needed. He nodded. "I'll keep my distance then."

Runa turned as though to leave, then stopped and gave him a sideways look. "Stefnir, don't trust Eirik. In fact, I suggest you just get out of Strand as soon as you can."

Before he could reply, she sprinted behind a hut and was gone, leaving Stefnir alone.

He considered what Runa mentioned. The fact that Eirik had given his true name rather than a false one made Stefnir ponder the man's integrity, for Runa clearly expected Eirik to lie. It was obvious that Valgard was the second Guardsman, given his and Eirik's contempt for Arnbjorn and, of course, Stefnir's encounter with him in Karlshus.

However, Runa's words created a hole in Stefnir's fresh confidence in the strangers. Had they lied about their intentions? Why was Arnbjorn really there? Or could Runa be trusted anymore, despite their childhood acquaintance? After all, she admitted to working for one of Magnus' men.

As Stefnir walked back to the camp, he resolved to trust only Olaf. And perhaps Ulfvalgr. Although the varl was brutal and cruel, he was too crass to be a liar. If the truth was painful to hear, Ulfvalgr relished inflicting it upon others.

Stefnir returned to find Arnbjorn still asleep. Valgard and Eirik had awoken and busied themselves with reigniting the fire. Ulfvalgr too had risen, having emerged from the cramped cellar. He rolled his arm as though relieving a shoulder knot, careful not to smack the ceiling with either his fist or horns. Olaf was nowhere to be seen.

Ulfvalgr frowned down at the boy. "Where were you?"

"I… had too much to drink last night." Stefnir kept his head turned toward the fire to hide his trembling lip. Ulfvalgr grunted. When Stefnir was certain his face was normal again, he glanced at the varl. "Have you seen Olaf?"

"He left about the time these two started working on the fire. Went to check the forum near here and get us some food. Said he'll be back in a while."

Stefnir studied Eirik and Valgard. The latter raised a brow and grinned at the boy before turning his attention back to their task. Stefnir bashfully waved Ulfvalgr closer. The varl obliged and knelt though he continued to stretch, tilting his neck to produce a powerful crack.

"I can't really trust these guys, Ulfvalgr," Stefnir whispered.

Ulfvalgr replied just as quietly. "Smartest thing I've heard you say yet, boy. When Olaf returns, we'll be off. Without them."

Stefnir nodded, feeling some relief. He had been wondering if Ulfvalgr had warmed to these men over dinner last night, as it was the only time Stefnir heard Ulfvalgr laugh. Thankfully, the varl was back to his old, cantankerous self.

"You alright?" Valgard asked.

"Fine," Stefnir managed without coming across as standoffish. He returned to his blankets, feigning tiredness. There was nothing to do but wait for Olaf.

Stefnir woke to Olaf's wide grin. The varl knelt, shaking him with a massive hand. "Time to rise, lad."

Stefnir sat up swiftly and drew a sharp breath through his nose. Sleep had ambushed him, but the fact that the fire lived again meant he couldn't have dozed for long.

"The boy's awake," Ulfvalgr said as he waved his hand. He stood over Arnbjorn and Eirik as he chewed at some mutton, speaking with his mouth full. "Now tell me what the faen you're so excited about already."

Olaf beamed at Ulfvalgr. "I've found an old friend of ours who may be able to help us. We're to meet him a little later today."

Ulfvalgr tossed the last of his mutton in his mouth, finishing his meal. Stefnir noticed Eirik perk with interest in Olaf's news. Ulfvalgr's eyelids drooped as he faced the three men. "Right, well. It looks like we'll be taking our leave then."

"Thank you for the hospitality," Olaf said, slapping a hand against his leg as he stood. Eirik rose as well and extended a palm to the varl, which Olaf shook.

"I hope you find what you're looking for," Eirik said.

"I think we will. Good luck with the hunting," Olaf replied.

Stefnir gathered his sleeping gear and equipment, bundling and stashing it in his satchel. He was glad the varl were on the same page.

As he slipped his satchel over his back, he noticed Arnbjorn eying him. The boy waved, and the man did the same. Try as Stefnir might to figure him out, Arnbjorn was his own enigma in the puzzle. The piece that was always there but whose importance no one volunteered or explained.

The varl ducked as they exited the hut, slipping through the door frame. Stefnir grabbed his mutton for the road, pausing to give Eirik and Valgard a final look. He coughed a bit, before finally bidding them adieu. "Take care of yourselves."

"You too." Valgard flashed him that grin. Unwilling to meet any of their gazes, Stefnir followed after Ulfvalgr and Olaf.

Chapter 6

Compared to the desolate slums, morning in the market districts and nearby neighborhoods was a livelier affair.

Merchants left wheel tracks in the snow-glazed streets, either by pushing carts or having them driven by yoxen. Children played with wooden sticks, dueling and shouting as though at war with one another. Men and women alike carried threshes of wheat, racks of fish, lumber, or buckets of ice to be melted into water. Beggars called for alms. Gothi, whom some called preachers, insisted to small and disinterested masses that the gods were not actually dead. Taller halls smelled of baking bread, roasting vegetables and meats, smoke wafting from their chimneys as the less desperate folks of Strand went on living their lives.

Several times, Stefnir watched Ulfvalgr check over his shoulder, eying the crowds for any signs of a tail. At last, Ulfvalgr took Olaf by the arm and slipped into a shady alley that the morning sun had yet to breach. Confused, Stefnir followed.

"Alright, I think we're not being tailed," Ulfvalgr said, scratching the base of his horns. "Good play to lose those three. Some of Valgard's jokes are a century old and I was getting sick of hearing them."

Olaf stared at him for a moment. "I was serious."

Ulfvalgr grinned darkly. When Olaf's face did not change, the red-haired varl's smile vanished. "Who the faen could we know in this yox-dung heap of a city?"

To Stefnir, it looked as though Olaf shrank a little as he next spoke. "Kjallak. We're to meet him at—"

"*Kjallak!*" Ulfvalgr's angry outburst drew the attention of a passing watchman, who peered down their alley. Olaf gave him a friendly wave to indicate everything was alright. Stefnir couldn't see the man's facial expression through the helmet he wore, but the watchman lingered for a heavy moment before moving on.

Ulfvalgr irritably scratched his beard. "Of all the varl we know, past and now, you just *had* to find the one that Torstein himself banished?"

"Oh, knock it off." Anger seemed to put Olaf on level with Ulfvalgr. He even pointed an accusing finger. "Like you're one to talk. I heard all the stories of you and Fasolt, the raids you pulled against human caravans back in the day. Now he's a loyalist in service to Grofheim. If Fasolt can change the tune he marches to, why can't Kjallak?"

Ulfvalgr's jade eyes rolled upside his head, which lulled backward, his jaw slack. A harsh groan grew in his throat until at last he spoke. "You just had to go and drag that sordid business out in front of the pup. Hadrborg dammit, fine. Fine! Just shut up and lead the way, wherever we're going."

"*The Shattered Shield*," Olaf said. "Come on, we're not far."

The meaning of the discussion was lost on Stefnir. He got that somehow, Olaf had one upped his friend into compliance. Suddenly, a vision of Olaf and Ulfvalgr as his parents quarreling made Stefnir snicker. He swiftly covered his grin as Ulfvalgr cast an evil glare at him. With his treacherous mouth covered, Stefnir realized he could lie with impunity. "Sneeze. Sorry."

Ulfvalgr grunted and followed Olaf out of the alley. Stefnir trailed along, prior thoughts of his parents disturbing him as he recalled his departed mother's face. Stefnir took a deep breath and exhaled slowly, controlling his emotions and forcing her from his mind.

Revenge would come. Soon.

"Eirik, old buddy of mine, we are wasting our time," Valgard chided. "They're just a couple of varl on personal business and we've better things to do."

They had turned their cloaks inside out again, donned their hoods and forced Arnbjorn to wrap himself in one of the blankets. With care, they stalked the varl, acting natural and blending with the crowd over the many times Ulfvalgr was vigilant for tails.

For a moment Eirik and Valgard lost them, but Eirik revealed himself to a city watchman, who pointed them to a nearby alley he had passed. There, they overheard Ulfvalgr and Olaf engaged in an argument. They did not catch the beginning of the exchange, but Eirik caught mention of the drinking hall known as *The Shattered Shield*.

"Arnbjorn, seriously." Valgard turned his attention to the scoundrel. "Just admit that you were hoping to rob them and we'll let you go. You didn't *actually* steal from them, and therefore you committed no crime. All this talk about Freystein wanting them was just something to deflect the blame, right?"

Eirik faced Arnbjorn, who appeared ready to speak. Instead the thief rubbed his throat, as though remembering the kiss of a cold knife, and remained silent.

Eirik sighed. "We can't ignore this. Freystein is too powerful, and we don't have any idea as to his whereabouts since our last attempt to take him. If there's something he's after, we have to know."

"I still say this is nothing but a wild goose chase. We should be checking out those shipments, or finding out how the raid against the Hilmir went."

Valgard's words affected Eirik. His friend was right. By now, Olvir should have something for them to investigate against the Aetla Hilmir. But as Eirik watched the varl walk towards *The Shattered Shield*, he couldn't shake the feeling that the giants were important. "If we don't find anything by noon, we'll cut Arnbjorn loose and return to our regular duties."

Valgard scratched his beard and squinted at the morning sun. Midday wasn't far away. He sighed. "Noon. Then lunch, which you'll be treating me to, then back to the Great Hall."

"What a dung hole," Ulfvalgr said as they scrutinized the structure that stood beneath a sign of a hammer smashing a shield.

Stefnir had to agree. The decrepit drinking hall sat between twin two-storied buildings. Boards were bowed, threatening to pop off the cracked walls. Some attempt at a paint job had left a mosaic of colored chips on the paneling. The roof was short a few tiles, like a smile with missing teeth.

As they entered, the door creaked on rusted hinges. Inside, such details of dilapidation were cloaked in a veil of shade, but the faint, musty odor of mold tickled Stefnir's nostrils. The aging ceiling, at least, was tall enough for Ulfvalgr and Olaf to stand without crouching.

"What kind of drinking spot is open this early in the day?" Stefnir asked as he pushed the remains of a smashed chair away with a booted foot.

An apron-clad bartender entered the hall from a passage behind the bar. "If you've got a problem with it, you can—"

The man stepped back when he saw the pair of horned giants.

Olaf bowed at the waist, putting his hands on his knees and looking the bartender in the face, like an adult speaking to a child. "We're waiting for a friend. Another varl, named Kjallak."

"I… he's already here," the man said. He jerked a thumb towards the back. "Upstairs, loft for special guests."

"Thanks," Olaf replied.

At the rear of the hall they found a staircase wide enough for varl to ascend with ease. Ulfvalgr went first, and the uneasy creaking of the floorboards made Olaf prudently wait for his taciturn friend to reach the top before following.

"Kjallak," Ulfvalgr said above, "It's been a while."

At last, as Stefnir ventured upstairs he saw another varl seated at a large table. A loft window behind the giant cast sunlight into the gloom, masking Kjallak behind a cloak of shadow. Stefnir could see the varl was not alone, as a man in black attended to the second story fireplace.

"Ulfvalgr, Olaf! Welcome my friends!" Kjallak rose and approached. In the warmth of the fire, Stefnir made out the giant's pale skin and dark features, black tips on his horns. His braided beard ran down his sagging paunch.

"Seems Strand has been kind to you," Olaf said as he took his old friend's hand with an audible clap of their palms meeting. "Hadrborg's blessing, Kjallak. You make Jorundr look a pauper."

Kjallak laughed and spread his arms to showcase his apparel. It was true his wardrobe was suggestive of wealth, as he wore a finely-stitched tunic laced with gold threading. His belt buckle bore a red jewel within a casing of silver. "Aye Olaf, Strand has welcomed me with open arms. But, at the least, I can shine some of that hospitality on you two and your little friend there. Come! Have a seat. Awful as *The Shattered Shield* looks, the mead is *liquid gold.*"

"I'm thinking Hrefna's," Valgard babbled on. "She makes that fine venison stew. The one with the leeks and potatoes, in that nice gravy…"

"Keep your voice down," Eirik bade. He peeked through a window with broken shutters that barely clung to the hinges. "I can hardly hear them."

They hid in the vacant building next to *The Shattered Shield.* From the second floor, they peered into the drinking hall's loft through an opened window. A large figure sat with his back to them, dark-haired with horns that rose and curled around and downward. Eirik figured this was the friend Olaf had mentioned. The trouble was, Eirik couldn't see the other stranger very well and could barely listen to their conversation.

Valgard lazily glimpsed at the sun, then back at Arnbjorn. The scoundrel sat on the wooden floors, crossing his arms and legs while wearing a bored expression.

"Sounds like I'll have to try the mead there sometime," Valgard commented after they overheard the dark-haired varl's statements about the beverage.

Eirik was about to chide his friend again when the other figure stepped closer to the opened window's light. Eirik only caught a half-glimpse of the man's face, but it was enough. "It's Skoegir."

Valgard faced the window. His eyes narrowed as he recognized the gangster, and he angrily sighed. "Faen. So much for lunch…"

Eirik cast a sharpened gaze at Arnbjorn. "At least one of Freystein's men is attending this meeting. Is that third varl a member of the Mársmidr too? Does he work for Freystein?"

Arnbjorn uncrossed his arms but said nothing. Eirik reached to his sheath when Arnbjorn finally spoke. "Knife, knife, knife. That threat is getting old, lawman."

Eirik studied the scoundrel for a moment, before drawing his blade. "You're just stalling for time."

"Let's get to it then," Kjallak spoke as he poured a mug of the mead. "Not a night passes where I don't hear about this crime lord, Freystein, and his desire for Torstein's heirloom. I've never seen the man, but he clearly knows his varl trinkets. And he knows enough to recognize that his men only returned with half of it, two weeks ago."

"Then maybe you could be of use," Ulfvalgr said. Stefnir noticed that the fiery-haired varl had not touched his stein even once, despite their host partaking from the same jug. "We need to find Freystein. Or at least get his half of the heirloom back."

Kjallak chuckled, and Stefnir couldn't help but feel some darkness in the varl's laugh. "Ulfy, that doesn't sound like you in the least."

Ulfvalgr's brow twitched at the nickname Kjallak gave him. Stefnir caught Olaf covering his grin with a hand, although the boy could still see his friend's cheeks rise from smiling.

"You're right, Kjallak," Ulfvalgr said with a tone that killed Olaf's mirth. "I want to find this Freystein and slam his head hard enough to bury it within his chest."

Stefnir heard another snicker, but this one didn't come from Olaf. Everyone's attention went to the man in black, who stood beside Kjallak.

"You'll have to forgive Skoegir," Kjallak said. "He has a morbid sense of humor. Good at what he does for a man, but strange by anyone's definition."

"How, exactly…" Olaf said, laying an elbow on the table. "Do you know this fellow, Kjallak?"

"Oh, you could say we're in the same line of work." Kjallak took a long gulp of his mead, finishing it off with a sigh of contentment. "Imports and exports, you could say. More importantly, he's one of the few men who have any idea where Freystein might be."

Arnbjorn grunted loudly through Valgard's gloved hand, which capped his mouth.

"Sorry? Didn't quite catch that," Valgard said as he moved his hand, careful not to touch the knife Eirik used to prick Arnbjorn just under the eyelid. Blood dripped down the blade's edge, not enough to cause death or even real injury but certainly enough to scare the scoundrel.

"Just stop! I'll talk!" Arnbjorn gasped. Eirik withdrew his blade as Arnbjorn felt the minor wound.

After a moment's respite, Eirik spoke. "Out with it."

Arnbjorn snarled and slashed a hand through the air. "Denglr damn you both! Freystein is dead!"

They were quiet for a moment, until Valgard broke the silence. "Yox-dung."

Arnbjorn checked the bloodstain on his palm before glaring at the Governor's Guardsmen. "It's the damn truth! Freystein has been dead for a year and a half now! His usurper took his name and runs the Mársmidr using it!"

"Dammit… it makes sense, Valgard," Eirik said as he turned to the window. "Think. We had a lead on the real Freystein. But before we got to him, he just disappeared. We lost him, but it was like he was still in Strand. Still running the Mársmidr."

"Skoegir!" Valgard drew his axe from his belt and the shield from behind his back, checking the window of *The Shattered Shield*. "It makes sense. He was supposedly Freystein's right hand man. He would have known all the Mársmidr's operations."

Eirik watched the meeting in the loft. Something in the demeanor of Olaf, Stefnir and Ulfvalgr changed. Their posture became defensive. Ulfvalgr leaned back in his chair, as though trying to keep his distance. Or trying to keep his war axe within swift reach. Skoegir walked towards the fireplace.

"No," Eirik said as he turned a perked brow to Arnbjorn. "It's not Skoegir, is it?"

Still clutching his cheek, Arnbjorn paled.

Stefnir watched Skoegir as he stopped before the fireplace, lifting a poker and setting it in the embers. In the warm orange light, Stefnir saw deep, aged scars across Skoegir's cheeks, the kind that only men of rough and dangerous work could earn.

Village bumpkin that he could be, even Stefnir knew that Skoegir was no businessman.

"So where can we find Freystein?" Ulfvalgr asked. "This man deserves what's coming to him."

Skoegir snickered again. "Freystein ain't no man, varl."

Everyone went silent as the meaning of Skoegir's words slowly dawned on Stefnir, Olaf and Ulfvalgr. Movement pulled Stefnir's gaze towards the staircase. The steps creaked softly. Someone, *several someones*, approached.

"It wasn't chance meeting you at the market this morning, was it Kjallak?" Olaf said. Stefnir realized that his friend's fingers inched towards his sword.

Kjallak just stared and smiled.

"Are you working for Freystein, Kjallak?" Olaf asked. Stefnir's friend gripped the handle of his blade, and the boy felt for his weapon too. "Why else would or could a human know or care about a varl relic? You told him about Torstein's heirloom, didn't you?"

"Almost, Olaf. Almost." Kjallak's grin grew as he reached both arms around the bench and drew a hidden war hammer.

Stefnir glimpsed behind them. Armed thugs gathered at the top of the stairs, while Skoegir drew the glowing poker from the fireplace. Stefnir noticed Ulfvalgr shudder, the varl fixated on Skoegir's heated weapon.

"I used to work for Freystein. Then *I* began calling the shots; telling the men of the Mársmidr what to do. Dealing with those who disobeyed me. Eventually, Freystein tried to reassert control. You, of all people, know I've got no patience when a prize is just within grasp."

Kjallak tilted his neck, which popped softly. "Sometimes though, you can get a bit more reach with a weapon. Which is good for grabbing a man's territory, his soldiers... And if it's useful, even his name."

Chapter 7

Eirik and Valgard leapt through the window, smashing the wooden shutters against the walls as they went. They sailed over the gap into *The Shattered Shield's* loft and crashed into Freystein's back.

Yet even as his axe came down, Eirik knew the strike would fail.

The varl stumbled forward and slammed into the table, his thick tunic split but the skin barely scratched. Stefnir, Ulfvalgr and Olaf jumped from their seats as flagons flew, sloshing their golden contents across the floor.

Eirik recovered and raised his axe, preparing to chop into Freystein's hind side again when a shaft of glowing metal speared towards him. He panicked, springing away from Skoegir's heated poker and tumbling into the already unbalanced Valgard, rolling over his back.

The desperate move saved them however, as an enraged and perhaps embarrassed Freystein swung his hammer over their heads. The weapon buried itself in the wall as Eirik and Valgard scrambled to their feet.

"Should have thought this through!" Valgard grumbled as he threw his shield up, protecting both of them from Skoegir's assault as they retreated into a corner.

"Shouldn't have missed," Eirik cursed. It was stupid and shortsighted, but when Arnbjorn revealed the varl's true identity, their window of opportunity was closing rapidly. There was no choice but to act.

Skoegir stabbed with the hot poker again and again, each shot blocked by Valgard. Eirik took the reprieve his partner provided him to examine the situation. Freystein's men were spreading out before Olaf, Stefnir and Ulfvalgr. Unlike Kollsvein's dregs, the Mársmidr were more numerous and better disciplined, trying to create a shield wall to cage them. Once their formation was complete, attrition would wear Ulfvalgr and Olaf down.

"We've got to charge them," Eirik said. He noticed Freystein clear his hammer from the wall and begin to advance on the cornered duo.

Valgard growled as another strike of the poker panged off his shield. In reply, he delivered a flurry of blows with his skeg axe that sent Skoegir reeling. Their path open, Valgard spat. "We take them together!"

As one they banked left, each bellowing a battle cry that would shame a bear. For a moment, Ulfvalgr gave them a hateful look that caused Eirik to fear the varl would assail them. At the last moment, the varl took advantage of the momentum the Guardsmen carried and stomped forth, adding his own axe to the rush.

The three struck the same shield-bearer with the force of an avalanche, the onslaught far too much for any man. The Mársmidr goon rolled back, leaving pieces of armor-debris and blood on the floors of the aptly named *Shattered Shield.* Another gang member tried to fill the gap, but Valgard threw a kick that forced him away, keeping their escape route clear.

Ulfvalgr dashed through the opening and immediately hacked the side of a Mársmidr swordsman, forcing him to his knees with a ghastly shoulder wound that slickened the floorboards red. Olaf and Stefnir followed and the three began descending rapidly, their footsteps threatening to shake the steps apart.

Eirik pursued but stopped immediately when he heard a cry behind him. He turned and caught Valgard as he fell, his friend's shield clattering to the ground. Eirik's hand came away scarlet.

Halfway down the steps, Olaf glimpsed back and fortunately realized the dilemma. The varl returned, covering them with his massive shield. One gang member charged, only for the varl to swat him backward, bowling the thug into a few of his allies. Sheathing his blade, Olaf helped Eirik carry Valgard down.

The Mársmidr thundered after them. As Eirik and Olaf bore Valgard to the ground level, Ulfvalgr twisted and chopped through the staircase itself. The axe pulverized the landing, sending aged boards and rusted nails scattering over the walls. The gang above stopped as the structure slanted, wood groaning as the weight shifted precariously.

As the staircase began to fall, Eirik and company ran to the exit.

Stefnir held the door for Valgard's bearers as they returned to the streets of Strand. Behind them, the Mársmidr howled from shock and injury as the stairs collapsed. It would not stop them, but would cause delays as they recovered and improvised a new descent.

Olaf grumbled. "We're not going to get far with Valgard's injury! Any ideas?"

"Leave him," Ulfvalgr spoke with grim pragmatism.

Eirik saw Stefnir's countenance pale when the boy faced him. The Guardsman realized whatever face he unconsciously made must have scared Stefnir good. Eirik shook off his anger and surveyed about.

Down the street, he saw a line of yoxen wagons with several guards walking alongside. Eirik regarded them a moment as an idea formed. "Olaf! Everyone! Follow me!"

Olaf and Eirik carried the injured Valgard down the street. Stefnir ran beside them while Ulfvalgr followed after a reluctant start. A few of the caravan guards noticed them and raised their round shields to block Eirik and Olaf's way. There were even a few varl among the traders, who gave the approaching band stormy, questioning looks.

"That's far enough," one of the guards commanded.

"I need to see whoever is in charge," Eirik replied, adjusting Valgard's arm draped over his shoulders.

The guards glanced at one another. Eirik snarled as he drew a silver from his pouch and tossed it at the guard who spoke. The man leaned back and caught the stud of metal, his features relaxing as his eyes darted between it and Eirik. He bit the coin, leaving teeth marks with his molars. A grin passed his lips. "Alright, hang on."

Eirik checked behind and saw a man standing outside *The Shattered Shield*. The figure spotted them and pointed their way, crying out something Eirik could not hear. Ulfvalgr's face tightened, and the varl raised his axe, preparing for a fight.

"What's the problem? What do you want?" An impatient-sounding robed man asked as he approached with the bribed guard beside him.

"I am Eirik of the Governor's Guard, and we are on official Strand business," Eirik said as the merchant regarded the weakened and barely conscious Valgard. "If you take us to the Great Hall, I will see to it that your duties during your time in Strand are waived."

"Eirik," Stefnir said meekly. "They're coming."

"How do I know you're telling the truth?" The merchant asked, scratching his mustache.

Eirik risked a fast glimpse toward *The Shattered Shield* and saw a group of armed men approaching. He grunted and drew his pouch, tossing it to the merchant's feet. "If I am lying, you can keep this as compensation instead."

The merchant scooped up and opened the pouch. His brow bounced as coins of silver and even a gold nugget spilled into his palm. He paused and lifted a piece etched with heraldic insignia, his features alight with recognition…

"Guards!" The merchant cried out. "These fellows are our guests."

The hired men gathered about them, forming a cordon of shields, spears and blades towards the advancing thugs. Eirik saw the group of Mársmidr, with Skoegir at the head, draw to a stop before the disciplined formation. A short fellow amongst Skoegir's men stared at Eirik rather intensely, before whispering something into the Mársmidr lieutenant's ear. Skoegir sneered.

"Come with me," the merchant said as he turned and walked beside the rows of yoxen carts towards the head of the caravan.

Stefnir, Ulfvalgr, Eirik and Olaf followed, Valgard leaving a thin trail of blood in the snow as he was carried. When Eirik glimpsed behind, he saw a frustrated Skoegir and his men beginning their trek back to *The Shattered Shield*. Eirik couldn't help but smirk.

"You're in luck," the merchant explained as he led them to one of the emptied wagon in his possession. A canopy stood over it, designed to keep precipitation from falling upon the bedding. "I just unloaded this and intended to have it refilled at a nearby lumberyard. But that task will keep till tomorrow."

"Thank you," Eirik said as he and Olaf carefully laid Valgard on the cart, resting him on his stomach.

"I will have my daughter run you some linens for your injured man. Climb aboard. I've made enemies here and have no wish to tarry."

They all boarded the cart, the varl hunching as not to puncture the overhead sheet with their horns. Eirik doubted that the single yoxen could draw them all, but the merchant ordered another beast attached to the yoke, ensuring that the wagon would be mobile. True to his word, a young woman arrived and provided Eirik with clean cloth to cover Valgard's bleeding back.

As he worked, Eirik realized that Olaf, Stefnir and Ulfvalgr stared at him. Ulfvalgr's scrutiny bore obvious suspicion, while those of Olaf and Stefnir seemed worried.

"I am sorry we lied to you about who we are." Eirik sighed from his nose as he unrolled a fresh bandage. "As soon as Valgard is cared for, I will tell you everything."

Arnbjorn smashed a fist into the wall of the abandoned building. Naturally, he did not follow Eirik and Valgard into the melee, yet he was a fool for involving them in the first place.

Everything, *everything*, was ruined.

The plan was good. No, the plan was great. It shouldn't have failed. Ottar had kept his word and called off the bounty on Arnbjorn's head, who in turn safeguarded the varl until Freystein could prepare his trap. Olaf and Ulfvalgr should have been Freystein's captives, and Arnbjorn should have been welcomed back and reunited with his brother.

Damn those bastards! Arnbjorn thought as he covered his stabbed cheek. He had only told the Guardsmen the truth to stop their torture, as it *shouldn't* have mattered. Yet his cunning had backfired spectacularly. The last thing Arnbjorn anticipated was the pair being mad enough to recklessly enter the fray, despite being heavily outnumbered and outmatched. Let alone fighting their way out.

"Skoegir!" Arnbjorn heard Freystein bellowing from the building over. "Here! Now!"

Arnbjorn grabbed his braid and tugged from frustration. He decided to wait until Freystein calmed. Perhaps the Lord of the Mársmidr didn't know of his involvement with the Guard. At least, Arnbjorn could beg for another chance to capture the elusive pair of varl.

"My lord," Skoegir spoke. "Our scout brings news."

Arnbjorn released his hair and dared to sneak a glance through the window, remaining low as the torn shutters now offered little cover to hide behind. He recognized the short man who arrived with Skoegir.

Arnbjorn dropped down and vehemently cursed, already knowing what was being whispered. It did not matter that Arnbjorn was unwillingly dragged along with the Guardsmen. Freystein was not one for mercy, not for such missteps.

He couldn't return to the Mársmidr after this, for Lord Freystein himself would probably crush Arnbjorn's skull.

He clenched his jaw, his vision watering. A tear trickled down his face, stinging his cut with salt before being lost in his beard. Arnbjorn blinked until he could see again, and noticed another figure approaching *The Shattered Shield.*

Ottar.

The Mársmidr lieutenant entered the bar and was undoubtedly climbing his way up to Freystein. A thought passed Arnbjorn's mind, and he leaned closer to the window to listen. They did not suspect his eavesdropping, and a little information would help Arnbjorn contemplate his next move.

"Ottar," Arnbjorn overheard Freystein say. "So glad you could come."

"My apologies, lord," Ottar groveled. "I drove my men hard in order to return the day before last. We arrived dead on our feet and I still had urgent work to be done."

Arnbjorn peeked over the windowsill again. Freystein drew a knife and set the blade in the fireplace. "Tell me again, whose idea was it to use Hallvard to track Ulfvalgr?"

"I…" Even from the distance, Arnbjorn could see Ottar blanch. "Mine, sir. The man may be a thief and a liar, but no one is better at tracking and infiltrating."

Freystein had his back to Ottar, rectifying the overturned furniture.

Ottar continued. "I saw an opportunity, and I to—"

In one motion, Freystein grabbed Ottar by the shoulder and slammed the man against the table. The varl raised one of Ottar's wrists, and Arnbjorn could see the henchman cringe painfully as his arm was twisted. Skoegir watched beside the fireplace, his features ashen as a whipped dog. The scout hurriedly departed.

"Let me see if I recall this correctly," said Freystein with morbid calmness. "You, Ottar, were the one who trusted Johan and his crew to fetch the faening shield. *You* let Johan run off with it instead of handing it over."

"He— he was trying to blackmail us into letting Hallvard back into the gang!" Ottar protested while squirming. "I had… Skoegir track him down and kill him for his insolence!"

Arnbjorn froze, a chill washing over his flesh. He heard a slight tapping sound and realized it was his fingers trembling, rattling against the floorboards.

"Oh, yes. No doubt," Freystein said as he slowly turned his gaze over to his other lieutenant. "Skoegir did indeed handle your blunder and bring me the shield, while *you* lost Ulfvalgr. Then you *enlisted* Hallvard, of all people, who crossed paths with those gods damned intruders while tracking Ulfvalgr."

"How, how can you be sur—"

"Yes Ottar! Our scout remembered them traveling with Hallvard. Their descriptions match his report the day before as well. And if Hallvard is at fault, so then are you!" Freystein reached and plucked the knife from the fireplace.

"Who? Who are they?" Ottar desperately asked.

"The caravan protecting them is heading for the Great Hall. Surely you're smart enough to figure it out." Freystein studied the softly glowing knife before slamming Ottar's wrist against the table.

The henchman yelped. "The Guard!"

"Aye, fool. The very last people we wanted involved. I've half a mind to cut your hand off for your plentiful faen ups. But unfortunately, you might need most of it." Freystein pressed his fist into the back of Ottar's hand until the man's fingers spread across the table.

"No, no! Please!" Ottar squealed as Freystein touched the hot tip of his knife to the man's knuckles, ticking down the row of digits until deciding on his ring finger. The varl shoved hard. Ottar screamed, and Arnbjorn winced as the man's finger was severed.

Arnbjorn covered his mouth as he slid against the wall to the floor, biting back tears. All along, he had been deceived. Tricked by those who held the cards and nearly being killed himself. Eirik and Valgard had unsuspectingly saved his life, for there was no way Freystein would have spared him.

Not just for his immediate or past failings but because Arnbjorn, better known as Hallvard, would have discovered the truth sooner or later— that his brother, Johan, was dead. At the Mársmidr's hand. And they would not risk Arnbjorn's vengeance.

Arnbjorn breathed heavily, the instinct to seek vengeance overwhelming. He cursed Eirik and Valgard for never returning his axe. But if they had, he would have mimicked the Guardsmen's earlier assault. Even though the futile act would end with Arnbjorn slain.

At last, Ottar's screaming abated. Arnbjorn forced himself to spy again. The heated blade cauterized the wound and left almost no blood on the table. Freystein released Ottar, who fell into a fetal ball, cradling his disfigured hand.

Freystein spoke to Skoegir. "Inform Magnus and Nikolas of our situation. Nikolas will likely offer his aid, which I will accept. When that's done, I want you down at the warehouse to ensure that our next shipment isn't delayed. Take Ottar with you."

"Yes Master," Skoegir said as he knelt to help his colleague off the ground. "Magnus will not relish hearing of our failure."

"Magnus is too invested to pull out of the plan now," Freystein said. "And Ulfvalgr and Olaf *will* be found."

Arnbjorn's fists tightened as he overheard their plan. He had a feeling he knew this warehouse they spoke of and couldn't believe the Governor's Guard hadn't found it yet. It was not the full revenge he desired, but it was a start towards the retribution Arnbjorn needed. He turned and slinked into the building, remembering where to go.

Skoegir was responsible for Johan's death and by extension Ottar and Freystein as well. Arnbjorn muttered prayers to Denglr, the god of good fortune, begging his aid in making the Mársmidr pay for the death of his brother.

Chapter 8

Valgard shook with the vibrations of the wagon as they were driven through the streets of Strand. He breathed uneasily, but the stained linens had stemmed the flow of blood from the wound in his back. In the corner of the covered cart, Eirik wrapped an arm over his knee and watched his friend. Nearby Olaf regarded him while Ulfvalgr crossed his arms. Both varl hunched over and barely moved lest their girth unbalance the wagon.

They had traveled for perhaps a half an hour and boredom, especially after their earlier escape, gnawed on Stefnir's patience. The boy averted his attention from his companions and lifted the canopy sheet attached to the side panels, just enough to peep through and watch the passing streets of the city.

Ulfvalgr grunted. "You promised us answers, if I recall."

Eirik straightened and drew a sharp breath before exhaling. "Valgard and I are members of the Governor's Guard, who protect Strand from all threats foreign and domestic. Unlike the City Watch who keep the general peace, we are the elite of Strand's defenses."

"Are you always so sneaky?" Stefnir couldn't help but ask.

"Valgard and I are shadow agents. We pose as lowlifes to try and get initiated into the organizations, sabotaging them from within." Eirik withdrew a leather wineskin from his side and pulled the stopper away, giving Valgard a sip of the contents as he continued to explain.

"The City Watch and much of the rest of the Guard prefer traditional tactics—kicking in doors, smacking lip-flappers about for information. That works fine against the rabble but not against the major players. Thus, a few of us have permission to use infiltration and subterfuge to accomplish our tasks."

"Does that even work?" Ulfvalgr asked. Although it sounded as if there was contempt in his voice, Stefnir thought there was a hint of genuine interest.

"At our least, we gather information which we pass onto the City Watch and Governor's Guard for later. At our best, we turn the gangs against one another, sparing our own men from the risk of violent arrests," Eirik replied.

"Ha!" Ulfvalgr smirked.

"So how did it come to this?" Olaf inquired, leaning forward and inspecting Valgard's wounds. "It's been decades since I've last been in Strand. How did the situation so degrade?"

"We had a harsh winter last year." Eirik returned the drinking pouch to his belt. "And the year before too. Many farmers and land workers decided to try and seek work here, to earn coin to pay for food rather than grow it themselves. At first it was a trickle, then a deluge. What few jobs there were got snatched up, and finding employment became hard. Theft and murders spiked, so we needed to raise levies and taxes to pay for more City Watchmen.

"These conditions were perfect for the smaller gangs and syndicates already in place, and gave rise to the worst of their lot. The Mársmidr, led by Freystein, made plenty of trade routes to peddle their smuggled goods." Eirik scowled. "The Skaflings, the Dreyri Runes and the Leidr Félagis. Worst of all are the Aetla Hilmir, sometimes called the 'Fated Kings.' They want the Governor dead, to turn Strand into an independent kingdom."

"Are there any others?" Stefnir leaned in, listening to every word.

"The Barði Fetill, who love their underground boxing clubs. And the Vak'auga, or 'Evil Eyes.' They formed a market for their joy houses and a smaller, quieter one for illegal slave trading." Eirik's gray eyes narrowed. "They like to bolster rumors that their leader, Magnus, never sleeps... hence the eye on their shields is always open."

"You're twitching, lad. Are you cold?" Stefnir realized Olaf was staring at him.

"Sorry," Stefnir managed, feeling sheepish.

"So if you're all-knowing and all-seeing of the events in Strand, why haven't you slain the Mársmidr yet?" Ulfvalgr asked.

"A year and a half ago we were ready to kill Freystein, whom our inside sources thought was a man. His was, and still is, the most powerful of the criminal clans. Removing him would have undone the cornerstone of several other groups."

Eirik crossed his arms and continued. "Just before we moved in, Freystein just... disappeared. We scoured the city and even got the City Watch to bust down doors and ask names. Freystein had vanished, yet the Mársmidr still ran as smooth as skis on fresh snow. Worse, the undercover Guardsmen in the Mársmidr surfaced, faces down, in the bay a few days later."

Olaf scratched his beard. "Kjallak happened."

"Arnbjörn said that the varl at *The Shattered Shield* had taken over Freystein's position." Eirik's gaze flitted between the two varl. "Who is he? Do you know him?"

"Our questions come first," Ulfvalgr intervened. "Who is Arnbjörn? Why was he with you before and not now?"

"He was a former Mársmidr gang member, who we caught tailing you three during your arrival in Strand. Sometime ago, his gang caught him pilfering portions of protection money. They put a bounty on him, and I suspect that he hoped to rejoin if he did Freystein this favor." Eirik offered an opened palm. "Now that I've been forthcoming, perhaps you could return the favor?"

Ulfvalgr and Olaf exchanged looks. When Ulfvalgr shrugged uncaringly, Olaf answered. "We knew him. He was a friend of ours… a former kendr to someone important to us. Adoptive family, you could say. We had a falling out long ago, and he was forced to leave our clan. However I ran into him this morning, and he invited us for morning drinks under the false pretense of lending aid."

Eirik nodded. "And he didn't try to recruit you? Then what did he want, exactly?"

At this, Olaf froze.

Ulfvalgr grimaced. "He offered to help us recollect some stolen property. Turns out, he wanted it all to himself."

Stefnir could see the clear-as-day skepticism on Eirik's face.

"That's very vague," the Governor's Guardsman offered. Stefnir knew Eirik was trying to discreetly persuade the varl to give up more.

"Yes, it is," Ulfvalgr replied. He gave Eirik a withering stare.

"I… see." Eirik didn't press any further, and turned his attention to Valgard.

"This does make trusting you difficult, Eirik," Olaf said.

The man seemed to consider this, and then nodded. "I admit that I lied to you, or misled you at least. So for whatever it may be worth, I'm sorry. I saw a chance to strike at Freystein and I took it. At least let us offer you hospitality and keep you safe until we figure out our next move."

"You figure out your next move," Ulfvalgr said with a grunt. "We'll figure ours."

Eirik's features became crestfallen but he nodded.

They traveled in silence, the only sound being the creaking of carts and the clumping of the yoxen' feet treading the stone streets.

Ulfvalgr drew a whetstone and took it to the edge of his weapon. Olaf scratched his beard and occasionally glimpsed at Stefnir. Eirik kept vigil over Valgard, while occasionally lifting the canopy to steal peeks of the city. Stefnir guessed the man was keeping lookout for trouble.

As time dragged on, Stefnir felt the weight of his eyelids. The gentle rocking of the wagon was not unlike a cradle, luring him to sleep.

Stefnir awoke sharply to the sounds of blades clashing and the roar of men fighting. He dived towards his axe instinctively. But his companions' calmness made him hesitate to draw it. "What is that?"

Eirik lifted the sheet a little. "Ah. Just the tournament."

The Guardsman's reply drew not only Stefnir, but Ulfvalgr and Olaf too towards the sideboard to watch.

In a courtyard in the afternoon, two groups met and fought. One handful of men preferred plain clothes of rough spun cotton. The other group had gone through the trouble of dyeing their attire a grass green. They engaged one another, round shields smacking together while axes flashed. One man yelped as a sword found his shoulder. He dropped, sliding back and away from the melee, leaving his companions slightly outnumbered.

The City Watch passively observed the battle. An audience of civilians stood behind them, drinking and cheering. Someone moved amongst the crowd, calling for last bets. A scuffle broke out in the sidelines, prompting the watchmen to disperse a fight between two ladies.

"I don't get it," Stefnir conceded. "Why would Strand host a tournament if crimes and the gangs make the city desperate?"

Eirik pursed his lips before answering. "Mostly to manage those very problems."

"Ha!" Ulfvalgr barked. "Clever."

Eirik sighed. "Almost."

Stefnir, confused, looked back to the skirmishers. The green gang was winning, as two more of their rivals fell. One was clearly dead, his skull split by an axe strike. Stefnir covered his mouth, horrified that the watchmen didn't even flinch at the gore.

The violent death of the fighter demoralized his allies, who lowered their weapons to forfeit the match.

"The larger clans don't fall for it," Olaf concluded.

"Indeed." Eirik's face became somber. "The syndicates know these bouts are a waste of time. Or they use it as recruiting grounds, grabbing the best fighters for their own ranks. They pay better than the City Watch."

Stefnir noticed Eirik's visage lighten as he appraised the varl, until a groan from Valgard drew their attention. Eirik stood on his knees. "Valgard, are you awake?"

"Just," the injured man said meekly. "By the gods, that's painful. Are we close?"

"Very close," Eirik said. He leaned back and pulled the canopy away, allowing a few tender snowflakes into the cart. Stefnir was awed by the sight which confronted them.

On a massive hill above, Stefnir saw a lengthy path caked in snow. It rose to a huge long hall, where several support beams gave the manor a triangular shape. The steeple on either side of the structure sported a curved beam, the ends carved into fierce animals. A massive flag stood on a pole rising over the manor, flapping against the endless gale that bombarded the hill.

"Gentleman," Eirik said with the softest of smiles. "Welcome to the Great Hall of Strand."

"Too much and too far. It never ends with Magnus, does it?" Leiknir asked, reading the missive.

Runa glanced at him from her candlelit meal of cod stew. They sat at a round table in Leiknir's private retreat, a quiet but luxurious little hut somewhere in the heart of the city. "Is something the matter?"

"A request. Magnus and Freystein have given their consent to the Aetla Hilmir for a task." Leiknir angrily crumpled the paper in his trembling hand.

Runa realized she held her breath and exhaled. Ever since the messenger had arrived, she prayed to the Loom Mother that it would not be a job specific to her talents. She didn't mind doing as Leiknir asked. Yet any request on behalf of Magnus always stung like salt to a wound. "That's all it said?"

"No. It says much more, both in words and implication…" Leiknir rubbed his eyes, reluctant to continue. He pushed his chair from the table and ventured to a wine cabinet.

Selecting a bottle from the impressively stocked rack, he poured himself a goblet. "Runa. How many months have you been in my service?"

"Near six I think," she replied. She hadn't really thought about it. She remembered the day that she was given to Leiknir. She had bit and clawed one of Magnus' men who tried to take her against her will. In no mood for her rebellious streak, Magnus cuffed her across the face, hard enough to scar her cheek with his studded glove. Yet instead of going any further with his discipline, Magnus turned about and offered the girl to Leiknir.

He happily obliged. However, once they arrived at his manor in the city, Leiknir unexpectedly gave Runa her liberty.

"You are free to leave my service if you wish and return home," he had said. "Unlike Magnus, I have no wish for slaves."

At that, Runa ran out. But she soon realized how hopelessly lost she was. Men longingly leered at her as she walked down the snow-trodden streets of Strand, cold and alone. Until she found her way back to Leiknir's manor after not even a day.

He welcomed her back into his service. Runa responded by telling Leiknir that someday, she would kill Magnus. Instead of striking her for insolence, Leiknir smirked and asked if she possessed any skills in the killing arts.

Runa's fate changed in ways unforeseen as Leiknir took her under his wing. In her old life she was a fisherwoman, harpooning catches from the streams near her village. Leiknir helped her hone those skills for combat, and taught her to read and navigate Strand's underbelly. She repaid Leiknir's lessons with service and loyalty.

In time, Runa became quite infatuated with the balding, widening and aging spymaster. It was love of a sort, though not the kind found in the sagas. Rather it had grown within her slowly, like the sprinkle of snow which becomes a blizzard. But her feelings were never truly reciprocated. Despite her youth and comely features, Leiknir always remained faithful to his distant, shrewish wife.

Leiknir took a long sip of his goblet before speaking again. "I grew up in a coastal village south of here, where I met and married my wife. One year, a bad storm cost us our fishing vessel and we were forced to start afresh in the city.

"We had so very little money when we arrived in Strand, but were fortunate. My wife's brother offered to share his home with us, freeing me of the burdens of rent. So, I could invest our meager funds into a tiny fishing boat to make a living."

Runa couldn't help but smile. "So *that's* why you were so amused when I came back to your manor… when I told you I used to fish."

"You remembered that?" Leiknir laughed. When his mirth abated he rubbed his reddened cheek, his grin still wide.

"Anyway, I searched hard and eventually found a small boat that seemed ideal. I inspected it myself and judged it sturdy and fit, if old. I bartered the price down and kept a few coins in my pockets for later. The next day at high tide, I launched with a few nets, hoping to catch my first haul."

He took another long sip of his goblet before sitting opposite Runa, his gaze on the candle between them. "It was during that maiden voyage that I accumulated water. It was nothing but a trickle at first. But when I was some distance from the docks, it lapped at my ankles.

"I pulled my nets and equipment aside, and saw. Someone had made a hole in the hull. The water was clear enough that I could see hatchet marks that were not there when I inspected it."

Runa felt surprised. "The merchant who sold you the boat tricked you?"

Leiknir shook his head. "I rowed back as swiftly as my younger arms could manage. But I was forced to abandon my newly-acquired vessel a stone's throw from the docks. As I swam to the nearby shore, I realized that several other sailors and fishermen laughed at me. One approached and offered a hand to help me onto the pier."

Leiknir leaned toward her, and Runa met his blue eyes. "The man who aided me whispered through a grin, and told me that I was fortunate to have survived. Fishing, he said, was their business, and new competition was unwelcome. He warned me not to come back again. And then he walked away."

"Bastard," Runa hissed.

Leiknir nodded, sighing sadly. "I did not return home that night. I was so furious I could barely see. I marched into the market forums and purchased an axe from a vendor. Then I found my way into the nearest meadery, and spent the last of my coin on some liquid bravery. When the bar finally closed late that night, I took my axe and returned to the dock, intent on inflicting similar harm to those who mocked me.

"Coming back long after dark, I came upon a few arriving longships, manned by armed folks. They worked entirely in the moonlight despite the risks of docking at night. My anger abated for a moment and parted way for curiosity instead. From an abandoned fisherman's hut I watched them. They forced dozens of thralls to march down the piers to a few waiting wagons."

Runa's shoulders tensed. Leiknir downed the last of his wine before continuing.

"As I slipped away, I thought long and hard about my situation. I could have run to the authorities. If they weren't on the take, they would have shut the operation down. And I would have been given a 'thanks' for doing my civic duty and nothing more. I would still be coinless despite my deed. Instead, I stayed awake all night, prowling about the docks and trying to get all the answers before deciding."

Leiknir set the goblet on the table. "And that's when I saw it. Another ship approached the other side of the docks. But it was like no ship I had seen in my life.

"It was massive, the height of two men from the surface of the ocean to the top deck. The moon shimmered off its hull, like the scales of a fish. Unable to fit into a slip, the captain turned her starboard side to the end of a pier to unload *dozens* of bound captives. Men, women, children…"

Runa swallowed, feeling flush with fury. She knew this strange ship intimately, having spent a few weeks chained within it herself. She remembered, however briefly, the oddly designed vessel with many decks and staircases between them, like a long-hall on the water. *"The Destiny of the Weak."*

"Aye," Leiknir said, sagging in his seat. "Despite my stupor, I realized that there not just one, but two cartels plying human chattel within Strand. Maybe more. As far as I could tell, they were oblivious to one another, the distance between their operations considerable. Near morning, I made my decision and marched to the captain of the second ship. I told him of his rivals.

"The captain, a man named Magnus, eyed me hard and sent two scouts to find out if I was lying or not. While we waited, he asked how I came to learn of this other operation. I spoke of my struggle to survive in Strand, and how I sought revenge after losing my boat. The scouts returned and confirmed my discovery. Magnus immediately ordered the attack on his competitors.

"A few hours before morning, the other slavers' ships were captured, and their captains disappeared into the depths of Denglr's Bay. As Magnus claimed the cargo, he asked why I should be allowed to live, as almost no one would ask if I vanished. And, I was a liability."

Leiknir hunched over, his elbows on the table. "So I told him, 'It's because no one notices or asks questions about me that I'm the best spy you could hire. After all, those captains operated without your knowledge, right under your nose. And their blood is on my hands as well as yours.'"

"And he hired you as his spy?" Runa asked.

Leiknir nodded. "I think my point made him recognize a weakness in his enterprise. Or perhaps his men would fear for their own security, if he slew me for the aide I conferred. Anyway, he hosted me in his cabin in the aft of his strange ship, somewhere below the top deck. Over drinks, we talked. He told me what was valuable to know in Strand. Shipments, patrols, happenings. I promised to keep him informed, to be his eyes and ears if he'd have me. And I walked out of there with a sack of gold and a new career."

Runa swallowed. Hate burned cold in her stomach. "I see why you're loyal to him then."

Leiknir's countenance softened as he leaned into his seat. "No. No girl, I am not loyal."

The silence endured a while, before Leiknir bowed his head. "I was angry that night and was drinking over thinking. I applied myself desperately to save my wife from the streets. And the rush, the taste of easy gold led me down a path that I didn't know I could never leave. For years, I spied for Magnus. I watched as merchants arrived and learned their departing routes. I tracked the number of guards they hired, noted their cargo and memorized their schedules. I measured the necks of honest men for Magnus' noose."

"And as I expanded my wealth and began to socialize with the nobles and merchants, I soon found new outlets for Magnus' haul. Sometimes I would provide private slaves for manor owners. Sometimes a merchant wanted to establish a pleasure house near a City Watch barracks and required young, fresh women. I dined and drank with people who bore false cordialities, eagerly trading gold for human livestock. All while this emptiness within me grew a little more every day, a listlessness with no outlet."

Leiknir swallowed, his cheeks rouging. "One day, I happened to witness a deal being finalized. A girl, perhaps not more than eleven winters, stared at me as she cried for her parents. It was only a few days after my wife told me of her pregnancy. A child of our own on the way! And I realized... that girl being traded could have easily been mine. How easy it is to peddle in human lives, until you ponder the possibility that it could be flesh of your own on sale."

Leiknir drew a shuddering breath and covered his mouth with a palm. Runa watched him for a moment and then rose, walking to Leiknir and placing a comforting hand on his shoulder. He took it and squeezed gently.

"I didn't want to work for the Vak'auga anymore. But when you're central to a criminal empire, retirement is usually delivered with cold steel. So I said nothing. I worked. And when my wife miscarried... I thanked the gods that Magnus could not gain another means to control me."

Leiknir stood, his tear-streaked face growing dark. "But Magnus' avarice has grown worse since the day we met. When the Aetla Hilmir first challenged the Governor's rule, and the Mársmidr changed leadership, Magnus saw a chance to make Strand his own. We are rats, Runa. Not territorial wolves, not nobles with a claim to this world. Our fortunes come from the flesh trade and that gives us no right to rule."

Runa felt the intensity in Leiknir's gaze when he turned to her. "Magnus would turn this city into his slave pen if left in charge. I have grown rich from this plague we've flicked on Strand, a disease of smuggling, strife and slavery. I am tired of it all. So when you say that you want Magnus dead, do not think I don't desire it myself."

Runa took Leiknir's hand. Pulling his knuckles to her mouth, she kissed them gently. It was strange, perhaps, that from the aging spy's exhaustion came the fire of passion. Yet when the warmer feelings mingled with simple human compassion, Runa's attraction to Leiknir ignited a bonfire within her.

But Leiknir pulled his hand away and left Runa wanting.

"I need you, Runa. I needed you to understand, hence why I squandered the precious time we have telling the story of an old, stupid man and his mistakes. And I need you to help stop the madness that's about to happen."

His words sent a shock of panic running down her spine. "Leiknir, anything. Tell me what's wrong and what I must do."

Leiknir gave her the crumpled note.

Chapter 9

Two watchmen approached as the wagon carrying Eirik and his companions arrived at the Great Hall. They startled at the sight of the giants, but still drew closer when Eirik waved them forward. After a quick word with Eirik, they vanished inside the hall and returned with haste, carrying a stretcher between them.

Olaf and Ulfvalgr carefully lifted Valgard from the cart and gently set him stomach down on the stretcher. Stefnir adjusted the man's arms to reduce discomfort. Without waiting for Eirik's orders, the bearers moved swiftly back through the grand double doors of the Great Hall, shouting. "Make way! Make way!"

Eirik wanted to follow them, and even took a step in their direction before remembering his guests. To have two unidentified and unescorted varl strolling through the Great Hall would invite calamity. To leave them alone in the central courtyard would inspire ideas of flight. And even if he followed Valgard, there was nothing he could do. Valgard's life was entirely in the healing hands of the menders.

Eirik sighed, trying to relax the knot of anxiety in his chest, and turned to Olaf. "If you'll follow me, we have guest rooms for visitors of your size."

Olaf nodded and Ulfvalgr gave Eirik a suspicious, narrowed eye. The Guardsman turned and stepped through the still open doors, his boots making a slight squishing sound on the stone tiles. The guards stationed there regarded Olaf and Ulfvalgr keenly as they entered. Unlike the medics who took Valgard to the menders, these guards were more accustomed to dealing with varl and were less intimidated by their girth.

They were about to shut the doors when Eirik caught sight of a robed man running forth. It was the merchant. "What about our agreement?"

Eirik groaned. "Guards, let that man in. I promised business with him as well."

The merchant barely hid his smirk as he entered. He stroked his mustache suggestively as he glimpsed the attractive furnishings of the Great Hall's foyer, the room lit by candles on yox horn sconces fixed to the walls.

Even as the guards shut the exit, Eirik found the room no warmer. He spoke reluctantly. "In our haste, I never even asked your name, sir."

"Frode. Of Boersgard."

Another pain in the ass from that city, just like the Mársmidr. Boersgard's chief export must be trouble, Eirik thought.

The tale went that a few corrupt Boersgard watchmen were relieved of duty several years back. Freystein— the man not the varl— treated the disowned men to drinks but refused to pay, claiming the city owed them for years of service. The bartender accused the disgraced watchmen of making nothing of value. In the lethal altercation that followed, Freystein claimed they "made corpses" as he slew the man. The name Mársmidr or "Corpse Smiths" stuck after they fled the city.

Eirik forced a false smile. "I must attend to my battle-worn guests first. Might we offer you some refreshment while you wait?"

"Oh, please." Frode took a seat in one of the fur-coated chairs, his posture far too comfortable with assumed hospitality. "And perhaps some for my men as well? It's cold out there and we aren't earning coin lounging about."

"I'll see what I can do." Eirik failed to keep his brow from ticking with annoyance for the merchant's pompous attitude. He faced Olaf, Ulfvalgr and Stefnir. "Please follow me."

They walked briskly through the kitchen, passing maids who tended hearths and cooks who diced vegetables, sweated over boiling kettles or yanked feathers from pheasants. Entering the lobby, servants dusted and cleaned the furnishings and tapestries. Then through a workroom, they bypassed valets cleaning and maintaining utensils, tools and weapons. And throughout each chamber, better dressed men and women occasionally helped, inspected or ordered about the plainly garbed folk.

While the varl showed indifference to the opulence of the furnishings and décor, Ulfvalgr yelled at Stefnir to hurry along whenever the boy lagged to study his surroundings. Eirik sympathized. He too felt awe when he first encountered such luxury, having come from such a poor background himself.

Eirik paused before a staircase and bade one of the servants with instructions. "I have a guest waiting at the courtyard entrance, a merchant named Frode. Please see that he and his men are offered food and drink."

As the servant left, Eirik turned to a maid. "Kari, please tell Steward Olvir I have returned. Inform him that Valgard is in the infirmary, and I will make my report as soon as my guests are shown their quarters."

Kari curtsied before dashing off to obey.

The companions ascended the stairs to the second floor, the balcony there overlooking the main dining hall. Eirik could see the Governor seated below, listening to the concerns of a few farmers. He suspected it was another appeal to reduce tithes for a season, a common request that the Governor often granted to the detriment of the City Watch's pantries. Mender Melkorka stood nearby, hunching over her cane as she whispered into the Governor's ear.

As they entered the guest wing, Eirik took a lantern from a hall table, guiding them to a handsome door. Pressing through the entrance, the Guardsman revealed a chamber with ceilings tall enough for Ulfvalgr and Olaf. In the center sat a prepared but unlit hearth. A beam of sunlight peaked through a huge, shuttered window near the room's corner, which shone on a pair of extremely large beds.

Eirik drew the candle from his lantern and touched the lit wick across a tall candelabra, warming the darkness without fully dispelling it. The varl and the boy entered. An elated expression spread across Olaf's face while Ulfvalgr cautiously tested one of the beds. "Full fur and not a lick of straw. They're certainly trying to make us cozy."

Stefnir checked left and right before grimacing. "There isn't a bed for me?"

"Varl often keep to their own, so you're somewhat unprecedented," Eirik said. "I'll have a servant bring some refreshments and water, and light the hearth for you. When he comes, mention the bed and he'll settle you in another room more to your size."

"I…" Stefnir started but paused uncertainly, looking to Olaf.

The varl caught the boy's reluctance and nodded. "We'd prefer to stay together if it's all the same."

"We have full beds and privacy for him in an—"

"The boy stays with us," Ulfvalgr cut Eirik off, glancing away from a small shrine to Hadrborg residing in the corner opposite the window. "He's a kendr's pet, after all."

"Hey!" Stefnir pleaded, but it was too late. Despite the strife of the day's events, Eirik and Olaf burst into laughter.

But Eirik felt guilt creep into his heart as he sobered, remembering both his duties and Valgard's injuries. He promised himself to visit his friend soon, hoping Valgard would be well enough to hear Ulfvalgr's joke. "We'll bring in a cot for now and see about a regular bed tonight. I have some business to attend, so please make yourselves at home."

"Thank you Eirik," Olaf said.

The Guardsman shut the door behind him as he exited. In the hall, a servant approached whom Eirik recognized as Wade, Olvir's personal attendant.

"I am pleased to see you well, Lord Eirik," Wade all but whispered.

Eirik grunted. Wade possessed a bad habit of addressing all Governor's Guardsmen as lords, but Eirik had long abandoned trying to correct the valet. "Thank you Wade. Any word on Valgard's condition?"

"The menders believe he is not in immediate danger and will survive despite the blood loss. However, the wound is deep and the pain impedes his movements. Even with their powers, he will need some time to heal."

Eirik sagged with relief, his tension all at once exhaled in a long, weary sigh.

"Olvir wishes to see you immediately," Wade continued. "He has urgent news of his own to share, and he commanded me to see to the needs of our guests for you."

Eirik nodded, dropping his voice to a hush. "They have been shown their quarters and need food and a cot for the boy. Please try to keep them in the room for now."

"And if they're inclined to leave, should I summon the guards?" Wade asked.

Eirik shook his head. "No. No, come and get me if they do, so I can talk them down. Violence will only destroy any goodwill we have earned today. Thank you, Wade."

Wade bowed as Eirik departed, seeking Steward Olvir.

Ulfvalgr pulled his ear away from the door. "He's gone. I think his boss wanted a word. And the servant slinked off elsewhere."

"Are we prisoners?" Stefnir asked, scratching his neck. The question had been on his lips since they arrived, his stomach churning with anxiety.

Ulfvalgr's face scrunched, but he shook his head. "No. If we push it, I think we can leave. Not that they could really stop us."

Olaf groaned as he raised his arms, leaning backward until Stefnir heard an audible pop from the varl's cracked spine. The giant sat down on the bed and rubbed his legs. "Good food and a fine bed for the first time in months, and you're already thinking about leaving."

Ulfvalgr snorted. "You should have stayed at the shrine if you needed a soft bed so badly."

"I would have had just that a few days ago if someone hadn't ruined *Broddi's Mead Hall*," Olaf retorted, scratching his beard.

A tense moment passed as Ulfvalgr regarded Olaf darkly and Olaf gazed back with half-closed eyes. It ended when Ulfvalgr harrumphed and smirked.

Stefnir's shoulders eased. "So what's our next move?"

Ulfvalgr clenched his jaw, his scowl returning. "We figure out the shortest path between my axe and Kjallak's face."

"That's it?" Stefnir asked incredulously. Ulfvalgr took the other bed beside Olaf, who cupped his forehead in his palms as though stressed.

"No lad," Olaf said. "We just need a moment to think. The odds are bad. We're outnumbered and I was wrong about Kjallak. I still thought of him as a friend even after Torstein banished him."

Ulfvalgr growled lightly. "I told you."

"Aye, and you were right."

Stefnir sighed and put his equipment on the floor, pacing back and forth. "What was he after anyway? What's so important that this former friend of yours almost killed us to obtain?"

"It was a long time ago, lad," Olaf started.

Before the varl could continue, a knock on the door interrupted them. A man pushed his way in, his features flat and unattractive. He bowed to them, careful to hold a tray upright, which he carried and placed upon a dresser.

"My name is Wade, and I am the assistant to the steward." The servant took a container of oil and a candle from the tray, taking it over to the hearth. With practiced ease, the man deposited the fluid on the set of logs and then touched the candle's flame against it. Within moments a fire started, warmth filling the room.

"We have brought you a decanter of wine, some cheese, fruit and bread. I will bring you the cot shortly. Dinner should be ready by sundown. Steward Olvir and Guardsman Eirik will attend to you then." The servant waited until a small flicker of smoke began to rise towards the slim vent in the ceiling. He rose and bowed again. "If you need anything more, I am right down the hall."

Olaf nodded. "Thank you, Wade."

As soon as he had gone, Stefnir turned toward Olaf. "So what happened?"

Olaf scratched his beard. "Well—"

"You won't be telling him," Ulfvalgr interrupted, swinging his feet over the bed and placing them on the floor.

Olaf scowled. "The boy has earned the right."

"Yes, he has," the red-haired varl said as he stood. "Which is why I'm telling it."

Olaf's countenance lightened and he laid back. As Ulfvalgr crossed the room to fetch the wine, Stefnir spotted a chair in the corner. The boy dragged it toward the fire and took a seat to warm his aching, stiff body.

"Did your parents ever tell you about the Second Great War?" Ulfvalgr asked as he poured a healthy measure of wine into a drinking horn.

"The one where men and varl struck an alliance?" Stefnir said. "My father told me some. How the Valka, the first of the menders, aided us in banishing the dredge back north."

"A lot happened during that war. There were many times we, the varl, were hammered. Hard. The dredge came from the icy steppes that we now call Valkajokull, and our kingdoms were the first on the butcher's block. Even after the war's end, we continued to endure raids against our newly won lands. And every varl who perished was keenly felt for Hadrborg, who created the varl, was dead," Ulfvalgr paused to sup from his horn.

"That's not how it goes," Olaf said with a scowl. "The gods had not yet died. Hadrborg, the god of the varl, was a disciple of the Loom Mother. She was not happy with Hadrborg using her gifts to create a race that could not birth. So he agreed not to craft anymore of our kind to sooth her fury."

"One, you don't know that." Ulfvalgr glared at Olaf with narrowed green eyes that sparkled with the firelight. He ticked fingers from his drinking horn as he spoke. "And two, you know as well as I that the gods had already perished just before the Second Great War."

Stefnir looked back and forth between the varl. Like some of the elders amongst his village, there were historical disagreements with no answers or evidence. He knew that if he didn't say something, the arguing could go on for hours. "So the dredge pressed hard against the varl, who dwindled in number?"

Ulfvalgr propped an elbow against the dresser as he continued, the furniture creaking under the giant's weight. "Aye. So Throstr, our king then, prayed to Hadrborg for help. He begged for something, anything that could help turn the tide against the dredge, and the inevitable death of varlkind. So from the realms of the dead, the god sent him a vision, showing Throstr the way to the deity's shield."

Olaf opened his mouth to interject, but Ulfvalgr raised his hand.

"Fine! *Fine!* Some idiots *say* that Hadrborg *gave* Throstr his shield. Other fools think it was actually given to the previous king, Skrymir, and handed down to Throstr who discovered its true importance. If you want to hear the gods damned details, I'll introduce you to that windbag Ubin someday. But there is no doubt that the shield belonged to the father of varl."

Both Olaf and Ulfvalgr stayed silent. All Stefnir could hear was the soft crackle of the fire. Ulfvalgr cast his gaze into his cup which he swirled, as though considering his next words carefully.

"It was this that Torstein's kendr, and his kendr after, have been charged to safeguard." Ulfvalgr said and took a sip of his drink. "The shield is a relic of our people. The weapon with which Throstr rallied the varl and gave us a future against the cold stone men.

"It was called… 'The Gift of Hadrborg.'"

Chapter 10

Eirik found Steward Olvir speaking to the Governor and a couple of his advisors in the dining hall. He approached, keeping a respectful distance, and stood with his hands clasped behind his back. If it were almost anyone but the Governor, Eirik would have felt it acceptable to approach. As he waited, Eirik surveyed the room.

Three long tables formed a U-shape about a long bed of coals in the center of the chamber. Over this, the servants would often hoist meats and kettles of soup, such that guests could be served meals fresh from the heat. Flags of crimson and gold hung from overhead rafters. Behind the Governor's seat the Long Banner of Strand draped over the wall, a partial imitation of the Great Banner in the capital city of Arberrang.

That particular tapestry was said to weave itself somehow, a gift from the menders that recorded the most important events of history and, it was whispered, foretold futures to come. Yet Eirik had also heard rumors that even the powerful Valka could not read the self-scribed runes woven into the Great Banner.

Eirik stared at the Long Banner of Strand, taking in images of the glorious battles between man and varl in the First and Second Great War, and the early peoples of Strand struggling to survive in the harsh climes. The growth of an ordinary village into a bustling city built upon trade, fishing and lumber. Quietly, Eirik wondered if he would live to see another event added to the heraldry, another knot in the rope of history and time.

Given how difficult life currently was, he doubted he would wish that on anyone.

"Eirik!"

He turned to the right, a smile spreading across his face as a slightly pudgy, stubble-faced teenager approached. The boy's fine clothes were parti-colored, green on the right and red on the left. Eirik pressed his right hand against his left breast and gave the young man a stiff bow. "Governor-Prince Ragnar."

If it hadn't been for the table between them, Eirik was sure that Ragnar would have swept him into a warm embrace.

"I'm glad you're back," Ragnar said. "I haven't heard you say in a few moons."

"I apologize, prince." Eirik shifted his weight to his left leg. "Valgard and I were hidden amongst gang ranks in the northeastern slums. We led them to solve our problems for us."

"What?" Ragnar asked, confusion clouding his countenance while his jaw slackened.

Eirik shook his head. "Never mind, my prince. How go the sword lessons?"

"Oh." Ragnar drew his mouth into a slanted line and nervously tucked some of his curled hair behind an ear. Eirik's gaze was always drawn to the birthmark resting upon the back of the Governor-Prince's knuckles, a blemish that ran in the Governor's family, though often jumping generations. "My father let me skip them for the week. The cold makes my chest scar ache, even if the girls do love hearing about how I got it."

Eirik kept his face neutral, but secretly he was disappointed in Ragnar. Eirik had been charged with protecting the Governor-Prince during a trip to Karlshus for town inspections a year before. There, the vanguard came under assault by warriors bearing crests of skeletal hands grasping at crowns. Ragnar was lacerated across the chest, and if it hadn't been for Eirik, the scar would have been a mortal wound.

When the surviving assailants escaped, Eirik swore he saw Leiknir amongst their number. When they returned later that day however, several witnesses came forth almost immediately, all swearing that the spymaster had been in Strand since the previous week. Even Ragnar, so enamored with notions of justice, was moved to believe them. The Governor's Guard was forced to let Leiknir be.

But Eirik wasn't fooled.

"I hope you take your learnings more seriously if you are to rule Strand with Arberrang's blessing one day, prince." Eirik kept his tone calm. "Men will always try to take what they can, and you may have to defend yourself."

"But you'll be there to protect me," Ragnar replied.

If some thug in an alley doesn't knife me first, Eirik thought. Cunning and care kept Eirik alive thus far, but sooner or later the odds would not go in his favor. Still, he nodded. "Of course, my prince. But that's no reason t—"

"Governor-Prince," Olvir said. Eirik turned and bowed to the approaching steward. "Not to intrude, but might I speak to Guardsman Eirik on a matter of some urgency?"

"Of course! Of course," Ragnar said, though his frown suggested otherwise. "Talk to you later, Eirik."

"By your leave," Eirik fell in step slightly behind Olvir's swaying robes as they marched to the dining hall's exit. As they departed Melkorka gave Eirik a sour and disapproving stare, her wrinkled face rather menacing.

Once they rounded a corner out of sight of the dining hall, Eirik whispered to Olvir. "Why does the mender look like she wishes to skin me?"

"More my fault than yours," Olvir said. "Apparently, she had placed a special order for some... components, of value to menders. One of the caravan wagons that you and Valgard marked yesterday happened to include the delivery of those goods, which are now impounded with the cart."

Eirik scoffed. "Then perhaps they should have paid the tariffs."

"That is part of the embarrassment to her." Olvir smiled, his wrinkled features pulling upward. "My position is all politics, with old men and women acting like spoiled children. Which is why I can't wait to give it all to you someday."

"And why I can't wait to turn it down," Eirik replied with a wry grin. *Maybe dying in an alley isn't such a bad way to go after all.*

Olvir stopped and faced Eirik, who checked about and realized the hallway was empty, save for them.

"So why is it I had to shell out a fifth of our wine stock to this merchant, Frode? And try to save face before Melkorka, so her menders will still heal an injured Valgard?" Olvir asked, his features calm. "And now, entertain two varl guests?"

Eirik was ready. "Yesterday, Valgard and I spotted some unusual activity. An old gang-spy who had left town returned on the trail of those two varl and a boy. Valgard and I felt the suspicion warranted investigation."

Olvir nodded. "And did it?"

"More than I would have dreamed." Eirik put a thumb to his chin. He started recounting the events to Olvir.

Olvir's eyes widened such that Eirik could see reflections of the candlelight in his pupils. "Impossible. Freystein is a man."

With that, Eirik explained to his superior of the false Freystein Kjallak, the escape from *The Shattered Shield* and their reliance on the merchant.

Eirik pointed a finger towards the end of the hall where the western door stood. "To evade capture, I had to give Frode something; relief from taxes within Strand. It was a deal made in haste. I am sorry sir."

Olvir stroked his white whiskers, clearly too deep in contemplation to even hear or care about the apology. "This changes… everything. Months wasted chasing Freystein and we didn't know he was dead. If anything, killing him and adopting his name was brilliant, as it badly misled us. What is he after?"

"I don't know," Eirik replied. "That's why I offered the varl, and this boy with them, asylum. I need to discover why Freystein or this… Kjallak, covets them. And I believe they can be bait to lure out the Mársmidr through the tournament."

"I'm sorry Eirik, but I have another assignment for you." Olvir reached into his robes and withdrew an object, handing it to the Guardsman. It took him a moment to recognize a piece of iron ore in the soft candlelight, with a faint crown-shaped mark of the Aetla Hilmir.

"We found some of this when we led the raid on the Hilmir yesterday. None of their gang were to be found. It was clear that they had managed to move much of what they've smuggled before we arrived, though not all of it." Olvir sighed and crossed his arms. "The Aetla Hilmir escaped, but I believe that we can track them down. Speak to Smith Gylfi. See if he can identify which mines could have produced this ore and begin a new investigation."

Eirik clenched his jaw, as well as his fist around the ore. "Can't we put one of the other Governor's Guard on this? Olin perhaps, or Brenda?"

Olvir opened his mouth to speak when he noticed a servant passing. He nodded to the hooded man and waited until the attendant left before continuing.

"Everyone else is engaged and on assignment, Eirik. You're all we have, all we can spare." Olvir put a hand on Eirik's shoulder, speaking in a consolatory tone. "I'm sorry. This was what you wanted anyway, right?"

"My guests aren't going to sit around and wait until we have the manpower to deal with this," Eirik countered.

"Then I will speak to them tonight and take charge of their case personally. I will make sure that Freystein does not escape, Eirik." Olvir leaned closer and spoke like a conspirer. "The Aetla Hilmir are the most dangerous threat to Strand at the moment, even more so than Freystein's lot or the Leidr Félagis. Can I count on you, Eirik?"

Eirik sighed with frustration before nodding. "Yes sir. I will talk to the blacksmith and then let our guests know of… the change of their handling. They should hear it from my lips so they don't feel bait-and-switched."

"Good man. Now, I'm off to get this merchant out of our hair." Olvir patted Eirik's shoulder, and turned to stroll towards the foyer. Eirik glanced down at the piece of ore, and then began to walk towards the smithy.

A servant passed by, having just left the smithy as Eirik arrived. For a moment, Eirik wondered if it wasn't the same attendant who passed Olvir and himself in the hallway not a few moments before, but dismissed the thought. He wanted to finish this chore and attend to Ulfvalgr and Olaf swiftly.

Pressing his hand to the smithy's door, Eirik felt the heat before he entered the room. A wide bed of lit coals sat in the center of the chamber. The orange embers shifted lividly like a bed of worms, illuminating racks of weapons and shields hung on the walls. The blacksmith paused when he saw Eirik, holding a pair of tongs that pinched a twist of metal over the heat.

"Eirik!" Gylfi grinned.

The Guardsman noticed an odd tick to the old man's face. "Gylfi. Have I caught you at a bad time?"

"A minute more and you would have." Gylfi set the warming metal beside the forge and the tongs down atop a bench. Eirik couldn't help but notice how the smith's left arm was visibly, asymmetrically larger than his right. "Shut the door, will you? Some of the maids think it fine to warm themselves in here while gabbing about who beds who."

"Doesn't it get too warm in here?" Eirik asked as he shut the entrance.

"I'll take hot and silent over warm and obnoxious. Besides," Gylfi replied as he indicated an opened window with a view of the setting sun. "That should cool the room well enough. It's been a while since I've seen you lad."

"That it has." Eirik stepped toward the window and put an arm against the sill. "I'm sorry Gylfi, they put me—"

"Out there, to cause trouble for someone or some gang?" Gylfi shook his head and walked closer to Eirik. "You deserve better, lad. You *are* better. And you've got a right to…"

"Gylfi, please." It was not the first time they had this discussion. "That's not how it works and never will."

The blacksmith drew a sharp breath through his nose, which whistled as he did. "Well, if you haven't come for your spoonful of reason, then what do you need?"

"Gylfi, you've been a blacksmith for how many years? Two dozen now?"

"Aye, something like that," he replied.

"So you'd have a pretty good idea where a piece of iron came from, right?" Eirik reached into his satchel and withdrew the metal-laced rock.

"I… might. Let me see that." Gylfi took the ore from Eirik. "I need some light."

The blacksmith stepped back towards the furnace and held the ore over the embers. In the fire's illumination, Eirik could have sworn he saw the blacksmith's face grow solemn, perhaps even sad. Gylfi ran a thumb along the marking of the Aetla Hilmir that crested the rock.

"Gylfi," Eirik said after a long, hard moment of waiting. "Do you know the originating mine or not? Even just the nearby mountain ranges are fine. I must attend to a couple of guests before I need to follow through on this, and I don't want to keep them waiting."

Gylfi took in the sight of his friend. His eyes glistened a little while his voice was almost melancholy. "Your varl guests?"

Eirik tilted his head, his brow perked. "How did you—?"

Before Eirik realized it, the blacksmith dropped the ore and plucked a spear from the wall rack. Eirik's hands found the haft of his shoulder-slung axe, but stopped when Gylfi leveled his weapon's tip at Eirik's throat.

"Step away, lad." Gylfi commanded, nodding his head to the side. "And have a seat."

"You're one of them," Eirik said unquestioningly as he moved to obey, lowering himself onto the bench. "The Aetla Hilmir."

"Given the current state of affairs, can you really blame me?" Gylfi said with a sullen countenance. "The gangs are bad enough. The Mársmidr running protection, while the Dreyri-Runes acting on their murder contracts. The Vak'auga grab girls off the street and whisk them away… to Arberrang. Boersgard. Or stick them in a brothel until they're too old to be worth a bowl of soup."

Eirik blinked. "And you think the Aetla Hilmir are the answer?"

"Dammit Eirik, why couldn't you have listened? Truly?" The spear wavered. "The Governor is too soft hearted to deal with the problems of his province. He spends too much food on the peasants instead of keeping the City Watch fed and alert. Too much coin goes towards city projects and not into stamping out corruption and crime. And if the Governor is bad, imagine what happens when your half-brother, Ragnar, takes charge?"

Eirik said nothing but felt a chill wash over him when reminded of what he tried for years to ignore. His mother had been alone, working a job as a bar maid. Yet somehow money trickled into her purse from another source. With it, she afforded Eirik a tutor to teach him numbers and writing. But when he was fourteen, a bout of the Northern Chills weakened her body.

Bedridden, she asked for a piece of paper and a quill to write a letter. She gave this missive to Eirik, its envelope addressed to the Governor. Then she instructed her son to deliver it to the Great Hall should the worst happen.

A week later, it did. Despite his grief, a teenage Eirik took the letter to the Governor's manor out of respect for his mother's words. Twice the guards turned him away, once mockingly, and then with pity when they realized his situation. If Olvir hadn't overheard and asked to see the letter, Eirik's life would have been considerably different.

To this day, Eirik wished he had not read that letter. Nor told Gylfi its contents during a night spent deep in their cups.

"So why expose yourself?" Eirik said, as his mind tried to devise how to incapacitate Gylfi without killing him, or being killed in the process.

"To save your life, lad. I was asked by a fellow for a key to the under hall. The Aetla Hilmir want your varl friends for whatever reason." The spear quivered again. "If you give the alarm or try to stop them, you and anyone in their way will be killed. I'm sorry lad, but trust me. You can't beat them."

"The servant from earlier," Eirik said, trying to recall the hooded man's face despite having seen it twice that day. "The one who visited you."

"Aye lad," Gylfi said glumly. "You were always bright, and that's what I admire most about you. But he'll be gone before you can do anything about him."

Eirik swallowed as he connected the facts and realized something horrible. Something he did not know before that only made horrific sense now. "Gylfi, listen to me… and listen well. I was with these varl when they escaped the grasp of the Mársmidr earlier today."

Slowly, Eirik stood and felt the tip of the weapon against his chest, a slight pain welling over his breast where the point pricked his tunic and skin. "There is only one reason that the Aetla Hilmir could possibly be after these varl, and that is if they are working alongside the Mársmidr. This is no coincidence. You may think the Hilmir are honorable, but they'll win at any cost. Even siding with the very men you want cuffed in irons or executed."

"That's a lie," Gylfi said, though the conviction had vanished from his voice. He took a half-step back, pulling the spear away from Eirik who stepped forward intrepidly.

"You remember the attempt on Ragnar's life, Gylfi. You trusted and believed me when I said Leiknir was there, along with the Aetla Hilmir. Why in the world would a band of raiders and thrallers care about the son of the Governor, unless they were currying favor with those who covet the seat of Strand?" Eirik asked, taking another step.

Gylfi shook his head and held the spear with two hands, pulling it defensively towards his chest. "Lad, stop now or I'll stab your knee. Better a limp for life than death at the Hilmir's hand."

"Gylfi," Eirik said solemnly. "I'm sorry."

The spear shot out. Eirik sidestepped the thrust and dashed forward, sending a fist into the blacksmith's jaw. It landed with power enough to scare Eirik, as Gylfi dropped like a stone over a bridge. Falling to his own knees, Eirik scampered over his friend and held a hand over his mouth to check for breath. He put a finger to the smith's neck to seek a pulse.

Gylfi lived, though the blood seeping from his lips suggested a few broken teeth. Eirik felt a pang of regret, but determination made him stand. He noticed a set of manacles on the blacksmith's rack and collected them.

"First Valgard, now you," Eirik sighed as he rolled the blacksmith over and bound his wrists behind his lower back. "I'm getting very tired of risking or losing friends today."

Once the smith was restrained, Eirik took off, his cloak flowing as he sprinted to the guest wing.

Stefnir paced back and forth. The cot had not yet arrived, and despite further questions, neither Olaf nor Ulfvalgr would speak any more about the Gift of Hadrborg. Stefnir was left with a wondrous sense of awe that someone could care so much about this relic and yet neither of the varl would speak of its abilities. What could be so valuable to justify these murderous plots to possess it?

A thought crossed the boy's mind when he passed the corner window. He approached it and opened the shutters, letting a gust of chilling air enter the room. Below, the city of Strand rested at the base of the hill. Thousands of hearth fires from homes and halls glittered like stars on earth. The light they cast robbed the night sky of some of its magnificence, as though there were fewer constellations above.

Since he arrived, Stefnir had never really *seen* the city, only pieces at a time from corners and alley. Staring down at it made him truly realize the magnitude of the metropolis, perhaps a hundred times the size of his village. How could civilization thrive in so clustered a state, with man clinging to man, even those who hated one another with such fierce passion? How could they stand it?

Stefnir turned as he heard what sounded like a stifled gasp come from outside the room. Olaf and Ulfvalgr shot up from their beds. Several soft footsteps padded just beyond the door, likely from more than one person.

"Guess my bed has finally arrived," Stefnir declared. He closed the shutters and began to head towards the chamber's entrance.

"No."

Ulfvalgr's simple, hushed word stopped Stefnir cold. The boy realized that both varl readied their weapons. Ulfvalgr saw Stefnir's questioning look. "One doesn't try to sneak around with a cot."

Stefnir's eyes widened. He reached for his axe.

Eirik drew to a halt as he found the carcass of Wade in the hallway, blood pooling about the deceased. His head rested on his cheek, the face a mask of pain. His back was a red ruin, where a blade had pierced the ribs. At a cursory glance, Eirik knew that the weapon must have nicked both the heart and the lungs, ending Wade's life with little chance to permit a scream.

A cry to the right caught Eirik's attention. A maid had dropped her linens on the floor, having caught sight of Wade's body. Eirik rose and pointed at her. "Get the watchmen! Tell them to meet me at the guest quarters! Hurry!"

The woman nodded frantically, rushing off to obey. Eirik was glad she did not go catatonic like too many other servants might have.

Eirik ran. As he neared the guest room, he overheard the metallic clash of weapons and the muffled crack of shields being split. Grasping his axe, Eirik rounded the corner. He spied a man staring into the chamber, holding both a blade and a buckler. The shield immediately drew Eirik's attention. Its mark was of a bony hand grasping a crown, a symbol of the Aetla Hilmir.

The rebel turned and shouted a warning as the Guardsman charged. Eirik's axe arced down, brushing through the man's upraised shield and slamming against his shoulder. Eirik heard the squelch of his victim's collar snapping and followed with a kick that sent the maimed man sprawling.

Eirik entered the room and witnessed the chaos. The varl were trapped in the corner with the closed window behind them, having pushed one of the beds over to create a barrier between them and their attackers. Stefnir stood sandwiched between their bulky frames, unable to really move. Meanwhile, four men tried to prod them along with spears and swords. The fifth commanded the rest, his features hidden by his hood.

"I think we got off on the wrong foot here," the hooded man said, whom Eirik recognized as the servant who passed him twice earlier. "Why don't you settle down and come with us? It'll be easier than having us stab your legs and drag you out."

Eirik, thinking that he might sneak behind the speaker, crept forward. But the hooded figure turned and flashed him a smile.

"Eirik, Eirik, Eirik," he said with a condescending tone. The false servant drew his hood away with gloved hands, revealing an attractive countenance and locks of blonde hair. "Why didn't you listen to your friend Gylfi? He tried to save your life, after all."

Eirik almost struck but something halted his hand. The unknown man had familiar features, but he couldn't quite place him. "Who are you?"

The false servant turned his body a little and then lashed out. Eirik barely ducked as the knife sped past his ear. Rising, Eirik leveled the handle of his axe to arrest the familiar man's descending sword.

Eirik swiftly scanned the room as he held death at bay. He came to a hasty decision.

The Guardsman pushed out, forcing his opponent to give ground and feigning a rising strike. As the fake servant posed defensively, Eirik swept his axe down and twisted his hips. The flat of his axe struck the hearth.

A cascade of embers erupted at his blow, spilling out across the chamber in a fearsome orange arc.

The Aetla Hilmir shouted as burning embers fell upon the beds, setting the furs ablaze. The familiar man screamed a curse and swatted a cinder that touched his neck. As the flame spread Olaf leapt back into the creaking window shutters, wide eyed. Ulfvalgr too portrayed dismay but took advantage of the distraction to swing his weapon into the arm of a spearman.

As the struck foe went down, Eirik charged and grabbed the flaming sheets from the other bed. With one hand holding his axe, the other whipped the fiery cloth like a whip towards the Aetla Hilmir, who hesitated to advance. Eirik realized that the fire had caught against the rug near the entrance, making escape through the door ever the more difficult. Only one option seemed plausible.

"Olaf! The window!" Eirik shouted.

"Are you crazy?" Olaf yelled in reply as he slammed his back against the shutters, trying to keep away from the encroaching flames.

Recognizing the varl's reluctance, Eirik had no choice but to act on Olaf's suggestion. The Guardsman leapt atop the flaming bed and bounced towards them, spinning his burning sheet overhead and yelling like a raving madman.

Olaf screamed and retreated into Ulfvalgr and Stefnir. The weight of all three broke the window shutters, and together they fell through the opening.

Eirik threw his flaming sheet aside and dived after them.

They landed across the slanted, snow-caked roof and immediately began sliding down. As he fell, Eirik noticed his cloak on fire and rolled, smothering it in the passing, icy white. With the motion, Eirik saw the sneering face of the familiar man from the window, before he turned and disappeared into the chamber. And standing next to the window frame was a feminine figure, perched on the roof itself with a short spear in hand, watching them fall.

"Runa!" Eirik heard Stefnir cry, before they all tipped over the roof's edge and dropped down the hill.

Chapter 11

Dagny pulled the cloak over her shoulders. Thus far, the heavy patchwork of mixed animal furs kept the freezing rain off her body, but she doubted it would last much longer. Hopefully, it wouldn't have to.

She cast her gaze about, trying to find the person that Vott, her adoptive father, had told her to seek. The huts of this slum were small, aging things, clustered together to stay warm despite the risk of fire spreading. Such was life in the Grárgróf, better known as the Grey Pits. It was another ugly slum in Strand, but the biggest problems here were occasional pickpockets and lesser thieves. Gangs didn't dwell in the area long, for most of the neighborhood's residents were lumber workers, and thus armed and hardened.

But the weather today undoubtedly kept even the hungriest rogues indoors. Dagny supposed that was a blessing, if the cold didn't kill her anyway. She sighed, her breath misting. "The least he could do is meet me at a public place with a hearth."

"Maybe next time, I will."

Dagny spun around, drawing a dagger. The man who spoke leaned against a support beam of some shabby home, his arms crossed. His hair was blonde with lighter locks over his temples, while his cloak was a darker brown against his tunic and pants. Dagny realized that he was attractive, if one were into men with wizened, grey eyes.

She didn't lower her blade. "Are you the Iron Turtle?"

"I am Eirik. Vott sent you?"

She nodded and slowly sheathed her blade. Reaching into her pouch, she drew a rolled parchment and held it out for him. "Vott was worried you were dead, by the way. He says everyone's been trying to find you for a day."

"And I'd prefer not to be found if I can help it." Eirik stepped off the creaking porch and took the missive. She wished he might read it then and hint as to its contents, for although Vott had taught her letters, the aging spymaster had used some secret code. Her hopes were dashed when he slipped the missive under his cloak. "You should go home before you catch the Northern Chills."

His mention of the pox made Dagny shiver a little and whisper the name of Radormyr for protection. "Aren't you a little old to be scaring girls?"

Eirik was about to leave, when he rounded and gave her a stern look. "If you want to be a girl, then get out of this game. Have Vott teach you a valuable skill and live your life, find a man, have many children. Pretend the ugly side of the world doesn't exist. But if you want to be a real woman, learn to use that knife. You'll need it in this line of work."

Dagny felt her spine bristle out of insult and shock. She opened her mouth to respond a few times, but wasn't quite sure what to say. Eirik spun and vanished into the morning mist and chilling rain.

She muttered a curse and began to venture home to Vott, and the heat of the hearth.

Sure he was alone, Eirik slipped through an alley and around the corner of an abandoned temple. Whatever god it was once dedicated to, Eirik could no longer say. The entrance had collapsed into a ruin of broken timber and poorly carved stone. But a hole behind the dilapidated structure was large enough for a man to enter and just tall enough for a giant to slip through. Eirik was thankful that the weather had swallowed his tracks.

Inside, the roof performed an unimpressive job of keeping the rain out. He found the varl and the boy in the corner closest to the ruined entrance and furthest from the only remaining windows. A small fire flickered, illuminating their tired faces. One of the giants held a gaze far more hostile than the rest.

"Well?" Ulfvalgr asked contemptuously.

Eirik approached the fire, his limbs trembling less in its warmth. He withdrew and unrolled the missive, angling its contents towards the firelight. His sight narrowed as he read, experienced enough to mentally rearrange the writing. Once he devised the true meaning, Eirik read it aloud.

Iron Turtle,

Gylfi has been arrested. They found him manacled beside his own smithy. Since Olvir knew you visited him, the steward figured the blacksmith had something to do with the attack. Interrogations underway, but the scriveners and guards checked his inventory. They found more iron and steel than records say was ordered. And a hidden cache of weapons. Huge weapons. Too big for a man to sensibly use.

Raiders got away under the cover of the fire. Two witnesses confirmed the Aetla Hilmir. Our sentries near the under-hall entrance were found dead. Signs point to inside job. We are questioning the servants and old hands, trying to deduce who it was and get a description of them. Fire was stopped but the guest wing is ruined.

Glad you're alive but we need to talk. Visit me soon, you probably need new clothes.
—Your tailor

Eirik hummed, thinking. It was true his clothes still carried the odor of smoke but the issue had to wait. There were more important matters to settle first.

"So Gylfi is the blacksmith. And your 'tailor' and Olvir are…?" Stefnir asked.

"My friend would rather I not disclose his identity." Eirik rolled the missive again. "And Olvir is the steward, who oversees Strand's security."

"Well he faening botched that!" Ulfvalgr slapped his knee angrily and stood, running a hand over the tips of his horns. Eirik harbored no illusion that the varl wasn't making a threatening display of strength.

Yet instead of being intimidated, the gesture only angered Eirik. Before he realized what he was doing, he slammed the missive into the fire, letting the flames eat the words.

"Yes, gods dammit! We faened up! But maybe now you have a better idea just how bad this city is and just how screwed you probably are!"

Ulfvalgr leaned back, tilting his head slightly. "What?"

"Think about it!" Eirik pointed his finger northwest in the direction of the Great Hall. "Those men who attacked you are the Aetla Hilmir! They've been trying to take down the Governor for more than a year. And last night, despite having a clear shot at the man, they went after you instead. You! Instead of their avowed goal! And this all happened after our little fight in *The Shattered Shield* with the Mársmidr. Why?"

Ulfvalgr glanced at Olaf, who returned his gaze steadily.

"Why, dammit?" Eirik clenched his fists. "Yesterday, we had no reason to believe the Hilmir and Mársmidr were working together. This is not a coincidence!"

Ulfvalgr growled, the sound like that of a threatened bear. "That's not a lick of your business, lawman. You promised us safety if we helped you break Kjallak's lot and you failed your half of the bargain. We're done here."

The varl collected his war axe, but Eirik was far from finished. "Just try Denglr's blessings out there. The City Watch will be searching for you, and plenty of them are on the take, courtesy of the Mársmidr. If they wouldn't arrest you for love of Strand, they'll sure as faen do it for a hundred silver!"

Ulfvalgr watched Eirik huff, trying to regain his composure. For a moment, Eirik feared the varl would smite him. Instead, the red-haired giant snorted and took a seat, rolling his jaw.

Eirik waited a moment until his heart slowed down. He took a step back and just breathed before asking. "What does Frey— Kjallak, want so bad?"

Both varl became inanimate, remaining still as statues and refusing to speak.

"Fine," Eirik turned his gaze to Stefnir. "You then. Who is Runa?"

The boy's eyes went wide. "Uh… She…"

Olaf blinked, staring at Stefnir. It seemed that everyone here had secrets.

"She, she is…" Stefnir stammered, scratching behind his head.

"She would be me."

The four rose as one, drawing their weapons and preparing to strike down a silhouette that stood at the hole in the wall. With surprising ease, the lithe figure slipped into the illumination of the fire. Eirik squinted, studying the intruder. She had brown hair with blonde streaks, bundled in a side braid and a sleepless gaze paired with a scarred cheek. She was covered with a white cloak. A bag at her side contained a handful of javelins.

"I remember you," Eirik said as he placed her features. "You were with Leiknir a few days ago. And if you're his woman, then you're under Magnus' command."

She laughed. To Eirik's ears it was a hateful sound. "I work for Leiknir, yeah. But Magnus? He could try to order me, but all he'd get is a skewered throat."

"How do we know you're not stalling us until reinforcements arrive?" Olaf asked.

"Look big guy, it's not hard to follow two giants in a human town. I've been watching you all since you fell from the Great Hall's roof. If I desired, I could have arrived in the middle of the night and taken you while you slept." A smirk spread across her lips. "It's amazing you all survived that drop."

"The servants always push the snow from the Great Hall's walkways down that side of the hill. It piles up after a while, becoming safe enough to land in." Eirik shrugged, though he didn't mention that the fall was unpleasant. The bruise over his spine began to ache again as he remembered their landing.

"Runa," Stefnir's voice was almost pleading. "What are you doing here?"

She scanned over them, one by one, before Eirik was sure her glare rested upon him. Runa exhaled meekly and dropped her javelins. Drawing a knife, she laid that down as well. "Let's chat, boys."

Reluctantly, they let her take a seat by the fire, gripping their weapons as they heard her story and proposition. When she finished, Eirik shook his head.

"No," Eirik said. "I'm not meeting with Leiknir. I don't buy that he's changed, and I don't believe he wants out of his business with Magnus."

"The lawman is right. Between our old 'friend' trying to capture us, and the Great Hall's hospitality casting us out on our asses, I've had about enough of bad deals, girl," Ulfvalgr replied.

Runa laughed and shook her head. She raised her opened hands. "Look, I understand. I've been listening to you all night. You got screwed by Freystein. The City Watch couldn't hack it and your old, faithful blacksmith chum betrayed you."

Eirik scowled at her. "You know about my friendship with Gylfi?"

"Come on Eirik. You guys aren't the only spies in Strand." She tilted her forehead towards Eirik. In the firelight, the fluctuating shadows made her features more menacing. "Leiknir sees the blizzard over the mountain. And he knows it's about to bury us all, Eirik. All of us. So why don't you just meet to hear him out?"

No one spoke until Olaf broke the silence. "It couldn't hurt."

"Maybe you should do it, Eirik," Stefnir pleaded.

Eirik covered his face with a palm, embracing the darkness as a chance to think. After a moment, he finally scowled at Runa again. "I'm going to speak to my allies here. We will send you on your way. If I change my mind, I will meet with Leiknir at the place you give me."

Runa smirked. "*Brenna Training Hall.* We'll be waiting there until midday tomorrow, otherwise we'll assume you're not interested… or dead."

Eirik turned toward Olaf, then Stefnir. When he checked Ulfvalgr, the varl nodded. At last, he returned his attention to Runa. "Fine. Go."

"Take care, Stefnir," Runa said as she stood and collected her weapons.

"Runa," Stefnir began. The girl ignored him and left.

Everyone stared at the boy, who gazed sadly at the flames. He needed no prompting to tell them the story they all wanted to hear.

"Runa was... from my village. She was a fisherman's daughter, who practiced spearing salmon from the river near us." Stefnir drew his knees to his chest, wrapping his arms around them. "About two seasons ago, my father and I were away on a trip to scavenge and collect game. When we returned home, the village was burned down to nothing. We found corpses. Most of them were our own people, but some were raiders. Those that attacked us had sigils of a great eye made from crossed weapons..."

"The Vak'auga," Eirik said, recognizing the symbol. "Raiders and slavers."

Stefnir nodded. "We figured that when we couldn't find several bodies but discovered a single file trail. I wanted to go after them, to save the rest of the villagers and avenge my mother, who was amongst the dead."

Stefnir's head lulled as he stared at the partially collapsed roof. Eirik saw a tear roll down his cheek. "But dad said no. He wouldn't hear it. So one day, several months after the raid, I finally snapped after another argument. I stole his axe and some gear and ran, trying to find where the slavers had gone. Sometime after, I caught the attention of a pack of wolves, who pursued me. And I was saved by Olaf."

Olaf's shoulders sagged as he listened. "So that's why you wanted to become a great warrior. And all along, I thought it was for what you men call 'a woman's love.'"

"I guess it was." Stefnir laughed bitterly. "I guess it was."

Silence reigned after Stefnir's story, as they reflected on the events of the last few days. It was broken for only a moment as Olaf added another piece of broken lumber to the dwindling fire, the cinders billowing above as he gave it fuel.

"I'm sorry I lied, Olaf," Stefnir finally said.

The varl rolled his shoulders wearily as he comfortingly touched the boy's arm. "There's nothing to forgive lad. It takes bravery to tell the truth. Something for which all of us should strive and admire."

Eirik almost seized the chance to ask about Freystein's goal but thought better of it.

"But vengeance is a flame. It consumes and twists, justifying itself by the pain the past inflicted on you. And when the moment of triumphant retribution has come and gone, all that remains is the shell of your life, of everything you built to accomplish a brief moment of revenge." Olaf drew his hand away. "At least with men, that tragedy ends naturally. With varl? It endures to the end of days. Don't waste what little time you have on it, Stefnir."

The fire crackled as the four endured the quiet. Little by little, something about Olaf's words touched Eirik in a manner he couldn't have foreseen, even if the wisdom was meant for Stefnir. He wondered if he also had wasted too much of his own life hating Leiknir for his attempt on Ragnar.

Perhaps it was time to abandon it.

Eirik finally stood. "I'll do it. I'll meet with Leiknir. We need information and allies."

"To do what?" Ulfvalgr asked.

Eirik drew a breath. "You still want Fre— Kjallak? We're not going to get him by waiting for him to come to us. We must turn the tide. Thus far, we've been at the mercy of the many schemes of others. Now I'm desperate enough to try one of my own."

"Oh?" Olaf perked a brow.

"I will meet Leiknir tomorrow morning, after I make sure that you are hidden," Eirik said, dusting off his tunic. "And then we'll figure out whose door we need to kick in."

Chapter 12

"I don't feel safe without Ulfvalgr or Olaf around," Stefnir said as they neared *Brenna Training Hall* under the midday sun. Eirik had told Stefnir how the arena was also a side business for enlisting fighters in underground boxing matches, from which occasional gang recruitment happened. Outside, Stefnir could hear the din of weapons meeting, both metal and wooden. A combatant howled painfully, and a cacophony of laughter chased after the victim's misfortune.

"I don't either," Eirik said, his tone like an admission. He rubbed his shoulder as he walked. "In the past few days, I've been through more brawls and fights than the rest of the year combined. The aches are starting to catch up to me."

Rapidly, Stefnir began to have second thoughts and slowed his step. "Maybe we shouldn't do this. I mean, if you're exhausted, and we have to hack our way out…"

Eirik shook his head. "I planned for that too, and I know this area well. In a few moments, a City Watch patrol will be coming down the road. Even if one of them is on the take, they can't all be. So we throw ourselves into their protection."

"But they'll take us awa—"

"Away, and Olaf and Ulfvalgr will be left to fend for themselves, but at least they'll be hidden. That's better than getting captured by Leiknir, and taken to Magnus." The varl had been moved to a new location, just in case Runa was trying to distract Eirik from his charges.

Stefnir swallowed and felt his hand close around the grip of his father's axe. They stepped under the awning of the arena's entrance and Eirik paused. Stefnir peered ahead to see why.

In the passage that led within the training hall, a table awaited them under a few arches. A candle on the furniture illuminated a chubby, long-nosed man in a seat opposite them, adorned in clothes trimmed with fine silver and wearing a wool cap over his head.

Runa stood next to him, her exhausted eyes keen on Eirik while her hand hovered over the pouch of javelins.

"Leiknir," Eirik said. Stefnir thought his tone decidedly neutral.

"Eirik," the seated man said, raising a worn mitten to indicate the table. Upon it rested a jug of some drink that steamed softly, a bowl of apples, a wedge of white cheese and some bread. "Gods man, you reek of smoke. Please have a seat and help yourself."

Stefnir felt his stomach rumble. For the last few nights he had sustained himself with nothing but the meager pickings of dried mutton and pickled vegetables, the last of the provisions from their travels. As he stepped forward, Eirik held his arm to block the boy. For a moment, Stefnir couldn't help but detest the Guardsman.

"Thank you, no. This place isn't very private for talk," Eirik said.

"I had hoped my discomfort would be seen as a token of trust," Leiknir said as he took the jug and poured himself a drink. Stefnir recognized the scent of mulled wine by the hint of steamed oranges and fragrant spices. Hunger made it hard to focus on Leiknir's words. "As for the lack of privacy, I know about the coming City Watch patrol, and I suspect you plan to throw yourselves into their custody if we attempt to apprehend you."

Leiknir took a sip of his wine and smiled. Eirik continued to regard him coolly, his voice equally calm. "Telling me you anticipated my escape plan doesn't endear me to you, Leiknir."

The Vak'auga spy sighed and set his goblet down. "Then how about I tell you a story? About a certain Governor-Prince and my involvement with that ugly affair almost a year ago?"

Eirik crossed his arms and twisted his head, his scowl distant and contemplative. Stefnir knew the man was checking behind them using his peripheral vision. At last, Eirik turned his attention back to Leiknir. "Go on."

Leiknir put his elbows on the table top, clasping his mittens together and leaning his double chin over his knuckles. "Back then, you may remember that the Aetla Hilmir were still forming. They barely even had a sigil. They approached Magnus with a deal; smuggled ore for coin and an alliance. Magnus was interested but wanted to know how far the Hilmir would go. If they really had the chops to take on the rulers of Strand. So, in order to seal the agreement, he wanted the Hilmir to try for what they claimed to desire."

"You're telling me you had nothing to do with it," Eirik said, doubt clear in his tone.

"Oh, I very well did Eirik." Leiknir sighed. "That's not to say I was proud of it, which I'll have you know I was not. I used my sources to discover that Ragnar would be touring the countryside. That wasn't enough for Magnus though. I had to go and *ensure* that the Aetla Hilmir made a sincere effort. I protested, but Magnus would hear nothing of it. In the end I observed the attempt, which cost the lives of several Governor's Guard, but was foiled because of you. I was convinced that the Hilmir were sincere about their efforts to overthrow Strand's leadership. So the Vak'auga and Aetla Hilmir became allies."

Stefnir found himself growing angry. It was so easy before to take Runa's word as a faded friend, but after hearing of Leiknir's conniving, control was difficult. He squeezed the handle of his axe, but he stayed himself when he noticed Runa giving him the faintest shake of the head. Her lips mouthed without sound, "Magnus. Soon."

The joints of Stefnir's fingers ached when he released the weapon.

Eirik tilted his head. "Who leads the Aetla Hilmir?"

"More, more, always more with you, Turtle," Leiknir groaned as he leaned back and took a long gulp of his wine. "Haven't I told you enough stories for one day?"

"I'm on the verge of believing you," Eirik said. "But you have a lot to answer for, if you intend to undo all the damage you've inflicted over the years. And details are a fine start."

Leiknir's seat creaked as he shifted weight, putting an elbow atop an arm rest. "If the rumors I've gotten about the fire at the Great Hall are true, you've already met him. A man named Nikolas. Some, particularly women folk, call him Nikolas the Beautiful."

A pained sound escaped Eirik's mouth. Stefnir looked at him and saw him bury his forehead in a palm.

"Well," Leiknir replied. "I'd say that's a confirmation of the scuttlebutt."

"Blonde hair?" Eirik withdrew his hand. "Attractive features, a full set of straight, white teeth? And fast with the throwing dagger?"

Leiknir nodded. "I know nothing about his origins, but they sure breed them pretty there."

"Thanks for ruffling my feathers, Leiknir. So good to know I was a chop away from killing the leader of the Aetla Hilmir." Eirik grunted. "Now for the thick of it. Why are you helping us? Runa said you've grown tired of obeying Magnus."

Leiknir regarded Eirik a moment. "Have a seat, Eirik. It's the least you could put forward in this parley."

Eirik rolled his jaw contemptuously. He reached out and took the two empty chairs, dragging them out. He sat with reluctance, as did Stefnir. Once they were seated, Runa pulled a stool from under the table and joined them.

"Now that we're all comfortable." Leiknir placed his forearms flat against the table. "Eirik, we are parasites. Fleas on a yox's hide."

"Indeed." Eirik snorted.

"Which means if the yoxen dies, we die. Magnus is working with Freystein and Nikolas to bring about something big. Huge. They all have a heavy part in this performance, which has only just begun."

"The triumvirate," Stefnir said before he realized it.

Everyone's attention went to the boy. Leiknir's jaw dropped a little. "How did you hear about it?"

"I," Stefnir cursed himself. It was Arnbjorn who had told him back at *Broddi's Mead Hall*. "I heard a rumor over the drinking horns."

"I must be getting lazy in my job then," Leiknir said glumly.

"Never mind," Eirik said, turning his attention back to the spymaster. "What's coming, Leiknir? What do they have planned?"

"I don't know all the details, Eirik. But what they're doing will kill Strand, that I'm sure of. I may be a thief, but I am no murderer." Leiknir's face took on a strange and serene element of sincerity as he spoke. "When Magnus and his allies meet, I am kept out of the council. And the last few months I have been given strange jobs. Morbid duties."

Eirik edged towards the spy. "Like?"

Leiknir swayed back into his chair, his countenance uncertain. "If I told you, you'd probably think me mad, at best. No, Eirik. No. I think this is where I suggest you let me show, rather than tell, you. Out of trust."

Stefnir could hear the sharp breath Eirik drew through his nostrils. A tense moment passed, and Stefnir wondered if Eirik wasn't about to flip the table and slay Leiknir then and there. Instead, Eirik sat upright. "Go on."

Leiknir slowly reached into his tunic. With no haste he withdrew a tiny piece of paper and slid it across the table to Eirik. "These are directions to a warehouse owned by the Vak'auga and staffed by both them and the Mársmidr. They use it as a temporary storage depot for most of their smuggled goods. You'll find something… unpleasant in the basement."

"You're not offering any assurances," Eirik said.

"Yes I am," Leiknir replied and rested a palm on Runa's shoulder. "She will be going with you. If I'm lying, she is your hostage to do with as you please."

"What?" Runa swiftly spun to face Leiknir, surprise dawning on her visage.

Stefnir realized this was not part of whatever script Runa and Leiknir had rehearsed. He scratched his head, perplexed. "What good is Runa as a hostage?"

"Surely, you can figure that out," Leiknir said.

When Stefnir didn't respond, Eirik turned to him. "Runa is known as Leiknir's aide. If she is identified while working alongside us, hard questions will be raised about Leiknir's loyalty." He focused on the spymaster again. "But if she fights with us, we cannot guarantee her safety."

"Hey," Runa started, her fist tightening over the grip of her knife handle. "I'm not s—"

"I can't even guarantee my own survival," Eirik interrupted, his glare shifting to the girl. "I've dodged a blade or two in my years, and a day ago my friend was less fortunate. He'll live, but Strand's foes are going to get another dance with me. Sooner or later, they're going to succeed."

"All true, Guardsman. But you've seen through Freystein's ruse and survived Nikolas' ambush. Treachery was their best shot twice over, and they failed both times. Denglr must live and love you, or your nickname is no misnomer... *Iron Turtle*," Leiknir said. "So will you agree to visit the warehouse?"

Eirik stayed quiet for a very long time before speaking. "When this is over, assuming we survive, you'll still have a fair bit to pay for, Leiknir. Attempted regicide, criminal acts..."

"Yes, yes." Leiknir waved his hand dismissively. "And I may exchange immunity for witness statements and evidence, so you can give some legitimacy to any trials you hold. I'll share every hideout and operations of every gang I know, so you can rid Strand of its scum. I want *out*, Eirik. For me, my wife and my closest associates. No more thrall taking, no more thieving, no more assassination attempts or spying or lies. I want out of this life for good with no threat of retribution. Is one missed dagger strike against Ragnar worth the price of a clean Strand?"

To Stefnir, it seemed like a tremendous act of willpower for Eirik to raise his hand from the table and extend it. Leiknir graciously accepted and shook it.

"Ha!" Leiknir slapped his palm on his lap. "One way or the other, at least we have a plot of our own."

Eirik was already standing. "Runa, Stefnir, let's go. We have a warehouse to raid."

"What will it take for me to earn your respect, Eirik?" Leiknir questioned the Guardsman as he began to walk away, the two youths trailing just behind him.

Eirik responded without breaking stride. "More than the gods could ever provide."

He led Stefnir and Runa away from the arena, ducking down an alley as the scheduled City Watch patrol marched in their direction. Eirik pulled up his hood and let Stefnir and Runa go first into the narrow lane, using the width of his cloak to make spotting his younger companions difficult. When they emerged at the far end of the passage, Eirik touched Stefnir's shoulder.

"Take Runa and go meet Olaf and Ulfvalgr," he bade the boy. "I have to go see my tailor and get some preparations for tonight. I should be at the meeting place before sunset."

Stefnir nodded, and Eirik took off down the street, his cloak bobbing as he walked. Alone with his childhood colleague, Stefnir flashed her a smile. "Glad we're working together."

The look Runa gave him caused his joviality to wither.

It was a considerable and silent walk to the hiding place. Stefnir had tried once more to start a conversation with the girl, but she would have none of it. Clearly, she felt slighted by how easily Leiknir gave her over to Eirik and his retinue. Stefnir wondered about the nature of her relationship with Magnus' treacherous spymaster, for her attitude almost suggested rejection.

She said nothing until they approached a very large drinking hall, the sign displaying a singing varl holding a flagon. "*The Caroling Giant?* Seriously?"

"Is that what it reads?" Stefnir smirked and shoved his shoulder against the huge portal, pushing inward. It yielded after a moment of effort.

The bar was filled with varl, laughing and guzzling. There were no men in the area, nor a fire in the hearth. Stefnir found it difficult to hear or even think, for the varl's voices were like the bellows of bears. Horns clicked together as giants roared with drunken revelries.

It had been Ulfvalgr's idea to hide here, for what few varl resided in Strand often congregated in this neighborhood. Should the City Watch try a raid, the drunk varl would have simply thrown them out on their asses. If the Watch asked politely, the owner would just comment on how many varl visit and how many faces pass through. Varl had to have strong, often personal, reason to tattle on their kind. At least in a city of men.

Covering his ears, Stefnir marched to the counter, Runa mimicking him as she trailed behind. After some searching, they found Olaf and Ulfvalgr seated on stools that were actually huge tree logs turned upright.

Olaf flashed Stefnir a grin and then turned his ash-colored eyes to Runa. "I take it the parley went well?"

Stefnir felt his back bristle fearfully as his friend yelled over the crowd, but he nodded.

"Where's Eirik?" Ulfvalgr demanded, brandishing a mug as tall as a man's shield.

Stefnir drew a deep breath and managed to get the word "tailor" over the carolers' singing.

"Well, guess we better finish and get back to the other hideout," Ulfvalgr said, his cheeks slightly rouged from imbibing. "Looks like the pups are going deaf, and one drink here would probably drown them anyway."

Dagny sighed as she folded another tunic. From the moment he entered, the previous customer didn't seem to have much coin on him, dressed in a cheap and gaudy outfit. And from the ogling he gave her, she realized his interest was more in imagining her in a state of *undress*. Fortunately, her cold demeanor and a stern rebuke from Vott had sent the lecherous man off after buying an inexpensive scarf.

Other than that, it had been a boring day primarily wasted cleaning the shop. She reached for a pair of trousers when the bell at the door chimed softly. She turned and gasped. "You."

It was the man she had visited yesterday, Eirik, standing half inside the door. "If you intend to have me try those on, might I suggest something more my size?"

She scoffed and put the slim pants back on the counter. "What do you want?"

"Vott," he said as he fully entered and shut the door.

"Eirik!" The aging owner stepped out from behind the curtains of the backroom, a few pins stabbed into the thick padding over his shoulder. "Please, don't mind Dagny's sourness. Our last visitor was a boor who I damn near threw out."

"Shame. I actually hoped terseness was her usual manner as time is short," Eirik replied. "Let's talk."

Dagny's adoptive father stepped to the side and held the drapes open for Eirik, who nimbly slipped past Vott's wide frame. When Dagny tried to follow, Vott shook his head. "Watch the front, dear."

"But da—"

The curtain closed with Vott beyond it. Dagny cursed and sneaked a glance of the door. Slowly, she crept towards the drapes and leaned her head towards them, brushing her dark brown hair from her ear to eavesdrop.

"… Leiknir wants out of the Vak'auga."

"You're serious?"

"Dead serious."

"Olvir will want him to come into custody for protection then."

"Olvir wants the heads of Freystein and Magnus on a pike. But he's going to have to wait for that too. Any news on the Aetla Hilmir attack?"

"Some. We interviewed the other servants. The man who is believed to be in charge—"

"Nikolas. Some might call him Nikolas the Beautiful."

There was a pause.

"How did you…?"

"Because Leiknir told me."

Another pause. "Did Leiknir know because of his connections, or are the Vak'auga an—"

The bell chimed again, bringing a curse from Dagny's lips. She hurried back to the showcase area to encounter a nobleman standing inside the entrance.

"Excuse me," the customer flashed a licentious grin. "You wouldn't happen to know the way to Hadd's stand, would you?"

"Soon as you leave, turn right, take another right at the intersection and it's there," Dagny replied irritably.

"Oh." He stalled a moment. "Hey, you wouldn—"

"No, and we're about to close," Dagny's tone was of ice.

"Oh," the nobleman replied, and finally left.

In no mood for anymore interruptions, Dagny rushed over and slid the bolt to the door. Assured the entrance was locked, she hurried back to the curtains to listen further.

"We know," Vott's voice said. "Gylfi confessed to being a member of the Aetla Hilmir."

There was a pause. "He was making weapons for them, wasn't he?"

"We think so, Eirik. Swords are uncommon for rabble. Ordinary men own axes for work and war, and a sword is only good for the latter. Witnesses say the attackers had spears, blades and even some helms amongst them. These were no thugs, but soldiers."

"Gods dammit. All this time…"

"Do not blame yourself, my friend. Melkorka and several of the other advisers have been pushing for Gylfi's release. They want him to resume production under supervision. Olvir is strongly considering it. Gylfi may be a traitor, but smiths are too rare to hang."

"And Valgard?"

"Recovering. He will fight again soon but not until then." A moment passed before Vott spoke again. "What will you do now?"

"Now I need your help. I need you to report all this back to Olvir so he can start making inquiries. I need clothes, fresh. For myself, a boy, a girl and two varl. And I'll need a yoxen wagon with a tall canopy and two beasts, so we can move about the city while hiding our large guests."

"A girl?" Vott waited before he resumed speaking. "My friend, I think you should seek Olvir and turn the varl over to his custody and protection."

"I can't, Vott. We didn't know about this triumvirate before, and learning of their alliance changes everything. Whatever Freystein wants, he's willing to burn Strand to obtain it. And if he's in bed with the Vak'auga and Aetla Hilmir, he has the means. Secrecy is a better armor than the thickest walls and broadest shields."

"Alright… Alright Eirik. So at least tell me what you intend to do."

"The varl aren't talking. But I have a lead to follow that might give us further answers."

"Where?"

"Near the western docks."

"Eirik… I should warn you. Olvir pulled the City Watch from select areas to increase security near the Great Hall. There is no one patrolling those docks tonight. If you get caught, nobody will answer your cries for help."

Eirik didn't reply. After a moment, Dagny heard footsteps growing close. Panicking, she flew to the counter and resumed folding some undone clothing.

Vott pulled the curtain aside and reached towards one of the shelves, drawing a piece of parchment and a quill from a small stack there. He scribbled something long on it as Eirik entered the showroom and began browsing clothes amongst the cabinets and tables.

"I will help you find something for clients of… that size in a moment," Vott said as he finally finished his message. Gathering a few tunics, her father turned to her. "Dagny, take these to Olvir in the Great Hall. If you hurry, you could be back before sundown and dinner."

"Yes pa," Dagny smiled as she accepted the bundle, content to pretend to be the good daughter. Inwardly, she smirked at the fact that Vott hadn't discovered her duplicity. That was until she pulled the handle of the exit to leave, and the door refused to open with a dull thud.

Her eyes went wide. She had forgotten to cover her tracks.

"Why is the bolt draw—" Vott stopped. Her father had figured it out.

She scrambled and managed to undo the latch. She ripped the door open just as a boot slammed against the doorjamb.

"You little sneak!" Vott shouted as he advanced, plucking the other boot from a nearby stand and preparing to throw it as well.

She took off running as the door shook from the second boot's impact. As she escaped, she heard him yelling at her over the sound of someone, probably Eirik, laughing.

"And make sure you get a receipt, girl! Or I'll tan your hide red!"

The door of *Vott's Consignments* slammed shut, the noise echoing down the street.

Chapter 13

Arnbjorn could only cry from his remaining eye. The other socket still dripped blood.

He was missing the ring finger of his left hand. His mouth tasted of copper and salt from a tooth violently shattered. He knew one of these wounds was bound to become infected soon. However that was the least of his woes.

His captors, the Mársmidr, had left him in a meat locker outside the warehouse. The cold weather seeped through the metal and wood, but Arnbjorn took some small comfort in the fact it kept the wind out. He pressed the shoulder they had burned with coals against the locker's metal wall, trying to soothe the cooked flesh. If he had the strength, he might have kicked and slammed his weight against the doors. But they hadn't fed him, leaving him too weak to act.

Through the wall, he could hear something coming. Arnbjorn pressed his ear against a wood panel and listened. It took him a moment to recognize the powerful clump of yoxen hooves upon stone streets with the roll of wheels behind it. If his sense of timing was correct, it was just after dark when they threw him in this prison after his beating. A strange time for a shipment.

For a fleeting moment, Arnbjorn wondered if it was passing civilians, close enough to hear him call for help. Just before he cried out he remembered that the warehouse— the very one he was captured within while trying to infiltrate two days ago— doubled as a smuggling front. It was quite possible the cart was just more contraband being delivered for storage.

Arnbjorn waited and listened, until the sound suddenly stopped.

"Hey, move along," a voice said. Arnbjorn was fairly certain it belonged to one of the Mársmidr who had been torturing him.

Arnbjorn dearly wished his heartbeat would calm enough to hear the wagon driver's voice, but all he picked out was a sonorous tone.

"That so? Well, I'll have to take a look."

Arnbjorn waited, his breath held.

A gasp outside was muffled by the locker. The din of a weapon clattering against the ground followed. There was a squelch, like steel through wet meat.

Arnbjorn weighed his choices. If he remained incarcerated, there was no question that he would die, slowly. If he misjudged this, he would simply be dead faster.

Or free, if he played his cards right. It was no choice at all.

"Hey!" Arnbjorn raised his clenched fists, ignoring the phantom ache of his missing finger as he pounded against the meat locker, shaking the walls. "Hey! Help! For the love of the Loom Mother, let me out! Please!"

"The faen?" A deep, powerful voice asked.

"Someone in there?" Another person inquired. "Check the guard for a key."

"Please, help me," Arnbjorn said meekly. Soon he heard the unlikely click of the lock being undone and the world, in all its splendor, revealed itself to the dying captive.

And then he realized who his saviors were.

"It's you again," said a varl with chestnut brown hair and wide, swept-back horns. The giant reached out and took Arnbjorn by his bloodied tunic. He yelped in pain, and the varl hesitated before carefully slipping his arms underneath and scooping Arnbjorn out. The scoundrel realized his hands were trembling, though whether from fear, elation or simply from knowing one of his captors was dead, he could not say.

"We don't have time for this," another varl in leather armor said. It took a moment for Arnbjorn's pain-riddled mind to recall the name Ulfvalgr, and that the one who carried him was Olaf.

"He's right." Arnbjorn knew Eirik's voice the second he spoke. The thief saw the man staring at him, dressed in darker clothes with colors that matched the night. "Leave him. If he can run, let him. If he cannot, then there's nothing we can do. But he made his bed."

There were two others. The boy, Stefnir, who regarded him with a pitying, sulky countenance and a girl. Arnbjorn remembered her traveling with Magnus' man, Leiknir, a few times. Her name eluded him, but the javelins at her side and the speared man beneath her feet clarified who was responsible for slaying his tormentor.

"You're…" Arnbjorn swallowed saliva with a lingering hint of blood. "You're trying to get into the warehouse?"

"We're not in a deal making mood, Hal— Arnbjorn," Eirik replied.

"There are only… t-two men at the warehouse's back entrance," Arnbjorn managed between breaths of cold night air, his recently learned claustrophobia dissipating. "Knock thrice on the door. The password is, 'See all, say none.' They'll open and you can take them without alarm if you hurry."

"Why the faen should we trust you?" Ulfvalgr asked.

Arnbjorn just gave them a weak grin, incomplete with a few broken teeth. Ulfvalgr was the last of his unlikely rescuers to look away.

Arnbjorn shut his eye and drifted between dark slumber and drowsy wakefulness. Somewhere in that state, he heard Eirik speak the password. The sound of a violent struggle ensued, followed by the scream of at least one man dying.

Whether it was a moment or a month later, Arnbjorn awoke to the kiss of water on his lips.

Immediately he slurped it down, reaching a weakened hand to the offered bowl and tilting it upright. Awakening, he realized he was in the warehouse kitchen. The back door laid open, and two dead Mársmidr thugs rested against the cabinets. Their fresh blood drizzled down the walls.

Arnbjorn felt gentle warmth from his right. He turned to a hearth with a pot of soup over it, while a loaf of bread warmed over a smooth stone. His hunger seized control and he began to crawl on all fours towards the warm food. Someone grabbed his wrist. Arnbjorn raised his gaze to Eirik.

"Are there anymore in the warehouse?" Eirik asked.

"I overheard that there are several that should be coming for a delivery from the docks tonight, maybe soon. Probably one or two in the basement, but they're likely sleeping at this hour. Since that's where you're going, be quiet and you can catch them off guard," Arnbjorn replied.

Eirik tilted his head. "And what do you think we came here seeking?"

"It's the same reason I did. You'll know it when you find it," Arnbjorn whimpered. Eirik released his wrist and Arnbjorn scrambled to the bread, the rest of the world forgotten. He shoved the loaf into his mouth, favoring the right side of his jaw where the molars were not crushed.

Never in Arnbjorn's lecherous, greedy and hedonistic life had something as simple as bread ever been so wonderful. He barely even tasted the softness of the leaven wheat, drawing a chaste man's pleasure from the sustenance it gave him. It satisfied the eternal ache of life's ravenous struggle against death, and smote the feral nature that all men felt on the cusp of starvation. The simple nourishment warmed a fire within him and ignited a remorseful tear from his sole remaining eye.

He began to choke.

A piece of bread stuck in his throat. His hand darted to the pot, grasping the ladle resting against the rim and pulling it directly to his lips without a thought of blowing away the heat. It was a thin, salty broth complete with a meager helping of carrots and potatoes that burned all the way down. But the moisture swept away the dryness of the lodged bread and rejuvenated his lost strength and yearning for life. His hand registered how hot the utensil itself was only after he gulped down the entire serving.

The ladle clattered to the ground as Arnbjorn dropped to his elbows, feeling his face burn from its proximity to the flame. The sheer act of eating left him exhausted, and the sudden influx of food made his once empty stomach cramp painfully.

"Stefnir, Runa, I want you to watch over the exit. As for Arnbjorn, keep him alive if you can, but put him down if he tries anything." Arnbjorn didn't see Eirik speak but heard him well enough.

"Why bother? He's worthless," Runa said.

"After what the Mársmidr did to him, he'll probably tell us more than we ever wanted to know." Arnbjorn heard Eirik step out of the kitchen and onto the footway that overlooked the greater warehouse area. "We'll be back soon."

The creaking grew much louder as Arnbjorn suspected the varl followed the Governor's Guardsman. A thought crossed his mind and Arnbjorn rolled over, putting his back to the hearth and sitting up to face the boy and girl.

"Do you two see any wine or mead?" he asked. The food had begun to revive his body, renewing the throbbing pains of a missing finger. His various cuts had also grown more agonizing.

Stefnir took a clay jug off the wooden table. After sniffing the top, he held it towards Arnbjorn.

Runa gruffly grabbed the jug from Stefnir's hand and dashed it against the far wall, pieces chattering against the floors while a stain of rich purple liquid trailed down the impacted surface.

"The faen are you doing?" Arnbjorn asked, feeling his brow knit together worriedly. He raised his left hand to show off the stump of his digit. "I'm suffering here!"

"Faen you." The girl sneered. "You lost a lot of blood and only just filled your belly. You really think we're about to mix alcohol in you too? Because we'll leave you here before we drag you out stinking drunk."

"You're all heart." Arnbjorn grimaced.

Runa faced Stefnir. "Who is this guy anyway?"

"I… I'm actually not entirely certain." Arnbjorn saw the boy's Adam's apple bounce as he swallowed. "He said his name is Arnbjorn. He claimed he was once a member of one of these gangs. But I don't know what to believe anymore because of all his lies."

Runa gave Arnbjorn a venomous glare. "Is it true?"

"Márs—" Arnbjorn hiccupped. "Mársmidr. Formerly. That part was true. And I'd been lying and being lied to about plenty of things until I learned the truth."

Neither of them responded for a while, until Runa asked with disdain in her voice. "That being?"

"Freystein killed my brother." Arnbjorn bent over and spit blood upon the stone floor. "I came here to make him pay by getting what's in the basement. Exposing him."

Stefnir took a cautious step forward. "And what's in the ba—"

A scream surprised them. Stefnir managed to raise his axe in time to parry a hatchet that nearly cleaved his head. Runa lifted her javelin to cast it. The assailant, a shirtless man with a heavy paunch and the red face of a drunk, angled Stefnir in her way to block her shot. The boy almost struck back, but instead threw himself aside to avoid the flash of the drunk's weapon.

Arnbjorn took a deep breath. Despite the protests of his body he forced himself to rise, gritting his broken teeth as he did.

The drunk grabbed Stefnir by the throat and shook him hard enough to throw the boy off balance. Runa stepped left and right, trying to aim a shot. Each time the drunk dragged Stefnir in the way. Inebriated as he was, the Mársmidr had a brawler's instinct and knew how to manage multiple foes. But he hadn't noticed Arnbjorn.

Arnbjorn screamed and flung himself at the man. Realizing what was about to happen, the drunk pushed Stefnir back and raised his hatchet.

Arnbjorn got within the man's guard. Instead of a chop in his back, Arnbjorn only felt the thud of the drunk's elbow. Arnbjorn kept driving, pushing him through the kitchen door onto the footway.

Then over the balcony.

The drunkard panicked and flailed his arms, trying to grab ahold of anything to arrest his fall. For a moment, Arnbjorn feared the man might cut him. But when Arnbjorn heard the clatter of metal on the floorboards behind him, he knew his foe dropped the hatchet. Instead, the drunk grabbed his tunic and clung tight.

For several breathless heartbeats the drunkard wrestled with Arnbjorn's tunic, like an anchor about his throat, threatening to haul the scoundrel over too. But Arnbjorn wriggled free of his loose shirt and slipped it over his head with the drunkard's 'aide.'

There was a startled yelp as both the tunic and his foe fell away.

Arnbjorn knew it to be a three-story fall. The abrupt crunch from below cut off the drunkard's yelling.

Arnbjorn wearily sank against the balcony, his arms shaking and bare back rubbing the balcony beams. Battle-lust washed over him. It sang in his ears and chest, and although his limbs felt weak, there was a fire within that could rejuvenate him at a moment's notice.

"Th-thank you, Arnbjorn," Stefnir said.

Arnbjorn realized that Runa and Stefnir stared at him from the door to the kitchen. He nodded. "Welcome, boy."

"Welcome nothing!" Runa pointed an accusing finger at him. "You said there were only two in the kitchen!"

"I also said sometimes a few sleep downstairs, so one must have…" Arnbjorn trailed off as he noticed something. It was dark on the footway, which made the light coming from the crack in the wall easier to spot. It was a hidden room.

Arnbjorn reached down and seized the hatchet the drunk had dropped. Runa raised her javelin defensively at Arnbjorn, but he put a finger to his lips and pointed to the barely visible door. She glanced to her right to see what he indicated and then nodded to him.

The three crept forwards, weapons ready to strike anyone who might emerge. Tentatively, Arnbjorn reached out and pressed the panel. The door gave, and inside they saw a candle resting atop a small drawer next to a clay pot. Arnbjorn caught a whiff of something fresh and unpleasant. He realized that the odor-filled chamber was a privy and likely from where the drunkard had emerged. He backed out, pulling the door shut as he left.

"Ugh," Runa moaned as she caught the vile stench, covering her nose. Stefnir waved a hand before his nose.

"Well I think we've solved the mystery," Arnbjorn replied. He rounded again only to face Runa's pointed javelin, aimed at his chest.

"I think you had best drop that weapon," she said. "I've given you enough leeway when we were in danger, but now that time has passed."

"Hey," Stefnir said, looking down at the warehouse itself. "Someone is coming up the road."

Runa remained vigilant of the thief, but Arnbjorn followed the boy's gaze and realized Stefnir was right. Through the massive and open double doors leading outside, he could see a distant group of torches approaching on a long stretch of road. The creak of carts could faintly be heard in the distance.

"Oh faen," Arnbjorn said and addressed Runa. "Lass, we aren't safe. Not by a long shot. You don't have to trust me, but those boys down by the docks will be back soon. If you want to get out of this alive, you'll come with me."

"We're not leaving Eirik and Olaf!" Stefnir said, his stance growing aggressive.

Arnbjorn was amused that Ulfvalgr wasn't mentioned but chose not to comment about that. "Then let's go get them before we're surrounded."

Runa and Stefnir looked at one another, before Runa tilted her jaw towards Arnbjorn. "Lead on. But you stray, you're skewered."

How the faen did that flabby Leiknir rein in a girl like this? Arnbjorn wondered as he led them down the footway and descended the staircase at the end, which shook with questionable stability and forced them to slow their steps.

The opened doors filled the warehouse's main floor with chilling air. Arnbjorn thought to slide them closed and lock them, both to reduce the cold and to buy them time. But the complex arrangement of ropes and pulleys that operated them were a four-man job, and he still felt weak.

Instead they ventured on, weaving past some chests and barrels to the basement. Arnbjorn cursed as he stepped in the blood of the fallen drunk, whose head had absorbed much of his impact. Arnbjorn spotted his dirtied tunic, which had fluttered near the blood pool but hadn't landed in the liquid. He procured and slipped it back on.

Behind a few shelves they found another staircase though made of stone. Candlelight shone from below. Arnbjorn padded as softly as he could, thankful that Runa and Stefnir recognized that subtly without need for explanation.

Below, they ventured down a short hall and discovered two more bodies. One's skull was brutally smashed with a red crater in his chest. The other was slain with more finesse, his throat sliced swiftly and precisely. Arnbjorn suspected the former was done in by Ulfvalgr, while the latter was the victim of a certain Governor's Guardsman.

They walked on, turning a corner. A blade came down, barely an inch from striking off Arnbjorn's head, before its wielder paused.

"Gods," Olaf breathed and lowered the sword. The varl exhaled sharply and cast his gaze at Stefnir and Runa. "What are you three doing down here?"

"They're coming back," Stefnir blurted out. "Too many to fight. We had to warn you!"

"Dammit," Olaf turned and called out. "Eirik! Ulfvalgr! Any luck yet?"

"No!" The gruff voice of Ulfvalgr responded from the room beside Olaf.

Eirik stuck his head out from another of the several chambers down the hall. "No luck. What are they doing down here? And why is *he* armed?"

"He saved Stefnir's life," Runa replied. "And we're about to be trapped."

"Hang on, I think I know where to look," Arnbjorn said.

Olaf shifted his attention to Eirik before returning it to the thief. He nodded, his horns scraping the ceiling and causing a small trickle of dirt to fall. "Go, hurry."

Arnbjorn slipped by Olaf and ran through the hall, counting doors. At the fourth entrance down he pulled the ring handle, yanking it open. The chamber within was dark, so Arnbjorn tucked his hatchet into his belt, plucked a candle from the wall sconce and ventured inside.

As far as smuggled and stolen goods went, there generally two kinds of contraband. The first type was often ignored by City Watch, for a substantial bribe of course. Smuggled mead, fine-if-pilfered utensils, or Tistelberries were all that variety. The second kind of contraband got a thief or smuggler incarcerated, interrogated and often executed. That was anything that might challenge the status quo, such as weapons or mushrooms that could cause illusions that whipped a man into a combative frenzy.

Or the object that Arnbjorn procured from the cache hidden under the chamber's floorboards.

He left the candle in the room, needing two hands to lift an item about the size of a kettle. Setting the discovered object down on the floor, he spotted a sheet in the corner and plucked it, wrapping his prize. "I've got it!"

The others wasted no time returning to the stairs once he was amongst them, although Eirik took the hatchet from Arnbjorn's side. The scoundrel frowned at this but was in no position to stop the Guardsman.

Back in the warehouse, they waited as the varl ascended to the footway first, trusting the stairs to handle their weight only one at a time. Arnbjorn twisted and saw the torches growing ever closer. He could even make out the shapes of men and realized they were but a stone's throw from the warehouse doors.

"Go!" Eirik pushed him. Arnbjorn dashed up the stairs, Stefnir right behind him. Runa and Eirik came last. Racing to the kitchen, Arnbjorn heard someone outside shout something akin to an alarm.

They reached the backdoor, and Arnbjorn felt the sting of a snow-laced gale as they stepped outside. Eirik grabbed Arnbjorn's arm and swiftly led him to a large wagon nearby. The Nautmot yoxen mounted to the yoke scratched the road impatiently, as though they felt the nervous energy of their masters' return.

Without prompting, Arnbjorn got into the cart, which was covered by a canopy of heavy furs to hide and safeguard them from the wind. Arnbjorn seated himself between Olaf and Ulfvalgr. Runa dived in after him, while Eirik and Stefnir went to the cab.

"Ya!" Arnbjorn heard Eirik cry out. "Ya!"

The wagon rocked a little as the yoxen tugged. After some effort, the beasts gained enough momentum to overcome the gross weight of two giants, four human passengers and the cart. Soon they moved at a brisk trot, their hooves clattering against the roads and splashing mud puddles.

The warehouse shifted from view as Eirik turned a corner and then another, their trail fading with each altered direction.

Before Arnbjorn considered his situation, Ulfvalgr faced him. "Uncover it. Now."

At that moment, Arnbjorn suddenly realized he was trapped on a wagon, with two varl who were bound to become very, very hostile. With growing apprehension, he unraveled the bundled sheet, unbinding a skull the size of a man's chest. Twin horns sprouted from the forehead just above the temples, curling about like a ram's.

Even Ulfvalgr gasped at the sight of the varl's skull.

Chapter 14

The return ride was sullen and silent by necessity. Eirik stopped the yoxen a few times in various alleys to ensure they weren't being followed, but there was never any pursuit. After perhaps an hour of travel into the night, the patter of snow on the canopy roof ceased abruptly. A little later, the wagon rocked and halted at their new hideout.

Olaf watched his friends and allies disembarking into the stables, their faces everything from haggard to exhausted to furious. Stefnir came about and propped Arnbjorn over his shoulder, helping the man limp into the house. Ulfvalgr had relieved him of the ghoulish prize they brought back with them, carrying it into the building.

Olaf regarded the large home. It was a two-story manor on the outskirts of Strand, fairly removed and isolated near a forest. Eirik had explained that the previous occupant died two weeks ago. The servants were dismissed and the land-claim awaited the return of the owner's heir, who was away on extended business and likely had yet to hear of their relative's passing. Eirik did not divulge how he knew of the place, but it hid them from both the gangs and the City Watch alike.

Here there was safety, fleeting as it would surely be. It was easy to avoid the cramped streets and the prying eavesdroppers who would report them to the Mársmidr in a heartbeat for a couple of silver. When he had seen it, Ulfvalgr claimed to hate it. Yet Olaf suspected he hated anything that took him farther from his foes.

Ulfvalgr stomped towards the homestead and parted the double doors with a gruff slam of his broad shoulders. On a long table made for men, he dropped the varl skull. Ulfvalgr ran his hands over the base of his horns and through his hair, before twisting and ramming a clenched fist into the wall.

"*Faen you, Kjallak!*" His voice echoed through the empty, cold halls.

No one responded for several agonizing moments.

Stefnir eventually led Arnbjorn to the table and set the injured scoundrel on a bench. Eirik passed them both and knelt beside the stone fireplace. Runa took a distant seat after setting down her weapons next to her.

Olaf ducked his horns below the overhead balcony as he walked towards the budding fire Eirik kindled. It was too small and too controlled to ignite the fear all of Hadrborg's children felt around flames. Slowly, Olaf lowered himself on the stone ground, staring into the crackling warmth as if it had all the answers.

Stefnir sought a pot of water which he placed over the fireplace. As the water was brought to a boil, the boy allocated thread, bandages and other supplies for Arnbjorn's injuries. The boy rested curled needles on the hearth to warm the metal, an old trick said to ward away spirits of decay. Everyone endured the silence for a long, long time.

"What do we do now?" Arnbjorn asked as Stefnir set the steaming pot beside him.

"What's this we?" Eirik asked, taking a rag and dunking it into the boiling water. "As far as I'm concerned, you're going into the City Watch's custody as soon as you're stable."

Arnbjorn laughed, but the sound died when Eirik placed the damp and steaming rag on his chest, scalding him. The thief gritted his ruined teeth and gave the lawman a stern look. "Eirik, look at me. You think there are any lies left in me after they took a finger and part of my face? After they murdered my brother? No, Eirik. I'm fighting for you now, and you know you're going to need my help to win."

Eirik said nothing.

"What were you doing there, besides finding odd lodgings in a crate?" Runa sneered.

Arnbjorn chuckled darkly. The scoundrel indicated Ulfvalgr and Olaf with his maimed hand. "I lied to you all because Freystein's boy Ottar promised me a chance to rejoin the gang, to be reunited with my family."

Eirik watched the man with a sunken gaze. Slowly, the Governor's Guardsman turned to the fire, drew his axe and set the head in the flame.

"But they were also lying to me." Arnbjorn shook his head. "They already killed Johan after he tried to steal off with something they wanted, to bargain for my return. They tracked him down and slew him for it. And once I ensured Olaf and Ulfvalgr's delivery to Freystein, I undoubtedly would have been slain too. I overheard Ottar and Freystein himself talkin' about the deal."

"What did Johan take?" Stefnir held a needle with a piece of cloth to prevent burning his fingers, trying to thread the eye in the weak firelight. "And how did you 'deliver' us to Kjallak?"

"I just had to keep tabs on where you were, so Freystein or whoever you know him as... would bait you himself once everything was in place. As to what Johan took, all I heard was something about a shield."

Ulfvalgr grunted angrily. Eirik flipped the axe over in the fire as he asked. "So what were you doing in that warehouse?"

"When I overheard Freystein talking about Johan's death, he mentioned that place. That's when I remembered. Shortly before I had to escape Strand, I did a cargo job for the gang and discovered varl bones amongst the arriving goods. A few of the other Mársmidr boys were pretty freaked over the shipment, but Freystein was calm like he had plans for them. He ordered the bones hidden somewhere close, so we stashed them in the basement.

"Yesterday, I tried to sneak in to collect the evidence, to expose them." Arnbjorn tilted his head towards the skull. "And then I got caught."

Olaf rolled his jaw, glancing about the room. Runa seemed indifferent, drawing a whetstone against the edge of the dagger she had unsheathed from her belt. Ulfvalgr stared at Arnbjorn with belligerent intensity. Eirik continued to focus on his weapon which heated in the fire.

"Serves you right for trying to trick us," Stefnir said. The boy wore a look of disgust.

Arnbjorn chuckled again, and covered the cavernous socket above his cheek. "I guess it does, lad. I guess it does."

Ulfvalgr's boots slapped against the floor as he approached Arnbjorn. The giant lowered himself, squatting down so his face was level with the injured scoundrel. "Kjallak. Where is he?"

"Freystein? I don't know. If I knew, I'd tell you so you could snap his neck. I'd even help, for Johan's sake."

Arnbjorn met Ulfvalgr's glare. For a long moment, Olaf feared that the thief would die at Ulfvalgr's hand. But the varl eventually stood and crossed the room to where an untapped barrel of mead awaited him.

Olaf knew how sour Ulfvalgr would become from drinking while angry. The varl understood how his friend needed a direction to focus his rage, lest it lead to a poor decision. "So Eirik, any ideas for us?"

"I have a plan. A terrible one though," Eirik drew his glowing axe from the fire. Arnbjorn paled. "Put your hand on the table. Stefnir, hold him down. He'll thrash."

They both obeyed, although Arnbjorn was reluctant. In the firelight, Olaf could see the gory root of the man's severed finger. It oozed with dark blood, thick as tar. Stefnir put both hands over Arnbjorn's wrist and held him tight.

Olaf turned his face away as the sizzle of cauterized flesh filled the air. Arnbjorn shrieked like a stuck hog.

The rest of Arnbjorn's wounds were nowhere near as serious, and their treatment was mercifully less drastic. The scoundrel wrapped a long cloth over his head, binding the disconcerting socket which once held a handsome azure eye.

"I think we can lure Freystein or Magnus out," Eirik said as he returned to the fireplace, the look on his visage haunted. "Or, at least, make them blunder so that we might find them."

Ulfvalgr stomped back towards the gathering, a horn of mead in his massive hand. "Go on."

"We bait a trap." Eirik adjusted his cloak over his shoulders. "We float a rumor that the varl are trying to get out of the city and are joining the tournament to claim the prize money to do so. If the Aetla Hilmir is willing to attack the Great Hall for their goal, then they'll come running if you're in the open."

Ulfvalgr snorted. "What's to stop them from simply coming in force?"

"He's right." Runa leaned forward in her chair as she spoke. "The Vak'auga and Mársmidr boast over a hundred fighting men at least. And they only want to capture Olaf and Ulfvalgr. They'll slaughter the rest of us and laugh doing it."

"It does," Olaf said. "Put us on the defensive."

"You're all correct. But the strategy can work if we play it right." Eirik knelt beside the fire and gave them all a focused look that assured them he was earnest. "We have the advantage of surprise, but not in a combative sense of the word. The Vak'auga and Mársmidr do indeed have the numbers. But it would take time to rouse and ready them, and to get them in position. Much less anywhere near the battlefield. So we bait them with a short window of opportunity."

No one answered at first. Ulfvalgr slowly scratched his beard. "Go on then."

"The tournament requires six men to enter," Eirik said. "The City Watch oversees and sometimes moderates it, as a means to manage the worst of the violence without actively getting their hands dirty. If nothing else, Freystein or Magnus will rush men there as a 'clan' to fight us, even if only to buy them time. One of these men is bound to be someone they trust. And we want to capture whomever they send for questioning.

"We take a few days to rest, train, heal and prepare. I will talk the steward into hosting this match. And we'll ready several City Watchmen nearby, besides the ones who regularly keep the 'peace' during the tournaments." Eirik turned his gaze to Runa. "Leiknir will inform Magnus at the last moment about this development. The Mársmidr or Vak'auga will have to scramble to send someone."

"But won't have time to get the rest prepared," Olaf finished. "So we'll smash them, grab their leader and escape before the rest of Kjallak's cronies fall upon us. That's actually not a terrible plan."

No one spoke, as though they were all contemplating the strategy. At last, Runa piped in. "You're sure you can get the City Watch to pick when and where the tournament bout will be held?"

"Not anywhere but certainly in a place to our benefit," Eirik replied.

"Then this plan, madness or genius it is, might actually work," Runa slapped her hands against her lap.

"No." Ulfvalgr shook his head. "I listened. I entertained it for a moment. But this plan is foolish. There are too many unknowns. We should pry the half-blind one for where the Mársmidr are hiding, what other flophouses they have, and then work our way up the river."

Arnbjorn opened a palm to Ulfvalgr. "That warehouse yesterday was the only real place they store anything consistently. Everything else goes on ships or caravans, and as you can imagine, they move. Besides which, they'll double security after what you guys did tonight."

"Also, if we mobilize the City Watch to raid them, one of their snitches will tip them off," Eirik finished. "We're either too small or too slow."

Ulfvalgr crushed the horn in his hand as he stepped forward. He pointed a thick finger at Eirik. "We have followed you enough! We obeyed before, and it damn near cost us our lives, our freedom, everything! We were foolish enough to do it again tonight, and still we are no closer to Kjallak! I do not trust your plans or your promises, turtle."

"You raided the warehouse with me, and now you've gained some knowledge as to what Kjallak is doing," Eirik countered angrily. "And do not talk to me of trust, for you're the one holding back about whatever he's pursuing."

"Because that's none of your damn business! All we have gained is a skull, no doubt stolen from the graves at Two Spears or the King's Barrow, and a loudmouth with an odd number of fingers!" Ulfvalgr gritted his teeth. "How is this getting us any closer to——?"

"Do you know what the difference between rage and wrath is?"

It was only when all eyes went to Olaf that the varl realized he had been the one to speak, as though possessed. The fact that Olaf voiced his thoughts without realizing it shocked him, but he put a hand to his knee and stood anyway. Ulfvalgr watched him coolly.

"Torstein once reduced Kjallak to nothing and sent him away, and I felt sorry for him. But the more I dwell on it, on how Kjallak has betrayed not only Torstein but his friends as well, the angrier it makes me. Yes, we were his friends once, and although I understand his feelings towards Torstein, he has made us to suffer for it as well.

"I am furious too, but our anger differs. Rage is imprudent and impulsive. Wrath is slow and calculating, a smoldering hatred that considers the long game. You may be rage, Ulfvalgr, but I am wrath."

Olaf shook his head. "Kjallak never learned the lesson Torstein gave him. I intend to teach him again, to grind him to dust. I want Kjallak, and I am willing to wait, to labor toward this goal and bend my will to the task, for as long as it takes. To take apart the house of crime he has built, one log at a time. Only this time, you can be there to make use of that rage of yours… and plant your axe in his *faening skull*. The last lesson he will ever learn."

Olaf put his fists to his hips. "Eirik's plan is the shortest distance to that end. We *are* doing as he says."

Ulfvalgr gave him a rictus mask of hate. But slowly his features relaxed, a devil's grin spreading across his face as though his anger melted into perverse delight. Like a cat slinking into the night, Ulfvalgr turned and headed towards the other room, where a massive pile of furs awaited him. He spoke as he went. "I'm glad you finally had the guts to tell it how it is, Olaf. Make it so."

Olaf watched him go, and couldn't help but wonder if Ulfvalgr had somehow twisted him, drawing Olaf into his realm of rancorous belligerence. Olaf rubbed a thumb against the base of his horns and grunted, trying not to dwell on the matter.

Eirik faced the rest of them. "We'll start figuring out the time and place tomorrow morning. I'll need to inform Olvir of this soon. Runa will go fill Leiknir in on the plan too."

"Can we trust Leiknir?" Stefnir asked.

Runa gave him a dark look.

"We'll wait until the last moment to tell him when or where. No sense taking undue risks," Eirik said.

The room went silent yet again, until Stefnir asked a question. "So what should we do now?"

"Now?" Eirik said. "Now, we sleep."

"And tomorrow, I show you how to swing an axe," Arnbjorn added.

Eirik gave Arnbjorn a sharp stare. "You're assuming that we've agreed to let you join us yet. For now, you'll sleep in a locked room, and we'll permit you to train with us. But we'll decide if you fight alongside us later."

Arnbjorn grunted but nodded. "Fine."

Olaf wasn't sure how he felt about allowing Arnbjorn that chance. He looked at the pitiful, maimed man and saw a beaten dog who growled and hated, and who wasn't about to give in. That vengeful single-mindedness could be as much of an asset as of a liability. Then again, so was Ulfvalgr.

Olaf relaxed his shoulders and spoke to the boy. "I keep my promises. Tomorrow I'm going to show you how to make a shield, Stefnir."

Olaf saw the boy curl his hand into a fist. A trickle of a smirk played on Stefnir's determined countenance. Despite the implication, Olaf couldn't help but cast a bittersweet smile. For he worried he wasn't the only one whom Ulfvalgr had corrupted.

Chapter 15

"Leiknir was right," Vott concluded after hearing Eirik's complete report. The merchant walked towards the curtain that separated the storeroom from the customer's area and opened it. On the other side, Eirik could see Dagny busy scrubbing the floors near the door, likely punishment for her alleged eavesdropping when last he visited. "Whatever Magnus is doing will destroy Strand."

Eirik had held nothing back, even revealing that Arnbjorn was cooperating with them now, but the explanation had taken quite a while. He rose from his seat, stretching his aching legs. Despite the long rest the day before, Eirik's body still felt bone-deep weariness. "I still don't know how all of it fits. Ulfvalgr isn't telling me what the triumvirate are after."

"Ha!" Vott laughed weakly as he faced Eirik, the fear clear in his dilated pupils. "Forget what they're doing. It's what they've done! Do you think the varl king, Jorundr, will take the desecration of his people's graves with compassion and good cheer?"

Eirik shook his head.

"The varl are a cantankerous, fractious lot at the best of times... But their race is dying, and they give tremendous respect to their dead." Vott exhaled, shuddering. "When Jorundr finds out, there likely will be retribution. He may even march against Strand. The alliance would be dead, with us sure to follow."

"We're so close to the north that it wouldn't be a difficult march for them. And Arberrang might allow Strand to burn if it meant staying in Jorundr's good graces," Eirik replied. "All this I know."

Vott sank rather than sat into his seat. He leaned forward and buried his face in his hands, saying nothing for a long time.

Eirik opened his mouth to speak but Vott cut him off. "Leiknir... that old spy has the right mind trying to get out of this game." Vott put his hands in his lap, shaking. "He made a good living off what he's done, but he knows when the ship is sinking."

"Would you have us rein on our deal once we have the triumvirate apprehended or buried?" Eirik asked. Though lying about his agreement did not sit well with him, the thought of arresting Leiknir was a soothing, pleasant one.

"No. Every third merchant in this city is a crook of some kind. Many smaller gangs can be persuaded to give us tips and leads if our promises of immunity are kept. And not every brothel owner beats his women into submission, for they need each other to ply their trade, believe it or not." Vott shook his head sadly. "Justice is a virtue, but sometimes it does not play well with pragmatism. If we take Leiknir in, those of shadier dealings will be reluctant to sell their wares or venture here. Or speak to us when they know something dangerous. Taking Leiknir to justice would cost us in the courts, law and trade. We cannot sacrifice what little trust we have."

Eirik's shoulders relaxed, his ambivalent feelings assuaged by the fact that the decision was not his to make. "Vott, I need your aide."

"Your plan in the tournament," Vott swayed back, drawing a long, tired sounding breath.

"Yes," Eirik said. "I need you to speak with Olvir. We'll need an influx of City Watchmen at a designated time at a location of our choosing. Can you get the steward to do that?"

Vott's gaze seemed to bore over Eirik's shoulder. "Why not ask him yourself?"

Eirik turned and stood. Olvir gently closed the hatch to the basement passageway, fixing his brown eyes upon the Governor's Guardsman.

"Sir?" Eirik asked. "How long were you...?"

"Actually," Olvir said with a warm smile as he took a seat beside them. "I just got here. Mind telling it all again?"

Eirik noted that Olvir made no remarks regarding Leiknir. But as he repeated his tale, Eirik wondered if perhaps the steward did not trust the tailor, if perhaps there was a stronger reason for him to visit *Vott's Consignments Shop*. It was very rare for Steward Olvir himself to come here.

"That's..." Olvir said when told of the varl skull they reclaimed, his face neutral. "Horrible. Was it only one varl?"

Eirik cast his gaze between Vott and Olvir. "I don't know. Arnbjorn said there was a collection of bones, perhaps enough for two or three full bodies. Maybe more."

"And you trust him?" Olvir asked, his tone somewhat incredulous.

Eirik drew a sharp breath. "No. But there's a difference between trust and truth. The Mársmidr cut him up, took a finger and half his sight. And if we hadn't intervened, he would have died a slow, rotting death. No mender can give him back what he lost. And he says they killed his brother, which was his motivation in the first place. I don't *trust* him sir, but I don't think he's lying."

"If only you had time to grab all the bones. By now, they've undoubtedly moved them." Olvir groaned. "So, what did you need from me?"

Eirik told him. Olvir crossed an arm over his chest as he listened, the other stroking the sprouting whiskers on his face.

"I approve of your plan, Eirik," Olvir replied when he finished listening.

"Even trusting Leiknir?" Eirik asked, but he knew the answer when he saw an almost amused look in Olvir's slight smirk.

"We have been receiving an influx of very, very accurate and detailed tips, about the locations of Vak'auga joy houses, smuggled mead shipments and gambling hotspots for underground fights. The person who gave us this information promised us that more would be forthcoming if we sit on it all for now. I'm having the junior Guardsmen verify it, but not act yet. A job they should be able to handle, I think."

"When?" Vott interjected. "And from Leiknir?"

"A courier arrived yesterday morning with a bottle of wine and a letter. Melkorka had spotted me receiving it and embarrassed me. She teased that I 'have a lover' amongst the court. The letter mentioned Eirik's name and was initialed 'L' at the bottom." Olvir uncrossed his arm. "I'd wager that Leiknir is quite serious about his retirement."

Eirik grunted bitterly.

Olvir edged forward. "Eirik, I can and will have the City Watch ready at the place and time you name. We'll need almost a week to prepare first, give or take a day. And when we have captured the man to interrogate, it's time for the varl to come into our protection. Where are they now?"

"Sir," Eirik began. "I don't think—"

Olvir raised a palm to stop him from commenting. "You're not stupid Eirik. You know that the grave-robbed varl remains will bring Jorundr's wrath down on our heads. The triumvirate took their best shot and missed, thanks to you. If you wish to keep their location secret a while longer then fine. But after the tournament match, we've played enough hide-and-seek. Olaf and Ulfvalgr need to come into our custody for their safety, and so we can discover what they know."

Eirik swallowed. It was another secret he would have to keep from the varl, another reason to justify their distrust of him. It took no small measure of effort for Eirik to say the words, "Yes sir."

Stefnir raised his shield at the last moment, stopping the axe from slamming into his shoulder. The sheer force sent him back some, his boots sliding across the ice. By bending his knees and keeping his stance wide, he maintained his balance.

"Good." Ulfvalgr grunted. "But do you know whether it would have been better to evade than block?"

"Evade," Stefnir managed after coming to a halt. Somehow, despite the power Ulfvalgr could put behind his leather-covered axe, Stefnir didn't feel as much strain in his shoulder as he feared he would. He wondered if he owed that to Olaf and his lessons.

"Why?"

"Recovery. If I had ducked that blow, you'd be within range of my axe."

"Ha." Ulfvalgr smirked. "Try it."

Stefnir raised his sheathed axe and round shield, which Olaf had showed him how to construct, and pushed off the ice. It was strange to fight on the frozen pond, but Ulfvalgr insisted that the effort of constantly maintaining one's balance would keep his leg muscles taut.

Stefnir grimaced as he rushed the varl.

The boy ducked, angling his shield to protect his head. The varl's bound axe struck the armor and deflected, swishing over Stefnir's hair. The boy realized Ulfvalgr was in striking distance. He raised his father's axe...

And barely blocked Ulfvalgr's right knee.

The blow knocked Stefnir upward and back. He landed on his butt, his axe clattering beside him while the shield landed on its edge and rolled towards the snowy shore. Arnbjorn, who watched from the pond's boundary, laughed.

"Dammit," Stefnir said as he rubbed his rear.

Ulfvalgr knelt and rubbed his knee. "Hmmm. Good work."

"Good work?" Stefnir said, incredulously. "You just floored me."

"That I did. But your reaction improved on three fronts. You both blocked and dodged because you realized that my low swing wasn't going to be easily avoided. When you were within range, you took advantage of my inability to recover my weapon in time. And even when I kneed you, you used your shield to make me pay for it," the giant explained.

"If a man did that," Arnbjorn shouted to them. "He wouldn't be rushing after you. Ulfvalgr's size lets him get away with things we couldn't."

"So, how would I counter that?" Stefnir asked.

"I don't know. I'm not a man. How would you?" Ulfvalgr replied, an amused smile on his face.

Stefnir stood and collected his weapons. His mind was tired of answering these questions after five days of grueling practice against both varl, preparing for a fight Eirik promised was coming but didn't know exactly when. "I... would, should, have waited a little longer on my attack. If my opponent's leg was rising, I would chop at that instead."

Ulfvalgr nodded. "That's one good counter. Maybe even the best if you hook behind my knee."

"But how would I know my opponent's intentions? Not all men would react the same, right?"

Ulfvalgr rolled his shoulders in a shrug and arched his back as though stretching. "Both varl and men who prefer two-handed weapons will try and keep their opponents at bay, for inside the reach of the blade we are vulnerable. The spear, however, is a unique exception."

"Why?" Stefnir asked.

"The handle," Arnbjorn said. Stefnir rounded and realized the scoundrel approached, a long staff over his shoulder. The thief spun the weapon vertically and stopped it, holding the handle at his hip with two hands. Then he jabbed the tip Stefnir's direction but stopped before poking him.

"The tip is the offense. The range and the shaft are the defense. A master spearman," Arnbjorn said, rolling the shaft in a circle with his back hand, keeping the tip at the same spot. "Can use the handle to block a blow, even while attacking. I once saw a man so fast, he simply *flowed* from stab to block to stab like water, needling his opponent down until he bled to death from a dozen cuts."

Stefnir's focus went from the end of the stick to Arnbjorn's stern face. "Are, are you a skilled spearman?"

"I dabbled with spears before but always preferred brawling, getting' up close. I was just practicin' to see if this would be better for us, given half my sight being gone and all." Arnbjorn shook his head, his face grim. "But it's too late to be changing my fighting instincts now."

"Why?" Stefnir asked.

He tapped the cheek under his makeshift eyepatch. "Can't gauge distance too well without two of these, and timing is more important and less forgiving when using a spear. Another shield will serve us better."

Stefnir nodded.

"Your friend might know a thing or two about timing and range though." Arnbjorn jerked a thumb over his shoulder.

Behind him, perhaps a dozen footsteps from the lake, Runa spun a bundled ball of fur around and around before tossing it into the air. As they rose, she snatched a javelin from her pouch and poised to throw. She waited until the bundle reached the zenith of its arc and threw. The tossed javelin sped through the air and lanced the ball, which flew on a new trajectory, landing in the snow some distance away.

"Hmph!" Ulfvalgr grunted and nodded with respect.

"She was always a great fisherwoman," Stefnir said as he regarded her with awe. "You need sharp senses and fast hands to spearfish salmon, and she was better than anyone else at it. Even the adults."

"Was she nicer then too?" Arnbjorn asked with a lecherous smirk.

"She was... once," Stefnir said. He couldn't hide the hint of sadness that crept into his voice. In truth, he barely knew her then. Once, after being mercilessly teased by the other boys, Stefnir was tricked into a bet: get Runa to kiss him and they'll leave him be. Rather than grow bashful or forfeit, Stefnir approached her and explained his problem.

Runa had laughed, but not in the cruel way that Stefnir knew her for now. "And they'll leave you alone if I kiss you?"

"That was our bet..." Stefnir replied, as second thoughts began to leak into his mind.

Instead she giggled a little louder, wrapped her arms around his neck and kissed him full on the mouth for all the boys to see. They hooted and shouted, jeering and singing taunts. Stefnir was angry that they wouldn't honor their deal. Yet Runa rolled her eyes and slapped Stefnir's arm playfully. "Come on, you really thought they wouldn't seize this for laughs? Besides, I'd say you're richer than they are for it."

At the time, it felt as though Runa was mocking him too. Stefnir had stormed off and never spoke to her again. But occasionally, he stared at her and wondered. When she spotted him she would wave back, and he would snub her friendliness.

Then their village came under assault. And Magnus took her.

Stefnir felt his jaw stiffen and his grip on his axe grow tight. He wondered if Magnus had taken his mother, would she have become so barbed and bitter as well? Was she the lucky one, to have died defending herself rather than be taken? Hot tears clouded Stefnir's sight as he considered it. He twisted away from Runa, for at that moment he loathed the girl for no fault of her own.

"Where are you going?" Ulfvalgr yelled as Stefnir stomped off.

"To make yellow snow," Stefnir lied, facing away from the varl so his quivering lip couldn't betray him. Instead of going about the corner of the manor, he entered.

Olaf rose from the hearth, where he readied the stew for that night's dinner. His face knotted with confusion when he saw Stefnir. "What's wrong, boy? Wind too fierce out there?"

"No," Stefnir choked.

Olaf tilted his head slightly, before stepping towards Stefnir and putting a large hand on his shoulder. "Well if there's a problem, say it. Is Ulfvalgr being an ass again?"

How can I relate to someone whose creator was a god, without a mother or father? Who doesn't know what family really is? Stefnir managed a deep breath and then another. His vision stung, but the tears had stopped. "No, it… it's not him. It's nothing. Just a hard hit."

Olaf nodded and returned to the kettle. He ladled a small bowl of venison stew and offered it to Stefnir. The boy accepted the food and forced himself to take a sip despite lacking an appetite. "It's… actually good. Better than the meal you made a few nights ago."

Olaf wore an exasperated countenance, putting his hands against his hips. "Like I said before, I don't work with fish that often!"

Stefnir failed to fight the grin against his cheeks and the accompanying chuckle. Despite himself, he did feel a little better.

They heard the squeal of the entrance's hinges as Eirik came into the hall and shut the door behind him. He wore a glum face, an expression that endured since his trip to the "tailor" almost a week before, after their flight from the warehouse. Stefnir wondered if it was bad news this time.

"Don't tell me you're saddened too!" Olaf said, making a pouty face.

Stefnir laughed a little. Eirik smiled, though it seemed more out of politeness.

"Stefnir," Eirik said. "Call the others. We have a fight in two days."

"Two days isn't a lot of time," Arnbjorn concluded as he stirred his piping hot bowl of stew. "Stefnir's getting better but he's still a liability, and I'm not quite used to dueling with a missing eye."

They sat in a circle around the fireplace. The varl had brought in a pair of very thick tree logs on which to seat themselves. Runa stirred the fireplace with a poker, distributing coals to better warm the room.

"We're under a lot of pressure," Eirik replied. "Those varl remains are a blizzard off the coast. If we had grabbed them all then perhaps we could have avoided this, but that's neither here nor there. Sooner or later, the wrong tongue will wag to the wrong person, rumors will run their course, and the varl will notice that graves were overturned. In fact, it may already be too late."

"Why is that?" Runa asked. Stefnir figured her intrigue was piqued about anything Eirik knew that Leiknir had not mentioned.

Eirik placed his emptied bowl on the floor. "There has been an increase in varl visiting Strand. We're trying to keep tabs on who they are and what they want. The biggest name amongst them is Vilmundr. Do you know him?"

Eirik watched the two varl. Olaf shook his head. Ulfvalgr leaned forward with his elbows on his knees, covering his mouth to finish a bite before answering. "Yes. He's a warlord. Walks a fine line between loyalty to Jorundr and being a self-absorbed mercenary arsehole."

"So he is someone important," Eirik concluded.

"By himself?" Ulfvalgr bobbed his horned head lightly. "Well, he can cause a great deal of damage if he so chooses. When he speaks, Jorundr listens at least."

"One of the letters Leiknir gave to Olvir mentioned that some, not all, of these varl have joined with the Mársmidr as hired thugs." Eirik crossed his arms over his chest. "We could very well be fighting some in the tournament."

Olaf and Ulfvalgr exchanged glances. Ulfvalgr dug into another bite while Olaf answered. "We can make do. Stefnir and Arnbjorn's training has prepared them somewhat for fighting opponents of our size."

"Well, they don't make them much wider than Olaf," Ulfvalgr quipped.

Arnbjorn, Stefnir and Runa laughed. Olaf glared at Ulfvalgr and slowly began to chuckle. Only Eirik wasn't amused, which sobered the mood swiftly.

"Eirik, what's wrong?" Stefnir couldn't help but ask, bending forth apprehensively.

The Governor's Guardsman slowly looked to Runa. "*Brenna Training Hall*, where we met Leiknir last week, burned down this morning."

Runa lowered her spoon for a moment but returned to eating. "He wasn't there though."

Eirik rolled his shoulders in a shrug. "Only two died, and their bodies certainly didn't match his description. But I thought you should know."

Runa nodded and said nothing more.

"That's not all though." Eirik grew solemn. Everyone watched as the Guardsman bowed his head before speaking to the varl again. "Steward Olvir decreed that, once we have our target, you two are to enter into the custody of the City Watch. The both of you."

Silence ruled. Stefnir feared for a moment that Ulfvalgr would cut the man down. Instead, the varl spooned another mouthful of the stew and chewed before speaking. "When did he *really* decide this? And why are you telling us?"

"He told me when last I met my contact. And I'm telling you because I lied to you once before, and made a promise to myself not to do so again," Eirik replied. "If you desire, I can create a diversion so you can escape with our prisoner. Give some orders that will confuse the chain of command."

"Tempting." Ulfvalgr rolled his jaw, before shaking his head with a contemptuous snort. "Tell your boss we'll go along quietly, just as long as I get a crack at Kjallak when the fighting comes."

"You may have to settle for being the headsman," Eirik replied. "I trust if you didn't tell me what Kjallak wants, you're not going to tell the steward?"

Ulfvalgr said nothing more.

"So any good news?" Olaf interjected.

"Yes," Eirik reached into his cloak and withdrew a parchment. Stepping into the center of the circle beside the fire, he knelt and laid out a picture for all to see, setting his bowl on a corner to keep the edge from curling. "This is a map of the area where we'll be fighting, including the location of the City Watch, escape routes if things go wrong and, above all, how we're going to take our man captive."

Everyone huddled in, curiosity clear on their features.

Chapter 16

The next two days passed as a blur. On the last day of training, Olaf and Ulfvalgr forbade Stefnir to exercise or practice, wanting the boy to rest his body. Instead, they reviewed the map layout and the battle strategy. They discussed axe-play techniques and proper shield reactions verbally. It felt wrong to Stefnir, but given that the varl survived for hundreds of years and had fought wars long before the boy had been born, it didn't seem right to question them either.

That night Stefnir asked Eirik questions about the tournament, such as why gangs fought in the matches. The reason had never been explained to him.

"Well, most of the gangs are nothing but rabble. Most of their crimes just petty robbery. Often they have a few drinks to ready their courage and then follow a merchant into an alley or just break into his shop. As the gangs get bigger, they sometimes turn to raiding." Eirik ran a thumb along his chin. "So, we offer the tournament as an alternative. Prize money or a trinket from the treasury to keep them fighting bouts, where we can manage them."

"And injure or kill those who would cause problems later," Ulfvalgr added.

Eirik pursed his lips. "You'd be impressed how many get a good cut or lose a finger and decide a life of crime isn't worth the risk. They learn that they're not as hard as they think they are. It also helps us track weapons in the city, who can cause trouble and who leads whom. We even mark tournament champions and try to recruit them into the City Watch. Better on our side than theirs, eh?"

"That sounds horrible," Stefnir responded with a sour feeling in his stomach. "Don't they have a better means to live?"

"I wish they did too." Eirik scowled. "Many goons are simply men with families to feed. But fair intent does not justify a crime."

Stefnir wasn't sure he agreed.

Runa returned the next morning from her trip to inform Leiknir of the fight. She was visibly shaken. "I did not see him but left a message and waited near *The Caroling Giant*. A courier delivered this note to me there."

Eirik accepted and read the letter. "So our message was received. Is there something wrong?"

"No, the mark is Leiknir's." Runa shook her head and swallowed. "I just haven't spoken to him face to face since the training hall fire."

"I'm sure Leiknir is just staying low, Runa," Eirik offered by way of consolation. Yet Stefnir recognized fear in her eyes. He felt pity for the girl, but had to deal with his own anxiety.

The fight was today.

Stefnir felt the gnawing uncertainty in every step towards the lumberyards, through a gentle dusting of snow. With every bootmark he left fading in the powdered white, Stefnir wondered if it would be the last imprint he made on this world. Save for his bones when he fell.

The dark thoughts caused Stefnir to watch Ulfvalgr, who walked with his war axe over his shoulder. The fiery-haired varl wore a grim expression, his dour countenance and gruff demeanor having returned in preparation for the looming battle. When the rising sun struck his features, the silhouette his shadow cast transformed him into caricature, a symbol of every varl soldier who had marched to battle.

Stefnir swallowed, the pressure in his chest and throat building. He heard war drums no one else could and his stomach churned. Eirik had forewarned them— as with any combative sport— that people died in the tournament. The City Watch were not always so swift to save the fallen.

Stefnir wanted to break and run.

A comforting hand fell on Stefnir's shoulder. He raised his brows to Olaf. The varl said no words, but fixed him with a level gaze that said, "All will be well."

Stefnir nodded.

Passing folks regarded them as they approached the lumberyards. Tall pines stretched to the heavens, coats of white upon their evergreen needles. Younger lads, trying to earn a trade, moved from tree to tree and used long poles to knock branches, causing snow to thud against the already covered ground. Cutting teams followed the boys and began to saw, adding to piles of huge, felled trunks. Harnessed yoxen were prepared to drag the produce away to be split and dried into firewood, cut into lumber, or carved and whittled into a variety of goods. Onto wherever and into whatever the markets of Strand demanded.

A couple of City Watchmen were there to sanction the fight, standing lazily beside a fire. A few of the lumberjacks distracted themselves from their labor to spy the forthcoming party of three men, a woman and two varl. One gave the slightest nod that Eirik returned respectfully.

"The Watch are hidden amongst the laborers?" Arnbjorn asked.

"A painful few are," Eirik spoke only slightly louder than a whisper. "The rest are involved in a training exercise, marching this way from the south. Only their captain knows of this match, and only when they arrive will they be instructed to interfere. Thus, no one leaks the secret."

Arnbjorn nodded. "Smart."

They stopped before the fire, receiving a stern glare from the pair of City Watchmen. After a moment's delay, Eirik stepped forward and cleared his throat. "We are here for the fight."

A watchman with pinched features grunted. "Names?"

"We are clan Óskorinn-Skjoldr," Eirik replied.

"Long name," the watchman said. "You've been expected. Please take ten paces back. If your opponents are not here by midday then they forfeit the match, and you will receive sixty silvers."

Eirik nodded and turned. As they marched the distance, Ulfvalgr hunched down to speak to their spokesman. "Óskorinn-Skjoldr... the unbroken shields. I like it."

"I needed a name to get their attention," Eirik replied. "And it has a lot of meaning. I thought it might tick them off."

"I think it worked," Olaf said. Stefnir stared at him, before following the varl's line of sight.

Six menacing shapes approached. On either side, two were clearly varl. Ulfvalgr edged forward eagerly until they neared, neither of their features belonging to Kjallak. Olaf's eyes narrowed as he examined them. "Do we know them?"

Ulfvalgr shook his head. "No. But that pinion the one on the right is wearing... that's a Raven mercenary."

"Bolverk's group?" Stefnir recognized a tinge of concern in Olaf's voice. "You don't think...?"

"No." Ulfvalgr grunted. "He must have been kicked out or left the Ravens. I doubt Bolverk would have the patience for this tournament. That varl and his ilk live for war, not just fights..."

"If we get through this, you'll have to tell me about them," Eirik said. "There. The man on the right. Is that who I think it is?"

He was dressed in black, thinning hair over a scarred visage that bore both cruelty and exhaustion. Stefnir did not recognize him, but heard Arnbjorn grumble under his breath. "Ottar."

Their foes were well-equipped, bearing shields and swords. There was a spearman amongst them and another even wore an iron helmet, a prized piece of armor few warriors possessed. The City Watchmen who proctored the match looked at one another, before one stepped forth to speak to their leader.

"Remember, we must take Ottar alive." The Governor's Guardsman regarded the nearby tree line, before gazing over his companions. "Does anyone need me to go over the plan one more time?"

Runa drew a javelin, resting the handle over her shoulder with the tip pointed down. "No."

Arnbjorn shook his head, pulling his shield to his chest.

"We've rehearsed the damn thing so much that Olaf mumbles it in his sleep," Ulfvalgr said, nodding his horns at his kendr.

"Ha!" Olaf barked and clanged his sword against his tower shield twice.

Stefnir drew a sharp breath, remembering everything they had strategized. When he said nothing, Arnbjorn swayed towards him and whispered. "Remember, if you take a crack or too much heat, tap my shoulder and back out."

Stefnir winced at the odor on Arnbjorn's breath. "Are you drunk?"

Arnbjorn smiled, displaying some of his broken and wine-stained teeth. "Liquid courage isn't just for approaching ladies or robbing mead halls."

"Fighters!"

Stefnir and the rest of his allies turned their attention to the City Watchman. The proctor had returned to the fire after a brief word with Ottar, holding the handle of his sheathed sword in one hand and a horn in the other.

"By order of the Governor of Strand, we sanction this tournament match on the sound of this horn." The watchman spoke loudly enough that even the lumberjacks ceased their work to watch. "The winner shall receive a total of sixty silver coins and shall be considered for a position within the City Watch."

All the fear that Stefnir felt before returned in force. His legs seized up, his muscles taut and ready to burst. His heart hammered his chest like a blacksmith upon glowing metal. Yet even as his body urged him to flee, he remembered running from wolves and escaping bar fights uninjured. He recalled brawling his way past a street gang, the ambush at *The Shattered Shield*, and being flung out a window to elude both fire and blade at the Great Hall.

Somehow, the memories kept Stefnir still.

Olaf took position on the boy's right, his shield raised and hips turned sideways, reducing his profile's exposure to the enemy. Arnbjorn took the left, keeping his shield-arm high. Ulfvalgr stomped into position behind the boy, ready to circle and crush the enemy's flank. Finally, Runa and Eirik stood at Olaf's rear, letting the varl's figure mask their presence.

Time slowed as Stefnir thought over his life. Had he survived all these adventures just to die here? His father told him once that no one truly knows what will happen in a fight. If wyrd— fate— coveted his death, it would have happened by now. What would have been the point of learning from Olaf and Ulfvalgr if there was such a thing as inevitability?

The question went unanswered, the thought echoing in his mind like a death cry in a valley. And somewhere between then and eternity, the horn of battle sounded...

Stefnir felt as if his soul had detached from his body. His legs began to walk him forward without his even acknowledging the movements. His arm rose stiffly, locking his shield with the others to maintain the wall that he, Arnbjorn and Olaf created as they marched as one.

"Too much time thrashing farmers and roughing up merchants for 'protection' money," Arnbjorn snorted, smirking.

The scoundrel was likely correct. Ottar's men had no discipline. They staggered, making no particular formation and failing to lock shields. Although they lacked structure, they moved eagerly to begin the fight, jogging towards Stefnir's allies.

Before starting to run. Before sprinting.

Despite himself, Stefnir glanced behind for a moment. Runa and Eirik were gone.

Stefnir panicked, his posture frozen. One of the two varl burst ahead of Ottar's mob, his massive hands gripping a giant sword. His visage bore rage, his beard gold like some furious storm god. Stefnir knew that one strike of that blade would shatter his armor, perhaps even cleave his arm.

He wanted to shirk and run. He stood firm anyway.

Just as the varl poised to strike, he stumbled, dropping to a knee. Stefnir didn't understand. Arnbjorn wasted no time flashing his skeg axe across the giant's neck, lacing the giant's gold beard with threads of red. The varl's face froze in shock as he dipped sideways and crashed into the snow. Only then did Stefnir spot the javelin sprouting from the dead varl's calf muscle.

The rest of Ottar's men halted, a few spinning toward the rearward woods. A couple of figures stood amongst the thin trees. One charged at Ottar's men with a two-handed axe, his countenance a snarl. Eirik shouted and swung his weapon against a foe's rising shield, battering his enemy back.

"Charge!" Olaf bellowed.

Stefnir obeyed. It was the maneuver they practiced for the last week, sweeping forward as one while maintaining their shield wall. The second varl howled and slammed his war hammer against Olaf's shield. Stefnir heard the wood crack threateningly. As Olaf recovered, Ulfvalgr stepped to his kendr's side, delivering a wickedly fast chop to their foe. The strike took the tip off the enemy varl's horn and left a deep gash in his upper arm, blood raining from the wound and crimsoning the snow.

A war cry drew Stefnir's attention back to the wider melee. The helm-clad swordsman charged him, shield and weapon raised. Stefnir swore he saw fury in his foe's eyes, despite the visor masking them in guarded shadows.

Stefnir snarled and yelled back, slashing his axe at his encroaching foe.

The last thing Stefnir expected was their shields crashing together. Stefnir's axe missed its mark as the swordsman pressed through, ruining the boy's balance and spinning him about. He shifted and realized the swordsman was behind him, his blade flipped to stab Stefnir's hind side. Stefnir twisted, slapping his round shield against his foe's arm, the sword skimming across the armor's surface.

Stefnir's axe followed.

The haft cracked and broke as the axe slammed home. Stefnir panicked, realizing he had lost his weapon even as the swordsman gargled blood. The dying foe fell to his knees, the axe's blade buried in his neck while blood cascaded down his tunic. He dropped his weapon and shield as his fingers clasped his ruined throat in vain, trying to halt his demise.

The swordsman tilted his head back, and Stefnir glimpsed inside the visor. It was the gaze of a man who finally faced death, not just the thrill of battle or inflicting death on another, but meeting such an end himself. To tumble into the grave after a life of sending others to such a fate.

With a pang of regret, Stefnir tossed the remains of his father's axe and plucked the dying swordsman's blade. Fearing his foe would desperately attempt something, Stefnir threw a kick that sprawled him against the ground. He returned to the rest of the fight, leaving the swordsman to his wyrd.

Stefnir barely raised his shield in time as another axe sped toward him. The force battered his armor aside and caused the boy to land on his bottom. Stefnir stared with awe as Ottar whipped his weapon around like a wheel to strike again.

Something thudded against the back of Ottar's head. The Mársmidr lieutenant wore a look of utter agony as he dropped, falling beside Stefnir and crashing face first in the snow. Eirik stepped forth, his axe reversed from striking Ottar with the blunt end, and offered Stefnir a hand.

Stefnir exhaled his relief and accepted the gesture.

Olaf's sword lashed against the wounded varl's other arm. The foe's hammer stuck in the muddied snow as the injured giant cradled his gushing shoulder, weakly raising his other hand for mercy. Meanwhile, the last thug went toe-to-toe with Arnbjorn. But when he took a step back and surveyed the situation, resignation crested his features. He let his shield and sword slide to the ground, accepting defeat.

A moment later, the City Watch's horn sounded, signaling victory for them. Arnbjorn shouted, stabbing his weapon to the heavens triumphantly. Ulfvalgr joined him, raising his war axe skyward. Stefnir shouted with joy. Eirik grinned at Ottar, before his features dropped. The Governor's Guardsman checked the south, the fields beyond white and empty. "Captain Dylan isn't here."

"Is something wrong?" Olaf asked, drawing mammoth breaths to recover from both his exertions and the victorious celebration.

"Yes," Eirik said. "That platoon of City Watch isn't—"

The thug who had surrendered jerked several times and fell against his chest. Arnbjorn raised his shield just as a shaft zipped through the forest line and lodged itself in his barrier.

"Runa! Stop!" Eirik boomed.

"It's not her!" Ulfvalgr yelled.

Then Stefnir realized they weren't javelins. The girl ran from the trees as more missiles followed. The City Watchmen turned to face the danger but were struck down as arrows rained upon them. Stefnir realized that a couple of the lumberjacks were being slain by others amongst their ilk, who began to rush towards them, casting off their jerkins.

One of them drew a round shield from within a sack. Stefnir recognized the skeletal hand, grabbing a crown.

"The Aetla Hilmir," Eirik breathed as their new foes advanced.

Chapter 17

"Fight or flee?" Arnbjorn shouted.

From the periphery of Eirik's vision, the scoundrel already shifted in preparation to run. For all the Guardsman's planning and strategies, he wondered if perhaps escaping was the only true answer. *Everything I try gets thwarted by them. Did Olvir betray me, or do we have a spy as high in the courts as he?*

Among the swarms of the Aetla Hilmir, Eirik saw him again. Nikolas the Beautiful smiled as he calmly approached with a blade in hand. So sure of his victory. Eirik felt his grip tighten around the handle of his axe and he spun to Olaf.

"Take Ottar and run! Forget the Great Hall and go with our backup plan!" Eirik commanded. The varl wasted no time in obeying. Stefnir almost dashed away but paused to loot the helmet of the swordsman he had slain, adding to his plundered sword.

"What are you going to do?" Runa asked.

"Distract them. Go! All of you!"

Olaf, Arnbjorn and Runa took off running towards Strand. Somewhere near the edge of the city, Eirik knew Dagny had stashed the yoxen wagon as their failsafe. However Stefnir hesitated, standing as though ready to join Eirik's fight.

"Go, kid."

Eirik realized Ulfvalgr had spoken, as the giant strode beside the Guardsman. The boy fidgeted uncertainly before sprinting to catch up with the rest of their fleeing companions.

Eirik was quite surprised that the varl would elect to remain. "You realize that if you're captured, everything we've denied them thus far will have been for naught."

"Oh, they'll never get what they're after. And these guys kicked us out of a fine room, with beds and free meals." Ulfvalgr batted the handle of his war axe against his palm. "I want to repay them with beds of their own, to rest on pyre boats and become fish food."

Eirik smiled softly. "You could find out where Freystein is hiding from Ottar."

"We'll do that anyway. And I'd rather remind Kjallak why he's smart to hide. You ready?"

"As good a day to die as any," Eirik replied.

They charged.

There was hesitation in the Aetla Hilmir's eyes, and their shouting faltered. Clearly the gang had expected their foes to bolt like hares on the hunt. The last thing they anticipated was for the rabbit to turn around and fight. Despite having a score of men, their courage floundered with Ulfvalgr's arrival as he smashed through shields, flesh and bone with wide sweeping strikes.

Three men fell immediately. Unlike before, Ulfvalgr was not confined by walls and ceilings or the threat of fire. As either death or loss of limb tempered the gusto of the gangers, they quickly learned to keep their distance. They trickled about, trying to surround the varl. Ulfvalgr moved and lashed, staying just outside the enclosing circle of men.

Eirik had only one foe, who smiled as he neared. "Eirik."

"Nikolas." Eirik almost hissed, taking the offensive with a lateral hack of his weapon. Nikolas skipped back, skilled enough to sway no farther than the reach of Eirik's swing.

The Guardsman swiftly recovered his weapon, choking on the grip to block Nikolas' counter slice. The gang lord's sword bit into the haft and Eirik recognized that he had few such parries before his weapon snapped in twain.

To Eirik's surprise, none of Nikolas' men leapt into the duel. Eirik jumped away, reevaluating the situation. A few gang members stood back observing, but the rest went after the varl. "An audience?"

"Perhaps." Nikolas dashed forth and sent a series of sword thrusts at Eirik. The Guardsman weaved and bobbed, evading every stab but absorbing scratches on his arms and tears in his cloak. At last, Nikolas made a mistake and committed himself too far, becoming unbalanced. Eirik slipped away from the strike and hooked the tip of his axe to the gang lord's knee. Nikolas grunted and slid back, leaving a trail of blood in the snow.

"Axe-men. Always with your tricks." Nikolas lowered himself to squeeze his cut knee.

Eirik resisted the urge to attack, the chance of earning the truth glimmering before him as he taunted. "We can't all have swords made for us by Gylfi."

"Ohhh, ho ho ho," the gang lord's wicked grin returned as he stood and brushed the blonde hair from his fair countenance. "Can you blame him, given how much of a failure the Governor is? His seat is there for the taking if someone has the claim, as I do."

Nikolas' words chilled Eirik to his core. The gang lord's familiar features suddenly began to make sense as Eirik could see traits of the Governor in the Aetla Hilmir's leader. "Who are you, really?"

Nikolas laughed and peeled the glove away from his left hand; a faint birthmark splotch ran along his knuckles. Eirik recognized the mark as identical to Ragnar's. "I am the son of Helvir, brother of the reigning Governor. And by that right do I claim what is mine."

Eirik barely escaped the sudden slash Nikolas threw at him, so thoroughly shocked by the invoked name and blemish. Instead of pressing the attack, Eirik danced back and glanced about, seeking a chance to flee.

Nikolas' men had begun to surround Ulfvalgr, cornering him with his back to a log pile. The few City Watch involved in the ambush were dead. Far to his right, Eirik saw what initially looked like a distant mob, until he recognized the helmets and spears of the City Watch. Captain Dylan had found them at last, but would not arrive in time to save them.

Eirik turned and ran, as Nikolas' sword nipped at his cloak.

The Guardsman leapt and brought his axe down on the spine of an unwary thug trying to contain Ulfvalgr. As their foe went down, Eirik cried out to his ally. "The log pile!"

Ulfvalgr twisted and slammed his axe into the post that kept the lowest log in check. The stake snapped and the bottom log rolled out from under the pile, the weight of those above pushing it outward. Ulfvalgr hopped over the first one as he dashed towards the opening in the Aetla Hilmir's line that Eirik had carved, leaving Nikolas' henchmen to deal with the rolling trunks.

Ulfvalgr and Eirik sprinted towards the mass of approaching City Watch, the Aetla Hilmir slow to follow. The two came to a stop between the approaching groups.

Ulfvalgr spun, glancing between the two forces. "If we fight, we could finish them."

"And then you'll have to be taken into custody…" Eirik replied between deep breaths that misted from his mouth.

"Is that not what you want?" Ulfvalgr asked as he sternly regarded Eirik.

Eirik took a moment but shook his head. "Dylan was supposed to be here earlier. Someone must have tipped off the Aetla Hilmir of our plan, for they hid amongst our own forces. There's a spy in the Great Hall, likely in high office. We can't let you get captured now."

Ulfvalgr smirked and the two began their flight towards Strand. Behind them, the Aetla Hilmir and arriving City Watch slammed against one another like ocean waves against the beach.

Olaf snorted, watching Runa creep about the corner of a hut to check for anyone watching. Across the street, Eirik's contact had parked their wagon. Olaf knew it on sight, as the prized Nautmot yoxen were more distinct than other breeds in Strand. The person stood near the beasts, and as far as Olaf could tell it was another girl.

Not for the first time, Olaf wondered how man got along with the other half of their kind. They could be gentle and a pleasure or they could be willfully strong to an extreme, like Runa.

Olaf felt a growing amount of trust and respect for the girl. Had there been more time to get to know her, and less blood spilled and ambushes the last few weeks, he might have even counted her as more a friend than an ally. However Eirik claimed she was fiercely loyal to Leiknir, whom Olaf did not know. This was strange to the varl, for he would never truly know Runa until he knew the Vak'auga spymaster. Although Runa would claim differently, Olaf wished she was truly her own lord.

Olaf shrugged and adjusted the weight of Ottar over his shoulder. The captive had awakened and shifted around in Olaf's grip.

"Stefnir," Olaf said, "gag him."

The boy stepped behind him and there were sounds of scuffling. Arnbjorn helped the boy, and Olaf heard the thump of someone being socked in the face.

"Got it," Stefnir said. "Thanks Arnbjorn."

"Thank you!" Arnbjorn sauntered aside with a wide, genuine smile.

Olaf said nothing about the scoundrel's joviality, for circumstances meant their original plan of going to the Great Hall was botched. Per their prior agreements, they would instead return to the manor to interrogate Ottar themselves and report what they learned.

But this contingency had sparked some debate over just who would extract the answers. Olaf and Stefnir couldn't. Eirik admitted a preference toward intimidation over interrogation; the lawman doubting that he possessed the sadism to brutalize a tough prisoner. Arnbjorn had rubbed his scabbed cheek and appeared oddly disgruntled at Eirik's statement. Ulfvalgr would have, but Eirik pointed out that a varl's tolerance for pain far exceeded that of a man's, a misunderstanding in which Ulfvalgr's strength could easily result in a permanent mistake.

"Finesse is the key," Eirik had said. That left Runa and Arnbjorn. The girl gladly left the job to the over-eager scoundrel.

Runa approached the contact and they exchanged words. Eventually the robed figure pulled off her hood, a tangle of dark brown hair spilling out. At last the girl gave the reins to Runa, who waved the rest of them over.

The three stomped from the shade of the hut. Stefnir opened the cart's canopy for Olaf to stash the bound Ottar. Arnbjorn jumped in and sat on the captured man's legs, but Ottar barely struggled. The prisoner's gaze darted amongst them, filled with equal parts terror and hatred.

"I'll drive," Runa volunteered as she stepped towards the carriage seat. Olaf noticed that the robed girl made a move as though to join them. Runa shook her head at her. "Go home. What happens next isn't your kind of work."

"You're just like that arsehole, Eirik." The girl pouted.

Runa laughed, the sound wicked and bitter. "I'm more an arsehole than he could ever be. Now faen off."

The robed girl's eye widened with shock. She turned and fled, covering her head with her hood. Olaf sighed at the exchange and boarded the wagon alongside Stefnir.

As the yoxen wagon began to move, Stefnir couldn't help but ask. "Do you think Eirik and Ulfvalgr got away?"

"It was foolish and stupid of Ulfvalgr to stay behind." Olaf slapped a hand against his forehead, disbelieving the mistake he had made. "Oh, what the faen was I thinking? I can't believe I listened to him. That idiot should have ran too."

"If he's captured, he could tell them where the missing piece of the Gift of Hadrborg is," Stefnir whispered while Arnbjorn was distracted. "He didn't tell you or anything?"

Olaf shook his head, his horns accidentally scratching at the overhead sheet. "Not a word. But they'll be forced to kill him before he ever talks."

He set his shield against the side of the wagon and studied the armor. One of the boards had cracked and would need to be replaced, another task to be done once they returned.

It was not a long ride. When the wagon halted before the manor, Olaf slung his shield over one shoulder before hoisting Ottar about the other. Stefnir ran along beside them and opened the manor's door for Olaf.

The hearth was still warm from the morning. Stefnir ran over and added another log with haste. The boy placed his plundered helmet and sword on a bench and plucked a candle from the table. Returning, he lit the wick against the livid embers before walking towards another portal. He opened it, both leading and lighting the way for the burdened Olaf.

The varl entered the revealed landing and began descending the stairs, taking their captive into the black cellar. The basement was lined with stone walls and no windows. Stefnir touched his candle to the waiting sconces, and finally the small, readied fire pit in the chamber's center. Arnbjorn opened vents along the walls for the smoke, and pulled over a chair for their guest.

Olaf set Ottar on the seat while the scoundrel fetched a rolled cloth and some rope from a shelf, then dragged a small cabinet over. He opened it, revealing a small collection of tools and blades. "Alright boys, I suggest you clear out. I've got a lot of work ahead of me."

"Just don't kill him," Olaf said.

Arnbjorn smirked, his ruined features seemingly impish in the illumination of the fire. Worse, Olaf could see a mad gleam in his remaining eye that disturbed the varl more than the thought of torture. Olaf and Stefnir said nothing, but ventured toward the waiting staircase to return to the main hall.

Olaf realized the boy had grown solemn as he reclaimed his looted sword, holding the blade with a slackened grip. "What's wrong, Stefnir?"

"I…" Stefnir started and choked. "When I, killed that man. I saw his face. I looked into his eyes."

Olaf listened, but realized that the fireplace needed more attention to remain glowing. He took a poker and maneuvered the fresh log to better sit in the heat, and added some dried twigs and leaves to replenish the flames. As soon as one of the leaves caught however, Olaf stepped back swiftly to distance himself from the blaze. When he spun about, he saw the boy staring into the visor of the helmet on the table.

A thought occurred to Olaf. He wondered if it was an omen that the axe, which had belonged to Stefnir's father, had broken and the boy was left with a sword. "Was that your first kill?"

Reluctantly, Stefnir nodded.

"So what did you see when you took his life?" Olaf asked.

"Fear. Terror even," Stefnir said glumly. "I guess when he couldn't breathe, when my father's axe was in his neck, it dawned upon him that he actually could die. That he had lied to himself that he would survive that fight."

Olaf nodded. "And someday that could be you."

"I really never thought about it," Stefnir confessed.

"Stefnir, you need to decide just how far you want to go." Olaf sat down on one of the cut logs he and Ulfvalgr used as seats, setting his shield beside him. "Every man who walks the path of sword and axe will eventually find himself on the end of one."

"It's… my fate to die like that too?" Stefnir asked, as if in denial.

"That's up to you. Every fight is a roll of the dice. Even if the odds are in your favor, you never really know what will happen. You have to know when fighting is no longer worth the risk, and walk away from that life." Olaf drew his sword and placed the pommel against the rim of his tower shield, trying to leverage it apart.

A sad smile crested Stefnir's features. "My pa said something much like that once."

"Perhaps he was one of the smart men, and got out once he had what he wanted, or discovered that another way is better. You are fortunate, believe it or not. Your," Olaf paused, trying to remember the word. "Parents, gave you a full life, whether or not you know it. They trained you in hunting and foraging, and other essential skills. As long as you don't succumb to the allure of a life of raiding, you can carve a good existence without slaying men or varl."

Stefnir sat down in a chair beside Olaf, who continued to tinker with his armor. "Do you want me to quit this and go home?"

Olaf turned his attention from his labor, staring into Stefnir's eyes. "Yes, boy, I do. Your life is a flagon's worth of mead, mine is a barrel. The difference is, you can have children where only my bones will remain when I am gone. I wish you'd forget Magnus and get on with your life. I want you to *live*, Stefnir, more than I desire our damn heirloom back.

"I want you to live, and not become the same vengeful shade that Runa and Ulfvalgr are, slaying with mirth until they're cast into early graves."

Stefnir turned away. Olaf realized the boy was staring at the helmet, which rested on the dining table. Slowly, Stefnir stood and gingerly took the helm. "Not until Magnus pays. And no more villages become infernos to fill his pockets."

Olaf was about to say something more when the doors opened. Eirik and Ulfvalgr sauntered in, bruised and battered, followed by Runa. Olaf rose from his seat.

"We lost them," Ulfvalgr declared. "Captain Dylan did come. We left the Aetla Hilmir to cross swords with the City Watch."

Olaf breathed a sigh of relief. "Glad you two are alright."

"Where is Ottar?" Eirik asked as he wearily sat down on a bench, setting his axe next to the table.

"With Arnbjorn," Stefnir replied.

Eirik nodded and pinched the bridge of his nose as though thinking. Ulfvalgr leaned against a beam, crossing his arms. There was tension in the air. Olaf felt it emanate from Eirik.

"Helvir," Eirik said. "I can't believe it. Nikolas is the son of the Governor's dead brother, Helvir."

"How?" Olaf could read the surprise on Runa's face as she spoke. "Leiknir mentioned Helvir while educating me about Strand's history. But no one thought he had children…"

"I thought as much too, Runa," Eirik said. "But Nikolas showed me a birthmark identical to Governor-Prince Ragnar's. And his features… Nikolas could easily pass for a younger version of the Governor. No, I think his claim to Strand could be sincere. And if the Governor and Ragnar die, difficult to contest."

Olaf listened for a while, but the talk of succession and Governors was not something he truly cared about. He focused his efforts on his damaged shield. When Ulfvalgr saw his kendr repairing the cracked panel he stepped away from the pillar.

"Olaf, let me help with that," Ulfvalgr said.

"No need," Olaf replied, ignoring his friend. He felt distracted and saddened that Stefnir refused to abandon his quest, and worried that the boy would die on Magnus' blade. Yet with the others around, it felt inappropriate to carry on that discussion. He wished Stefnir understood his sincerity, and would rather the boy survive than be involved in this mad obsession to reclaim the Gift of Hadrborg.

"Olaf…" there was urgency in Ulfvalgr's voice.

The damaged panel of Olaf's shield buckled and cracked, falling from the rim. As it did, Olaf heard something chime against the floor, as soft as a tiny bell. Ulfvalgr moved with haste towards Olaf, but the latter varl reached down first and snatched the fallen object from the ground.

The others gathered about as Olaf held the item to the light. In the dull radiance of the fire, it revealed itself to be a metal amulet or talisman, about the size of a man's palm. A face was etched against its surface with a vacant expression and a tongue jettisoned from a snarling mouth. Runes were carved along the talisman's rim.

Olaf felt the anger rising within, growing uncontrollably as he cast his reddening gaze at Ulfvalgr. His fist clenched the Seal of Hadrborg.

Chapter 18

Ulfvalgr stirred. Stefnir realized the varl was not dead. The boy could have sworn the crunch earlier was Ulfvalgr's neck when Olaf punched him.

The downed varl spat a bloody tooth as he sat up. Stefnir noticed the tip of his right horn had snapped off against the stone floor. Ulfvalgr ran the back of his fist against his split lip and grinned pink teeth.

"Maybe I deserved that..." the varl said.

Olaf seethed, his breathing ragged. He clenched his fists so tight his knuckles were white as snow. Blood ran from the hand holding the discovered amulet, the source of the conflict. Stefnir had never seen Olaf filled with such ardor. If his friend pummeled Ulfvalgr, Stefnir wasn't sure they could or would stop him. And because of Olaf's levelheadedness, the boy partially accepted the violence as justified.

Olaf opened his mouth, preparing to speak when a man's scream rose from downstairs. Eirik was reluctant to glance away from the standoff, but another pained cry sent him scrambling to check on Arnbjorn and Ottar. Runa followed, her steps swift as if glad to vacate the scene.

Stefnir wanted to join them, but he didn't. He had to witness this.

"All this damn time running around in circles," Olaf managed through gritted teeth. "And I was carrying it all along. And you *knew*. The faen is wrong with you, Ulfvalgr?"

The varl said nothing, remaining on the ground.

"Torstein disowned and exiled Kjallak for his ambitions, yet he ignored the fact that you led raids against men." Olaf pointed a finger at the downed varl. "What the faen is the difference? You both lie and betray people who trust you to obtain what you desire, regardless of the cost. What difference did Torstein see in you that he didn't in Kjallak?"

Ulfvalgr bent forward and put an arm on a knee. "You never got it."

Olaf's nose and brow creased into a mask of utter fury. "Got *what?*"

"Loyalty to those who call us kendr." Ulfvalgr rose. "Doing what it takes to keep our people's history safe."

Olaf and Ulfvalgr faced off for a moment before the latter finally explained. "You're right. I was a bandit who enjoyed preying on men. We got good, then lazy. We barely bothered to scout our targets anymore. One day, we hit the wrong caravan as it headed north. It wasn't merchants selling trading wares from the south. Rather, it was an emissary of men, protected by a vanguard led by Jorundr himself."

The varl ran a thumb along his reddened lips. "When I realized what I had done, I surrendered. Rather than execute me, Jorundr pulled me and Fasolt aside. He asked why we raided. We told him, without batting an eyelash, that it was for the good of varlkind. That we did it to prove the superiority of Hadrborg's children, and that we never forgot the First Great War between men and varl.

"Jorundr shook his head. He reminded us that Hadrborg was dead, that his power was gone. And we were the last varl who would walk under the sun." Ulfvalgr rolled his jaw a little. "Jorundr took us to see the bridge at Einartoft. You ever see it Olaf?"

Something in Olaf's eyes softened. "Once."

"Once," Ulfvalgr repeated, grinning. "That bridge will outlive us. When the last varl has perished, our deeds will echo through time. This world will not forget that we existed. Even if men live on, we will be remembered."

Ulfvalgr sat down atop one of the large logs. Stefnir could see Olaf's shoulders slouch, the anger gradually fading.

"So I went home and told Torstein what had transpired. He understood, Olaf. He was just like our king, which is why it's important to keep the Gift of Hadrborg safe. Torstein wanted the varl to leave their mark on this world after we vanish.

"Before he died I told Torstein our plan to guard it. He didn't like the idea of separating it, and I didn't want to be bogged down in the middle of nowhere. I wanted to venture out, to carve new history for our people. To create the past, not just protect it. So I made a decision to hide the second piece nearby, in a place that you'd eventually find if I died."

Olaf glared at him.

"But don't mistake that for not caring, Olaf. I admit I was greedy for new glory. Yet Hadrborg's gift... it's our legacy. It's Torstein's legacy. And to keep that safe..." Ulfvalgr lifted a clawing hand. "I'll lie, cheat, steal and outright murder anyone who threatens it. If you imperiled Torstein's legacy, I'd kill you as swiftly as I'll kill Kjallak."

Olaf stepped back, shock dropping his jaw.

"You tried playing nicely and giving men the benefit of a doubt, like Karl during the First Great War. All that has accomplished is earning us a cellar full of problems, keeping us in check, and worrying about the fate of a city… when the only thing I give a faen about is retrieving what is ours. Now ask yourself a damn question Olaf. Would you have the guts to do what I've done if it was the only way to safeguard Hadrborg's gift?"

Olaf's mouth opened and shut a few times like a fish out of water, before the varl finally shook his head.

"Course not." Ulfvalgr forced himself to his feet. "I'm going downstairs to check on our friend. Because we're going to get the heirloom back. Then I'm walking away from this pathetic city, even if it's burning as I do."

With that, Ulfvalgr departed, descending the steps into the basement.

Olaf fumed, clenching and unclenching his fists before casting his dark gaze upon Stefnir. For a fleeting moment, the boy feared the varl would strike him. Instead, Olaf raised the talisman, holding it towards Stefnir. The amulet was bloody from where the edges cut into his friend's palm.

"This is the Seal of Hadrborg, the centerpiece of the shield. I need you to hide it," Olaf said.

Stefnir didn't accept the fetish, fidgeting uncomfortably. "Olaf… I can't."

"You can, boy." Olaf choked a little. "Ulfvalgr is right. I've run about this city painting a huge target on my back this whole time, and never knowing it. If we can't reclaim the shield, then we should keep them from gathering the entire thing. Take it, and tell no one you have it. And if we fail, I want you to toss it into the damn sea."

"You can't be serious!" Stefnir said.

"I am, boy!" Olaf's tone frightened Stefnir. The varl's following words were kinder as he tilted his head towards the wall. "Look there."

Stefnir obeyed. On a shelf, the ever grim and grinning horned skull watched the room. Its empty eye sockets seemed to absorb and judge all they saw.

"That's Kjallak's doing. He doesn't care, lad. He doesn't care at all about how history will remember the varl. Whatever he's really after, he's willing to piss on the graves of our people to achieve it. I'd rather our father-god's gift be lost than fall into his hands."

Stefnir saw the sadness in his friend's eyes, raw from exhaustion, as though this very act hurt him. Before he realized his actions, Stefnir felt the seal pressed into his open palm. The boy stared at the ugly visage of the fetish, which mocked him with its sprouting tongue.

The boy drew a leather strap from his pouch and threaded it through a nail hole in the seal. When it was complete, he tied the ends of the strap and looped the bloodstained necklace over his head, tucking it beneath his shirt.

When Stefnir raised his head again, Olaf was gone.

Stefnir awoke to the sound of a fresh scream. The fire in the hearth had weakened, but was far from dead. Stefnir suspected he had not slept long, but he noticed that his sleeve was slightly wet as though he had been crying into his arm.

He did not remember why he might have wept, until he rose and felt the cold touch of a god's face against his chest. Only then he recalled the responsibility and weight that Olaf had thrust on him. How angry his friend had been. How the few good things in his life always soured.

A powerful whimper came from the basement. Stefnir grunted, having had enough. Slowly he stood from the table and sauntered towards the stairs.

As he descended, Stefnir realized the basement reeked of quintessential fear. The dank smell of sweat and the odor of piss contributed to a musk of terror. When he reached the ground level, he saw Arnbjorn shirtless, sweating from the heat of the fire. Stefnir's view of the chair-bound prisoner was blocked behind the scoundrel. Olaf observed from a corner with crossed arms.

Arnbjorn shifted. Stefnir gasped as he saw the ruined man.

Every injury that Arnbjorn had suffered while incarcerated had been paid back; a bloodied stump of a finger and crushed teeth, a fresh cavity within his head where Arnbjorn had plucked out an eye. Ottar writhed, trying to sway away against his restraints.

"No, no no no no," Ottar's voice rose in octanes as he endlessly muttered the meaningless word. The pleading crested into a fresh scream as Arnbjorn jabbed a stick with a smoldering end into the prisoner's groin.

When Arnbjorn pulled the heat away, Ottar bent forward. If he were crying, then the tears were lost in the sheen of sweat. Even the blood from his taken eye was thin and runny as he soaked in perspiration.

"For the love of the Loom Mother," Ottar choked, his mouth muffled by blood. "Just ask me a question! You call it interrogation and you've inquired nothing!"

His entire body shook as he sobbed pitifully. Stefnir covered his mouth and fought back the rising wave of nausea. Somehow, the swordsman he had slain at the lumberyard was not so horrific, but now rather merciful.

"I just wanted it be understood that I am serious as faen, Ottar," Arnbjorn responded as he tossed the stick into the fire. Stefnir swore that Arnbjorn wore the face of a demon as he snatched a pair of glowing tongs from the flames. "Joke is, you're kind of expendable. You might die from infected wounds anyway. And I couldn't care less, really, but I'm listening if you think you can change my mind."

Ottar's mouth chewed wordless for a moment as the gleaming tool neared him. "I... I don't know where Magnus or Freystein are. But—"

Ottar swung back as the tongs grew closer, keeping himself as distant from the radiating instrument as he could. "But! But! I know... I know where some of their operations are. I can't guarantee they'll be there, but it's your best bet! Just give me over to the City Watch so this ends! That's all I want! Now please, please stop..."

"Who said I'm in the deal making mood?" Arnbjorn asked.

"Skoegir..." Ottar croaked. Arnbjorn hesitated.

"Just when I was having fun." Withdrawing the tongs, Arnbjorn drew a breath through his nostrils and turned to Olaf. "Go get Eirik."

Olaf stepped away from the wall and nodded to Stefnir as he lumbered up the stairs, each floorboard creaking under the giant's weight. Arnbjorn returned the still glowing tongs to the fire.

"I'm sorry..." Ottar whispered.

Arnbjorn regarded him, his face something between contempt and amusement.

"I'm sorry about your brother, Johan. Skoegir was the one who—"

"Killed him. You think I don't know?" Arnbjorn wiped his brow with his wrist as he shifted his attention to the fire. The scoundrel kept his back to Ottar, and Stefnir could see Arnbjorn wince from agony best unseen.

The stairs creaked as Runa and Eirik came down. As soon as Runa saw the ruined shell of a man that was Ottar, she covered her face. A moment later Olaf descended the stairs, followed by Ulfvalgr. All six gathered about the man with varying looks of disapproval.

"Olaf tells me you have information that you're willing to confess in exchange for more… legal custody and protection," Eirik said, his gray eyes reflecting the firelight. "You do realize that even if I grant it to you, the best case scenario is banishment from Strand or several years' hard labor in the mines. Decades even, perhaps longer than you'll live."

"I don't care…" Ottar whimpered. "Just get me away from him. Anything is better than this."

Eirik clasped his hands behind his back. "Alright. I think you know what happens if you're lying to us, of course."

"N-ninth pier, off the Left Foot of Denglr's Bay," Ottar said. "Tonight, there's a critical shipment arriving a few hours before midnight. It's your… your best chance of capturing either Magnus or Freystein… or both."

"That settles it," Ulfvalgr said with a smirk across his bruised face.

"Excellent," Eirik replied. "I'll take Ottar in and alert the City Watch."

The room went silent, save for the crackling of the blaze. Eirik regarded them all with a perked brow.

At last, Olaf spoke. "Eirik… I don't think that's a good idea."

"If it wasn't for the Watch, Ulfvalgr and I would not have escaped earlier today," Eirik replied with a scowl.

"Aye," Ulfvalgr said with his fists on his hips. "And your Captain Dylan was fashionably late. I won't deny they helped keep us out of Nikolas' grasp eventually, but the Watch failed to safeguard the plan."

Eirik's gaze grew hard as he studied Ulfvalgr. "Coming from a varl who intended to be taken into custody."

Ulfvalgr's laughter was a cruel bark. "I lied. I planned to escape your vigil once Ottar gave up Kjallak. But by good fortune, the City Watch failed to show. So I fought the Aetla Hilmir to make certain Olaf escaped with the target and the seal, but I was never going into Olvir's protection."

Eirik tensed, his grip tightening into fists.

"The varl are right," Arnbjorn piped in as he donned his tunic again. "The plan leaked and someone infiltrated the City Watch, posing as lumberjacks."

"The lapsed security in the Great Hall," Stefnir realized he had added to the list. The ill feeling of betraying someone did not sit well with him, but he couldn't deny the sense of distrust he had for authorities given their failures.

One by one, Eirik sized them all up. His sight even fell on Runa, who shrugged. "Eirik, even Leiknir hasn't been able to account for the information leaks in the City Watch. Either someone else is playing the game, or we've been having yoxen-dung for luck whenever the Watch is involved."

"You all cannot seriously think to take on the Vak'auga and Mársmidr without the ranks of the City Watch," Eirik said with a stern glare. "We can gather trusted men, keep it tight lipped for a few hours…"

No one spoke, until Ulfvalgr responded with an empathic tone. "Eirik… no. We've put our faith in the city's guardians only to see them fail us tirelessly. You're a good seed, I'll give you that. But this city is rotten, and you can't change the facts."

"There's too man—"

Ulfvalgr waved a hand. "You don't seem to have trusted them either. Does Olvir know where this manor is? If so, why aren't he and his men here to collect us by now?"

Eirik's jaw dropped. His fists clenched tightly.

Ulfvalgr moved to ascend the stairs when he stopped and regarded the Governor's Guardsman. "In fact, since you're so determined to involve the Watch, I think you'll understand when we take the yoxen wagon. And leave you to walk back to town."

Stefnir was shocked. The journey to Strand was quite a distance from the manor, especially on foot. If Eirik moved swiftly, he might arrive sometime after nightfall. But it also meant that he would have precious little time to convince and mobilize the Watch. Ulfvalgr and Olaf weren't just betraying Eirik's trust, but abandoning him as well.

"This is a damned mistake and you know it," Eirik replied. "Just ask the others."

"Oh," Ulfvalgr murmured, and Stefnir could hear the return of his snide ways in the sound. "Show of hands. Who wants a chance to get vengeance on Magnus and Freystein? Tonight?"

Ulfvalgr, of course, raised a palm. Arnbjorn and Runa followed soon after. Olaf's hand rose with reluctance.

Stefnir considered the situation. There was no shaking their disappointment with the City Watch. Every move of the city's defenders continued to fail, their every play and strategy going badly. It was difficult to meet Eirik's eye when Stefnir raised a hand, joining the others.

"Shall I even bother to ask who wants to join you in your walk?" Ulfvalgr asked, wearing a triumphant smirk as he jerked a tip-less horn towards the captive.

"I offered to help you escape custody once," Eirik said through the grinding of his teeth. "To cause a distraction and let you flee with the prisoner. Why didn't you just accept then?"

Ulfvalgr shook his head. "Do you really think you or your boss would have let us bolt with so vital a prisoner? It was a test of trust, and I just gave you the answer you wanted to hear."

Eirik said nothing.

"Goodbye, Eirik," Ulfvalgr said as he rose up the stairs. Olaf appeared as though he wanted to apologize to the Governor's Guardsman, but instead followed his friend. Arnbjorn flashed him a grin and trailed the varl as well. Runa hesitated.

"If you thought outside the law, maybe you would have caught Leiknir all those years ago," she said with neither rancor nor sympathy, and took to the stairs.

That left Stefnir with Eirik. Stefnir felt self-hate when he saw the older man's pained and defeated features. "Eirik, I'm… I'm sorry."

"Go on, Stefnir." Despite the boy's fears, there was no bitterness in Eirik's voice. "Ottar and I have a great deal of running to do."

As Eirik began to prepare Ottar for transfer, Stefnir returned to the main hall. On the table, his helmet and sword awaited him.

Chapter 19

Runa took the reins as she rubbed the exhaustion from her eyes. Although Arnbjorn had driven much of the way, he awoke Runa for the last leg of the trip. She cursed that Eirik wasn't there to share the burden. Stefnir was worthless with animals, and the varl could not leave the concealment of the canopy for risk of being identified.

Not that sleeping in the back of the bouncing wagon provided much rest anyway.

As she guided the yoxen towards the Ninth Pier, she couldn't help but wonder about the group's decision. Eirik was clever and skilled at intimidation and misdirection. Yet when he gave his word to accomplish anything he fought hard to keep his promise, walking that fine line of balancing deceit and lies against a core of honor. And he had whisked the varl away from situations that she doubted her own abilities to escape. She would regret abandoning the lawman and his talents if tonight went poorly.

But Eirik's faith in the system was a liability that Ulfvalgr did not share. And Leiknir's messages— the ones she hadn't shown Eirik— stressed the importance of Magnus and Freystein's capture, which the Guardsman risked by relying on the authorities. Eirik may have struck the deal with Leiknir, but it rested on Olvir's approval. Leaving Eirik behind only cut out the ambiguous middle man… or so she told herself.

The sun seemed to take forever to dip behind the horizon. They arrived at the Seventh Pier sometime after dusk. Although she was unsure of Ulfvalgr's leadership, she felt him wise to order her to scout ahead.

Dressed in her white cloak, she climbed the stairs of the abandoned wharf warehouse and then ascended a ladder. She emerged at the top, treading carefully as roof boards creaked with questionable stability. She prudently stuck to the load-bearing beams, avoiding the slippery and aging tiles already burdened by heavy snowfall.

It was a short but treacherous jump across the chasm to the storage hall of the Eighth Pier. The heavy snow clouds masked the moon, which was a blessing for maintaining stealth but a curse for placing one's foot. As she cleared the steeple of the dock's warehouse, she saw several lit torches amongst the piers below.

Runa recognized the anchored ship.

She had seen it once before in her life, perhaps a week after she was taken from her village, when she was loaded and shipped to Strand like any other cargo. Its bow was carved in the image of an open and terrifying eye. The ship was large yet sleek, blending speed with capacity. During that voyage she heard a rumor that the vessel's hull glittered with the scales of the dead god Marek, endowing the vessel with incredible quickness, allowing it to glide over the ocean. The pitiful illumination of the sailors' torches glimmered off the ship's frame, suggesting a hint of truth to such accounts.

She counted the fires that moved and whatever shapes she could tell were centurions and dockworkers until a sudden flash of distant lightning forced her to duck down, camouflaging her position with her cloak's pallor. In that moment she saw the deck of the vessel clear as day.

His silhouette was impossible to miss. His arms were bulging, his chest wrapped in rare plated armor. His horned helm rose to the sky.

Magnus. Warlord and Master of the Vak'auga.

For a moment, Runa entertained the thought of casting a javelin at the slaver-lord. But if the great distance wasn't enough to dissuade her, the sudden gale was sufficient. She hugged the roof and began to retrace her steps. Runa felt relief from the chilling wind when she finally slipped back through the ruined ceiling of the Seventh Pier and descended the stairs towards her waiting allies.

"He's here," she spoke with soft breath.

"Who?" Stefnir asked.

"Magnus. He's on the docked ship."

Ulfvalgr stepped forward from the shadows. "You're sure? What about Kjallak?"

"Frey… Kjallak, no. I saw no varl amongst the men down there."

"Hm." Olaf scratched his beard as he glanced at Ulfvalgr. "I'd wager my horns that Magnus will know where Kjallak is."

Runa crossed her arms. "These aren't rabble. Vak'auga are skilled fighters, well-versed in close quarters. And they have experience fighting varl—"

"Down!" Arnbjorn hissed. "Get down!"

They all dropped, seeking shelter behind crates and boxes. Runa peeked out from behind the stairs and watched as torchlight neared. The two centurions didn't enter, but passed by the entrance, glancing inside for but a moment. Each of their shields bore painted spears and blades arranged like a narrowed eye.

Arnbjorn eventually gave the "all clear" and the team huddled together. Runa told them what she saw; about the vessel, the number of armed men working and patrolling the pier, and the coming weather.

"Listen boys," Runa said as she knelt, a forearm against her leg. "We don't have a lot of time. Lightning snow is fast approaching and the winds are starting to get bad. Magnus isn't a fool. He risked docking, and the only reason is to unload. He'll be rushing, trying to beat the storm before it dashes his ship against the shore."

"There's nowhere to beach it?" Olaf asked.

Runa shook her head. "I've been to this shore once or twice. It's a rocky cliff that runs for a few leagues. There's nowhere nearby that Magnus could take the safety of land, not without being noticed by the City Watch. But there's a path along the rocky cliffs. I could lead us under the docks."

"What if we take a rowboat and try to board her?" Arnbjorn asked.

"Boarding the vessel from a rowboat is tricky business and will take too long," Ulfvalgr replied. "But it's a decent escape plan, if we're not dashed against the rocks ourselves."

"They're coming again," Stefnir said.

The team vanished once more. Only this time Ulfvalgr rose as the sentries passed, stepping behind them.

They turned too late. The varl smashed his axe against their heads with one stroke. One was slain instantly, his blood sloshing against the snow. The other slammed against the wall of the warehouse and fell still.

"Runa, take us to this damn path along the shore," Ulfvalgr said.

"Eirik," Olvir breathed, shock clear on his face as the mentioned man burst into the lobby of the Great Hall.

Eirik panted hard. It had been a marathon of a run, made worse by pushing Ottar. The captive's leg was badly wounded by the injuries Arnbjorn had inflicted, and Eirik was forced to craft a sled to take him along. Eirik thanked Denglr when he came across a vendor wagon heading into the city and convinced the man to bring him to the Great Hall as swiftly as possible. The driver agreed, but only went half-way up the hill when the threat of the lightning snow made him turn back.

Eirik opened his mouth to speak but only coughed, doubling over. Olvir put a hand to his shoulder to help Eirik stand.

"Someone get this man water!" Olvir commanded. Eirik waved his hand dismissively.

"We need…" Eirik coughed again. "We need men down at the Ninth Pier. City Watch, Governor's Guard, anyone we can spare."

"What's going on?" Olvir said. "And what happened to the varl?"

"Order the men armed and assembled and I'll explain as we go." Eirik pointed at the maimed prisoner bounded in the ski cart. "Take him to the menders and keep him under protection. That is Ottar, one of Freystein's lieutenants."

Olvir eyed the captive. A look of recognition passed the steward's gaze, as Ottar was difficult to identify given his swollen face and missing eye. Olvir gave the orders and a few guards rushed to obey. When a servant returned with a pitcher of water, Eirik drank deeply and wished only to sleep. However there was no time.

Once he had recovered, Eirik and Olvir walked swiftly through the barracks. Eirik told the steward of the attack after the tournament match, the torture of Ottar and the discovery of the docking ship. Eirik spoke of Ulfvalgr's betrayal and how he was left to rush back to Strand on foot.

As he gave his story, Ulfvalgr's words haunted Eirik as they had a dozen times throughout his long run back. *He was right to ask. Why did I not tell Olvir where our safe house was? Do I no longer have faith in him?*

When it was over, Olvir shook his head as he opened the doors to the stables. "In truth, Ulfvalgr may have been right not to trust us."

Eirik stayed silent for a moment.

"I must confess. He made me begin to suspect you had betrayed us," Eirik said as they rounded a corner. As they did, Eirik saw a familiar face smiling at him. "Valgard!"

His friend embraced him but winced when Eirik did the same. "Easy brother. I'm not ready to go dashing into the fight yet."

"I'm just glad you're alive," Eirik replied, relief washing over him.

Valgard stepped back and nodded at Eirik. "Looking at you, I'm inclined to say the same."

"Why isn't he in bed, Steward?" Eirik said, turning to Olvir. He couldn't help but feel some anger towards the old man.

"Valgard wanted to help badly, so I had him make inquiries once he was in better health." Olvir explained as he raised a hand defensively. "Captain Dylan's fight with the Aetla Hilmir went well, but we failed to take any living prisoners. Nikolas the Beautiful and a few others escaped. Dylan told me that the orders he had received were deceptive. Valgard checked into it."

"About Nikolas," Eirik said, feeling himself weaken. He wanted to ask about the false orders, but his news seemed direr. "I have terrible news about who he is."

Olvir and Valgard said nothing as Eirik explained. When he finished, Eirik could read the disbelief on their faces.

"Helvir was barely twenty years old when he passed," Olvir replied as he blanched. "He could have fathered a bastard but I have doubts."

"It doesn't matter. He must be stopped," Eirik replied as they stepped into the back of a cart, awaiting the snap of the driver's reins. Soon they were moving. "How did Captain Dylan receive bad orders?"

Valgard scratched his beard. "From above."

Eirik raised a brow. "What?"

Olvir sighed and reached into his robe, slowly withdrawing a small piece of paper and holding it out. Eirik accepted and unrolled it.

Captain Dylan,

Ignore your previous orders. The situation has changed. The landing point remains, but you are to take your men and march south along the waterfront until you encounter the tournament match.

By order of the Governor,

—Melkorka

Eirik read the note. He read it again. His hands shook and he forced himself to give the note back to Olvir. "All along... all along we thought there were spies amongst the servants... perhaps the nobles."

"But we never once thought to check the council," Olvir said. "Melkorka has been missing for the last few hours. We've had no choice but to detain all the menders and interrogate them."

Eirik's eyes widen. "You surely cannot mean—"

"No." Olvir shook his head. "There are limits. Anything worse than questions would destroy our standing with the Valka and endanger Strand. Still, this might not bode well with Arberrang. And none of them know where Melkorka has gone."

Eirik's head spun. There were so many details, so many elements of the mystery before them that he couldn't see the whole picture. Something was coming together, but he wasn't sure what. He knew he was close to figuring it all out. Melkorka was only another piece of the ever-expanding enigma.

As exhausted as he was, as angry as he was... Eirik had a fight ahead of him at the Ninth Pier. The wagon came to a halt. The three Guardsmen stepped out into the courtyard to face the assembled ranks of the City Watch.

If there is one good thing about taking the wet path, Runa mused, *it's that there's no need to keep quiet.*

The restless water splashed hard against the sharp, moss-coated stones and lapped against the rotting boards that paved their way. Runa wished there was another route, as the conspicuous varl were likely to be spotted. Yet she could think of no other alternative. Olaf and Ulfvalgr cautiously followed her sure-footed steps from afar, with Arnbjorn in the middle and Stefnir just behind her. To their right, Magnus' ship rested alongside the dock. Its name, *The Destiny of the Weak*, was carved on either side of the bow.

Looking at the vessel conjured foul memories and Runa cursed inwardly. Being around Stefnir was beginning to make her wish for that old life in the village again and the peace that accompanied it. The reminder of everything she had lost stoked the rancorous fire she felt for Magnus. The cold whisper of revenge cooled her rage and brought her mind back to the task at hand.

"This ship is far larger than any I've ever seen," Olaf said. "Where are we going to find Magnus on it?"

"It has several layered decks, like stories of a home. But I have a pretty good idea where we'll find him once we're aboard," Runa replied. She stopped before a corner. Around it, she knew there to be some steps carved in the stone.

Runa peered around warily. Her eyes narrowed as she spotted something red glowing in the dark. Distant lightning illuminated a lone sentry leaning against a post halfway down the stairs, smoking a long pipe.

Runa turned to her comrades and put a finger to her lips, drawing a javelin. She waited until the waves receded noisily and then spun about the corner, twisting her whole body to hurl her weapon.

The javelin found its mark with a wet thud and she waved them on. As she passed the dead man, she wrenched it free of his skewered neck.

"—ants to know how long it'll be. She's gotta be gone before the storm strikes."

Runa paused and held out her palm for the others to do the same. Despite the sea battering against the rocks, she still managed to hear the speakers, even barely so.

"One more load and we're finished sir," another worker said. "The other carts are already underway."

"Excellent. I'll have the deckhands prepare the oars."

Runa waited with bated breath as a thug walked past the top of the stairs. When he had disappeared, she turned to the varl and drew another javelin. "We have no time. They're leaving in a few moments."

"Let me lead then," Olaf volunteered. "Stay behind me and keep close. Runa, kill any horn-blower you see. It's too early for any alarms."

Runa nodded as she stepped down and slipped passed the varl. Olaf lifted his shield and Runa couldn't help but notice the unpainted replacement board the varl had nailed in place. Stefnir nestled near her, ready to block any incoming arrows with his shield.

Olaf ran to the top of the stairs, the others rushing behind him.

Almost immediately they came across a sentry. He yelped in alarm as he was slammed with Olaf's shield, knocked from the pier and sent tumbling into the depths.

With the threat dispatched, the companions ran down the docks, the varl's weight stammering the boards with each footfall. No one seemed to notice them yet. As they stepped on the gangway, a deckhand glanced their way from a bundle of ropes and went for his horn.

Runa pushed Stefnir down as she launched her javelin. It sailed steadily but a stiff breeze caught it and fouled her aim, sending it through his shoulder rather than his heart. The deckhand dropped, his horn clattering against the floorboards.

The wounded man tried to reach for the signaling device but Ulfvalgr intercepted him. He tried to shout as Ulfvalgr jerked his neck, which sounded of an egg cracking. The varl tossed the fresh corpse over the railing, sending him to join the sentry in the bay.

The topmost deck was clear. Runa realized that Magnus had not expected anyone to infiltrate this close to the ship.

"Where do we look?" Stefnir asked.

"Captain's cabin below," Runa declared, making her way towards the stern. They found stairs that led down, the varl dipping their heads to keep their horns from being caught by the overhead rafters.

As they descended they heard the din of working laborers towards the bow, far enough away not to notice the interlopers amongst their midst. Olaf risked a glimpse around the bulkhead and watched with suspicion. He waved his friends towards the captain's quarters after a moment.

Arnbjorn and Stefnir took either side of the door with Runa in the center. The varl stood just behind. "It'll take too long for Olaf and me to get in there," Ulfvalgr said. "We'll cover the escape. You three will grab him."

Arnbjorn smirked at Stefnir and Runa. "Ready children?"

Runa scoffed. Stefnir shook his head and raised a foot. Arnbjorn did the same. As one, they kicked.

The door swung outward, splinters flying free of the jamb. In the cabin, a figure turned from a desk where a helmet rested. In the soft candlelight, they could see the plated armor over his shoulders and back.

"Who the faen...?" He asked.

"Magnus of the Vak'auga," Stefnir said as he entered and slipped to the side. Arnbjorn followed and went opposite the boy's lateral step, as Runa covered the rear.

Even in the dim light Runa instantly recognized the warlord's face. Scars ran under his right eye. He possessed a large, bulbous nose and ruddy cheeks with thick stubble. His snarl bore yellow teeth.

"I know you, pig," Runa spoke through bared fangs. There was no question it was him.

"And I don't know you," Magnus replied, drawing the sword from his belt.

"Wait…" Runa said as it dawned on her. That detail was wrong. Her memories always portrayed the horned warrior carrying an exquisite axe, carved and marked with totems and war trophies. He was no swordsman.

"The faen are you waiting on?" Ulfvalgr inquired from the door.

"Ulfvalgr," Olaf said.

"What, dammit?"

Magnus' sneer turned into a smirk. Runa couldn't resist turning around.

Between the varl, she saw another figure. He too was dressed in plated armor and a horned helmet, and through the helm's opening she could see features that mirrored the very man whom they had cornered. An axe, the very axe from her memories, was in his meaty fist.

"Two of them?" Ulfvalgr gaped.

"Intruders!" the axe-wielding Magnus screamed. "To arms! To arms!"

Runa turned back as Stefnir took off running towards the first Magnus. The warlord had slipped behind his desk, grabbed his helm and pulled a chain. Through the window, a rope ladder descended outside his cabin. The warlord deflected Stefnir's blade with his own and twisted to leap through the pane, shattering and raining debris into the sea as he caught a rung and began ascending to the stern deck.

"Dammit!" Runa cursed.

"Runa, Stefnir, go after him! We'll get the other one!" Arnbjorn commanded and ran back through the doorjamb to join the varl. Runa obeyed, rushing to the window where Stefnir grabbed the swaying ladder to give chase. She held the ropes so he could find footing.

Once he had made some headway she began to follow. As she climbed she swore she heard a distant horn despite the whistling wind and waves that rocked the vessel. They crested the railing of the stern, and Stefnir didn't bother to turn and assist her. As she clambered aboard, she paused, stunned.

A fire had broken out over Ninth Pier. Against the flames she saw men crossing blades and heard the chorus of battle. Someone else had come in force for the Vak'auga. Runa didn't understand, until for a moment she saw a distant cloaked figure taking his two-handed axe to a Vak'auga goon. A heartbeat later, she saw the sigil of the City Watch on one of the attackers' shields.

Shaking off her shock, she chased Stefnir. The boy put a foot against the port-side railing and leapt to the wharf below. Briefly, Runa feared he would tumble over or break something. Instead Stefnir wisely dropped and rolled on landing.

As she neared the railing, she noticed a Vak'auga raider charging her right. She drew a javelin. The man instinctively raised his shield high. Runa's missile sailed low, plunging into his leg without resistance. As he reactively dropped his guard Runa skipped forward, drew her knife and sliced. Blood sloshed against the deck as her dying attacker fumbled feebly at his ruined throat.

Sheathing her weapon, she couldn't help but wear that wicked grin of hers. The spear-low-slice-high trick never got old.

Careful not to slip on the fresh blood, Runa vaulted over the railing and carefully scuttled down the netting, unwilling to take the same risk Stefnir did. But when she neared the dock she dropped, bending her knees as she landed.

Rising, Runa saw Stefnir engaging Magnus alone. The Vak'auga leader had rounded on the boy after realizing he was the only pursuer. One look at the deepening notches in the boy's shield proved he had but moments before Magnus ended the mismatched duel.

Runa advanced cautiously. Stefnir's unskilled footwork showed as he bobbed and weaved and spent too much energy trying to stay out of Magnus' sword reach. It was too easy to strike the unwary boy. Yet if she didn't do something, Stefnir would be dead. And her chance of catching *this* Magnus could be gone.

She picked her moment. Her throw was reflexive and she didn't feel the javelin leave her grip.

The flying weapon grazed Magnus' bare left shoulder, scoring a thick red line through the meat, debilitating but far from lethal. Magnus glared with a sneer as the blood gushed freely.

Runa smirked and clenched her fists, anticipating victory.

Stefnir's inexperience slew her hopes however. The boy foolishly gaped at her appreciatively.

"Stefnir, turn around!" She screamed.

It was too late. Magnus recovered and swept his blade across in a backhanded motion. Stefnir managed to lift his shield, but the force of the warlord's attack sent him stumbling off the dock planks. On the slippery rocks Stefnir tumbled, unable to remain upright, and plunged into the ocean.

Runa's eyes shot back to Magnus. She went for another javelin. As she did, Runa saw him raise something from his back.

She twisted and threw herself down as a throwing axe spun towards her. She felt the air whoosh as the blade passed her head, but mercifully felt no kiss of cold metal. Landing roughly, she realized Magnus stomped towards her. Another flash of lightning made his sword gleam. Runa reached for her javelins.

The pouch was empty.

Her javelins had scattered after her fall, pitched over the wharf's edge. Cursing, she drew her dagger...

"Oh, I remember you alright! It was my brother's fool idea to give you to Leiknir," Magnus boomed. "I'll dice you into chum, little girl!"

Runa swallowed. She was a killer of renown; no one could throw javelins like her or find the way to a man's throat as she could. But Magnus was something else. She had seen the warlord fight before and knew no weakness in his technique, not that a dagger could hope to match a longsword in a fight. If he was unaware maybe she could slit his throat, but Runa couldn't match him face-to-face.

No matter how she envisioned it, she knew this was a fight she could not win.

As her thoughts turned to escape, several figures crept forth from the fiery pier. A brief glance revealed Vak'auga, trying to return to the ship and cutting off that route in the process.

She knew to remain would be death. And her vengeance would go unfulfilled.

Runa cursed and did the only thing she could think to do. Spinning her torso, she cast her dagger at Magnus. The warlord swayed to avoid the blade which chimed harmlessly off his armor. While he was distracted, she sprinted and threw herself into the sea.

Chapter 20

Eirik cursed while a few City Watch and Governor's Guardsmen took a knee at the edge of the waterfront, drew their bows and fired. *The Destiny of the Weak* completed hauling anchor as long oars pushed it away from the shore. If it hadn't been for the chaos of released slaves confusing and slowing them, the City Watch might have been able to board the ship in time.

"There's nothing we can do to catch it?" Eirik asked as Steward Olvir stepped up from behind.

The steward shook his head. "The storm will be here before we can get a vessel in the water. But they'll be fortunate if they're not dashed against the rocks before they reach Denglr's Bay."

A powerful wind whipped and whistled through the air, carrying large flurries. The gale threw the aim of several bowmen and was frigid enough that Eirik had to draw his cloak about his face. When Eirik regarded the vessel again, he noticed a large hole in the bow of the hull just below the topmost deck but well above sea level.

Eirik tilted his head at the sight of the damage. "What the faen caused tha—"

"Guardsman Eirik!" A watchman cried over the gale from farther down the cliff, where the land sloped closer to the waterline. "We have a situation."

Eirik stepped in the messenger's direction. "Can you elaborate?"

"A pair of varl and a man who won't throw down their weapons. We don't think they're Vak'auga or Mársmidr since they asked for you by name."

Eirik took off running in the messenger's direction. "Stand down! Stand down *now!*"

He arrived on the scene to find several watchmen encircling Ulfvalgr and Olaf with Arnbjorn between them. They shivered and looked disheveled, wet from a plunge into the turbulent seas. Their shields and weapons were raised defensively. Ulfvalgr bore a plank impaled at the end of his broken horn, the panel's gray-brown surface glittered like a serpent's scale.

Eirik entered the circle and placed a hand on one of the watchmen's spear-shafts, forcing it earthward. "Stand down men. They're with me."

The watchmen withdrew their spears and dispersed. Arnbjorn's wrists flopped open-handed as he shook his head. "S-see? N-next time listen to me when I drop names."

"That's assuming I don't have you three thrown behind bars for a while," Eirik said, crossing his arms. "After what you've pulled, I might as well."

Ulfvalgr snorted and rested his war axe upon his shoulder. Arnbjorn turned his sight away and Olaf sagged as he spoke. "Eirik, we're sorry. We feared the City Watch would flummox this."

Eirik rolled his jaw, but felt some shame in the varl's words. "You were right to do so, I think. We've found out who the last traitor was, who tricked Captain Dylan into almost missing the tournament match."

"Who?" Ulfvalgr asked.

"Mender Melkorka. A senior adviser to the Governor. She gave bad orders and then vanished." Eirik's gaze narrowed. "We're still looking for her."

Ulfvalgr growled. "I can't believe your Governor trusted a mender of all people. They fiddle with Ingrid's runes, the very language of gods, and we all suffer for it!"

Eirik ignored the outburst as he examined the area, his brow perking. "Wait, where are Runa and Stefnir?"

Olaf paled a little.

"They're not...?" Eirik felt cold in his stomach. He liked the boy and respected the girl.

"W-we don't know," Arnbjorn spoke with a stutter, rubbing his arms to stay warm. "We got split up. Magnus... Magnus has a twin."

Eirik blinked, very slowly. "I beg your pardon?"

"We cornered Magnus, *a* Magnus, in the captain's quarters. But just as we took him, we ran into another Magnus. S-same armor, same helmet," Arnbjorn explained.

"But different weapons," Ulfvalgr went on when Arnbjorn paused to catch his breath.

"Runa and Stefnir w-went after the one in the cabin," Arnbjorn said, shuddering as a fresh blast of snow-speckled wind struck them. He continued after the gust had abated.

"Olaf, Ulfvalgr and I pursued the other one, but we got cornered when his crew arrived. So Ulfvalgr... improvised. Through the hull."

"Ah," Eirik said, touching a finger to his forehead while speaking to the varl. "You've still got a little bit of ship on your horns."

"What?" Ulfvalgr reached above and found the plank, his face turning beet red as he plucked it off. "So I do."

Eirik couldn't help but crack a weak smile which faded almost instantly. He suddenly noticed Valgard coming downstairs towards them.

"Any news?" Eirik called out.

"Most of the dead are Vak'auga. Some Mársmidr but not many."

"Valgard!" Olaf waved, a broad smile on his face. "You're alright!"

The Guardsman grinned but leaned forward to rub his injured back. "You guys are terrible at staying out of trouble."

"Valgard," Eirik quipped. "Ask the men if they've seen Stefnir or a girl amongst the fighting or the... the dead.

"And if they're not among the causalities, order the men to begin searching in pairs for them, Guardsman."

Eirik spun about. Steward Olvir perched on a boulder above them. A pair of Governor's Guardsmen stood at attention at his side, their rare metal shields gleaming with embroidery of flying hawks. Their swords remained in their sheaths, although gloved hands gripped the handles.

"Steward Olvir," Eirik breathed more than he spoke.

Olvir glared at the injured Guardsman. "Valgard, go and do your duty."

Valgard saluted the steward and ventured off. Olvir and his bodyguards rounded the cliff's slope and descended to the gathering. The steward scratched his white whiskers as he spoke. "So these are the varl you've risked life and limb to protect through these troubles, Eirik."

Eirik swallowed and remained silent.

"I think it's time," Olvir said as he perused Olaf and Ulfvalgr. "That you two told us just what the faen Freystein thinks is worth turning over half of Strand to procure. This city has never faced such turmoil in all my years."

Eirik studied the varl. Ulfvalgr sneered. However Olaf shook his head glumly. "Ulfvalgr... enough. Tell them."

Ulfvalgr growled, turned his head and spat. He snarled at them all, until at last Eirik noticed a hint of defeat in the giant's posture. The red-haired varl gritted his teeth as though the very act of speaking ached, as if every word was a struggle. "It's a shield. A gift from our god, Hadrborg. During the Second Great War, it was discovered by our king, Throstr."

Ulfvalgr jutted his jaw out defiantly as if he had already conceded enough. Olvir's eyes narrowed, and finally the varl continued. "The Gift of Hadrborg was said to be able to create new varl. With it, we could have... replenished, our numbers. Our race would not die at the end of our long lives. The gift rallied the varl, for the shield was more than a weapon against the dredge who came from the north. It was a promise, a future for all varlkind."

Ulfvalgr's words brought a chill to Eirik's bones that could not have been the wind or flurries. The facts clicked together at last. "That's it."

Everyone's attention went to Eirik, whose brow creased in worried realization. "Think about it! Everything! The varl bones in the warehouse. Gylfi making weapons too large for a man to wield, but definitely a good fit for a giant. Warlord Vilmundr and his visiting band. And now this boon, this blessing of Hadrborg. Don't you all see...?"

Olaf gasped. "If they show the power of the shield by conjuring new varl... they'll win Vilmundr's loyalty. Then Kjallak will likely be able to challenge Jorundr for the throne of Grofheim."

"Gods," Olvir said, his features aghast. "With him in charge of all varl, Nikolas the Beautiful will have both a powerful ally as well as a rightful claim to the governorship of Strand."

"And if the fight is nothing but a succession struggle, the capital of Arberrang won't be inclined to get involved." Eirik slapped his palm over his brow. "They'll hope to stay on Freystein or Kjallak's better side to maintain the alliance of varl and men. Except that Arberrang..."

"Is just a short march down Longhalr Road from Strand," Ulfvalgr concluded, a look of utter horror washed over his face. "But Olaf still has the seal that makes Hadrborg's Gift whole. So Freystein hasn't won yet."

Everyone faced Olaf. But the varl didn't say anything. He didn't need to. The look of pure despair that crested his countenance spoke volumes louder than anything he could have uttered.

Ulfvalgr seemed to try and disbelieve it. "Olaf... you, you do have it, right?"

Olaf's lower lip trembled pitifully. Until he found his voice and told them the truth.

The first thing Stefnir did after crawling on dry land was check under his tunic. Beneath his drenched shirt, the oddly shaped talisman pressed against his chilled chest. Assured he still possessed it, Stefnir shuddered from both the freezing dampness and relief. He was thankful to be out of the sea. Thankful to be alive. Thankful he still had the seal.

He rolled over on the cold-hardened sand and stared out over the sea's horizon. As he did, he noticed a strange shape in the water. For a moment he feared it was one of the gang members, perhaps thrown over and drifting his way. Stefnir had lost his shield and helmet in the ocean, but he had been quick and fortunate enough to sheath his blade before the tide battered it from his grip.

It took more than one try to rise to his feet though. His body was weakened from struggling against the waves, and he had barely managed to swim to shore. Eventually he stood and stumbled towards the figure in the water, drawing his sword and preparing to finish them off.

Until he spotted a white cloak and auburn hair on the interloper.

Stefnir stabbed his weapon into the beach and ran, splashing as his boots treaded the water. As he ventured deeper he could barely touch the seafloor with his toes. He persevered and grabbed Runa's shoulder, kicking outward as he tugged her to shore.

After his tenuous effort, he draped the girl's arm over his shoulders and walked her away from the rising waves. He realized the water was dragging his ankles and that the sea was drawing in on itself dangerously. He reached behind her knees, hoisted and cradled her then began to run to escape the undertow. A massive wave crashed down as he rushed farther up the beach. The rolling water missed them but propelled Stefnir along with a washing of foam.

He knew they were safe when he felt nothing but a gentle lapping beneath his feet. He set her down and put an ear to her mouth. She was breathing although her lips were blue. He placed a hand to her shoulder and began to rub it vigorously, hugging her body and trying to keep her warm.

Runa awoke with a sputtering cough. She expelled dribbles from her lungs, turning her face toward the sand. After a moment, her ragged breathing became steady.

Stefnir shivered. They were wet, and the snow was falling in earnest. The water felt as ice, and he possessed no means to warm them.

"Are you two alright?" A bashful voice asked.

Stefnir rose and saw an aging man staring at them. Over his shoulder was a set of nets; his clothing was nothing but patches. He wore a bent old cap at an angle from which wispy white hair sprouted from the hem, running down his thin face.

Stefnir cast a sidelong glance toward his sword, still erect in the sand nearby. He said nothing.

The old man, whom Stefnir guessed to be a fisherman, twisted and surveyed the horizon where black clouds gathered. He returned his attention to them. "Listen kids. Yer wet and it is frigid out here. It's about to get uglier. I don't know who you are, but I... I don't think it right to leave people to freeze."

Stefnir looked at Runa who quivered and couldn't focus, as though dazed. She eventually shrugged. Stefnir collected his sword from the shore and sheathed it. The boy figured that if he could take on Mársmidr swordsmen, then an aging fisherman was unlikely to cause much trouble. Stefnir slipped an arm under Runa's shoulders as she put one over his. They rose and began to follow the elderly man.

The fisherman's home was not far from the beach. As soon as they entered, the fisherman set to work lighting the hearth at the center of the single-room home, cracking flint against steel until a spark caught dried branches and began to smoke. When the fire finally came to life, he sought a pair of blankets from a corner and gave them each one.

Stefnir was instantly grateful. He knew that the fisherman had almost nothing. Yet despite this he drew a kettle and set it over the flame. A bottle of red wine was poured into the pot and a few spices were added. A few moments later, the sweet smell of mulled wine spread throughout the tiny hut.

"I'm sorry I don't have much," the fisherman smiled uneasily as he held his hands towards the warmth. "I don't get many visitors anymore."

They heard the sound of snow pattering against the stone streets outside. Runa huddled close to the hearth, holding the patchy blanket close to her shivering frame. "You're trusting to take strangers in."

The fisherman smiled sadly. "It would have been what I did with my life, if things went differently."

Stefnir waited. When the man said nothing more, he couldn't help but take the bait. "What do you mean?"

"Oh," the fisherman said, as though surprised anyone was interested in listening to him. He rubbed his palms together and sat back. "Well… I was raised in a village to the south. Closest city was um… Whithagr. It was on the sea too."

The wine bubbled slightly. The fisherman reached over for a trio of bowls and a wooden ladle that rested on a small cabinet near the wall.

"So we didn't get many visitors out there. It was pretty boring, mostly just fishing and trying to make lives for ourselves. But my mother, she loved telling me stories. Stories of the gods. Hridvaldyr. Ingrid. Radormyr and the Loom Mother." He sighed as he spooned the wine into the bowls and handed them to Runa and Stefnir.

"She loved telling me those tales again and again." The fisherman peered into his wine. "But of all the gods, I feared Marek the most. As any smart fisherman did."

He sipped. Only after he did, Stefnir tasted his drink as well. It wasn't the finest wine with notes of sourness, but the spices helped.

"Anyway… one day my dad gets into an argument with my mom when I said I wanted to become a priest. Or gothi, as we sometimes called them. To host and heal strangers, lead sermons in praise of the gods. To care for the sick and feed the glorious poor. And dad, he turns to me and tells me the gods are dead. And there was no more time for these silly stories." The fisherman gazed into the fire for a hard moment. "And it was time for me to face my fears and get on with my life because there wasn't another waiting for me after this one ended."

The fisherman's eyes lowered and he supped heavily of his wine. When he lowered the bowl, he ran a fist over his darkened lips. "So gods, who looked so much like men, could die like them too. But something bugged me about that. There were… so many gods. And every god is so different. So unique. What they did, what they lorded over."

The fisherman paused as the wind whistled by the shut door. He lifted a hand, with a thumb pressed to his curled forefinger. "They each gave something to men, and I began to wonder about it. Why would gods be so different? Each of them taught us a different way to live. Another way to look at life. A special view or way of thinking."

Stefnir couldn't help but watch the elderly man as he became spirited in his discussion. The fisherman pressed a finger to his cheeks, his mouth open. "What if that's all a god really was? An idea about how to live our lives? An avatar of who we aspire to be? Almost all of them appeared so human on the Godstones that my thought made so much sense... until..."

"Until you remembered the gods who were nothing like men or varl," Runa said.

"Exactly." The fisherman pointed at her. "Radormyr and Marek... maybe a few others. We are most certainly not in their image and yet they watched over us anyway. The mystery endured for me. Every time I tried to live my life like my father intended, I couldn't help but return to that mystery and wonder why. I guess that's why I'm here. Because they took the shapes of beasts... and the only purpose for the life of a beast is to live, as simple and pure as that. It was a lesson I hoped to understand."

They grew solemn a moment as the fisherman buried his chin in his palm as though lost in thought.

"The dead... god, varl, men... always try to teach us, even from beyond the grave. They always want to be remembered. For the songs to echo on. The tapestries to never come unwoven. For their stone carvings to never shatter. The security of knowing that there is one true immortality. One true constant in the world... that defies death and time. And that is our story."

Stefnir opened his mouth to say something, but he felt flabbergasted by the strange wisdom. He tried hard to wrap his head around the fisherman's words. As much as they seemed to make sense, his exhaustion and inexperience collapsed any understanding that he tried so hard to craft.

In the end, they dozed. The fire warmed and dried their clothes, and the strength ebbed back into Stefnir's body. At last he rose and helped Runa to her feet.

"I want to thank you for helping us," Stefnir said.

The fisherman waved it off. "Think nothing of it. Thank you for hearing an old fool's thoughts. Guess it sure beats talking to myself."

"I... what's your name?" Runa asked.

The fisherman's brows dropped, his mouth drawing into a line. "I'll tell you what. If we ever meet again, I'll tell you. And you can tell me yours."

Stefnir extended his palm politely, smiling. "I hope we will."

The fisherman shook his hand, grinning in return. Runa and Stefnir left.

Outside, the storm had long ended. A fresh dusting covered almost everything but was no deeper than one's ankles. The morning sun began to peak over the east. Stefnir and Runa rounded the hut and took to the streets. As far as Stefnir could tell, they were in the northwest part of Strand.

"That way?" Stefnir asked, pointing to what he guessed to be south.

Runa nodded and the two of them began to walk. The roads were empty. Several homes stood dark.

"Why do you think he was reluctant to tell us his name?" Runa finally asked after they distanced themselves enough from the fisherman's home.

Stefnir thought over his answer before speaking. "Maybe he... forgot his name."

Runa laughed.

"I'm serious!" Stefnir said with a grin, raising his opened hands defensively. "That man has probably lived on his own for years. A decade or two maybe. Shaping his life after the gods that hid and avoided men and varl."

They traveled in silence until Runa spoke, her voice strangely sweet. "Stefnir. Promise me that you'll never become like that."

"What?" Stefnir stopped.

Runa took a few more steps and then faced him. Her countenance was calm. "That you'll find a good wife, make a good living by hunting and farming. And have lots of kids. Because I don't think you're cut out to be a violent avenger."

"Oh what, you are?" Stefnir huffed angrily. "First Olaf, now you."

"First Olaf what?" Runa asked, her head tilting.

"Telling me that he doesn't want to see me fighting. That I should drop the sword and go make a new home." Stefnir shook his head and began to walk again. "Faen you both. Was this why you leapt into the ocean too? To make sure I was alr—"

"No."

Her response was instant but not harsh. Stefnir didn't doubt her sincerity.

She gazed at him and brushed her auburn hair from her eyes. "I tried to kill Magnus after you fell into the drink. But I slipped and lost my javelins."

"Sometimes I feel like we have the world's worst luck," Stefnir replied.

"I could believe it!" Runa's brow wrinkled from a worried expression. "By the way, the next time someone gives you an opening, use it to kill your foe."

Stefnir sighed, his cheeks warming from humiliation. "You're right. I acted stupid and should have used the advantage you gave me."

She shrugged. "We'll probably get another chance soon. Anyway, after losing my javelins, I got surrounded. I knew I couldn't best Magnus, not blade to blade. So I tossed my knife at him and followed you into the water."

"You really think you couldn't beat him?"

She shook her head. "Leiknir taught me to see things clearly, no matter what I want. No matter how badly I want to see Magnus' guts spilled. If I hadn't jumped, he would have handed me my own head and I would have died for nothing. I want to live to see that man suffer."

Stefnir's mouth twitched a little and he couldn't help but ask. "You love him don't you? Leiknir?"

Runa went silent a moment, focused on the frosted street. "I do. I never… admitted it to anyone. I never wanted anyone to know— least of all Eirik— that stabbing Leiknir's heart might as well be ripping out my own."

A little smile crept on Stefnir's face. "You know. This is the closest thing to human I've seen you since I came here."

"Well hey, you got to thaw your heart sometimes." Runa gave him a wide-eyed look and stuck her tongue out at him.

Stefnir laughed. But when the moment passed, a well of guilt sprouted within him. They carried on solemnly before he spoke again. "I hated you for making me remember my mom, for making me wonder if she was better off dead than… whatever happened to you."

Her head bobbed as though considering this sentiment. "I hated you for reminding me of home and everything I lost. I think it made me detest everything and almost everyone worse than ever before."

"Well when this is over, you're going to make Leiknir one amazing wife," Stefnir said with a hint of sarcasm. "I mean, with all your javelin skills, you clearly aren't going to let his stomach get any smaller…"

Runa punched him in the shoulder, her uncontained smile huge. "You are such an arsehole!"

Stefnir guffawed and she joined him in the revel. Their laughter died as a figure dressed in black stepped out of the alley before them, a blade in hand. Stefnir went for his sword, but realized other figures surrounded them from behind, their shields bearing marks of skulls over anvils or skeletal hands grasping crowns.

"Why hello there," Skoegir said, a smirk spreading over his face.

Chapter 21

"Still no sign of them, sir," a watchman reported, saluting Eirik. "We've had teams running up and down the shores all night and have found neither a body nor a soul who has seen them."

Eirik rubbed his exhausted eyes and looked with jealousy at Valgard. His friend rested peacefully beneath a thick blanket under the shade of a wagon canopy, alongside a few other Governor's Guardsmen. Valgard had needed to lay down when his back pain grew too strong and sleep found him soon after.

Valgard was not alone in this. Fearing the search could take until morning, Olvir had ordered several of the Guardsmen to grab a few hours of rest while the remainder took to the shores. Thus far, half the City Watch who accompanied them had been sent back with prisoners to recover, being replaced by fresher men.

"Any word from the naval captains about the fate of *The Destiny of the Weak*?" Eirik asked as he reluctantly tore his sight from the cart.

The reporting watchman shuffled his feet around. "No sir. Magnus' ship hasn't been sighted, but neither has any debris. The commander of the seas is beginning to believe that Magnus has escaped through Denglr's Bay entirely."

"If no sign is found by nightfall, have them call off the search," Eirik replied.

The watchman saluted again and ran to attend to his duties. Eirik passed the wagon and walked down the streets on the edge of the shores, approaching Olaf who was seated in the cold sand. The varl peered at the eastern morning horizon as though in a daze.

Eirik could hear Olaf's soft wheezing. As the varl slowly raised his head Eirik's way, the Guardsman could see purple bruises along his neck. After Olaf admitted to giving Stefnir the missing piece of the heirloom, Ulfvalgr had tried to kill him in a fit of rage, grabbing and choking his kendr with his bare hands.

It had taken Arnbjorn, Eirik and the two Governor's Guardsmen to pull Ulfvalgr from Olaf, whose face had gone blue during the attempt. The red-haired varl thrashed and fought, as Olvir called for more men to pin him down. It had taken a plea from both Eirik and even Olaf, of all people, for Olvir not to arrest Ulfvalgr.

"Ready?" Eirik asked.

Olaf nodded and slapped a hand to his knee, rising. Eirik pulled a rolled parchment from his satchel and opened it. It was a map, a rough sketch of the neighborhoods and streets that pinpointed the households whose occupants they had yet to ask. Or kick down the doors and investigate the hard way. It was a slow, terrible approach that thus far had yielded strange results.

Most were family homes and the inhabitants had not seen anyone matching the description of Runa nor Stefnir. One man was violently resistant, and Eirik felt they had no choice but to ram the door open and inspect the premises. Stefnir and Runa weren't there. But the City Watch found three barrels of silver salts, a substance used to mask the scent of spoiled fish. When a few of the City Watch recognized the owner for selling poisonous "fresh catches" in the city's eastern forums, Eirik ordered his arrest.

"One more block, and we'll get a few hours of sleep if we can," Eirik said.

"No." Olaf's voice was weak from his injuries and sounded raspy and fatigued.

"We've been on our feet for a day and a half, Olaf," Eirik said. "We need to rest or we'll be worthless in the fight to free them."

Olaf didn't say anything, but nodded.

As Olaf and Eirik neared the next city block, Eirik noticed Ulfvalgr and Arnbjorn amongst a few other Guardsmen just farther down the street. The watchmen accompanied Ulfvalgr both to assist him during a fight and ensure that he did not run off. Although Olvir permitted him and Olaf to participate in the search, the steward's terms were strict to the point of inefficient. If they stumbled across a gang stronghold by accident, Ulfvalgr would be quite the boon. But giving him an escort reduced the ground they could cover.

Olaf stopped as Ulfvalgr faced him with narrowed and accusing eyes. Olaf tried to match Ulfvalgr's hateful glare as long as he could, but eventually cast his gaze down.

Eirik gently touched on Olaf's arm in a consolatory manner. Olaf didn't acknowledge it; instead he stepped beyond Eirik's reach. The Guardsman wondered if the varl, with their incredibly long memories and lives, ever forgave one another.

Eirik shook off the thought and returned to the search.

Their wrists had been bound with rope and, of course, Stefnir's sword had been taken. As they were frisked, Skoegir found the amulet under Stefnir's shirt. The boy kept a calm face, though he feared the game was over. Instead of taking it, Skoegir wore a look of disgust. "The faen is this ugly thing?"

Skoegir didn't see Stefnir breathe easier when the crime boss dropped it back under his tunic. Yet when one of their captors tried to "search" Runa's underside, she had responded with a knee that nearly found its mark.

"None of that now," Skoegir said to the struck man as he danced away from Runa, uttering promises of violence towards her. "These two have firmly pissed off every one of the bosses. They'll want to tenderize this fresh meat themselves. Now, no more mistakes. Blindfold them."

They stumbled along unable to see, as Skoegir's men pushed them down paths unknown. Stefnir tried to keep track of the directions they went, the sounds and the smells, but it was all unfamiliar to him. Until at last they felt wood creak beneath them, and they were marched upstairs where they were each tied down to a seat. Only then were the blindfolds removed.

Stefnir recognized one of the men present as the same who led the attack on the Great Hall. He was there during the ambush at the lumberyards as well, though Stefnir wasn't sure if he had overheard his name. His attractive countenance was ruined by a slowly healing cut across his cheek.

"I ask for the bulls and all you bring me are the calves," the man said, drawing a knife from his belt.

"You'll hold, Nikolas." Skoegir sneered at the man contemptuously. "He belongs to Freystein. And Magnus wants the girl."

Nikolas pointed the blade at Skoegir. Stefnir caught a glimpse of something in the insulted man's pupil and began to think him truly mad. "Who the faen are you to order me around?"

Skoegir laughed.

"He's done more right than you," a booming voice sounded from behind Stefnir. He and Runa tried to twist about to see who it was but their restraints prevented them. A Magnus stepped out from Runa's left, and another from Stefnir's right. They held their helmets under an arm and still wore their armor, each of which bore marks of battle. The one near Runa sported a bandage across the shoulder where she had nearly skewered him.

"You failed to capture them at the Great Hall despite being so close," one of the Magnus brothers said.

"And then you failed at the lumberyards despite everything being in your favor," the other twin added.

"Oh, like you two have any reason to brag." Nikolas spat on the ground. "Fetch a little mead, smuggle in some goods. Throw a few coins at the right people and drop some varl off so they could march into Strand without being connected to you. And when you actually needed to perform some heavy lifting, you let Ulfvalgr and Olaf get away!"

Stefnir saw one of the Magnus twins twitch, and the two of them slowly reached for their weapons. Everyone halted at the sound of heavy footsteps falling on the staircase, before a burling feature ducked its horned head to step inside the chamber. Brushing his dark hair behind his shoulders, Freystein stood taller than any of them.

"We've all failed in some way," the varl said, his deep voice silencing the others. "But Magnus bears no blame. They ambushed him, and the blood of his Vak'auga and the City Watch alike was spilled."

"This entire plan will be for naught," one of the Magnus brothers said, putting a fist against his hip. "Those varl are in the hands of the City Watch, and the meeting with Vilmundr is tonight. Can't we forge the missing piece? Or try to do without it?"

Freystein shook his head. "Vilmundr is a veteran of the Second Great War. He witnessed the shield Throstr held in the height of his glory. He will know a fake and doubt damaged goods."

"So what do you want done?" Skoegir asked. "Cut them up and get them to talk?"

"I suppose torturing women is your specialty, Skoegir," Nikolas baited.

Skoegir gave the upstart a look, but a Magnus raised a hand. "No need. Fiske! Bring him in!"

Freystein stepped away from the door as Magnus' henchman dragged in a fat figure, forcing him to his knees. Fiske grabbed a handful of thinned hair and yanked his head back, revealing a face ruined by cuts and swollen, bruised flesh. Runa immediately sat up, a look of dismay passed over her features as an anguished cry escaped her lips. "Leiknir!"

"Runa," Leiknir moaned the name, a trickle of blood escaping his split mouth.

Freystein gave the Magnus twins a perked eyebrow. "This… is your man, isn't it?"

"A traitor," one of them said. "We think he revealed the warehouse where we stored the varl bones. And was no doubt feeding the City Watch information about us."

"But this one," the other brother said as he gently stroked Runa's cheeks. "This was a gift I gave him almost a year ago, something fresh and warm to keep him loyal to us. She loves him."

Runa rapidly chomped at Magnus' fingers. Stefnir heard the audible snap of her teeth clicking. Magnus pulled his touch away and responded with a backhand that snapped her face about, leaving a red mark.

Anger rose in Stefnir. But the boy knew he was powerless.

"So we torture Leiknir until the girl talks," the Magnus who had struck Runa said.

"And if she fails, we torture her until the boy talks," the second brother said. "Meanwhile, you can demand an exchange with the City Watch."

"Mm," Freystein scratched his chin. "So let's have it then. Either of you two. Ulfvalgr hid something I want…"

Stefnir gulped. He cast his sight at Leiknir, who breathed gasps through his mouth while Fiske grasped and held him by a braid. The spymaster's eyes darted between the boy and Runa, pleading and helpless all at once. Runa bit her lower lip, her face turning flush with anger and perhaps embarrassment.

"An object. About the size of a man's fist. Carved with an image of Hadrborg himself, sticking out his tongue with an angry face," the varl crime lord continued.

"Wait, boss!"

Stefnir felt his entire body go cold when Skoegir spoke. The boy tried to shuffle and fight against his restraints as Freystein's underling grabbed his tunic and reached inside with a black-clad hand. Following Runa's example, Stefnir bit Skoegir's forearm. But the man retracted the item anyway and struck the boy for his insolence. Stefnir spat blood on the aging floorboards as Skoegir presented the fetish to Freystein.

The joy that spread across the varl's face and echoed in his laughter was the second most crushing moment of Stefnir's life, and was so connected to the first; the death of his mother.

"Yes!" Freystein took the amulet from Skoegir, throwing his head back in a victorious roar as he raised a clenched fist towards the ceiling. "Yes! Well done, Skoegir!"

Skoegir grinned and slightly bowed as Nikolas glared at him with pure hatred.

"Tell me boy!" Freystein boomed as he beamed at Stefnir. "Ulfvalgr would never have given this to you. Too much hate in that one to trust a man. It was Olaf, wasn't it?"

"Was it worth it, Kjallak?" Stefnir couldn't help but demand, his tone full of anger. "All the lives, all the people who died, just so you can get your mitts on this? The faen does it matter? Vengeance against Torstein? Gold?"

The triumphant expression seemed to vanish from Freystein's face. In its place Stefnir saw something sad and distant. "Boy, if I told you… I doubt you'd believe me."

It was the sincerity in Freystein's voice that disturbed Stefnir the most.

"Lord, what do you want done with this one?" Fiske asked, jerking Leiknir's neck and earning a moan.

The brothers exchanged looks, wearing dark smirks as they began to draw their weapons.

"Hold," Freystein said. "The plan still needs all of us to work, and the near decimation of the Aetla Hilmir was quite an injury heaped with insults. Leiknir has betrayed you, yes. But none have suffered more than Nikolas. Perhaps letting him have the honors will assuage some damaged pride?"

The brothers glanced at one another again, clearly reluctant to allow an outsider to carry out their vengeance. But they nodded, returning their weapons to their sides. "Nikolas," one said, "If it would help maintain our friendship…"

The beautiful man flashed a sneer that was equal parts amusement at the suggestion of bloodletting and satisfaction that the Magnus brothers were humbled. Instead, the man sheathed his knife and dusted off his tunic. "You are all correct. The deaths of so many of my men have led to bad blood between us. Still, if I am to be Governor of Strand, I must do more to control my anger and maintain alliances. Leiknir has betrayed your confidence. Justice is yours to administer."

"No," Runa breathed.

The Magnus twins bowed to Nikolas and drew their arms as they stepped forth. Fiske skipped back as the brothers finished the task their torture began. One Magnus slipped an axe across Leiknir's neck, slitting the edge across his throat from ear to ear while fresh blood cascaded down his tunic. The other stabbed his heart with a squelch, the sword slipping through the spymaster's ribs to find the beating organ. Crimson spurt on the Magnus' forearm.

All Stefnir could feel that moment was Runa's pain. She leaned forward in her chair, her face flush from screaming. The frustration felt palpable and real as Runa's love fell to his side in a spreading pool of his own blood. Leiknir breathed like a fish out of water. Stefnir could see the spymaster mouth something to Runa, unable to utter words. Until at last he laid still.

"Such is the fate of traitors," the Magnus brothers said in unison over Runa's sobs.

"What do we do with these kids then?" Skoegir asked, stepping away from the encroaching blood.

Freystein rolled his shoulders in a shrug. "Leave them here under guard for tonight. If something does happen between now and our meeting, we can use them as leverage. There's no sense in wasting a bargaining token."

"And after?" Skoegir asked. Stefnir could see the man's hand twitching beside his weapon. "I wouldn't mind trading them for Ottar."

A burst of cruel laughter rose from Runa and all turned to her. She scowled wrathfully with reddened eyes, her cheeks stained with tears. "Eirik and Arnbjorn turned him. He betrayed you, gave up Magnus' landing in exchange for safety and protection. So tell us again of this fate of traitors."

With that, she spat at Skoegir.

Mad grief on his face, Skoegir grabbed the handle of his sword. He drew half of it from his sheath when Freystein laid a palm on his lieutenant's shoulder, staying him.

"It is done, Skoegir. Ottar does not know of the location of our meeting tonight." Freystein considered the two hostages a moment. "We'll decide their fate after."

"The girl should be ours," one of the Magnus twins said.

"As she was property of Leiknir," the other added.

"We have guests to prepare for," Nikolas said, stepping forward. "And these two are going nowhere. Let us take our victory and deal with the petty details on the morrow."

"Aye," one of the Magnus twins spoke reluctantly. The other turned to Fiske. "Stash the body and have a few guards on watch, and keep loading the carts. You know where we're going?"

"Aye sir," Fiske replied.

All of the crime lords departed. Fiske grabbed the cadaver of Leiknir by the ankles and dragged him out. Stefnir could see the spymaster eerily staring at them as he left a trail of crimson behind him.

Runa shook and sobbed, but fought against crying. Stefnir turned as far as he could despite his restraints to examine the room. The attic was barren. Motes of dust fluttered in the thin sunbeam that poured through a broken shutter hanging over the room's sole window.

Stefnir started jumping about, trying to get closer to Runa. He nearly lost his balance and tipped over. After some maneuvering, he put his bound wrists against Runa's, back to back. Unable to see the knots, he fumbled about with his fingers, feeling the bindings and trying to visualize them.

"We're going to get revenge Runa," Stefnir cooed. "We're getting out of this, we're getting Ulfvalgr and Olaf, and then we're going to crush them all."

Runa stilled. Slowly, her fingers brushed over Stefnir's, who thought it was a moment of compassion, before they found his own ropes.

"A narwhal's horn knot," she said, her voice hoarse. "Pull the line underneath the bottom loop. The rest will make sense."

Stefnir remembered that as a fisherwoman, Runa must have learned a fair bit about knot tying. He found the spot she had mentioned and tugged. It did not undo the entire knot, but after a little fumbling he realized the complexity of the bindings had dropped considerably. Stefnir felt the rope loosen and give, the threads slipping away.

With her wrists freed, Runa turned her attention to the ropes about her ankles. As she neared her freedom, Stefnir heard the sound of footsteps coming upstairs again. Someone approached.

"Runa," Stefnir hissed. "The window. Go and tell the others."

"Don't tell me what to do," Runa replied as she stood, liberated. She sauntered to the wall and put her back next to the door, waiting.

Fiske entered and paused, staring dumbfounded at the empty chair and pile of slack rope. Runa stepped behind him and deftly snatched the dagger from Fiske's sheath. The henchman turned just in time to take the blade full in the throat as Runa rammed it through.

Fiske's lips turned blue as he ceased to breathe. His hands flailed as blood sprouted like a geyser from his torn esophagus. Runa snarled and jerked the blade out, reversed the handle and stabbed deep into his belly, ripping downward.

Stefnir winced and turned his head away as the stench of half-digested food filled the room. Fiske dropped to his knees, dying and unable to call for aid with his ruined diaphragm. Runa reclaimed the dagger from his gut and stomped toward Stefnir.

One glimpse at the fury in Runa's countenance put Stefnir on edge, fearing without rationale that she was about to deal him a similar death. The instinct died as she cut away the ropes about his ankles and wrists, freeing him.

Stefnir rubbed his wrists a moment, returning sensation to the skin. He spun towards the shutter and pulled it open as Runa examined Fiske's clothes for anything of value. Stefnir studied the shabby roof. It was covered in snow but seemed sturdy enough to hold their weight. He realized it would be a two-story drop, so he gathered the discarded ropes and began to fasten them together.

"Nothing on him," Runa said as she stood beside the door on lookout. "I should have kept him alive and questioned him about where they're meeting Vilmundr tonight."

"We can't do anything about it but escape and get help," Stefnir replied as he tugged, testing two combined pieces. Confident the twine was secure, he used one end to fasten the two chairs together and push them to the opened window. Climbing the seats, he stepped on the roof, bundling the rope in his hands to rappel down. Runa followed just behind him.

A little way down, Stefnir suddenly felt his purchase falter. He slipped and banged his knee against the tiles, biting his tongue to keep from shouting. Ice had compacted beneath the snow, and had he not griped the rope tightly he might have fallen. Changing his approach, Stefnir decided to crawl on his knees instead of his feet. Runa, having seen what happened, did the same.

As they neared the edge Stefnir peered over. Below, he spotted yoxen wagons being loaded with barrels and boxes of various goods by grumbling, rough-looking men. Changing his mind, Stefnir padded the roof towards another side. There the street was empty, the huts dark. Stefnir let the rope drop, took a deep breath and began to climb down, his feet against the building's wall. He kept his grip tight despite sweat dangerously spreading across his palm, until he safely touched down on the snow-coated ground.

Stefnir took a second to breathe a sigh of relief. He reached above and gently took Runa's hips, letting the girl slide down the rest of the way. The innocently intended assistance warmed something in Stefnir, but he ignored it and glanced around the corner at the carts.

"What are you doing?" Runa said. "We have to go."

"Remember what Freystein said. Something about how those carts are bound for the meeting place or where ever the triumvirate are next assembling. Maybe if I can stow aboard one of them and find out where they're going…"

Runa's eagerness suddenly shifted as she approached the corner. "Let me do it."

Stefnir shook his head, extending an arm to stop her. "You know Strand better than I. You need to run and get Eirik and the City Watch and lead them here. We can't risk me getting lost, or this will be for naught."

"Wait," she said, her brows lowered stubbornly. "I just had second thoughts. This is a bad idea."

"We're running out of time," Stefnir replied. "If they find Fiske's body and us missing, they'll take off immediately."

"How are we supposed to find you even if I lead them here?" Runa asked. "The snow tracks could easily be lost before we arrive."

"Give me your dagger and watch me." Stefnir couldn't help but smile as Runa hesitantly presented him the blade. Staying low, he surreptitiously moved towards the carts, pausing for a moment to hide behind a crate as two laborers carried a fresh haul from the house to add to the loaded wagons. When they re-entered the building, Stefnir snuck out from his hiding place and leapt into the cart, slipping behind a few barrels. He gently shook one and heard the contents slosh within.

"Last load," one of the laborers declared as they approached again and threw a shank of salted boar meat and sack of apples aboard. Stefnir held his breath, but none of the laborers noticed him.

As the workers rounded the wagon towards the driver's seat, Stefnir took his blade and pressed the tip into one of the barrels, exerting just enough pressure to make a hole.

A thin trail of mead began to trickle down, slipping between the cracks of the cart's panels and into the snow below.

Stefnir heard the snap of the whip and felt the cart shake and rumble as it began to move. He waited as the cart rounded the corner of the hut. There he caught a glimpse of Runa, who put two fingers towards her eyes and then pointed at the mead-stained road. She finished by flashing Stefnir a thumbs up. Small as the leak was, she had clearly seen the golden trail Stefnir had created.

"Follow the yellow snow," Stefnir whispered, feeling the edge of his lips turn a little upward.

Chapter 22

"Excuse me," Eirik asked an elderly couple walking past him. "Have you seen a boy and a girl come through here? The girl would have had auburn hair and a white cloak."

The old woman hugged a basket of market goods close to her chest and shook her head.

"I am sorry sir, we have not." The aged man put a protective hand upon his wife's arm. "We must be off. Another storm is on its way and we've dinner to prepare for the family."

Eirik sighed and waved them off. It was the afternoon and they had no luck. Two leads had proven false and while the sun was not yet set beyond the western horizon, gathering clouds had masked it anyway.

The sound of crunching snow caused Eirik to check behind him. Olaf approached, looking despondent though his voice sounded hopeful. "Any luck?"

Eirik shook his head. "The snow has kept people away from the forums. And with another blizzard on its way, the few open shops will close their doors soon. I had hoped for more of a crowd to ask."

Olaf groaned. "We've scouted everywhere in this neighborhood. I overheard Olvir mention something about calling off the search tonight."

"Yes, he did." Eirik swallowed. Another snowfall would destroy any tracks or trails and force potential witnesses to seek shelter again. With every hour that a City Watch patrol was dragged into the search, another neighborhood went without law and order. Soon every gang in the city would realize it and start carving out fresh turf…

And they were still no closer to finding Stefnir or Runa.

"I've failed everyone," Olaf said, his features appearing crushed while his shoulders shook. "I let Ulfvalgr down by losing the seal of Hadrborg. Stefnir and Runa are lost or dead. Arnbjorn will not avenge his brother and Strand is under a terrible threat. Eirik, I'm sorry."

Eirik put a hand comfortingly on the varl's forearm, unable to reach his shoulder. "Olaf."

The varl looked at him with red eyes.

"It's still too early to despair. This is our last chance to make a difference and stop Kjallak's plans. You cannot give in now," Eirik told him.

The varl said nothing, but glanced above Eirik's head. Immediately, his features brightened. "Runa!"

Eirik rounded. Valgard and Olvir neared with the disheveled girl between them. Her hair was frayed and her white cloak covered in dried blood, but she was alive and apparently uninjured. However, she seemed haggard and shrunken somehow.

"So she was telling the truth," Valgard said as he raised a hand.

Olaf stepped forward and scooped the girl into a massive bear hug. Eirik felt that something was wrong when the girl didn't smile, her visage as dour and spiteful as ever.

"Put me down," she commanded. "I'm alright."

"Where is Stefnir?" Eirik asked as he noticed the group of soldiers with Arnbjorn and Ulfvalgr coming toward them. Eirik called out to them. "We've found her!"

"We were captured," she explained. "And brought before Freystein, Nikolas and the Magnus brothers. They were about to interrogate us when Skoegir found the piece of the heirloom on Stefnir. They killed…"

Olaf put a hand to his forehead in dismay. Eirik felt his heart freeze as Runa choked, her face under duress as she tried to exert the words. The name took forever to come out.

"They killed Leiknir," she finished.

Eirik felt the chill pass over him. He hated himself for it, but the fear he felt was reserved for the boy's life, not Leiknir. "I'm sorry, Runa. And what about Stefnir?"

"Stefnir and I managed to escape. But he stowed away on a yoxen wagon bound for where ever they're meeting that varl… Vil… Vilm—"

"Vilmundr," Ulfvalgr said as his group neared. "And did you say they have the seal?"

"I'm afraid so," Eirik said, his heart sinking a little. "So our suspicions about the varl warlord were correct. Do you have a plan, Runa?"

She nodded. "Stefnir left us a trail from the house where they stashed us. I know the way back."

"Alright," Ulfvalgr slammed a fist into an open palm. "Tell you what Olvir, Eirik, I'll even let you bring the City Watch in on this one…"

"Not that you could stop us," Olvir scoffed. "But we have a problem. I've ordered half the Watch to return to the barracks and their regular duties, as we cannot leave Strand's streets without the presence of the law."

"I never thought I'd say this," Arnbjorn said, scratching just beneath his eyepatch. "But what about the other half of the Watch?"

"The rest are scattered in the search. And even when we get them ready, they'll be exhausted and dead on their feet. We played our strength yesterday and dwindled what we had today." Olvir grunted, rubbing his chin. "We have all of Strand's finest at our beck and call and no time to ready them."

"Dammit." Eirik growled. "So it's just us and whomever we can muster. Do you know when this meeting is taking place Runa?"

She shook her head. "Tonight is all I heard. We have to go now or we may miss our only chance at turning this around."

Olvir turned to Valgard. "Have a runner inform the Watch that the search is over. Send back the exhausted units and get me anyone fresh. Have them arrive here and await a messenger to lead them to this meeting."

Valgard saluted and took the three watchmen who were part of Ulfvalgr and Arnbjorn's squad. He delegated duties and set each man running off to complete his assigned task.

"You're coming too, sir?" Eirik asked.

Olvir nodded. "This is the end game, Eirik. Our last chance to stop Freystein and Magnus. We either take them down tonight or we have lost Strand for good."

They turned to Runa. She put her hands on her hips, scowling. "I'll need something to slit Magnus' throat…"

Olvir turned and called out to Valgard, who was dashing away to obey orders. "And have someone get this girl a weapon!"

Dusk approached as the sky became a heavy orange. Just as Stefnir began to wonder if he would have to leak a third barrel, the yoxen wagon slowed and ceased moving. In the dimming afternoon light Stefnir peeked through the cracks of the cart's sides.

The wagon drew to a stop near some stone building. Stefnir could feel the cart shudder and hear the sound of snow compacting as the drivers exited. Stefnir's hand tightened about the handle of the dagger, prepared to stab the man if the boy was discovered.

"Faen, it's cold," one of the workers grumbled as he began to pull back the cart's tarp.

"Hold on," the other said. "It's starting to snow 'gain. We don't want no water getting mixed into the salts or the dry goods."

"Right," the previous worked replied. "We'll roll it over bit-by-bit as we go."

Stefnir breathed a little easier as they took a couple of crates from the edge of the cart and left, his presence still masked by the sheet over him. As he heard their footsteps fade, Stefnir peeked out from underneath to ensure the coast was clear before vaulting over the side and out of the cart.

Like the worker said, it had begun to snow. A light sprinkling fell upon an aging blóthus, a temple to one of the dead gods. Light came from the door, devoid of anyone's shadow. Stefnir scanned about and snuck towards one of the stained-glass windows along the side of the building. From a missing panel, he eavesdropped.

"I will require these benches cleared," the voice of an aging woman said.

"It will be done. And the components you requested for this have just arrived." Stefnir was certain it was the voice of Freystein.

"Good. Vilmundr is due here shortly and we must hurry," the woman said again.

Stefnir sank down again as the laborers came back. He hid himself beside a stone strut of the blóthus, waiting until the laborers took in the next load. Suddenly, Stefnir noticed the trail of mead he had made slowly being covered by the floating snow. At the rate it fell, his markings would soon be gone. Stefnir cursed.

"You two!" Nikolas called from the door. "One of you get Skoegir and have some of his men assist you. We haven't time to dawdle."

"Right," one of the laborers said. A moment later, he mumbled to his companion. "I seriously hope someone guts that arsehole before he becomes the new Governor."

"Likewise," his partner replied.

As soon as they were gone, Stefnir rushed towards the cart. The temple was surrounded by a wall. The boy was about to follow the track towards the exit, but as he passed the driver's seat Stefnir noticed a sheathed blade innocently hanging from a hook. He plucked the sword and retraced the wagon's path.

Stefnir came to a small stone bridge that stretched over a tiny stream, which had frozen over save for a thin trickle. Stefnir crossed over and neared one of the pillars. He was suddenly glad that Eirik had taught him some writing during their week of training.

However bad his "penmanship" was, Stefnir knew just enough to scratch "Eirik" against the stone, his dagger leaving a white mark against the rock. When he finished, he added an arrow pointing towards the blóthus.

The effort was harder than Stefnir thought it would be as he hacked the stone a few times to craft the desired effect. Originally he had thought to follow the trail back and carve more markers, but he began to think it a bad idea as it required too much time.

"What are you doing?" Someone boomed behind Stefnir.

The boy turned and saw a helmed and cloaked sentry approaching. The shield over his arm bore the mark of the Mársmidr. Stefnir saw the man pause and reach for his sword.

Stefnir kicked into a sprint, drew his blade in a fluid motion and slashed. His weapon bit into the sentry's shield, taking a chunk of wood with it. As the sentry got his blade out, Stefnir changed tactics and threw himself at the man, ducking the intended shield bash.

Inside the sentry's reach, Stefnir dropped his sword and hugged the man with one hand. The other planted his dagger in the sentry's kidney. The Mársmidr went stiff and Stefnir pulled the dagger along his oblique, the weakened blade breaking off somewhere under the ribs. The sentry dropped to his knees as the snow blemished beneath him.

Stefnir lowered the dying man carefully, steam rising from the inflicted wounds. The sentry shivered, his body in shock. With equal parts pity, fear and need, Stefnir dropped the dagger handle and snatched his fallen sword. He flipped the blade downward and grasped the handle with both hands. The boy forced himself to avoid the dying man's eyes as he thrust the sword into the sentry's chest, finishing the job.

Stefnir huffed hard. He felt nauseous but the sensation was not as horrible as when he slew the swordsman during the tournament. He forced himself to relax, knowing that to spare his foe would have been death. As he leaned back, Stefnir caught a glimpse of something.

Above the second floor of the blóthus was a horn tower. He stared at it a moment, the realization dawning on him. To sound that horn would bring the City Watch faster than slowly carved signs, as its massive size would undoubtedly be heard several neighborhoods over.

Working swiftly, Stefnir rolled the dead sentry over and began to unfasten his cloak. Taking and crunching bits of snow, Stefnir rubbed the compacted ice against the fabric, causing the blood to either freeze and come out or be diluted by water. Moisture could be explained, but blood stains raised questions.

When he finished cleaning it, Stefnir donned the cloak and took the man's helm as well. He slipped the sheath into his belt and slid his sword inside. Finally he picked up the shield and slung it over his back.

Grabbing the body, Stefnir dragged it towards the bridge. Only then did Stefnir remember that he could not hide the cooling cadaver under the mostly frozen water. Instead, he stashed it behind one of the bridge pillars, piling on snow to cover the corpse and hoping no one would immediately notice. Then he gathered the red snow and dumped it over the bridge, letting the trickling stream melt and carry the evidence away.

Content that the hidden body would raise no alarms for a while, Stefnir began to casually walk back towards the wagon. It was critical that nothing appeared out of the ordinary so he took a moment to regain control of his steaming breath, which was as visible as it was audible.

The sun was on the cusp of setting. Before the temple the two workers emptying the cart had become several and were nearly finished unloading it. Stefnir accepted a crate full of shanks of venison. The worker who handed him the box gave a small nod of respect. "Take that to the kitchen. Thanks for your help."

Stefnir nodded back and followed the others into the temple.

He entered the foyer, passing some dilapidated furnishings and religious paraphernalia. Stefnir almost stopped when he saw a decorative ball that wore the face of Hadrborg. Stefnir realized that the halls were large enough to accommodate varl and many of the seats were clearly of a size fit for a giant.

When Stefnir entered the kitchen however, he crossed into a scene of hot chaos. Dozens of worried men and women hustled furiously. The fires cast warm colors about the chamber, which bore a myriad of pleasant but confusing scents. As servants diced vegetables and fruits, whole boar and deer were butchered and pheasants plucked and alleviated of their feathers. Young girls wiped their foreheads as they ladled and stirred bubbling kettles that smelled of boiling soups, or shoved paddles bearing kneaded dough into a stone oven before retrieving hot, fresh bread. In the corners and exits, a couple of men bearing markings of the Vak'auga watched them all sternly. Stefnir suspected that these kitchen workers were likely slaves.

The boy kept his gaze away from the Vak'auga guards and set the box of venison down, which a couple of men wearing blood splattered aprons gathered and carried away to be prepared. Stefnir couldn't help but notice how they kept their heads bowed, avoiding him as they shuffled about, cowed.

Stefnir returned to the foyer but turned away from the entrance. It was critical he found a way to that horn tower. He took a right and sauntered down the hall until he heard the booming voice of Freystein. Panicking, Stefnir noticed a door to his right and entered the random room.

The room was lit by several candles along the walls. Stefnir didn't see anyone inside but he spotted three large bundles covered by sheets in the center of the chamber. When Stefnir heard Freystein's voice again, he anxiously looked about and noticed a chest in the corner. Stefnir opened it swiftly and checked for any contents. Finding it empty, he stepped within and knelt, lowering the top quietly.

"Are you certain that your men can pull this off?" It was not Freystein who spoke but an aging woman, almost certainly the same Stefnir heard earlier. Through the chest's keyhole, Stefnir saw a bowing, hooded crone shuffling into the chamber with an elegantly carved staff. He knew he had seen her somewhere before but couldn't place it.

"Of course Melkorka. I've had them practicing with weights and stilts for a month to master this puppetry. They are prepared for tonight." Freystein stepped towards one of the piles and pulled the sheet over. The rolls of the wrapping prevented Stefnir from seeing what they hid.

"Hmmm. Yes." The crone cackled. "That looks grand, Lord of the Mársmidr. You are a clever one indeed. I trust you will honor our agreement despite my son's behavior, of course?"

"Indeed. I need your son to claim the Governor's Seat and provide us his aide. You need me to place and keep him there," Freystein replied. "And I of course, assume you can provide what we require? Magnus obtained what you requested."

"Kings and Governors futilely ask menders to gaze into the future, make them fly or even live forever. Compared to that, a little light show is nothing," Melkorka said.

The sound of someone knocking on the door drew their attention away from the uncovered objects. Nikolas entered, dressed immaculately in a tunic and trousers stitched with gold lace, not unlike the varl. "Lord Freystein, mother. Warlord Vilmundr has arrived."

"Excellent," Freystein pulled the sheet over the pile again. "And the food?"

"The slaves Magnus provided us are quite skilled. Drinks and hors d'oeurves are ready. The rest of the courses will not be much longer," Nikolas replied.

"I'll have Skoegir and some men carry these to the sanctuary," Freystein said as he and Melkorka made their way to the exit, shutting it behind them.

Stefnir's curiosity peaked. Quietly leaving the confines of the chest, Stefnir made his way towards one of the piles and drew back the wrapping.

The boy leapt back in shock, barely clapping a hand over his mouth to keep from yelping.

It was the skeleton of a varl, carefully arranged and resting on what appeared to be a stretcher. Properly sized clothing covered the reassembled bones from skull to toe. Resting atop the rib cage was a massive blade, and finger carpals clasping the handle as though the giant was prepared for burial.

Stefnir studied the remains and realized that someone had constructed very fine hinges that connected the joints. Stefnir tried to lift one of the fingers but discovered that it unyieldingly gripped the blade. The other wrist moved freely however and Stefnir raised it, studying the neatly connected carpals. Unable to resist, Stefnir lifted the skeleton's shirt and found an array of straps and belts inside the ribs and along the arms and hips.

Boots clomping against floorboards outside alerted Stefnir, who pulled the shirt down and returned the sheet to its former position. He hurried back to the chest and managed to shut the lid just as someone entered the chamber again. In his haste, Stefnir had his back to the keyhole and couldn't see what was happening. He heard Skoegir's gruff voice well enough though.

"Two men carry each puppet. These go to the room behind the altar like we rehearsed. Once they're prepared, take your piss breaks and strap yourselves in boys…"

Stefnir heard a soft rattling and more booted steps. Soon the room was silent. Stefnir lifted the lid to peep and realized he was alone in an empty chamber. Slowly, Stefnir rose from the chest and moved to the exit, peeking through the door to ensure the coast was clear before stepping out. As he took a left down the hall, he came across a staircase that led to the second floor.

"We're losing it," Arnbjorn said, cursing to himself. The snow started to fall harder and the thief was growing fearful they would lose the trail.

A little earlier, they had found the home where Runa and Stefnir had been kept. Runa insisted they keep going but Olvir demanded a fast search for any clues that Runa and

Stefnir might have missed. They had found nothing save the bodies of Fiske in the attic and Leiknir in the basement.

The latter event prompted a moment of silence from Runa. And, as far as Arnbjorn could tell, one from a solemn Eirik.

"Are you actually mourning him?" Arnbjorn couldn't help but ask Eirik, incredulously.

"I don't know." Eirik tilted his head away. "All this time I spent hating him. And it turned out that the man was more genuine than I thought. I cruelly told him that it would take more than the gods could give to make me respect him. Now, he's with them. Leiknir played a dangerous game and lost. I hated him, but he didn't deserve this."

"He spoke highly of you," Runa said, not averting her grieving gaze from the slain spymaster. "He told me you came very close to catching him after the assassination attempt against Ragnar. Once, he said that if you two weren't enemies, you could have been the best of friends."

Arnbjorn heard the breath catch in Eirik's throat. The lawman put his back to them all, a hand covering the side of his face. After a moment, Eirik managed to talk with a level tone. "Runa, I'm sorry for your loss. But we must hurry and save Stefnir, or Leiknir will have died for naught."

Runa nodded, rising from the pitiful form of Leiknir's ragged remains.

As they exited the abandoned hideout, Olvir ordered one of the Governor's Guardsmen off to lead Valgard to the house. Soon they were on the trail but a light snow had begun to fall.

"Dammit," Ulfvalgr muttered. "We shouldn't have stopped. Hurry!"

Runa led them on as best she could despite the fading trail. However the snow and the foot tracks from unwary pedestrians had eroded the tracks and the mead stains until they could no longer find the path. Eventually they were amongst one of the quietest neighborhoods Arnbjorn had ever seen with nothing nearby except an old stone blóthus just a few blocks north.

"The trail is gone," Runa finally declared. "Since they were heading farther north, there can't be many places for us to check."

Olvir shook his head. "This neighborhood alone accounts for several dozen homes and halls. If they turned east, there could be hundreds of locations."

"And only seven of us to search," Olaf added.

"Six," Olvir said, turning to the remaining Guardsman. "Head back the direction where Valgard will be coming and lead them here. We need reinforcements nearby or we'll just be cut down if we find them."

"Sir," Eirik said as the other Guardsman departed to fetch the City Watch. "We cannot afford to wait for them."

"I know, Eirik! I know," Olvir put a hand to his face, grunting with exasperation.

Arnbjorn narrowed his remaining eye as he stared at a pillar next to a bridge. He could swear there was something familiar about the way the marks on the stone appeared, as though someone had been working to etch something on the surface. "Hey Eirik. Is that, um… is that writing?"

Eirik followed Arnbjorn's pointed finger and peered at the carvings. "Unless stones have suddenly started saying my name."

Eirik began walking in the bridge's direction when Olvir called out to him. "Wait for reinforcements."

Arnbjorn cast a hard, angered glare at Eirik and then at everyone else. Runa's grip tightened on a spear she carried, a smaller one over her back. Olaf drew his blade while Ulfvalgr choked up the haft of his war axe. When Arnbjorn looked back at Olvir, the old man blanched. "All of you, just hold on! If we run in there, we may spoil our only chance to capture them all. Guardsman Eirik!"

"Sir." Eirik coughed. "We need to scout the perimeter and assess how much time we have left. Also, I'm fairly certain I cannot stop the varl from charging in there and killing everyone they can."

"No offense," Arnbjorn added. "But it could be hours before the City Watch shows. And if they take too long, I might not get the chance to kill Skoegir."

"And I Magnus," Runa said.

"And reclaim Hadrborg's Gift," Olaf added. "And rescue Stefnir."

"And snap Kjallak's neck," Ulfvalgr said.

"If Nikolas is in there," Eirik replied. "I have to take him down. I'm sorry sir, but you can wait. We must go."

Olvir sighed and reached for his sword. Arnbjorn briefly thought the old man was going to take them all on, but instead he opened the satchel next to his sword handle and drew a piece of chalk. He tossed it to Eirik. "Mark that wall for Valgard, Guardsman Eirik. If we're going to do something stupid, then at least mitigate risk."

Eirik nodded and swiftly chalked the wall with an arrow, spelling out in white strokes something Arnbjorn couldn't really read. He knew enough to tell it started with V.

They crept toward the bridge carefully. The varl grunted and held their horns down beneath the stone walls as best they could despite their girth. As they neared the brook, Runa glanced over the corner of a pillar and faced them, whispering. "I think there's someone on the other side of the bridge, but they're hunched over."

"I'll check it out," Arnbjorn said and began a cautious advance. He crossed over the water and halted. On the opposite bank someone was hunched over, examining a leaning figure on the other side of the parapet. The latter shape was a body, bowing forth as though about to rise from a mound of snow. The other figure rose from behind the parapet.

Arnbjorn attacked.

Somehow Skoegir managed to get his blade up, blocking Arnbjorn's axe. As the two grinded their weapons together, a spear sped past Arnbjorn's head. It lodged itself in the neck of a man who stood beside Skoegir, his blade raised to chop into Arnbjorn.

Arnbjorn skipped back, creating space between Skoegir and himself.

"I can't tell whether it's grand or strange luck that I met you here," Arnbjorn said to the Mársmidr lieutenant.

"Oh, it's bad alright," Skoegir replied. He backed away, his attention elsewhere.

Arnbjorn heard the others encroaching from behind and thrust an arm out. "Stop! This one's mine."

Skoegir gave him a look of equal parts contempt and amusement.

"Arnbjorn," Eirik said. "We can't afford to leave him alive."

"This is between us, Eirik. I owe this arsehole for Johan's life," Arnbjorn said with a growl. When Skoegir chuckled, Arnbjorn spat in the snow. "I'm the one who sliced Ottar apart and maimed him, just as you did to me. I made him talk and rat you out, you milk gurgler."

Skoegir's smirk disappeared and Arnbjorn could see the rage building in the ugly man's visage. "Hallvard is right. This is between us."

There was a pause. Then Eirik and Ulfvalgr wished him good luck. He heard them all hurry off, never taking his focus away from Skoegir. The two of them had no more words for one another. There was nothing left to share but their hate.

Arnbjorn studied his opponent. Skoegir was in fighting shape, his leather outfit filled with a lithe, muscular form. He held his sword with two hands, his stance strong and ready. Every fighting instinct in Arnbjorn's psyche screamed that this was a fight he could not win. Skoegir was more experienced, stronger, in better shape and still had full sight and all his fingers.

The rational voice in his mind warned Arnbjorn that fighting Skoegir would cost him his life. Arnbjorn ignored his doubts.

Kicking snow, they charged each other.

Chapter 23

Stefnir stayed low on the catwalk above the prayer hall. The few times he had dared to glimpse down, he saw that the shrine's sanctuary had been transformed into a banquet hall. Long tables were decorated with food and utensils. A coal pit sat in the center of the room, the embers livid. Thus far, only servants had gone in and out of the chamber. Yet Stefnir could hear the laughter of approaching company.

At the far end of the catwalk was the ladder that led to the horn.

Crawling, Stefnir made it less than halfway across when the doors below opened. Risking another glimpse, Stefnir saw Freystein enter. The Lord of the Mársmidr led a gray-haired varl, behind whom trailed two giant bodyguards.

"Well! You've certainly prepared enough to satisfy Hadrborg's hunger," the elderly varl exclaimed after inspecting the prepared feast. "And here I was, fearing you'd spent so much time amongst men that you'd lost your appetite."

"Only the best for you and your varl, Vilmundr." Instead of offering his guest a bench, Freystein pulled one of the few, more ornate chairs from the main table. "Please."

As Vilmundr took his place, men began to gather in the dining hall. Before withdrawing behind the floorboards of the catwalk, Stefnir could see the Vak'auga slavers and Freystein's Mársmidr. Stefnir saw no sign of the Magnus twins amongst the congregation, but Nikolas appeared alongside Melkorka, escorted by a couple of men bearing shields of the Aetla Hilmir. All in all, Stefnir counted almost a score of heavily armed men.

"Where's Skoegir?" Freystein asked one of the Mársmidr.

"Checking on a patrol. A few of the men here will replace him shortly."

"Grab something to warm yourselves and replace him now," Freystein commanded. "I need him here."

Stefnir crawled on as Vilmundr spoke again. "Kjallak, I appreciate all this, truly. But I want to see it."

"Patience, Vilmundr," Freystein cooed. "I assure you, it works."

"I knew Torstein, Kjallak. Oh, he was a real stickler for honor. Whenever I suggested something more clever or crafty when fighting the dredge, he insisted on fighting them with the horns first." Stefnir heard Vilmundr laugh. "No. No, pup. Torstein threw you out and denounced you, his kendr, for a reason. And I suspect that it's because you're too smart for your own good. I'll not be hoodwinked. Show it to me. Now."

Everyone below went silent. Stefnir stopped, fearing they would hear his shuffling. He even held his breath. Over the edge of the catwalk, Stefnir could see Freystein face off with Vilmundr. The former rested his fists on his hips as his stormy features challenged the elder, who was nothing if not bemused as he popped a torn piece of bread into his mouth.

"So be it," Freystein declared. The varl stomped across the room, keeping a wide berth from the coal pit. As he neared the altar which stood underneath Stefnir, the boy heard a whooshing sound as though someone had rapidly tugged a sheet or tarp.

"The Gift of Hadrborg," Vilmundr said with reverence. "Bring it here."

At last, Stefnir couldn't resist spying. At the risk of being spotted, he leaned over and observed as Freystein neared Vilmundr. One of the warlord's bodyguards audibly awed at the sight of the shield. Yet with Freystein's back to Stefnir, he could not see it.

"Yes," Vilmundr said as he leaned on the table, keenly examining the details of the shield. "Down to the oldest scratches. This is Hadrborg's boon to Throstr. The salvation of all varl."

"I suppose then that you couldn't help wondering if it still works," Freystein asked.

"Of course it cannot. Hadrborg is dead!" Vilmundr slumped in his chair, his visage one of dismay. "Without the gods, the power in their gifts has waned. There is no way such an important relic could still bring new varl to life."

"But we," Melkorka declared as she stepped forth, snapping the butt of her staff against the floorboards. "The menders understand the words of the gods. The divine are dead no doubt. But there is still power in their names, in the air they once breathed, to again forge life itself."

Vilmundr glanced between Freystein and the old woman, then back again. "Impossible. Even the skillful Valka could not do such a thing."

"I forgive you for being mistaken, Vilmundr." Freystein began to turn. "You're old. And though the elderly are rarely wrong, it is either disastrous or fortuitous when they are."

Stefnir swore he could see Vilmundr bristle, but the aged varl kept a level tone as he replied. "Then I suppose you won't hesitate to show me, to show all of us."

"Not at all. Nikolas! If you would be so kind as to summon the components."

Nikolas bowed and ordered a dozen of the men to the altar. They passed beneath the walkway, directly below Stefnir. Unable to see them, the boy heard a door creak open. The men returned, each holding a handle of one of the three stretchers, clearly struggling with the weight. Stefnir's brow rose, as before only two men were required to carry the remains. Gently the bearers set the cargo down near the coal pit and stepped away.

Melkorka hobbled towards the pit as Nikolas set to work drawing the sheets away. Vilmundr and his varl gasped at the massive skeletons revealed.

Freystein held up a hand. "We are the children of Hadrborg. From the ice and earth we were formed, and to the ice and earth we return. You know that the cycle of life leads to death. And for every other living thing, death paves the way to new life. Our kind are the only exception to that rule. To see that truth laid before you can be shocking, but recall that these are the words of the god himself."

Freystein's statement seemed to calm some of the anger Vilmundr bore. The aged varl sank back in his chair with a contemptuous scowl, his arms crossed. "Proceed then. But this will bode quite ill for you if you are wrong, Kjallak."

Freystein nodded and turned to the assembled sets of bones. Slowly, he raised the shield. Stefnir beheld the details of a tower shield crafted of unknown metal, though trimmed with gold. The ugly face of Hadrborg rested in the center, its tongue sticking out almost mockingly. Freystein began to chant.

"Hadrborg, gone as you are, your power resides in your gift to Throstr. Hear me from the other side. Hear my pleas and know that your most beloved children wish to live on, that we desire the prosperity promised to all other livings things. Lend us your power, so that varl can endure eternally."

As he spoke, the shield began to glow.

Stefnir caught his breath, almost gasping at the sight before him. The golden trim shined with Aurelian luster. Stefnir couldn't be certain from afar, but it was as though runes written in light began to appear along the shield's surface, circling the centerpiece which began to radiate like fire.

The varl bones began to rise.

A cry of shock arose amongst all who watched. One of the skeletons stirred and moved, putting a forearm against its femur and forcing itself to stand. The others did as well, carefully rising to rigid attention.

And all the while, Stefnir couldn't help but notice Melkorka's lips softly moving. When she finally stopped, the glow coming from the Gift of Hadrborg ceased.

Vilmundr stood. His mouth gaped at what he saw, his features an unhealthy pallor. The chamber was silent as a tomb, until at last he managed to speak. "This, this is… unprecedented. Is it only within the shield's power to raise these… draugr?"

"This is only from a cursory study of the shield," Melkorka said, sagging meekly. "At first, we could barely get the bones to rattle. Now we can get them to stand and stay for a while, for our study is incomplete. There are many runes on the shield left to translate, but we are certain that the entire ritual of creation is there. With time, we can create flesh and blood…"

"So," Vilmundr relaxed a little, though he still wore a disturbed countenance to the revelations. "We can, in fact, revive our race."

As Stefnir scrutinized the skeletons, he noticed that there was a head of hair just between a collar bone and the shoulder blades inside one of their shirts. He doubted Vilmundr or anyone else could see through the ghoulish disguise. It was naught but a mummer's show.

The doors suddenly burst open and a man of the Vak'auga stood there, fidgeting with panic.

"Lord Freystein," the messenger said, his tone ringing with fear. "Steward Olvir has arrived with two varl and a couple of men. Our patrols are fending them off but cannot match them!"

"How?" Nikolas said, shock rippling on his countenance. "How many?"

"We count only five, but they are skilled!" The messenger gulped. "Several of our men have already been slain!"

"It does not matter how. It is. And even if there are only five, they must be a vanguard to the rest of the City Watch, who are undoubtedly on their way!" Freystein growled, his fist balling. He pointed at his championed heir. "Nikolas, take half the men and deal with the intruders. The rest of you, we will escort Vilmundr and Melkorka to safety. We must get away before they arrive!"

Stefnir knew that he had no choice now. Aid had arrived, but Freystein was preparing to bolt. Only one thing could stop them, could prevent them from fleeing, and it was not by blowing the horn of the blóthus. Stefnir rose and drew his sword, which hissed as it was freed from the sheath. Putting his hand on the balcony, he knew he had only one chance to get the drop right.

He vaulted over and plummeted below.

Stefnir crashed into one of the skeletal varl. The sound of its puppet master yelping from surprise shifted everyone's attention to the confusing spectacle. As they tumbled, the skeleton collapsed with a small cloud of dust and the crack of brittle bone. A short man of thickset muscle rolled out of the large tunic, wrestling with straps and belting over his limbs.

Stefnir leapt from the crumbling varl remains, grabbing onto the shield in Freystein's grasp. The varl held tight as Stefnir knew he would, and the boy stabbed hard into his forearm. Freystein roared as the blade took a healthy chunk of flesh from his wrist and relinquished his grip of the shield.

The first thing Stefnir realized as he fell to the ground was that the Gift of Hadrborg was very, very heavy. It took a strenuous act of balance and strength to arrest it before the armor fell flat on its face, or onto him. Stefnir's helmet tumbled off and rolled across the floor as the boy's head dipped too far. With one hand holding his sword upright, Stefnir dragged the tower shield back, scratching the floorboards as he placed his back to the coal pit, feeling the heat through his cloak.

Everyone was on their feet, weapons drawn and bearing faces with murderous motives. Freystein drew the hammer from his side, stomping forward with lethal intentions. Stefnir glimpsed into those eyes and saw a glimmer of utter madness; a touch of insanity mingled with quintessential rage. Stefnir heard the clash of swords and axes and suddenly believed himself caught in a war dream.

"I should have killed you, boy," Freystein muttered. "I should have *killed you!*"

"*KJALLAK!*"

Freystein froze as his true name was roared throughout the banquet chamber. His rage vanished as his countenance became one Stefnir could only understand as horror. The varl turned about.

Stefnir followed Freystein's line of sight and felt elation at the timely arrival of his salvation. Several Vak'auga were already down and Nikolas shuffled away from the united arms of Olaf, Eirik, Runa and an aged man that Stefnir did not know.

But at the heart of the group was a red-haired juggernaut, wielding a war axe. The hatred on his face was more becoming of a being of fire than ice, and he stomped forward with a rancorous leer aimed at the terrified Freystein.

If in their existence there was a god of reckonings, his avatar was Ulfvalgr.

Arnbjorn was losing.

Even if he still possessed his lost eye, he was fairly sure he wouldn't win. Despite Skoegir's vengeful ardor, he was patient and opportunistic. The Mársmidr lieutenant kept his distance and conserved his energy, settling for scoring small cuts on Arnbjorn's arms and shoulders while evading any attempted retaliation. Twice, Arnbjorn dodged a coup-de-grace that would have ended his life. But the scoundrel grew tired and wounds wore him thin, the snow reddening with his blood. Sooner or later, Arnbjorn would fall to the superior swordsman.

"Come on Hallvard," Skoegir said with a sneer. "Johan was a better fighter than you."

Arnbjorn tightened his muscles and tried another advance. He feinted to the right and when Skoegir moved to deflect, Arnbjorn swept his foot around. It found Skoegir's knee, causing the man to stumble. But as Arnbjorn zipped in for the kill, Skoegir's blade slipped passed Arnbjorn's arm and left a deep gouge below his ribs.

Arnbjorn cringed, clutching his fresh puncture. Blood splattered against the bridge, and he realized the wound was a grave one. Arnbjorn glimpsed at Skoegir, who pulled away limping. Time was running out. He had to beat his foe now, or never.

Then, the thought occurred to him. And Arnbjorn laughed.

"The faen is so funny?" Skoegir demanded.

"You're right. Johan was the better fighter. I was always stuck outsmartin' folks. Lying and tricking them," Arnbjorn said. "But thing is, I've already beaten you. You're just too faening stupid to realize it."

Skoegir stared, his brow ticking impatiently.

"Think about it. When Ottar failed Freystein, he took one of Ottar's fingers. After this, after failing at exactly the moment of truth, do you think Freystein will spare you?" Arnbjorn shook his head. "You ran into several intruders, us. You should have given the alarm, should have screamed. But you didn't. They're going to see that you and I danced here, that you dallied about on some personal duel rather than perform your duty. If Eirik takes Freystein down, you'll be on the run. And if Freystein lives, he'll put a bounty on your head for your failure. You're already dead Skoegir. You and I are just the dancing dead..."

Skoegir froze, his visage that of a man who realized he had wrought his own demise. Then, his face began to grow red, flush with anger. Skoegir raised his sword to rush Arnbjorn.

Arnbjorn snarled and slashed his axe in an uppercut motion.

It caught Skoegir in the stomach, stopping the man and causing his sword to thud against the ground. He groaned. Arnbjorn heard the sloshing of liquids against the street, followed by a squelch and the stench of bowels voided. Arnbjorn slipped away and caught sight of the pink mess that Skoegir plopped into, a river of blood cascading over the trampled snow.

Arnbjorn grunted in satisfaction and limped towards the parapet of the bridge. He turned, dropping his axe as he sat against the wall. The pain ebbed but the bleeding had not as he felt it seep into his pants and down his leg. He suspected it was his kidney, a fact he found somewhat amusing. How many other foes had he slain with a finely timed dagger to the same spot?

The air left his mouth in a fine mist, and Arnbjorn knew that he could count the number of breaths he had left. Without aid, he would soon see his brother Johan on the other side. His vision blurred but the sound of marching made Arnbjorn lift his gaze. He caught the fading sight of several approaching figures, armed with spears and shields. The allegiance of whom he could not guess. Not that he could truly bring himself to care.

Arnbjorn... no, Hallvard shut his eye and began to pray silently to Denglr, dead as the god was. He prayed that Eirik and Olaf would succeed. For Stefnir's safety. That Freystein would be stopped. For the memory of his brother and for Strand, as the city had always been good to Hallvard and Johan. Never before had he actually prayed for the odds of the law, least of all Eirik. It made him smile to remember the day they met, when Eirik grabbed Hallvard during a theft. And another encounter, when Eirik and Valgard warned Hallvard to leave Strand before Freystein found him.

Strand, for all its best and worst traits, deserved to live. It deserved a chance to thrive.

Arnbjorn prayed, and knew with satisfaction that his brother was avenged with Skoegir's death. He prayed until the darkness swallowed his consciousness.

Eirik's axe sailed into the rear of an unwary foe's head. As the thug went down, the Governor's Guardsman surveyed the battle.

Despite being heavily outnumbered, the melee had gone in their favor. Three men had rushed Ulfvalgr, only to be torn apart by the varl's axe as he charged towards Freystein. Vilmundr and his bodyguards had withdrawn into a corner, remaining neutral and defensive the entire fight. Runa and Olaf made a surprising team, with Olaf fending off blows and Runa striking from behind the varl's protective shield. One Vak'auga had already died after writhing with a spear-pierced stomach.

Olvir engaged the two men who stood between Melkorka and his sword. That was when Eirik spotted Nikolas sneaking behind the steward. With little time to act, Eirik grabbed the weapon of the freshly slain man and flipped to hold it by the blade. He arched his arm back and threw it.

The flying blade missed, landing next to Nikolas' foot. Eirik cursed and wished he had Valgard's skill. Yet it had succeeded in grabbing Nikolas' attention. The would-be successor scowled darkly as he approached Eirik.

"This is where it ends, cousin," Nikolas said. He raised his sword and kept his shield at the ready.

"I couldn't agree more." Eirik lifted his axe.

"Weak, always weak." Nikolas dashed in to deliver a slash. But Eirik struck with proper timing and caught the sword with the flat of his axe, metal singing with the blow's deflection.

Nikolas countered with a swipe of his shield which Eirik skipped away from, giving ground. The Guardsman was tempted to strike, but knew Nikolas was ready to counter. Parrying with axes was a risky game that gave the advantage to the swordsman, and was not something Eirik could chance again.

"It was always there for your taking, Eirik! Gylfi wasn't the only one who would have backed your claim for the throne." Nikolas leveled his sword above his shoulder, the point aimed at Eirik. "And you deny it for what? So some princeling snob can have his 'rightful' due?"

Eirik snapped. "Better than a spoiled madman who murders and connives his way to power!"

He reversed his axe and performed a rising chop. The blade caught the rim of Nikolas' shield and forced it upward. As it rose, Eirik reversed his grip on the haft and slammed his axe down, hammering the shield into Nikolas and blasting him back.

"The law exists so men can live without fear of unjust rulers!" Eirik screamed as he recovered and chopped again. Something was wrong for Nikolas, who gave ground but did not counter. Eirik continued. "You're nothing but a hypocrite! To flaunt the law and still demand, by law, your place on the throne!"

Eirik struck again and again, the shield cracking with every swing. Nikolas jerked wildly before the blows, and Eirik realized the would-be heir had accidentally wedged the tip of his blade in the back of his own shield. Nikolas struggled desperately to free it, his eyes wide in realization of his peril.

"The law means *nothing* to you, yet you demand everything from it! A child's whim, for the scales that measure justice are the same that weigh our trade, our daily bread! And the very lives of *everyone* in Strand!" Eirik screamed with every blow. The fury welled within him as the Guardsman twisted his entire body, hurling the full force of his axe against Nikolas' armor. *"You aren't worthy to be Governor!"*

The shield gave. Eirik's weapon passed through the barrier with a burst of splinters and debris. The axe-head struck something behind it.

Nikolas screamed.

Eirik kicked out and freed his weapon from his nemesis, whose smashed shield and sword clattered against the floor. He saw the ruined mess that was Nikolas' face, a deep gouge in his forehead where the axe had maimed him. Nikolas sank to his knees, his cupped hands trying to stem the gush of blood.

Eirik's instincts veered towards mercy. His heart begged him to stop the anguish he had wrought upon his own flesh and blood. But a voice within his mind spoke with a sage's tone. *If he lives, Ragnar and Strand will never be safe. And neither will I…*

Eirik swallowed and knew he had no choice. He turned, taking a stance as though felling a tree.

And struck his axe through Nikolas' throat.

The screaming endured, though its source changed. Eirik glanced to Melkorka behind her henchmen, whose shriek shriveled into a hateful glare. She heaved and sobbed and pointed a finger at Eirik.

Something sparked and a rune drawn of light appeared in the air. Melkorka hissed as she drew a pouch from her robes and slammed it against the letter, bursting the symbol into flames which flew through directly at him. Eirik couldn't help but watch, dumbfounded. He felt the heat spread across his face and knew he was dead.

Something crashed into him. Eirik struck the ground as the burning figure bowled over, a spreading trail of flames chasing it.

Eirik rolled and saw that the henchmen who had defended Melkorka were aflame as well. Runa disengaged from Olaf and rushed passed Eirik, spearing one of the burning henchmen as she tried to reach the mender.

The aging woman screeched and threw another object at the ground, which burst into smoke. Runa danced away from the black cloud, coughing. The cloud swiftly dissipated, and the mender was nowhere to be seen.

A thought struck Eirik and he turned. He panicked and removed his cloak, desperately beating the flames off Steward Olvir, his savior. The fire smothered swiftly enough, but one glimpse at the steward told Eirik how far gone he was. Wherever blistering wounds didn't cover his shriveled frame, charred fleshed clung to thinned features. Eirik gagged at the stench of charred meat.

Olvir coughed, his voice weak. "Eirik."

The Governor's Guardsman knelt, reluctantly taking the steward's outstretched hand for fear of further hurting him.

"You're... the steward... now," his raspy voice struggled for breath his lungs were unable to hold.

"No, no," Eirik said, panic rising within him. "The menders can sav—"

"Captain Dylan... knows. Several others too. Others will reject it. Work with them," Olvir managed. "Strand... needs you... Eirik."

The steward's breathing stopped. His wrist went limp. Eirik clenched his jaw angrily. But when Eirik shifted his attention to the scene, he realized the fire was fast spreading. Already, it had devoured a trail towards the walls and begun climbing towards the rafters. The situation had ignited panic from everyone. Vilmundr and his varl bodyguards were already making their way towards the exit. Many of the surviving gang members had begun to escape as well.

Olaf and Runa rushed towards Eirik, the varl shouting. "Where's Stefnir?"

When his friends had made their entrance, Stefnir saw an opportunity to take a corner, better protecting his rear. The boy regretted putting his back to the wall as he noticed the blaze spread, growing near. He tried to move laterally and get away but the Gift of Hadrborg slowed him. Part of Stefnir wanted to drop the shield and run, but too much blood had been spilled to abandon the relic now when they were so close to reclaiming it.

Something shuffled Stefnir, grabbing hold of the shield. Above him, he saw Freystein place his meaty hands on the rim. Stefnir raised his sword defensively to swipe at the varl's fingers. The giant slashed down with his hammer, ringing Stefnir's blade as the varl tried to smite the stubborn boy.

"You don't have a clue, child!" Freystein screamed, madness clear in his tone. "I'm trying to save us! All of us, man and varl! The darkness is coming from the north! And we need this power more than ever to be united!"

Suddenly, huge palms slipped around Stefnir, dragging him away. The boy desperately clung to the shield handle, but felt his fingers scrape and relinquish the cherished relic to Freystein's delight. Stefnir screamed in anger and frustration, kicking and striking wildly as his captor sailed over the flames. Only when they cleared the fire did a familiar lock of red hair fall on his face.

Ulfvalgr landed near Olaf, Eirik and Runa, and set Stefnir down. The varl twisted and immediately patted out his burning leather armor. He and Stefnir looked back over the flames and saw Freystein clutching the shield, surrounded by the dancing blaze. The Lord of the Mársmidr was unable to escape as panic and fear washed over the varl's features.

Stefnir faced Ulfvalgr, who keenly regarded Freystein with his jaw clenched.

"The shield will be destroyed if we don't do something!" The boy pleaded.

"We've got to get out of here," Runa declared. Olaf seemed apprehensive, clearly wanting to leave but honor bound to remain.

"Dammit, I don't see any means to get the shield!" Eirik shouted as he scanned the scorching, infernal chamber. "I think Runa is right. We have to cut our losses and run!"

Ulfvalgr said nothing. He snarled, clenching and unclenching his fists as a trickle of sweat cascaded down his brow.

"Ulfvalgr, we've got to go!" Olaf said at last as the waft of smoke made the varl cough a little. "We've tried! The gift is lost!"

Ulfvalgr showed his kendr a momentary grimace before turning his gaze to Stefnir. The boy recognized his own face reflected in the varl's pupils. "When we meet again in the home of Hadrborg, tell me what you learned this day."

"What?" Stefnir asked.

"Ulfvalgr, no!" Olaf screamed, reaching towards him.

Ulfvalgr didn't heed his kendr. He crouched and sprinted from Olaf's grasp. Before hitting the wall of flames, the varl vaulted over the heat at the screaming figure of Freystein.

Stefnir and the rest of them could only watch as the two varl grappled and fought one another, their flickering shadows growing great in the fires. Stefnir witnessed the flames spread and crawl over his friend's back. Yet the giants grappled on, their horns clacking loudly as they wrestled. Ulfvalgr's curled fingers grappled for the shield and ripped it from Kjallak's grasp. With a shout Ulfvalgr threw it, tossing the Gift of Hadrborg over the fires.

It clattered as it landed. Olaf dropped his own shield to snatch the relic, screaming as the heated metal rim sizzled his palm with a puff of smoke. But the varl refused to relinquish it, not now. Not after all they had been through.

"We have to go!" Eirik shouted as he finished wrapping Olvir's body. He took the dead man in both arms and carried him. Runa grabbed Nikolas by an ankle, and Olaf sheathed his sword to grab the other leg, dragging the heir along. Together, the four of them rushed to the exit, their way clear as the rest of the Vak'auga and Mársmidr had preferred life over valor.

As they fled, Stefnir couldn't help but glimpse back just once. He could not see the two varl. Rather he saw great horned shadows, choking the life from one another in the flames. Locked in the last moments of their existence in an embrace of mutual hate.

Stefnir felt the sting in his eyes and tore them away from the sight.

They rushed down the smoke-filled halls and past fleeing slaves. Until they emerged outside in the falling snow, where they discovered the City Watch surrounding the remaining gang members, and Vilmundr with his bodyguards.

As they came into the clearing of men, a spurting cough brought their attention to Nikolas. Eirik set Olvir's corpse down with respect and stepped towards the leader of the Aetla Hilmir, rolling him over. Nikolas was not yet dead, but clutched feebly at his throat.

"You're weak," the heir somehow spoke, his throat gurgling with bloody bubbles. "Weak as Ragnar, too weak to sacrifice lives for a greater goal. War built civilization, Eirik. War is what makes the shield that is a nation. And only nations with strong leaders survive…"

Eirik said nothing as Nikolas' chest rose and fell for the last time. Stefnir looked between the dead heir and Guardsman, seeing the likeness between them that Eirik had mentioned.

The boy's head spun as he remembered everything that happened that night, trying to connect Nikolas' last words with Freystein's, to make some sense of the insanity he had been witness to. At last, Stefnir shook his head. "The darkness."

Eirik and the others focused on him and Stefnir blushed.

"What did you say, Stefnir?" Olaf asked.

"When Freystein grabbed the shield from me, he said he was doing it to save us all. To save us from the darkness of the north," Stefnir said.

"Madness and lies," Runa replied.

Eirik and Olaf exchanged expressions with one another, saying nothing.

"Yeah," Stefnir answered. The boy turned to take a final look at the bonfire that was the blóthus, and resting place of their friend. A giant pillar of black smoke rose into the night skies of Strand. "You're probably right."

Epilogue

It had been nearly two weeks. Eirik rubbed his eyes as he prepared his report, the first in his career as Steward of Strand. Dagny glanced at him from the unrolled scroll, her quill at the ready. They were seated at a table in the steward's quarters of the Great Hall.

"Need a rest?" She asked.

"No," Eirik said. "Let's finish this. And thank you again for recording."

Eirik had taken care of most of the report himself, but his writing wrist was exhausted. He had detailed almost everything; the encounter with the varl and Stefnir, meeting Arnbjorn. The attack on the Great Hall, hiding from the Aetla Hilmir to the deal with Leiknir. Gylfi's deception and Melkorka's manipulations. The capture of Ottar, who was alive but in captivity, to the raid against Ninth Pier. Vott had been kind enough to offer the services of Dagny to help, and the girl was eager to engage in what she referred to as "real work."

Eirik ran his fingers through his hair and finally went on. "At the end of the ordeal, Nikolas the Beautiful and the Aetla Hilmir were destroyed. Freystein, better known to the varl as Kjallak, was slain alongside Ulfvalgr during the fire that consumed the temple to Hadrborg in the northern district. The remainder of the Mársmidr, whom we suspect is naught but a meager score of men, have either escaped Strand's justice or have fallen in with other gangs. Although the Vak'auga are weakened, the Magnus twins have fled the city. Their whereabouts, and that of their vessel *The Destiny of the Weak*, are unknown."

He waited patiently until the girl finished her sentence before continuing. "Melkorka, who was revealed to be the mother of Nikolas, eludes justice as well. The man's birthmark and appearance strongly suggest that he is indeed the son of the Governor's brother, Helvir. Out of respect for our liege's bloodline, we have agreed to give him a small and private funeral with royal honors tomorrow."

Eirik sighed as Dagny scribbled. Although the funeral for Nikolas was tomorrow, today he had not one but three funerals to attend.

"We knew you as Hallvard," Valgard said, holding a torch. "Before, we thought of you as a scoundrel, thief, a liar and a charlatan. But we learned that in Strand's darkest moments, you too could shine as brightly as the best of men."

Valgard stepped back into the circle. Olaf, Valgard, Eirik, Stefnir and Runa had gathered about the wooden funeral boat they constructed to honor the dead man. The City Watch had discovered him cold on the bridge, a smile on his lips as he nursed a fatal kidney wound that caused him to bleed out. Skoegir's body was nearby, and Eirik felt some satisfaction that his ally had earned revenge before passing to the other side.

Arnbjorn laid in the boat with an axe and shield set across his chest, dressed in fine slacks and a tunic. Several jugs of mead and a few tokens to the gods rested alongside him, ensuring that the redeemed man would drink deeply with Denglr, Bjorulf and Dundr in the next life.

Olaf stepped beside the burial ship. "In the short time I knew you, I truly only saw the good. I wish... that you survived. That perhaps you would carry on and become a great man. And I hope that you and Ulfvalgr will go into the afterworld knowing that we succeeded and your deaths were not in vain."

Olaf returned to his place in the ring. Runa didn't step forth. They had already buried Leiknir earlier that day and Eirik doubted the girl possessed anymore tears to shed in this life.

Stefnir strode forward, his face tight as though trying not to weep. "Arnbjorn... thank you. You taught me how to survive and how to fight. I wouldn't be alive if it wasn't for you. And I will miss your lessons and jokes."

The boy lingered a long moment before returning to the ranks. A tear ran down his cheek.

Only Eirik remained. The new steward moved reluctantly, feeling a degree of guilt. He rolled his tongue about the roof of his mouth before speaking. "Hallvard... was a terrible man. A deceitful fellow who betrayed even his employers. Yet Arnbjorn... though a trickster and scoundrel, found something good in him. Something that mattered. I regret... the way I had treated you. For despite the guile, you found decency and redemption in our eyes. Farewell, Arnbjorn."

There were no more words left. Valgard put his boot against the rim of the hull and pushed Arnbjorn's boat into an inlet with a gentle current, bound for Denglr's Bay. He tossed the torch into the ship and set Arnbjorn's body aflame.

The floating funeral pyre reflected off the water's surface as it glided its passenger out of Strand and into the life after.

The five stared at the departure of their friend. Until at last Olaf coughed. "Eirik..."

The steward nodded. "You three should probably be going. It would be best not to be seen at Olvir's funeral, as I don't know if there are others who covet the shield. Vilmundr may have hired a spy to watch you."

It still irked Eirik that they had no choice but to release the varl warlord. Vilmundr had stormed and fumed, warning them that he was a powerful figure with the support of Jorundr. To keep him imprisoned when he was, in fact, guilty of no direct wrongdoing was a violation of the truce between man and varl. He was even bold enough to demand the Gift of Hadrborg, declaring the relic of historical value to varlkind and unworthy of those who had the shield in their possession.

Eventually Eirik had no choice but to escort Vilmundr and his bodyguards from Strand. He warned the warlord never to return until the men who might remember him were dead and his face forgotten.

Olaf nodded, adjusting the strap on his back. The bag contained the Gift of Hadrborg, carefully wrapped to hide it from greedy eyes. "I wish there was more I can do for you."

"You've saved Strand. And that letter you wrote explaining everything to Jorundr should keep Vilmundr from spinning his own truth against our city," Valgard said with a smile. "If you did anymore, we would look like helpless children."

"Yes. Between Kjallak's ruse as Freystein and his puppet show, I think that letter will dissuade Jorundr from believing much of Vilmundr's ranting." Olaf flattened his mouth. "Still I doubt Vilmundr will even be punished. But I think Jorundr will probably find some... distant task for him."

"You don't fear that Jorundr will want the shield for himself?" Eirik asked. "Couldn't it have the power to again raise varl?"

Olaf shrugged. "Truth be told, I don't even know if the shield ever truly created varl, or if it was just a rumor Throstr used to save our people, to rally us. But with Hadrborg dead, the power in it has long waned to nothing... if there ever was any."

Eirik bowed and turned his gaze to Runa and Stefnir. "And you two... are you sure about going with Olaf?"

Runa's fingers tightened around the strap of a satchel which contained several freshly crafted javelins, a gift from the Governor. "The Magnus brothers are out there, hiding. I intend to find and finish them."

Stefnir nodded. "During the fighting, I... I realized that I don't really know how to use a sword. For some reason, I never considered how different it would be compared to an axe. That was a mistake. But Olaf offered to teach me."

The varl stiffened a little, scratching his beard. "Stefnir, Runa, could you give Eirik and I a moment to discuss things?"

The two stepped away. Valgard joined them, granting Eirik and Olaf some privacy.

Eirik raised his face to Olaf. "You don't seem pleased about these lessons."

The varl groaned, his countenance drooping as though drained of vitality. "Given everything that's happened here... would you believe that Stefnir survived while Ulfvalgr and Arnbjorn had not?"

Eirik hummed and shook his head. "I know from experience that close calls are no way to make a living."

"I don't know why I care so much. Maybe because I still see some kindness left in him, some willingness to hold back rather than take life with reckless abandon. Eirik, I see so much *hatred* out there. Arnbjorn, Ulfvalgr, Runa. They've poisoned that boy."

Olaf sighed. "When he came here, that axe was his father's, a working man's axe. Now he has a killing man's sword. You're right, that's no way to live. And I only hope that someday he'll outgrow his vengeance before it's too late."

Eirik swallowed. He was, at heart, a man of action. But the steward knew the value of every man who waged an honest living under the promise that Strand's finest would protect them. It was his duty to stop the blatant cruelty of men like Nikolas and the Magnus brothers. Yet Olaf's goal was truly more difficult, for the varl persevered to prevent one more blackheart in a cold world overrun by them.

"Where will you three go?" Eirik finally asked after pondering the varl's words.

"We're going north," Olaf said, placing a hand on the satchel at his side. The pouch contained the mingled ashes and bone fragments of both Ulfvalgr and Kjallak that the City Watch had carefully collected from the blóthus inferno. "I have to find a suitable resting place for my friend, and our enemy still deserves respect in death."

"And then?" Eirik inquired.

"Valgard gave us a tip he heard from a caravan yesterday. He suspects that Magnus is lying low somewhere around Ridgehorn. If not, we will build a new shrine to hide the shield, then seek him out. Otherwise, he could return to try his luck again. Hadrborg's Gift would be a prize the Valka would pay handsomely for, and I fear the Magnus twins will be desperate enough to attempt to reclaim their losses."

The varl pointed to the distant and waiting forms of Runa and Stefnir. "And since these two numbskulls aren't giving up, I'll see if I can keep them breathing."

Together the five walked to the gates of the city. For a long moment, Eirik wanted to throw aside his position as Steward and venture with them. But his place was amongst his people. He *lived* to protect Strand.

However, a nagging thought disturbed Eirik as they neared the city's boundaries. He couldn't help but voice his concerns to Olaf before they departed through the yawning gates. "Do you think there was some truth to what Stefnir mentioned?"

"About what?"

"The darkness of the north," Eirik replied. "What Frey— Kjallak, said."

Olaf hesitated. "I don't know, Eirik. After Torstein banished Kjallak, he did go farther north than was sane, well into the territories of the dredge. It could have been that he feared another invasion of the stone men. But as long as the alliance between men and varl holds, we can beat them. If I find anything during our travels, I will send word."

Eirik bowed and waved. He watched long and hard as Runa, Stefnir and Olaf journeyed away from the city, fading into the tundra.

Valgard slapped a hand on Eirik's shoulder. "Come on, we're going to be late for Olvir's funeral."

Eirik was exhausted after laying Olvir to rest in the bay. He wanted to go back to the Great Hall and sleep, but Valgard insisted they take care of some reports and plan the itineraries for the City Watch and Governor's Guard.

"Come on. I'll treat you to dinner at the *Skald's Scribbling*," Valgard promised.

"You sure about that?" Eirik asked with a tired but wry smile.

"Why not?" Valgard replied.

As they sat down at the establishment for dinner, Eirik cupped his forehead in his palm. Two steins had been laid before them, but neither man partook more than a sip as they studied the letters and reports.

"Gods be good," Valgard grumbled.

Eirik groaned irritably. "The tournament needs restructuring. The funds we've seized from the Vak'auga and Mársmidr operations will, at least, replenish the City Watch and provide restitutions for the families of slain watchmen."

Valgard shook his head. "We have to be careful. It's too easy for former Mársmidr to accidentally slip into the ranks of the City Watch once we begin recruiting. They could want vengeance."

Eirik hummed in thought, remembering that not every traitor had died. Gylfi, for one, might spend the rest of his life behind bars. Perhaps in a decade, the Governor might be persuaded to offer the blacksmith a pardon. Eirik remembered speaking to his treacherous friend in the dungeons.

"Steward Eirik," Gylfi had said with a sad shake of his head. "You'll be protecting a weakling."

"A weakling protected by strong men, who bested the Aetla Hilmir and Nikolas the Beautiful," Eirik replied.

Gylfi laughed bitterly then. "A shield is only as strong as its weakest panel. And this city is *rotten*, Eirik. The Aetla Hilmir and Mársmidr are dead and gone, and the Vak'auga on the run. But others will come and take their place. There's always a blade not far from the Governor's head."

Gylfi was right. Almost immediately after the destruction of the triumvirate, another gang called the Skaflings was gaining ground fast. Reports gave rise to suspicions they had already infiltrated the City Watch.

"Also," Valgard said after taking a swig. "Some of that plunder has to be set aside for next month."

"Why?" Eirik asked with exasperation.

Valgard slipped a paper forward. Eirik scanned the missive and slammed a fist on the table, causing his stein to jump.

"We just finished saving Strand and Jorundr already wants his tax dues?" Eirik cursed. As part of the agreement of the alliance, the strongholds of men provided taxes to the varl king to fund the defense of the northern borders from the dredge. The contributions were due once every one or two years, depending on when the varl representatives made their rounds.

"Their collector Ubin is due in about a month," Valgard said as he leaned back, crossing his arms.

"Hello Valgard. Remember me?"

The two Guardsmen looked to a blonde bar maiden, who placed her fists on her hips and wore an unimpressed scowl. Eirik swiftly covered his uncontrollable grin as he remembered her from Valgard's bedroom weeks ago, just before the whole mess with Olaf and Ulfvalgr began.

"Um. Of course!" Valgard quipped with a false smile. He paused. "Astrid... right?"

"Asta, you arsehole!" The bar maiden said as she took Valgard's mug and dumped the contents into his lap. He howled in shock as the bar patrons, including Eirik, burst into laughter.

When Eirik opened his eyes, he glimpsed out the window. His laughter slowly died.

"I just have to bed the wild ones," Valgard grumbled as he took a napkin to his stained trousers. "Anyway, back to Ubin. I know it'll be rough Eirik, but we have an obligation—"

"What time is it?" Eirik snapped.

Valgard paused. "I... dinner time?"

"Then why is it still light out?" Eirik asked. "It's as though it's almost midday."

Slowly they rose and stepped out of the mead hall. Glancing to the heavens, the sun shone as if nearing noon. Their own shadows were still as long as they were tall. A few other passing folks looked up as well, their voices hushed yet worried.

"This, this isn't correct," Valgard said as he shaded his gaze with a flat hand to his brow. "We had lunch today, right?"

"No, because it fell over Arnbjorn's funeral," Eirik replied, his brow furrowing as stared into the sky.

For the sun itself had stopped.

About the Author

James Fadeley lives in Arlington, Virginia, where he conducts the misdeeds of Thunderbird Studios (http://tbirdstudios.com). A part-time skald, he has written a dozen or so short stories for various publications. *The Gift of Hadrborg* is his first novel.

He can be followed on Twitter at @JamesFadeley.